FAL

When I was fifteen, and opened the gift delivered to me by The Man, I learned that I was two people. And one of me was dead.

The gift was a black metal box with a handle on the lid, latched with a tiny lock. The key was taped to the lid, the tape sealed with the signature of The Man. Until I opened it, the box hadn't been opened in thirteen years. It had once belonged to my mother. My real mother.

Inside was a sheaf of papers, including two birth certificates dated one year apart, and a death certificate . . . for me. It was the beginning of the mystery that drove me, the secret that obsessed me for so long. The secret for which so many died.

Also by Gwen Hunter

Stolen Children
Ashes to Ashes

False Truths

Gwen Hunter

NEW ENGLISH LIBRARY
Hodder and Stoughton

Copyright © 1995 Gwen Hunter

First published in the USA in 1995 by Pocket Books,
a division of Simon & Schuster, Inc.

First published in Great Britain in 1995
by Hodder and Stoughton

First published in paperback in 1996
by Hodder and Stoughton
A division of Hodder Headline PLC

A NEL paperback

The right of Gwen Hunter to be identified as the Author of
the Work has been asserted by her in accordance with the
Copyright, Designs and Patents Act 1988.

10 9 8 7 6 5 4 3 2 1

All rights reserved. No part of this publication may be
reproduced, stored in a retrieval system, or transmitted,
in any form or by any means without the prior written
permission of the publisher, nor be otherwise circulated
in any form of binding or cover other than that in which
it is published and without a similar condition being
imposed on the subsequent purchaser.

All characters in this publication are fictitious
and any resemblance to real persons, living or dead,
is purely coincidental.

British Library C.I.P.

Hunter, Gwen
False Truths
I Title
813.54[F]

ISBN 0 340 61731 4

Printed and bound in Great Britain by
Cox & Wyman Ltd, Reading, Berkshire

Hodder and Stoughton
A division of Hodder Headline PLC
338 Euston Road
London NW1 3BH

This book is dedicated to my own Tante Ilene and Tee Dom –
Aunt Nell and Uncle John Hedgepeth . . . wherever you may be.
All my love.

ACKNOWLEDGMENTS

I am grateful to the following, without whose help this book could not have been written.

In Louisiana:
Gilbert Johnson, Public Relations, New Orleans Police Department. Lanea Primeaux, of French Quarter Realty on Bourbon Street. Laura Miller of the Ponchartrain Hotel. Pat Bourque, of Les Vieux Temps, Breaux Bridge, Louisiana, for sharing the story of her search for her mother and family. Houston's Restaurant of New Orleans, and Petunias of the French Quarter. Irene Wheeler of Westlake for soap recipes.

In South Carolina:
Dr William C. Oliver for Physiological Mydriasis. Detective Taylor from Rock Hill Police Department's Crime Scene. Joyce Prater Turner and Joy Robinson for assistance with art and artistic techniques. Jim Connell of Winthrop College for technical expertise with ceramics. Mike Prater for computer assistance, as always. Benson and Susan Prater for being my research team after hours. Bobby Prater for information on bayous. Lynn Hornsby for points on correct etiquette. S. R. Stockes, for the use of her last name.

Special thanks to Edna Ann Belk and her French class at Westminster Catawba Christian School: Wendy, Rhonda Lynn Tyre, James McDonald, Joshua David Reinhardt, for the French place names.

And to Beth McKnight for meeting my deadlines when my own fingers couldn't.

In New York:
Jeff Gerecke for all the support and for believing in me. I can't thank Brigid Mellon enough for all her help in fine tuning this manuscript – reading it over and over and over.

And great thanks to Jane Chelius, my editor, for working to make this a stronger and more chilling novel.

In London:
Carolyn Mays, my editor, for being such a darling and so easy to work with. Andi Blackwell for sorting out the paginating and age errors. All the people at Hodder for their enthusiasm and professionalism. To Vanessa Holt for bearing with me when I was all tarted up.

PROLOGUE

Most people know who they are – at the very least they know their own name. I was two people, with two different names. Bonnibelle Sarvaunt and Carin Colleen DeVillier. I knew myself as Bonnie Sarvaunt, the niece of the elderly couple who raised me, or rather, allowed me to grow up in their home. The two people who hid the truth of my identity from the world. And from me.

When I was fifteen, and opened the gift delivered to me by The Man, I learned that I was two people. And one of me was dead.

The gift was a black metal box with a handle on the lid, latched with a tiny lock. The key was taped to the lid, the tape sealed with the signature of The Man. Until I opened it, the box hadn't been opened in thirteen years. It had once belonged to my mother. My real mother.

Inside was a sheaf of papers, including two birth certificates dated one year apart, and a death certificate . . . for me. It was the beginning of the mystery that drove me, the secret that obsessed me for so long. The secret for which so many died.

Yet, even before the gift of the box, I had always known I was different. Fair-haired and pale-complexioned in a world of dark hair and eyes and olive skin. Too tall in the midst of a short, stocky people. Anglo in a Cajun domain.

Yet, it wasn't only the physical differences, it was other things that set me apart. Mainly, my love of this magical, watery land.

I was born knowin' the magic of the south Louisiana landscape. Magic that comes from earth and storm, the sound of rain on a tin roof. The magic of migrating birds and mating alligators and the danger of poisonous snakes. The fierceness of survival in a world that gives no quarter.

A magic ignored or discounted or even complained about by others. A magic which, it seemed, only I could see.

The magic of bogs and swamp and quicksand, and rain from a clear blue sky. The beauty and mystery of the bayou. In reality or on my canvases, this mystery and magic was the cadence and rhythm of creation, constantly renewed in the depths of my twin beings. Bonnibelle and Carin Colleen.

I was different in other things as well. Little things that set me apart from the human world in which I lived. The piano lessons twice a week in town with a retired music teacher. Ballet, art, languages and speech lessons. Science and history and math. My schooling was private. All of it. With one tutor or another and no other children to distract or disrupt or to play with.

And when I turned fifteen – the year I received the box – I began lessons in finance and stock management with the vice-president of the LaRoque National Bank. My education was the only evidence of money in the dirt-poor town of Khoury, Louisiana. A shabby, faded, backwater place peopled by old, grizzled, timeworn Cajuns, a place where unemployment often reached fifty percent. Where the US government was the biggest provider, issuing Social Security and welfare checks on a regular basis.

Not that I lived rich. I didn't. On the surface, I lived just as poor as the next family. Poorer than some. There were no new clothes at Christmas or birthdays unless Tante Ilene made them herself. No new shoes or hat at Easter. Nothing to make me stand out as different.

Yet I was. I knew it.

If for no other reason than The Man. The Man came to see me twice a year, driving down the potholed ruts of the drive in winter, in the wet and cold of 2 January; motoring up to the dock in the humid heat of late summer, on 10 August.

He brought me an allowance each time he came. The extravagant sum of one thousand dollars twice a year, to be spent any way I wished. Not on clothes or videos or music. But on canvases and oil paints and expensive brushes from France. Oh yes. I was different. I knew it.

We lived on the Bayou Negre in the summer months, away from town and away from our three-bedroom mobile home.

Throughout the steamy heat of summer we stayed in a three-room shanty on creosoted pilings. No air-conditioning. No electricity. And a toilet out back.

My room was the loft, the roof so low at the sides I had to duck beneath the rafters when I grew too tall. A small space under the low-pitched roof beams, barely ten by twelve and broiling hot under the tin roofing. But all mine.

The ladder up was a flimsy thing, too brittle for Tee Dom to risk his bulk on. Too steep for Tante Ilene's gouty knees.

Unlike my trailer room which they entered at their leisure, and where my treasures were always under the scrutiny of the old couple's rheumy eyes, the loft room was totally private. It was here that I worked my art. Here where the scenes in my mind found life, becoming paintings and drawings, visions of the dark water and mist of the swamp and the magic of bayou which I so loved.

If I had nothing else in my life, I had my art. It filled up the dark places in my soul. Like the mystery of my life, the world I painted was a hidden place, full of secrets and shadows and unexpected beauty. Or sudden death.

CHAPTER 1

It hadn't rained in weeks and the heat was more than oppressive, it was dangerous. The local news carried by KMK in Khoury reported that the water level in the bayou was down, domestic violence was up, and the Khoury Clinic was full of heat-stroke cases. It was the driest summer in years.

The locals scanned the sky for rain, muttering about drought and withered cane crops and dried-out rice fields. Muttering as the sky stayed clear and blue and the heat remained intense. And after weeks of worry on the part of farmers and complaints on the part of freshwater fishermen, rain was finally coming. Maybe today. Maybe tomorrow. Until then, the normally wet world would remain parched and pungent.

Even the swamp was drying out as the water level dropped, a thick scum of green algae sliding down the trunks of trees and cypress knees and settling into the muck of rotting flora, silt and eroded topsoil. The stink of the swamp was a heavy sour miasma, rank with the scents of earth, and mold, and stagnant water. Alligators stayed beneath the black water in the midday heat. Snakes clung to the shadows and nooks and burrows in the dry, cracked ground. Nutria – nine-pound water rats with razor-sharp teeth – were being driven from their no-longer watery swamp homes in search of food. I had shot two the day before with a twenty-gauge shotgun while Tante Ilene and I made soap on the outside cookstove.

We weren't low on soap, but Tante Ilene was set in her ways. We made soap twice a year, regardless of supply, chamomile in February, oatmeal in August. And if the weather wasn't cooperative, well, a little heat or cold never hurt anybody – that was Tante Ilene's philosophy, and at twenty-one years, I still did as she wished. My sunburned neck and lye-blistered hands disagreed, but then minor discomforts were inconsequential to the people who raised me. A pinched leaf from our aloe plant was a cure-all for most minor skin complaints. Even lye burns. And it was true . . . we had never run out of soap.

It wasn't difficult to make soap, just time consuming.

Tante Ilene always saved her bacon grease in a three-pound coffee-can until the coagulated stuff reached nearly to the top; about a three-to-six-month process. The day before the soap-making began, Tante Ilene lit up the propane cookstove outside the shanty and heated water, sitting the grease-can in the center of the water when it reached a strong boil.

Ten minutes later, the grease had melted through, making it easy to see old food particles and trash. Using padded gloves, Tante Ilene lifted out the grease-can and set it overnight in an ice-chest filled with ice. This was all the warning I ever had that my plans for the next day were to be canceled. Tante Ilene had never wasted words on something so obvious.

In the morning, she scraped off the purified grease and discarded the rubbish that had filtered through to the bottom. Over the cookstove, my job was to heat a quart of water to a slow simmer and add one can of lye. This was the dangerous part of making soap. The part where, if you weren't careful, you were likely to get burned. If you let the water get too hot before adding the lye it would boil over or spit at you. If you let your mind wander or if you were angry at having to change the day's itinerary, you often sported a burn thereafter to remind you to pay attention. I had never yet made soap without getting burned.

When Tante Ilene determined that the lye and water had reached the right consistency, she poured in the purified grease and stirred the mixture until it turned the rich brown shade of raw honey. When the color was perfect, I scooped in the cooked oatmeal, slow spoonful by slow spoonful, as Tante Ilene stirred. This thick mixture was then dipped into muffin-tins and put aside to set. Only a few hours of hot, sticky work in the sun, but enough to spoil my schedule.

Making soap wasn't the way I had wanted to spend my last fully sunny day. I had plans for that day. Big plans. Plans interrupted by soap recipes and burned grease and a hot flame. And Tante Ilene blithely ignored the irritation that caused me to splatter and spill and grumble all day long.

A day late, I was finally in position, deep in the bayou. On the first day in weeks that rain was expected. Waiting out the afternoon, hoping the clouds would hold off. Hoping the rain which we needed so badly would hold off just a little longer. And hoping that when it finally came, it would be the slow rain we needed and not a howling storm to catch me unprepared on the bayou water.

So far, the sky was cloudless and still, sweltering hot and dripping with humidity as only Louisiana can be in August. The aluminum of Tee Dom's johnboat was blistering to the touch, the ribbed, backless seat a torture to muscles held stationary too long.

Slowly, I put down the book that had kept me company throughout the long afternoon, eased my legs out along the floor of the boat, extended my arms toward my toes and flexed my fingers. I stretched my back, curving my body forward and holding the position till the burn of tight muscles forced me to slowly release the tension. I repeated the stretch. Next I tightened my thighs, held and repeated. Then my arms and hands. Then my calves and finally my buttocks where they rested on the seat of the boat. The stretch relaxed me, yet was done so slowly, with so little actual movement, that it hadn't startled the two egrets fishing in shallow water only feet away.

Still moving slowly, as if my hands were only leaves brushed by the breeze, I found the aloe leaf pinched from Tante Ilene's massive aloe plant. Massaged the open end once more over the lye burn on my right thumb knuckle. The gel instantly eased the day-old sting. I sipped a bit of tepid water from a capped plastic cup, a 7–11 memento that had once held cooler refreshment.

For two hours I sat, reading a paperback copy of *Momo* by Emile Ajar, that I had ordered from a French publisher. Except for turning pages I scarcely moved, dripping with sweat as dusk approached, and with it, the return of the egrets. Almost a thousand of the snowy white birds nested in this bend of the bayou, and at dusk, in a thunder of wings and raucous cries, they would all return to the rookery for the night. A huge screaming, shrieking, writhing, joyous cloud beating the air with living wings.

My old camera and my new 35mm Nikon were ready, both fitted with special attachments and 70–150mm focal length lenses. The cameras were chunky-looking things, each with bulky exposure units on either side. The new Nikon had a specially fitted motor drive for speed filming. All new equipment in the hopes that I could finally capture the birds' reappearance.

No time would be wasted changing film during the precious seconds of the return. I'd had a photographer in town specially wind my film for me, giving me nearly a hundred exposures in each camera.

The boat thumped beneath me as something large swam under the shallow draft bottom. *Alligator?*

I touched the .20 gauge stored in the side pocket running along the port side of the boat. The metal was scorching hot in the late-day sun, and I hoped I wouldn't have to use it. Nothing like a shotgun blast to scatter the wildlife to the four winds.

I had chosen my location last week after two previous attempts to film the egrets' return had ended in failure. Hidden between the immense trunk of a fallen chenier – Cajun for a storm-battered oak – and the smaller trunks of the dead oak's seedlings, I would likely not be noticed – that is, if I could only hold still an hour or so longer.

The old chenier had lain in the black water for as long as I could remember, the odd-shaped boat-tie screwed into its slimy rotting bark inches below the surface. Now, with the drought, the boat-tie was above the water line, its triangular anodized shape easily available, the bark dried and cracked and falling away.

The tripods for the cameras were leveled on the bark of the chenier. I would be uncomfortable, sitting in the boat, leaning my arms on the tree to take the pictures, my body twisted to accommodate the shots I was hoping to take. The chenier itself, however, would carry at least some of my weight, easing my back. I hoped I had thought of everything.

Twenty or so egrets, white-feathered wings stroking strongly to slow their decent, landed early, beating the rush. The birds separated into pairs and settled into mounded nests or valleys between mounds. The occasional lone bird kept watch perched up higher on a sturdy branch, one seemingly shoved into a mound for just that purpose.

My presence caused no alarm, the leafy protection of oak shielding me even from the sky.

I didn't film it, this beautiful display of white bodies beating the air. I held still for the pilgrimage to come. I merely stored the paperback in the side pocket of the boat and stretched again.

The sun dropped slowly, a scarlet ball in a plum-colored sky. The air changed texture, becoming lighter, softer, not merely cooler. The water grew even blacker. Shadows took on depth and vibrancy.

I slipped off the sunglasses that had protected my eyes throughout the afternoon, tucking them into the mesh bag I always carried. Slowly I stretched, taking longer this time to pull through the motion. Flexed my fingers. Bent over the cameras. And waited.

And the egrets came. By the hundreds.

The air was suddenly crowded and close, filled with the screams of a thousand birds rocking on the artificial breeze of their collected wings. Dipping and soaring and banking and breaking and a hundred near misses, far fewer collisions. They settled into the trees, onto the mound, all around me, up high and down low. Fluttering white bodies against the green-black of foliage. Alligators thrashed and roared, catching the unwary, disappearing without a trace. Feeding in the black water. A rain of white feathers settled around me, onto me, feathering my camouflage in the copse of young oaks.

The boat rocked beneath me as alligators fed.

I started with the old camera and black and white film, because it was familiar against my face, the worn leather of the case as comfortable as an old shoe. Almost instantly, I abandoned it as too slow, nearly knocking the old camera and its tripod into the black water, luckily catching its unbalanced weight on the strap around my wrist. Seizing the Nikon in shaking fingers, bending my face to the viewfinder, I settled to work with the 35mm clicking as fast as the motor-driven shutter would move, adjusting the settings as the light changed.

Egrets were tinted flamingo pink and dusty white and gray,

and the communal mound of nests writhed with the pecks, stabs, and mock fights over territory and mates. Wings thrashed the shadows. The noise was incredible, the thunder of wings and bellow of alligators, the raucous chorus of birds.

Mosquitoes swarmed, disturbed by the screaming birds, thousands upon thousands, seeking a blood-meal. Even their slight buzz seemed amplified in my ears.

I switched back and forth between cameras, ignoring the cramps in my fingers and calves and back. I ignored the alligators feeding on careless egrets, thrashing in the water around me, bumping the boat bottom like a hollow drum.

The water reddened as the sun sank, a scarlet ball bleeding into the bayou. Foliage blackened on the shore, birds flew into dark silhouette against the vermilion sky and ruby-tinted water. Scarlet sparkles, like precious gems flung from the bayou, scattered and rippled in the dying light, tossed from the struggles of alligators and prey. Nature painted the scene around me in harsh and glorious color I'd never be able to reproduce.

Long before full dark I was nearly out of film. But I stayed on, hidden and still, watching the birds settle for the night.

I had saved half a dozen shots for time exposures, hoping the almost-full moon would be free of clouds. Sitting on the hard boat seat, I adjusted the shutter speeds down to bulb, a term which meant I would have full manual control. I could leave the shutter open for a full minute. Then for a minute, fifteen seconds, followed by a minute, thirty seconds. Bracketing the shots for the best light as I photographed the bayou moon and black water.

I smiled and sighed, remembering the rush as wings whipped the air. Persistent mosquitoes buzzed and landed, delicate little wings and minuscule legs touching my skin before they flew away, frustrated. A layer of poison between them and a delicious bloody supper.

Again I stretched and sipped my water. Patient. Waiting.

An hour after sunset, the moon broke through the tops of the trees, lighting the world with a silver-gray light. Adjusting the settings for each shot, I took my last six of the sleeping mound and moon-touched water, clicks and whirrs of the slow-moving shutter lost in the night. I finished just as the front, which promised long-overdue rain, began scudding the black sky with clouds.

Slowly I settled into the boat bottom, feeling the creak in muscles unmoved in hours. There was a sting in one calf, charley-horse coming on. Rubbing it gently, I blinked into the night. Brushed away the mosquitoes still buzzing around my ears. Scratched a few bites where the mosquito repellent had not covered me sufficiently, or the mosquito had been hungry enough to risk the quick nibble. And remembering how to breathe, I grinned. I had done it. It had taken a month in preparation and timing and planning. But I finally had the egrets' nightly return on film.

I covered my eyes with my palms. My heart beat unsteadily for a long stretch before it smoothed out. I laughed softly.

As silently as possible, I stowed the cameras and tripods, and untied the aluminum johnboat from the boat-tie screwed into the fallen chenier. Slipping the oars into the makeshift oar-locks, I moved down the black water of Bayou Negre toward home.

Only when I was far from the egrets' nesting ground did I unlock and secure the oars, just as Tee Dom had shown me the first time he had brought me here so long ago. By moonlight, I wrapped the starter rope around the old Evenrude engine, flipped the switch and pumped gas through the gas line. The engine started on the first pull, shattering the silence with its roar and fuming breath. I reached home just before 11 p.m.

I cut the twenty-horsepower motor, gliding up to the dock in a silence I couldn't appreciate for the ringing in my ears, and secured the johnboat under the dock. The water level was higher already as rain upstream ran toward the Gulf, preceding the storm front. It was always sudden, this swelling of the waters. Dangerous for the unknowing and the foolish.

Picking up the mesh bag that held my supplies, draping the camera straps over my shoulder, and cradling the .20-gauge shotgun beneath my arm, I climbed the makeshift ladder to the dock and entered the shanty which had been my summer home for as long as I could remember. Tante Ilene rocked slowly on the uneven floorboards in her place beside the long table. A hurricane lamp lit the right side of her face, leaving the left in shadows. She didn't speak.

Hanging the mesh bag and ungainly cameras on the ladder that led to my loft room, I broke open the shotgun, removed the shells, and placed it on the gun-rack below Tee Dom's .30 gauge, locating the wooden supports by feel in the total black near the door. Aware of the long day in every slight pull of muscle and the stink of sweat that hung around me like an odorous mist, I longed for the hot shower I couldn't have. Not in the bayou, where our water came from a spring and was carried in by the bucketful. Tonight, even a cold shower would have been welcome. Instead I went to the pie-safe for my dinner.

The shanty lacked modern amenities, but was well equipped with worn, but useful antiques. Up north, the pie-safe alone would have sold for several hundred dollars and graced the kitchen or breakfast-room wall of a rich collector's home. It would have sat in a prominent place, doors open to display crockery and pottery and handmade stoneware dishes. Here the pie-safe was shoved in a tight corner behind the back screen door, hidden in the darkness. It was crammed with Melmac and chipped china and jelly-jar glasses, and my supper wrapped in a reused piece of aluminum foil.

As I moved in the lightless kitchen, finding stainless-steel tableware and a plate, and filling a glass with spring water, I could feel Tante Ilene's eyes on me. Eventually, she would speak, and I would answer. Some inane and useless comment from us both. It was what passed for conversation in the Sarvaunt household.

'You see in de dark too good, girl.'

So it would be sooner than usual tonight. 'Yes, ma'am.' I drank down the cold spring water and refilled the glass. 'Where's Tee Dom?'

'Sleepin'.'

I looked up from the cold étouffée and rice, surprised. Tee Dom was a night owl, like me. The rocker squeaked rhythmically across the hollow floorboards, a deep sound like a primitive drum. Tante Ilene was crocheting another afghan, her nimble fingers moving through the delicate and intricate motions with no conscious effort.

'Hem an' Mishu Pilchard goin' to slaughter a hog in de mornin', befo' de sun rise. You lef' gas in de boat?'

'Yes, ma'am.'

Tante Ilene grunted.

'Is he going to help smoke it too?' If so, I'd be stuck in the shanty all day. Thunder rumbled in the distance. Tree frogs suddenly became raucous and bull frogs added a bass note. Crickets sang tenor. Rain was coming.

'Yah. Yo' wan' take him, you can keep de boat. He leaving at fo'r.'

'Fo'r t'irty,' Tee Dom bellowed from the black hole of his bedroom.

'I'll take him.'

The formalities were fulfilled, conversational requirements satisfied. There would be silence in the shanty till four. Tante Ilene grunted again and I swung a leg up onto the bottom ladder rung, carrying my dinner and an aluminum bucket of cold spring water up to the loft.

Lighting the hurricane lamp, a chipped cut-crystal edition I had picked up in a junk shop, I turned down the wick to a faint glow, stripped off my sweaty T-shirt and shorts. Water left from the day before had heated under the tin roof all day. It was warm and I soaped as well as I could, the scent of Tante Ilene's chamomile soap a delicate perfume to my sweaty body. A cold spring-water rinse revived my tired mind and revitalized me. Although I had scarcely moved for the greater part of the afternoon, sitting still for hours had created its own form of exhaustion.

A cool night breeze blew through the open shutters of the window beneath the eaves, cooling me further. I pulled a short cotton shift over my head and sat in front of my easel. It was too cloudy for me to work on the night view of the bayou that snaked around the shanty and the old chenier that seemed to anchor the water in place. I turned my back on the scene outside the window.

Opening Titanium White and Ivory Black and Green Earth, I squeezed out a small, pea-shaped smudge of each, and with a tiny palette knife, a metal blade made for mixing, I mixed the shade I called Bayou Moon. Sometimes I added a bit of linseed oil to thin the paint color, but tonight, with the rain smell in the air and lightning flickering its white strobe through the window, I used thick, undiluted paint and the mixing blade to apply it with a heavy hand.

This was the magic I was born knowing. The magic that soothed my soul. The magic that, if ignored too long, began to die within me like a beast in agony. The magic of oils and shadow and perspective. The magic of shape and form and texture. The magic of my art.

I had taken lessons all my life, learning all that my teachers had to teach me and then surpassing them. And it *was* magic, the creating of something out of almost nothing. And I knew without being told that this magic of the brush and pigment was part of the secrets that surrounded me.

Quickly, by the soft light of the lamp, I added the strong highlights of the moon on black water to the canvases I had started in late July. Referring often to the black and white photos tacked long ago to the rafters around my makeshift easel, I added light to a black night scene, touching the blade edge along the chenier's limbs, the flat of the blade along the clouds and through the water.

The paint was still wet, and working the highlights into the black of the landscape was a simple matter. Often it took weeks for an oil to dry in the bayou, the damp air allowing me time to work and rework a scene.

Lightning struck nearby, shaking the shanty and filling the air with an ozone scent. Rain thundered in behind. The sound on the tin roof, only inches over my head, was a deep pitched roar enclosing the loft in an oasis of sound.

After an hour, I placed one canvas in the rack I had made between the joists and pulled the half-finished egret scene out, setting it on the easel. *Empty Nests* was the working title: with the night scene fresh in my mind, I applied the highlights of Bayou Moon into the blackness with knife and brush.

At 4 a.m., as the long day finally began to settle across my shoulders like a meaty hand, I opened the gallon-jug of mineral spirits and added a fresh amount to the cleaning glasses. These were tall jelly-jars with screw-on lids and a ball of window screen crumpled in each bottom. I tapped and lightly stroked the sable bristles onto the screening to release the paint. The mineral spirits quickly became cloudy. The second cleaning jar became less cloudy than the first, and when no more cloudy haze swirled up from its screening, I moved to the third.

Only the slightest pale fog tinted the spirits as I closed off the last jar.

A metal garbage can, lined with a thick black Glad garbage bag, was the final part of my cleaning process. Holding the brush firmly, I snapped downward, letting gravity and inertia force the remaining spirits from the bristles. I had learned the hard way not to use a cloth to clean my brushes. Sable couldn't take a cleaning with cloth, and I had ruined a dozen expensive brushes before I hit upon my current method.

I didn't sleep. During the summer, I seldom slept at night, preferring naps in the bright of day when my eyes sought relief from light and my body grew drowsy from heat.

It was still dark as I dressed in jeans and fresh T-shirt, and gathered up my dirty clothes in a duffel. Scuffings and thumps came from downstairs, and the smell of propane, as Tante Ilene used the cookstove to fix black coffee and oatmeal, our usual breakfast when it rained. I braided my hair and climbed down the ladder, hanging the canvas duffel beside the mesh bag which held the cameras and mosquito repellent and water bottle from the day before. The rain had died outside, it was silent in the shanty.

Tee Dom, a massive short man, emerged from the back bedroom and hung his own duffel of dirty clothes over the ladder rung. Throughout the summer months, whenever I went to town, I took our dirty clothes and dropped them off at the Khoury Washerette. Three hours later, the clothes were ready for the trip back up Bayou Negre to the Sarvaunt Shanty.

For the Sarvaunts, the service was free. I had painted a portrait of Eloise Deen, the proprietor of the washerette. It had pleased her so much, she offered free laundry for two years as payment. Eloise was portly, gray, and had bags under her eyes plump enough to support the blue orbs like pillows. The portrait showed a thinner, younger, smoother Eloise than she had seen in the mirror in a decade. Maybe two.

We ate in silence, Tante Ilene, Tee Dom and I, gathered around the long table that served as work table, dining table, and occasional foot prop. The coffee was so strong it could peel the enamel off my teeth, and the oatmeal was diluted with reconstituted powdered milk. A ghastly mixture, but it *was* sweet. Tante Ilene believed a bowl of oatmeal was properly served with three tablespoons of cane sugar. It was the only way I knew how to eat it.

'De Man. He come tomorr',' Tee Dom said.

I paused, spoon halfway to my mouth. A small electric shock passed through my upper body. The Man was my mother's lawyer, the executrix of her estate and the administrator of my trust fund. The keeper of the secrets. I smiled and finished the bowl of oatmeal, nodding slowly. Eventually I answered. 'Yes, sir.' I had always wondered how much the Sarvaunts knew about my real history. Whenever I asked they ignored me. I no longer bothered.

Tee Dom nodded with me, then sucked the last of his coffee out of the bottom of the cup, a syrupy, wet sound, loud in the silence. 'Le's go, girl.'

Rain drops again pelted on the tin roof, a sharp sound, like a snare drum, as we slipped into rain slickers. Thick yellow plastic, so old they were cracked and stained, the rain slickers nevertheless still kept out the rain. The clips were ancient, stiff aluminum instead of modern plastic; they snapped into place with loud clicks.

We stored our supplies in the johnboat, added a tarp to keep the boat bottom free of water, and Tee Dom started the Evenrude. It was recalcitrant in the damp air and required three tugs before it finally turned over and spluttered to life.

Mishu Pilchard had a covered lean-to where local men gathered to slaughter animals, smoke them, and get drunk on his homemade brew. The men would need the lean-to today.

Fat splats of rain beat against the slickers, the tarp, and marred the smooth surface of the bayou. Black rings on black water, almost invisible in the darkness.

I had better eyes than Tee Dom – I had better vision than most people, especially at night – so I took the tiller and glided the johnboat out into the bayou and downstream toward the Pilchard Place.

We passed the Roberts Place, the Terrell Place, the abandoned Plauche Place, and the Fiongas Place. Lights were on in about half of them.

Father Alcede was drinking coffee on his covered porch, the

plain windows of the Holy Ghost Church of the Madonna, to his left, dark. The good father would most likely be at the pig slaughter later today, partaking of Mishu Pilchard's free brew. Father Alcede preached against sex, drugs, movies, cable TV, rock-and-roll, and the evils of New York and Los Angeles with great frequency. But never against the evils of drink. Most sermons, in fact, were delivered with his strong voice liberally coated with alcohol. However, no matter how drunk he was, he never failed to stir the congregation of the Holy Ghost Church of the Madonna into a frenzy. Tee Dom and Tante Ilene never missed a meeting.

I had stopped going to church regularly the day The Man gave me the box that held my secrets. Secrets that Tee Dom and Tante Ilene refused to explain away. Refused even to talk about. Perhaps refusing to go to church was the simple adolescent rebellion that Miss Taussig, one of my tutors, proclaimed it was, but to me it was more. If the people who raised me were going to hide my past from me, I wasn't going to give them anything of myself. Adolescent rebellion be damned.

The black box given to me by The Man contained the memorabilia of my mother's life and the clue to the secrets in my own. Amongst the ticket stubs and receipts and mementoes, there were several official pieces of paper. Two birth certificates, one for Bonnibelle Sarvaunt and one for Carin Colleen DeVillier. The babies were born almost one year apart. There was a marriage license for Marie L. Smith and William Marc DeVillier. And there was a certificate of death for both Marie DeVillier and for Bonnibelle Sarvaunt. Me.

I could have looked at this information in a thousand different ways. My death certificate could have been in error. Or it could be a case of mistaken identity – one child declared dead when it was really the other. Or Bonnibelle Sarvaunt and her mother, Elizabeth, might both really be dead, while the DeVilliers might both really still be alive, living under the Sarvaunts' assumed identities. I had no death certificate for Elizabeth Sarvaunt, the mother I had never known.

There was no way for me to know unless my aunt and uncle finally opened up and shared the story. The years of silence and frustration had taken their toll on our relationship.

Father Alcede lifted his cup and nodded his head. We nodded back. Bayou dwellers were seldom more demonstrative, at least not from a distance. Or when they were sober. By day's end, it would be a different matter entirely as old men, flush with liquor, took their leave of one another. Then it would be traditional French exuberance and back slapping and massive hugs.

The sun had tinted the sky overhead a faint gray by the time we reached the Pilchard dock. As usual, Tee Dom was the first man there, ready to help Mishu Pilchard start the coals and sharpen his knives and open his moonshine. For his help, Tee Dom always took home an extra portion of the meat. And got started early on the shine.

Mishu Pilchard was one of a handful of men always referred to by the honorific Mishu – the Cajun version of Monsieur. The few so blessed had land, power, age, and money. Lots of it by Cajun standards.

I pushed off from the dock and raced the hard rain to the Khoury public landing. I beat the deluge by minutes, for once letting Elred help me dock the johnboat and unload. Elred was always at the public landing, running the small park for Khoury Township. He seldom, however, unbent from the high prominence of his trusted position to help a patron dock or unload. I was the exception. Elred was always available to assist me in any way I desired, and he hoped one day to arrange for me to desire him. It wasn't likely.

Elred also ran the local bait-and-tackle shop, occasionally running errands for the rich fishermen who tried the waters. It was rumored that he also ran a little moonshine and marijuana on the side for the local boys who needed transportation for their wares. He was taciturn, closemouthed, and meaner than a papa gator in mating season. Elred would shoot his own mother for a fiver. At least he was predictable.

He carried my dirty laundry up to the parking lot, no doubt fantasizing about the contents of the laundry bag. If Elred was envisioning lace and satin and merry-widows, he was far from the plain white-cotton truth.

Tee Dom's truck started with an unmuffled roar, drowning Elred's final words. I waggled my fingers at him and drove off into the deluge. Elred was a pitiful figure reflected in the rear-view, standing in the pouring rain, staring at my retreating laundry in the back of the pickup.

It was barely dawn when I got to the three-bedroom trailer we Sarvaunts call home. I turned the air-conditioner to high, lit the natural gas hot-water heater and stripped off my clothes. I kept half my clothes in the trailer so when I came to town I'd have something to wear.

While the water heated for my first real bath in days, I beat up an egg and fried French toast from the meager food supplies I kept in the fridge. The milk was a bit sour, but anything was better than the powdered stuff we drank on the bayou.

There were fresh mouse droppings along the counter top so, after I ate, I set traps and washed dishes. This was routine for me. At least once a week I came into Khoury, got a hot shower, dropped off the laundry, picked up the mail, bought groceries, and ran errands. It was a responsibility I accepted the summer I turned twelve.

I always used my own money for groceries and supplies, giving the receipts to Tante Ilene for reimbursement when I got back to the shanty. No receipt, no cash, no excuses. I only forgot the receipts once.

I washed my hair in the shower and shaved what little body hair I possessed. There was a black mold growing up the fake-tile corners, but housekeeping was Tante Ilene's provenance. According to her, I didn't know what clean was.

After a three-hour nap – I seldom needed much more – I dressed and closed up the trailer, shutting off the air-conditioner, the water heater, and tossing out two dead mice which had found the baited traps as I slept. Before I left, I reset the spring-loaded traps, smearing on a mixture of peanut butter and Cheeze-whizz.

Eloise was open for business when I dropped off the laundry, sitting on a three-foot-tall square stool behind the counter, making change for the washing machines and folding clothes. The portrait I had painted of her hung on the wall behind the register. She had framed it in gilt with three-color matting so heavy it looked like a shadow box. A tasteless thing to do to an oil of any kind.

Leon Harless was loading his wife's dainties into the dryer, keeping one eye on Eloise as he worked. The first time Leon saw the portrait over the counter, he had asked Eloise where her pretty daughter lived. Eloise had chased him from the washerette with a hot iron causing him to leave the family clothing behind. Leon had learned how to keep his mouth shut since.

'Bonnie,' Eloise's face wreathed itself in a smile so big that the pouches beneath her eyes nearly met her brows. 'You look pretty as a picture. Come here, girl.' She folded me in her ample arms, against her ample bust and hugged me. Hugs were uncommon experiences in my life, so rare that I had to stop and think about where my arms would go, left up, right down, and where my face would end up. But I had decided that I rather liked hugs, and wanted to develop a proficiency with the skill.

'Hello, Eloise,' I said, my mouth pressed against her well-padded shoulder. 'You look right nice yourself. You on a diet, Eloise? I swear you look like you lost at least ten pounds.'

'Now, Bonnie, your know better than to swear,' but her pleasure at my comment was obvious. 'Father Alcede and your aunt and uncle, I know taught you better.'

I grinned at her. 'This is the last month of free laundry, Eloise, and it's a big load this time, I'm afraid.' I heaved the damp duffels onto the counter. They landed with a squishy thump. The tarp from the johnboat, which Elred had tucked around the duffels, had blown off as I slept. The clothes were soaked.

'La, child, look at all this. And it's wet too.'

'Got caught in the rain this morning in the back of the pickup. You want me to pay you something on it anyway?'

'Of course not.' Eloise paused in her sorting of Tee Dom's gardening clothes. 'A bargain is a bargain. Besides,' she glanced back at the portrait, 'it's been worth every load. I do believe that business has gone up since the portrait was hung.'

Business had gone up, but only because the White Star Laundromat on the other side of town went out of business. I was smart enough not to say so.

'I'll be back in about three hours. That long enough?'

'I'll have them ready for you in two, child.'

I smiled. 'Thanks, Eloise,' and headed for the door.

My next stop was the drug store on Main Street. The pharmacist was a photography buff, and had taught me all I knew about cameras and film. Dr Boddie had a photography studio and darkroom set up in back for the rare citizen who wanted a family portrait and had the cash to pay for one. Even Boddie's cut-rate prices were high in Khoury. Ever since the LaFargue Refinery shut down in seventy-eight, the median income was too low to support luxuries like family photographs.

Still, there was the occasional need. Business had actually boomed during the Middle East War as hopeful local girls sent letters 'To Any Soldier'. One girl had actually received a proposal from the experience and went around in a delighted daze until she discovered her soldier fiancé was already married.

I waited while Dr Boddie finished up with Miz Lawas. She was complaining – again – about the fact that her blood-pressure medicine didn't seem to be working. She felt the same whether she took it or not.

Dr Boddie was explaining – again – that she couldn't and wouldn't be able to tell the difference until she quit taking it altogether and stroked out. Then she'd end up in a home like her sister. Miz Lawas grumbled, but paid the fee, collected her pills, and grumbled on out the door. It was the same argument every time she came into the drug store, an exchange unchanged for the last ten years.

While they argued, I spun the paperback display, searching for any novel I might have missed. I had learned about the world outside Khoury and the people who inhabited it through books, magazines, and the occasional film. Studying the way the rest of the world interacted, the way they lived. It wasn't the same as living out there, but it was the only vista allowed me. There was nothing new in yet and I sighed. The Emile Ajar novel was the last new book I had, and though it had won awards in France when it came out in 1975, it wouldn't last forever.

Boddie looked up and clapped his hands together once. 'Bonnie. Wha' I can do fo' you t'day?' He braced himself on the pharmacy counter. It was an old-fashioned, family-owned store, not a big national chain, and Boddie was on the same level as the customers instead of on a raised platform. Boddie ran the store alone ever since his daughter took off for college and never came back home. That was before I was born.

'Got some film for you, Boddie.'

The druggist's eyes opened wide. 'You go' de egrets comin' in? Down in de bayou wha' ya tol' me 'bout?'

For answer, I cocked a brow at him and handed over both cameras. Boddie had loaded the cameras for me with surplus 400 film, and removal would have to be done in the darkroom. There was no special Kodak casing to protect this film from light.

'Good enou'. You use all hunner'?'

'In both cameras. You think you can have them ready for me day after tomorrow?'

'Sho' I can. But it goin' to cost yo'.' Boddie's brows went up. 'Yo' got de cash fo' dis?' There was no such thing as credit in Khoury. Not with the economy so bad.

I never bragged about my allowance, and I never carried large amounts of cash around, but Boddie knew I always paid cash for everything. It must have been going to cost a bundle if he had to ask. 'I think I can manage.'

'Den I can have dem for yo' day f'om tomorr'.'

'Thanks, Boddie.' I backed slowly down the aisle, my sneakers squeaking occasionally on the waxed-tile floor. 'And Boddie, the last six or so in the Nikon are all time lapse. Full night.'

'Okay, yeah. I push it for you. Develop at eight hunner', 'stead of four hunner'. Increase de negative contras'. I do dem same size a' las' bunch?'

I nodded. The light had been poor on the bayou, and pushing the developing process would serve to uprate the film's effective speed. 'Thanks, Boddie. That'll be fine.' I had my hand on the 'out' door. If I stayed too long, Boddie would start into Cajun jokes and I'd never get out of there.

'Yo' wan' take yo' aunt her medicine?'

I stopped. 'Medicine?'

'It near 'bout time for her bloo'-press' medicine. Her call in fo' it las' week.'

'Blood-pressure medicine.' Tante Ilene was on blood-pressure medicine? 'Sure. I'll take it.' The Sarvaunts never took medicine. Except for Mishu Pilchard's shine.

I walked back up the aisle and took the paper bag. A large plastic bottle was inside. 'Can I pay for it when I pick up the film?' I backed slowly up the aisle again.

'Yeah, sure, okay. Bonnie, I tell you de one 'bout—'

The door opened behind me, letting in damp air and one of the Boudreaux boys. There were six last time I heard, and they all looked so much alike that no one bothered to learn their names, even in a town where children were a rarity. The town of Khoury had emptied of its young people when the last refinery shut down in the seventies. Those who wanted to work had packed up and moved, following the jobs to other parts of the south. Their departure left Khoury composed of the old, the decrepit, and the lazy. I took my chance and slipped out onto the sidewalk.

There was still a misty rain, the kind that evaporates as fast as it falls in the summer heat. The slicker would have been an encumbrance. Moisture dampened my T-shirt and re-wet my braid. I'd have curls for tomorrow. For The Man.

The pills rattled in the plastic pill bottle as I climbed into the pickup. Tante Ilene was on blood-pressure medicine . . . Secrets. My whole life was secrets.

Driving around to service windows, I paid the electric bill and natural-gas bill before I bought groceries. Canned goods and dried, boxed and bagged. Nothing fresh. Tee Dom raided his half-acre garden for fresh foods daily, and we ate what was available. Popcorn rice was on sale, and I hefted one of the twenty-pound bags onto the grocery cart's bottom rack. The pills rattled in the child seat with the shock of the weight. Secrets. What else did I not know?

I stowed the groceries in the back of the pickup and secured the tarp over them with bungee cords, leaving room for the laundry. The tarp kept them dry as I ran several errands, and then visited with Eloise while she folded our clothes. The well-padded woman talked of soap operas, TV stars, and her favorite recipes for an hour as the sky continued to pour an inconstant rain. She hugged me again as I left. A typical run into town . . . except for the pills still rattling in their bottle.

The trip back up the bayou was no trouble, even with the intermittent rain and the rare buffeting breeze. The trick was to place everything in the bottom of the boat with care, keeping the weight evenly balanced.

I munched a Dairy Queen burger and fries and drained a large

Coke on the way back, delighting in the fast-food taste and the greasy film that coated my lips.

Even with the bottle of pills and Tante Ilene's health preying on my mind, an occasional electric flush of excitement whispered in my veins as I maneuvered the johnboat through the mist, over the dark water. A visit from The Man always did that to me. It was a twice-yearly contact with the outside world. And this particular visit was especially significant.

Khoury was an isolated town, off the main roads, located down in the toe of the boot that was Louisiana. There were no roads passing *through* Khoury. Any further south and you'd hit the Gulf of Mexico. State road number 1372 moved south from Houma and dead-ended in Khoury. We had no movie houses – they had been boarded over ten years earlier; no cable – the cable company cut its service when it couldn't make a profit; no arts, no entertainment, no news.

If you needed a cop, there was only the LaRoque Sheriff's department to call, and a forty-minute wait on average. But then Khoury had no crime. The criminals left when the money did, in the seventies. An entire generation of youth followed soon after.

And if you needed an ambulance, good luck. There was a saying in Khoury. If you could survive the hour-long wait for an ambulance, you probably didn't need one anyway.

As far as I was concerned, Khoury was the end of the world. Yet, because of the specifications of the small trust fund set up by my mother, I stayed on in Khoury. My little world for twenty-one years.

I licked my fingers clean, swallowing the last salt, fat and ketchup. Fast food was my weakness. I prayed daily for the local Dairy Queen's financial success.

There wasn't much to do in Khoury, and no one to do it with. Needless to say, The Man's visits were the high points of my year.

The Man was Mr Alex Duhon, a lawyer who practiced in LaRoque. He controlled my education, my access to the outside world, my allowance, and my future. He also controlled my trust fund in accordance with my mother's wishes, making investments with the funds entrusted to him for my benefit. And this year I would learn who I really was and who my mother was. All the details about my past. This year Mr Duhon would explain the contents of the little black metal box he had given me six years ago.

I had tried to show him the contents of the box on two previous visits, offering up the sheaf of papers that proclaimed a mystery waiting to be solved. Both times he had refused to even look at the papers, saying he had strict orders to answer no questions until 10 August the year Bonnibelle Sarvaunt would have turned twenty-one. This year, had she really lived.

My hand was sticky on the tiller, making it difficult to steer the boat through the turn into Bayou Negre. Bayou water was always black except after a rain when silt and mud painted the surface a swirling brown, like today. Yet even after a rain, the Bayou Negre was blacker than the water it poured into. No one had ever explained it to me, but for some reason, even the mud was darker here.

Twenty minutes later I pulled up at the Sarvaunt Shanty. I had always called the small house the Sarvaunt Shanty instead of the more pretentious 'Place'. The title simply fitted better.

Tante Ilene met me at the dock as the roar of the twenty-horsepower engine died away with the fumes. Reaching down, she held out her hands and I handed the groceries up to her. When the water level was higher, it wasn't much of a stretch; I could tie up the johnboat and simply off-load the supplies. After the dry summer, there was a three-and-a-half-foot difference between water level and dock.

Once the johnboat was empty I put my foot on the lowest rung of the makeshift ladder and started up.

'Yo' goin' ge' Tee Dom.'

It wasn't a question, and I knew Tee Dom was most likely ready to come home, but I climbed up anyway. When I stood on the dock, my face half a foot above Tante Ilene's, I handed her the paper bag and her blood-pressure medicine. The pills jostled in the plastic bottle, an abrupt sound like a dropped baby's rattle.

Her face underwent the most imperceptible change. A slight tightening of the loose skin around her mouth. A faint narrowing of her black eyes. Nothing more. Her hand closed over the bag and with a single quick motion she shoved it into a pocket of her skirt. 'Yo' goin' ge' Tee Dom.'

'How long have you been on blood-pressure medication, Tante Ilene?'

'Yo' goin' get Tee Dom,' she said stiffly, even managing to pronounce a final consonant in her agitation.

'How long, Tante Ilene?'

'Yo' go.' She flapped her fingers at me, waving me away as if I were a bird raiding in Tee Dom's garden.

'How did you call in for a prescription renewal?' We didn't have a phone on the bayou. Neither did our neighbors.

'Yo' go.' She was emphatic this time, her eyes focused on the johnboat below us.

'No.'

Her eyes widened and for once met mine. They glittered like moonlight on bayou water, black-on-black. I had never said no before. I was almost as surprised as she, but I managed not to show it.

'Not until you answer me, Tante Ilene,' I said softly.

A silence stretched between us. I was so close I could smell the onions she had chopped for supper. I wondered fleetingly what it would feel like to hug Tante Ilene. Except for the rare moment when I helped her into or out of the boat, we never touched. It was an odd thought.

I was curious what Tante Ilene would do about my small refusal, my minor rebellion. She looked away, twisting her hands in her pocket. The stiff paper bag full of pills crinkled. Rain pattered down on us. A turtle splashed.

'Two year ago my bloo' press' go high – two fo'ty on top one twen'y. De med'cine keep it down.' Her lips pressed together a moment, releasing the words reluctantly. 'Miz Bourque call for me.'

Three entire sentences. I couldn't remember the last time she volunteered three sentences to me, and she wasn't finished.

'I . . . s'pose pick dem up . . . when Tee Dom and I go to town nex' week.'

She looked deeply into my face and I had the sudden impression she was seeing me for the first time in years. For a moment, she looked surprised. Her lips pursed, and her usual stern expression took its place on her features.

'You don' tell Tee Dom. No hes bizness.'

I was so startled that I agreed. 'Yes, ma'am.'

Tante Ilene nodded her head once, sharply. 'Yo' goin' ge' Tee Dom, now.' She turned and went into the shanty, leaving me staring at the empty space where she had been.

CHAPTER 2

The room was lit by a computer screen, the green glow reflecting dimly off a polished desk top, a small bronze statue, and a wine glass filled with dark liquid. Papers, both from the computer's tractor feed and from a legal pad, were scattered across the desk top and the floor. A fan, turning energetically above, ruffled the pages softly.

In the remote corners of the room, buried in shadows, was a carved antique bed from Italy and small seating area. The bed was eighteenth century, its four posters and elaborate headboard covered with the unyielding faces of long-dead saints. Legend claimed the bed had once belonged in a monastery, the nightly resting place of the head of the order himself.

A soft beep sounded from the computer, and the young man sitting before it leaned over the keyboard, his fingers dancing across the keys. Again it beeped, the screen changed and the man sighed, a long breathy sound of almost sensual delight. His lips lifted gently in the darkness, a smile as angelic as the carved saints on the bed behind him.

'So. We have activity.' He laughed softly. 'Do you hear? There is activity in the account.'

A rustle sounded behind him. The sound of sheets sliding over flesh. A woman's voice answered.

'I hear, McCallum dear. How long before we know something concrete?'

McCallum shrugged, his naked shoulder lifting in the emerald light. 'All we can do is follow the deposit. Perhaps tomorrow. Perhaps next week. Perhaps never. If she chooses to cash the check or takes it out of the country, we might never find her.'

'Find her and she's yours.' Her voice was silky with promise.

McCallum smiled at the screen. Her promises were worth everything. Her promises could give him the world.

'Now,' she said sharply. 'Come back here.'

His smile faded as he padded silently back to the bed.

There was paint under my nails and ground into the skin of my hands, Cadmium Red and Brown Madder and Lamp Black. By the light of the flickering wick my skin looked mottled, like a leper's hands must look in the last stages of disease. Once again I shuffled through the stack of papers I still stored in the little black metal box. The two birth certificates, two death certificates, a photograph of two gravestones, and two baby pictures – one was me.

There was no mistaking my features, long of face even as an infant, yellow-green eyes. I had called them hazel when I got my driver's license, but hazel didn't come close to describing them. They were the color of leaves in fall, green with yellow and amber and brown flecks. And huge pupils, wide open even in bright sun. At an age when most newborn's eyes are milky blue, mine stared back at the camera solemn and self-possessed and seemingly adult . . . yellow-green.

The other infant had milky blue-black eyes, and splotched red skin, and hair which stood straight up, like a black rooster's crown. The child looked like Tee Dom, but wasn't. Big ears and a flat nose. Neither photograph was labeled or dated, but both were taken at Merciful Savior Hospital in Petit Chenier, Louisiana.

I stacked the edges of the papers and the photographs neatly and slipped them back into the aged manila envelope. There was an address on the envelope, and a name. M.L. DeVillier. The same name that appeared on the gravestones. DeVillier.

Using the papers in the box, I had been recreating my past for six years, trying to explain to myself who I was from the meager clues. In my imagination, my mother was Marie L. Smith DeVillier, on the run from my father, William Marc DeVillier. She had met and befriended Elizabeth Sarvaunt and taken Elizabeth's identity as her own when Elizabeth died, burying beneath the graves in Petit Chenier her own identity and that of her baby, Carin Colleen. When the real Elizabeth Sarvaunt died, Marie DeVillier ceased to exist.

The story answered all the clues I had so far, but it was just a guess. Just a dream. It wasn't proof.

And for all I knew, I might really be Bonnie, and the death certificate with my name on it might have been an error of the state which my mother had never had time to correct before her own death. There were many possibilities that would fit the clues.

The Man had promised to tell me the truth when he came this time. Tell me all he knew about me, my mother, and my past. Today. As of today there would be no more secrets.

My heart raced a moment, an uneven clip of beats before it settled. I checked my watch for the hundredth time. Still not quite four and black as pitch outside. I knew about pitch. I cleaned the stuff off my lamp from time to time. Lamp Black, like the paint ground into my skin. I closed and locked the little box, hanging the key around my neck on its leather thong.

Shadows flickered with the breeze through the window, a waltz against the rafters, great rough-hewn things softened by faint light. The shanty was over a hundred years old, a survivor of hurricanes, drought, high winds and time. The ax blade which had shaped the thick lengths of wood still marked the oak which supported the tin roof.

I tried again to lock away my thoughts and concentrate on the wet painting resting on the easel shelf. *Empty Nests*. The egret rookery, Desolate and deserted by quarter moon.

Rain shushed down on the tin roof and into the bayou, a soft water-on-water sound, a slick and liquid den, vibrant and rich. Dark, like the scene on my canvas.

It was an odd shade to add to Lamp Black, but on impulse I mixed in a faint smear of French Ultramarine Blue, and with a fitch brush, touched at the water edge. Moonlight with shadow. It worked. Suddenly *Empty Nests* came alive, a moving, breeze-touched scene where even the shadows had life. The new shade went everywhere, on the white feathers, on the water, on the black sticks of nest.

And suddenly it was morning, with smeared shadows on the rafters and Tante Ilene stirring, and *Empty Nests* seemed to die. Only in faint light was it alive. I smiled and stretched, resting the paint-smeared fitch in the first cleaning jar. And stretched again.

I moved the easel back a pace and stretched more fully, an entire series of yoga moves. From chest expansions, to rishi's posture, to the triangle, to the dancer's posture, and finally into the plough.

My dance instructor, Miss Taussig, had been a firm believer in yoga as a part of any dance discipline. At eighty-something, the nimble woman had been agile as a cat. And almost as peaceful. When they found her dead, she had a smile on her face and her body was in full lotus.

Rumor was, the funeral had been delayed until rigor mortis had passed. It was the only way she could be pried into a coffin. According to her will, no bones could be broken to force her into the proper supine position. She was a stubborn old woman.

I stretched out on the floor for a moment and breathed deeply before I rose to my feet. Opening the mineral spirits, I cleaned my hands with an old, worn diaper. The tart scent quickly filled the shanty, but Tee Dom and Tante Ilene had never complained about the smell.

Breakfast was eggs over easy, biscuits and fresh pork sausage from Mishu Pilchard's hog slaughter. Tee Dom and Tante Ilene stirred the eggs and spicy ground pork into a yolk-yellow medley, scooping the damp meal up with a spoon, dipping in the biscuits to sop up the left-over grease and yolk. It looked wonderful, but I had never been allowed to eat that way. I had to use Proper Manners. Proper Etiquette. If I didn't, I got the back of my hand smacked with one of Tante Ilene's wooden spoons.

Rain started back almost immediately after breakfast, and I returned to the loft for another few hours of painting. Tante Ilene gave me a fresh cup of coffee, black and strong, to carry up with me. I wondered what it would be like to have actual conversation over breakfast.

The light was dull enough to continue work on a night scene, dark trees, dark water, dark shapes which seemed to twist and writhe. A full moon lit it all with faded gray light.

The sput-putter of a boat moving through the lily-choked bayou downstream pulled me from the depths of the night scene. A hiss of excitement sizzled through my bloodstream like far-away lightning. Nine thirty. He was early.

Washing my hands with mineral spirits and again with Tante

Ilene's chamomile soap, I cleaned the oil-based tint from my nails and cuticles and the creases between my fingers. I poured spring water into the chipped bowl and washed my body. The sound of the engine smoothed out as it neared. My hands were shaking. I changed into the cotton print dress hanging from the rafters of my makeshift closet. Slipped on sandals. Unbraided my hair and ran a comb through the thick curly mass. Lipstick, pale coral, the color of the flowers in the yellow print, brightened my lips. Mineral spirits was my only perfume.

I tried to calm my breathing, but Miss Taussig's lessons in control slipped away, forgotten. The boat engine cut out, popped once and fell silent. Bumped against the dock. I swung my leg over the low railing and made my way down the ladder. At the last second I paused and grabbed the black box, carrying it down with me.

Tante Ilene looked up from her coffee cup, steaming on the table before her. Tee Dom was on the front porch, visible through the screening which let in light and air but not the mosquitoes and night pests. He was staring down at the muddy waters of the bayou, his body strangely tense and hard. A long stream of tobacco juice shot from the side of his mouth into the dark water below.

'De Man. He here.' Tante Ilene scratched the pitted skin of her nose.

'Yes. I heard.'

Soft voices sounded from the front porch which was also the dock. Tante Ilene opened her mouth as if she might speak. Closed it uncertainly. Her eyes looked away. I had never seen Tante Ilene uncertain of anything, ever. Surprised, I waited for her to speak. When she didn't, I shrugged and turned away from her silence, pulling out my sunglasses and checking them for smudges.

Sunglasses had been a part of my outdoor life for all of my twenty-one years, a necessary precaution to protect my eyes from developing cataracts at an early age. I had Physiological Mydriasis, a fancy medical term for enlarged pupils.

Alex Duhon's pudgy frame appeared through the screen, an odd sight in his sweat-streaked dress-shirt and his loose silk tie. A suit coat was draped over his arm. Only on Sundays and for funerals did any bayou dweller wear dress-shirts. A few of the men owned suits, but seldom wore them.

I picked up my bag, the mesh carry-all I carried into the swamp and into town, and went out into the sunlight. Blue sky beaded with gray clouds blinded my eyes and I slipped on my sunglasses, cutting the glare.

Alex held out his hands to me, took my wrists and gave me a perfunctory hug. 'Bonnie. This old geezer taking good care of you?'

Tee Dom spat a stream of brown into the muddy water. It blended in instantly. The old man said nothing, but stared out over the water. His jaw worked, clenching and releasing as he chewed the wad of tobacco; his face was tight as he studied the familiar landscape.

He had never been a demonstrative man, silent and taciturn. As much a part of the bayou country as one of the cypress knees that jutted up from the swampy water. And almost as communicative. I had learned to read his body language over the years, discerning his mood from his posture. At the moment, Tee Dom was upset, angry. But I might never know why. Body language wasn't that precise a science. He spat again, ignoring The Man.

'Well.' Duhon patted my back and stepped down into his boat. It rocked slightly on the water. I handed down the black box and my bag and while The Man's hands were full, stepped down gingerly beside him.

I was wrong. It wasn't Duhon's usual johnboat rented from Elred at the public landing. This was a sleek bass boat, the kind with two raised swivel seats sitting side by side, a front-mounted trolling motor with twenty-four-volt battery and foot pedal controls, a one-hundred-and-fifty-horsepower Mercury motor on back, and a real steering wheel. There was a cooler for beer and a second cooler for fish, expensive-looking rods were secured into the side walls, with two bright orange life preservers. The floor of the boat was carpeted in green, which matched the upholstery on the swivel chairs.

I had seen out-of-towner fishermen any number of times on the bayou trolling past at a snail's pace or whizzing past at what looked like seventy miles per hour on their way to the nearest secluded fishing spot. However, I had never been in one of those expensive boats.

On the bayou, fishing was a sport only to tourists. To the residents, it was a survival skill. Johnboats and the occasional pirogue were daily transportation, not a rich man's toy.

I took the seat to the left, although I really wanted to drive the boat. Duhon started the Mercury motor with a key – no rope pulls for this plaything – pulled into the bayou and pushed forward on the accelerator. The shanty fell into the distance, left behind in a swirl of smoky exhaust and gas-filmed muddy water.

I grabbed the mesh bag, untied one of the rubber bands from the handle, and quickly rebraided my hair before the curl was lost to the wind. And then I sat back and watched the world speed by. Egrets and a blue heron took off in a startled flutter of wings. An alligator raced into the safety of the water, his clawed feet tearing into the muddy earth, leaving deep scratches on either side of the slick furrow left by his tail. It was a big gator, at least eight feet.

Waterlilies were blooming, a soft purple in the intermittent sunlight. I had always loved the thick carpet of lavender blooms, but they were a real problem to boaters, choking out the waterways, contributing to the decreasing number of fish in many parts of the bayou. The broad green leaves of the plant were closing off parts of Bayou Negre, and some day soon some anonymous person would ride by and spray them with a herbicide, not caring what the chemical did to the environment or the food chain.

A light rain started and Duhon slowed the bass boat, handing me an umbrella while maneuvering carefully through the narrow channel left by the lilies. He opened a second umbrella over his own head and sped on, much slower this time in deference to the umbrellas. The man-made breeze created by the boat's progress whipped the black fabric of the umbrellas, and tried to snatch the feeble protection away. I put the umbrella in front of my body as a shield from the blowing rain. It was ridiculous to think of using an umbrella at thirty miles per hour. It was clear that Duhon wasn't a bayou dweller.

Finally The Man pulled up at an abandoned and sinking dock, tossed a rope over an unsteady piling, and cut the big Mercury.

We drifted on the still water, raindrops splattering into the water and onto the greenery around us on shore. Exhaust blew away slowly, leaving the faint smell of dank water, rotting vegetation, and Duhon's sweat to mingle in my nostrils.

This sinking, rotting dock was one where we had stopped for the last eight summers. The place where we carried on our summertime conversations about my schooling, my medical needs, my plans and Duhon's plans for me.

The abandoned Plauche Place – the siding blown off the ancient house, the roof fallen in – was set back from the bayou, engulfed in leaves and vines and overgrown bushes. I had once thought the house itself might be significant to the mystery that was me. I had combed the grounds and the mildew-covered rooms inch by inch one summer after Duhon left. Nothing. Whoever lived there had left nothing behind when they moved.

In the years since, I realized that Duhon stopped here simply because he was set in his ways. If he stopped here once, he would stop here every time. Duhon was not exactly an imaginative man.

'Sorry about your hair. I know you young girls always want to be perfect. I have two daughters myself.' He beamed at me, his face full and fat. Duhon had put on weight in the last year. His dress-shirt pulled at the buttons. 'So. Are you ready to hear what I know about your mother?'

A liquid shock of electricity ripped through me, and I had to force myself to remember how to breathe. Slowly, I tilted back the umbrella, resting it parasol-style across one shoulder, watching The Man.

His mouth curled up making great mounds of his cheeks, like a happy Buddha. His ruddy skin was a bit sunburned, his hair a wind-blown tangle. It looked like the kind of smile a favorite uncle might bestow on his niece's birthday. As if he had a surprise for me.

My heart did a strange little leap. There had been scant reason to feel excitement in the years of my life, except for my art or my lessons. Few gifts as a child, fewer toys, no birthday or Christmas celebration of note. So it was strange, the behavior of my heart.

'Tell me about her. How you met. When. What she looked like—'

I stopped, aware the words had stumbled over one another in their haste to be said. 'Tell me everything.'

Duhon laced his fingers and swiveled back and forth in his tall bass boat chair. Rain made an uneven pattern of gray spots on his dress-shirt.

'Exactly sixteen years ago today your mother came into my office. You know I keep my main office in Houma now, but back then I kept a second small office opened in LaRoque, two mornings a week in the back of McMillan's drug store. Well, in walked your mother one day with a sheaf of papers and the request that I provide her child – you – with the necessary certificates to secure your custody at her death.'

'What did she look like?' I had been taught it was impolite to interrupt, but Duhon seemed to be stuck like glue to the inconsequential.

'She was tall and graceful, like you, with blonde streaked hair. Green eyes. Long legs. Very classy dresser for LaRoque, let me tell you.'

There was a tone in Duhon's voice when he said, 'Green eyes. Long legs,' that made my scalp tingle. She had gotten to him, my mother. 'Big pupils, like yours. Must run in the family, your condition.'

I blinked my eyes behind the dark lenses, surprised. *A familial trait. Was Physiological Mydriasis genetic? . . . My eye doctor had never hinted at the possibility.* Duhon was still talking.

'She wanted a trust fund set up, and she wanted me to administer it for her on your behalf until you reached the age of twenty-one.'

In a long rambling monologue, perfectly in character for a lawyer who billed his time by the hour, Duhon went on to explain the terms of the trust – pretty standard – and the terms of my custody to the Sarvaunts. But this wasn't what I wanted to hear. I wanted to know about the woman, my mother. I wanted to know about her hair, was it natural blonde or dyed? What colors had she worn when she came to his office? What did she smell like, how did she walk? . . . I wanted him to tell me she was still alive.

Duhon wanted to talk the law. I wanted answers.

I had little practice with conversation, but I had learned the finer points of negotiation with my teachers over the years. *I'll learn tap dance, if you'll teach me the Tango. I'll learn Proper English if you'll teach me to curse in French and Spanish. I'll watch the boring foreign film with subtitles and write an essay on it if you'll take me to see* A Few Good Men *or* The Firm *or anything with Tom Cruise or Harrison Ford in it*. So I listened, sifting through the self-aggrandized legal mumbo-jumbo for the kernels of truth I wanted.

He knew my mother as Elizabeth Sarvaunt. He had never heard of DeVillier, it wasn't a name my mother had mentioned to him. I tried not to let my dismay show when he casually dashed my hopes.

'She was taller than you, but not quite so graceful. All your lessons have polished your natural grace into something like a professional dancer's. But hers . . .' His eyes were far away. 'Hers was a wilder kind of . . .' He stopped, scratched his head and wiped his face with a handkerchief pulled from his pocket. He cleared his throat.

Hers was a wilder kind of what? . . .

He glanced back at the coolers longingly, and I knew suddenly that one held beer. Duhon sighed and swiveled his chair back to me. 'She seemed sad sometimes, like when I would be talking to her and she would be miles away in thought. Pensive. A couple of times when she showed up in my office to sign papers she had paint stains beneath her nails.'

My heart did its queer little jump. *My mother had painted. Like me.*

'She wore a hint of perfume. Like some kind of flower. She was twenty-one, I think, or maybe twenty-two, I'd have to check my records, when she signed over custody of you to her aunt and uncle. It wasn't a matter for the courts, as a few simple legal papers were all it took to arrange the details, giving you to your nearest relatives. She was dying even then, you see.'

My heart jolted and my hands closed on the arms of the swivel chair as my world swam, all watery and dark. No. No! NO! And his voice floated around me in this watery world, telling me more about my dead mother while inside me something began to laugh. She had fooled even him. Even her own lawyer. *I knew she was alive. I knew it.*

Yes, he thought it was odd how little she looked like a Sarvaunt, but there were explanations for that. Perhaps Tante Ilene's sister had fathered Elizabeth elsewhere, not in the insular little Cajun community of Khoury. Polite little phrase. 'Fathered elsewhere.'

I showed The Man the contents of the black box, hoping the photographs and the legal certificates would dislodge something in his mind. Help him remember some fact. *My mother wasn't dead. She couldn't be.*

He flipped politely through the ticket stubs to plays and jazz concerts in New Orleans and the matchbooks from Felix's and the Absinthe House Bar. Nothing. He had no comment and no speculations. She was dead, he knew that much. Elizabeth Sarvaunt had died in Gloree, Louisiana. He had a death certificate to prove the fact, and it was '. . . useless and futile to speculate about the possibility that she might be alive.'

He had a death certificate . . . I demanded to see the official form, which he produced. It was a photocopy, but I assumed that Duhon had the original. He was far too thorough a lawyer to accept a photocopied one. With the proof of Elizabeth Sarvaunt's death, my theory of my own origins floundered. But then, my mother, if she were hiding me, might have become someone else by the time of the death, leaving another young woman to die with the identity of Elizabeth Sarvaunt. It was possible. And I had lived for so long with the belief that I was not Bonnibelle, that I couldn't let go of the thought.

Duhon wouldn't consider the possibility of an error in the official documents. Not even when I showed him the death certificate for Bonnibelle Sarvaunt. His face turned a bit red as he fingered the certificate, and he pursed his lips as if he was trying to spit out a reason for the paper's existence. Finally he simply shrugged and set it aside, wiping his fingers fastidiously on his handkerchief. And he had no interest at all in the photographs of the graves marked DeVillier.

At that point, Duhon soulfully patted my hand, like one might pat a deranged child. A youngster who sees fairies or leprechauns. A 'Yesyes' to calm the deluded. And that was all. Nothing else.

Nothing about the kind of woman she had been, or what she

had wanted out of life or even how she had supposedly died. As attractive as she had been, his interest in my mother had died long ago.

The conversation took the better part of two hours as the back of the bass boat drifted away from the dock and the sky cleared. I asked questions about my mother and Duhon answered. I rephrased questions and Duhon rephrased his answers. And I learned nothing.

Duhon and I smeared sunscreen into our skin, handing the pink plastic bottle back and forth as we talked, my eyes hidden behind the dark sunglasses. After an hour Duhon finally broke down and went to the cooler, twisted the top off a beer bottle and swigged down half in one swallow. No wonder Duhon's shirt was pulling at the buttons, I thought unkindly.

When I finally ran out of unanswered questions, Duhon sensed something in me and fell silent himself. He patted my hand again, consolingly, and said something stupid like I'd get over it and I'd go on with my life. I ignored him and managed not to claw his face for the inanities. He took my silence for acquiescence and perhaps delayed grief for the mother I had never known and never would. I don't think he suspected the fury, the cold rage that burned inside me.

'She isn't dead!' I wanted to scream. *'She was hiding me. She was running from something. She was afraid.'* But I couldn't. I couldn't give her away to this pompous jerk. And besides . . . what did I really know about my mother?

There were a thousand unanswered questions. Questions about my mother and her past. Who was Marie L. DeVillier? Was she my real mother? And if so, why had she given me the identity of a dead baby?

But Duhon was hungry, and I had the feeling he never let anything stand between him and a good meal. Or a bad one, for that matter.

With dinner obviously in mind, he started the motor and drove downstream into the Gulf and up into a second bayou. I was lost, but Duhon seemed perfectly comfortable with his heading. The rain had stopped, and we made good time, probably covering thirty miles inside an hour, into unfamiliar territory.

We were on Bayou Frivole, farther north than I had ever been.

Bayou Frivole was deeper than Bayou Negre, a home base to shrimpers and fishermen, drug dealers operating out of the Gulf, and tourists. Frivole rolled right through LaRoque Parish into Moisson Parish and served several towns with livelihoods and transportation.

We passed docks where shrimpers and small-time commercial fishermen off-loaded their catch. Ice houses and sorting sheds whipped by. And over everything there lay the harsh stench of dead fish and shellfish.

There were restaurants and public docks and campgrounds for the tourists. There were even several small motels with both land and water access and dock storage for fishermen's boats. Bayou country in economic up-swing.

Better times hadn't made its trickle-down way into Khoury yet. Perhaps never would.

We pulled up at a nondescript little dock and moored the bass boat to an empty piling. Three other bass boats were moored at the same dock, decked out in the finest fishing gear known to man. Depth finders and fish finders and electronic fish callers. All the gee-gaws the rich sports fisherman thought he needed to bring in a big catch.

I followed Duhon up the rickety steps and down a path lined with hibiscus to a little house, a small, four-room café. It was little more than weathered, unpainted wood siding, dirty windows and a sagging roof. The café was nestled onto a spit of land, Bayou Frivole flowing behind, a narrow paved road out front. Ancient and worn as the couple who ran it, it was a café only because they insisted it was.

Duhon ordered Boudin and cracklins, jambalaya and fried catfish. He even ordered a beer for me and a huge order of fried onion rings.

I had always been told I looked young for my age, like a teenager instead of an adult, but the old woman never even asked for an ID. Although Louisiana officially conforms to the federal standard drinking age of twenty-one, in practice, no one adheres to it. If you look at least eighteen, you can always buy alcohol. Especially during Mardi Gras, when the cops look the other way as a matter of course.

The Boudin was livery – full of finely ground organ meat and rice – the cracklins crisp and the beer cold. I had never drunk dark beer, and I particularly liked the thick yeasty texture-taste of the St Pauli Girl. We ate for several minutes in silence, as the café cleared of the lunchtime crowd. The jukebox fell silent. The smoke thinned out. In a clatter of sound that seemed far too loud for the few dishes, the old woman cleared away paper napkins, chipped plates and cheap tableware from the deserted tables around us.

'Now.' Duhon took a bite and wiped his mouth, leaving behind a smear of ketchup just above the corner of his lip. It quivered when he spoke. 'I have something for you to handle.' He handed me two envelopes, one with SARVAUNT typed on the front, all in capital letters. The other had BONNIBELLE SARVAUNT typed on the front. Neither was sealed. From the Sarvaunt's envelope, I pulled a cashier's check.

Duhon chuckled when he saw my face. 'For services rendered,' he said, and drained his beer. Ordered up a second. I looked at him, wanting to wipe off the ketchup. It looked like blood, glowing in the smoky air.

'Fifty thousand dollars for your aunt and uncle to be delivered on 10 August, the year you turned twenty-one according to your mother's specifications.'

There was a strange sensation in the pit of my chest, a tiny electric jolt of pain, a twinge of grief. Feelings that I didn't want to touch. Didn't want to look at too closely. I carefully replaced the check and put it beside my beer. Water beaded the outside of the dark green glass and trailed down onto the scared wooden table top. I lifted my beer and drained half of it at once, forcing down the musty-tasting liquid. Trying to swallow back and down the peculiar emotions pushing at my heart. *'For services rendered'!*

I placed the beer back on the table, and carefully reached for the envelope marked BONNIBELLE. My fingers were pale and shaking in the dim café light. Within, was a second cashier's check for fifty thousand dollars. The shock still tingling in my blood began to soften, began to ease as I stared at the check. I turned it over, stared at the smooth, pale green paper. Turned it back upright. The figure was still the same. Fifty thousand dollars.

A bit of something was kindled deep inside me. Heat. Anger. And something else I couldn't name.

The strip of paper smelled like Duhon, sweat and coffee and tobacco, as if he had carried it close to his body for some time. My fingers slid over the raised lettering of the amount. Red dots, mounds like measles across the paper, in the shape of words and numerals. My future.

I folded the check and tucked it into my pocket; it was warm against my thigh like the lover's touch I had never felt. I wanted to laugh. Or cry. Or break something.

Rain started to fall again, a soft summer mist that clung for an instant and evaporated. A common rain, typical to sub-tropical regions. Soft. It dribbled down the windows outside and disappeared. Duhon wiped his mouth.

I swallowed and took a deep breath. The air seemed to burn as it entered my lungs, like breathing smoke. Something hot and sweet pumped its way through me. And I resisted the urge to giggle like a child. Resisted the urge to jump up and run out of the café, waving my arms like a windmill and shouting to the world that finally something had happened in my life. Something had changed. Finally, after all these years of Khoury's sameness. Khoury's nothingness . . . I resisted the urge to cry.

Duhon didn't even look up. He dipped a fried onion ring into ketchup and popped it into his mouth. I closed my eyes and took another shuddering breath.

Over the meal, Duhon opened my portfolio. He tried to explain about growth funds and long-term investments, income dividends. Things I probably knew as much about as he did. Halfway through his little seminar I seemed to waken, suddenly heard what he was saying.

My small trust fund wasn't so small after all. I was wealthy. Not fabulously wealthy – not Princess Di wealthy – but well enough off. And suddenly I understood the reasons behind my exotic education. I had been groomed all my life to handle money. To comport myself in a society totally unlike that which existed in Khoury, Louisiana. To live differently from the poor, closed lifestyle offered me by Tante Ilene and Tee Dom. And this was why. This trust fund.

If I could someday have control of the trust, if I could wrest the monies from Duhon's grasp, I would handle the funds in a much less conservative fashion. I could make my fifty thousand double in three to five years; I had done as much on paper, using play money for years. I had an eye for the market and a knack for investments. If I controlled the trust in its entirety I could do even better. I could—

'In three years, just after your twenty-fourth birthday, 10 August, you will take control of your portfolio. Which, by then, providing growth continues as I predict, will be valued at five hundred thousand dollars.'

The slow swirl of emotions that had pulled and wrenched and burned in me from the moment I saw Tee Dom's and Tante Ilene's check, steadied and cleared, like wind calming after a storm. The feelings washed away at the sound of his words. It would be mine. All of it. In three years' time.

'I want a copy of everything,' I heard myself say, 'and I'd appreciate it if you would keep me apprised of all future transactions. It would give me a chance . . .' My voice trailed off.

Duhon put down his fork, a thick mouthful of spicy jambalaya untasted. His eyes looked odd, as if I had just slapped him, or told an obscene joke.

'For my financial education,' I added. 'If I have to make decisions in three years' time about how to handle investments, then I need to see how you manage them.'

Duhon still looked a bit strange. Uncomfortable. As if his collar was too tight. I suddenly wondered just how much money Duhon made administering the trust for me. And if he had found some rather unscrupulous means of making more than he was entitled. Or had I simply insulted his pride when I asked to see the books?

Duhon pursed his lips, and swallowed, his eyes on his near-empty plate. 'I suppose it would be a natural progression for your studies. How are your sessions at the bank, with Mr Kirby, going?'

Duhon was asking about my financial studies, the once-a-week seminar held in nearby LaRoque, where I was taught the finer points of national and international finance. Over the years, I had been taught about futures and commodities trading on the commodity market, arbitrage trading on the international markets. I had studied the New York Stock Exchange, the American Exchange, the Texas Stock Exchange, the Pacific

Exchange, NASDEQ, and the foreign currency markets. Even trading on the NIKO – the Japanese market.

'Well enough,' I said shortly. Although he was a good teacher, I had never liked Rufus Kirby. He put his hands on me too often when I was first his student in financial matters. The day I came to the branch bank with Tee Dom's .20-gauge shotgun and threatened to shoot off his fingers and anything else big enough to aim at, he had put a stop to the hugs, pats, and caresses. I suppose he could have put me in jail for all manner of charges, but he didn't. In fact, I don't think Kirby ever mentioned the incident to anyone.

'He does say that you show unusual promise in your studies.'

I smiled. Kirby would have said as much to Duhon even if it weren't true. Kirby was scared to death of me.

It was something I had noticed in several of my tutors. Not that I had ever been violent or even rude with any of them. Even when I threatened Kirby, I had been polite. But they had all expected me to be a kid. A teenager, typical of the day, interested in MTV and Madonna and the latest fashions.

They expected me to *think* like a teenager – and I had been an uncomfortable surprise. Even as a child, I had been an adult thinker with a well-developed mind of my own. Opinionated and quick – at least in the subjects that interested me.

No. I had never acted like a teenager. Perhaps because I had never been around kids my age even when I was growing up. I had been alone, or with older children like Elred or the Gastineau girls or the Boudreaux boys, fishing and crabbing and playing pranks on Father Alcede.

But that had been when I was an adolescent, before Louise Gastineau got pregnant for the first time and her sister took off for the evils of Los Angeles and the Boudreaux boys started looking at me differently. So except for the two years before I turned twelve, I had always been with adults or books. I had never been a kid. I had never thought like a kid. And my tutors either respected and acknowledged that fact, or they were nervous and uncomfortable around me.

Duhon was gabbing away about my studies, my well-rounded education, and the fact that with my GED and the advanced-study courses I had taken since I turned eighteen, I could take any college entrance exam anywhere in the state and be accepted. Most likely as an advanced student.

I smiled and fingered the check still warm against my thigh. 'I'm not going to college.'

Duhon stopped midway through the process of closing up his briefcase, his hand held motionless in the air, his mouth slack and eyebrows pulled together over his nose. It was as if I had said the unthinkable. 'But that's what the money is for.'

'The check is made out to me.' I tapped it in my pocket although he couldn't see the motion where my hands were hidden beneath the table. 'I'm twenty-one, and I'll use it anyway I please.' I said it calmly – even sweetly. But I meant it. I meant it as much as I had when I threatened Kirby with the shotgun. Perhaps more.

Duhon patted my shoulder and sat back in his seat. I hated that paternal mannerism, the pose of automatically assumed superiority. Okay, Duhon was older than I was. But not necessarily smarter.

'Now, Bonnie. We both know your mother always intended you to go to college. That's why she handled your education the way she did. You can't just—'

I leaned in close to Duhon and slipped off my sunglasses, effectively cutting him off mid-sentence.

'Mr Duhon. My mother didn't have the slightest concern about my education. She raised me the way she did because she *was* hiding me from someone. You know that. I know that.'

Duhon's eyes widened a fraction and he sat back from me in the rickety chair. His hand lifted from my shoulder like I had flamed up suddenly and burned his flesh.

'If she had wanted me to use this money only for my education, she would have had you administer the funds that way, and pay them out only to an educational institution. And she would have begun that when I turned eighteen, not now. Instead she gave them to me, to use any way I wanted. To sink or swim. Right, Duhon?'

He hated it when I used only his last name, and he pursed his lips again. It occurred to me that Duhon would have made a great maiden aunt, always disapproving and handing out advice a generation old and out of date.

'I have fifty thousand dollars to live on for the next three years. My mother wanted me to have it. And I'm not going to college.'

Duhon blinked, focusing on me strangely. I had the feeling he was seeing me for the first time, like Tante Ilene when I first said 'No'. None of them had ever really expected me to grow up. None of them had ever really thought I had a mind of my own. But I had grown up years ago. And thanks to the unconventional education my mother had devised for me, my mind had always been my own.

A long moment passed. Duhon drummed his fingertips across the table top several times, then, as if the movement gave away something I wasn't supposed to see, he put the hand on his lap under the table. We looked very proper, I'm sure, sitting at the plastic checked cloth, our hands in our laps.

'No college.' He looked at me speculatively. 'What will you do, instead?'

I sat back from him. Duhon took a deep breath. He seemed relieved when I moved away, releasing a pent-up breath. I filed the reaction away to analyze later.

'I'm not sure yet.' But I was. I had known what I would do the instant I saw the check. 'I'll contact you when I decide.'

Duhon nodded.

'My mother. She was hiding me, wasn't she? She was protecting me from something. Or someone.'

'She never said.'

I waited, patiently.

'But yes. I got the impression she was hiding from someone. And someone was trying to find her. She was hiding *you* from someone. I do know that.'

'My father.'

'I don't think so.'

I was surprised. Opening the little black box, I pulled out a marriage license from the sheaf of papers. 'Marie L. Smith married a William Marc DeVillier on 7 July—'

'Yes,' he interrupted. 'But you were already born. Look at the year, Bonnie. Besides, your mother's name was Elizabeth.'

That paternal sound was back in his voice, and I wanted to slap him. Because he was right. Bonnibelle Sarvaunt was born one year before Marie L. Smith married. But what if I wasn't

Bonnibelle Sarvaunt? What if I was Carin DeVillier, and Marie L. Smith DeVillier, my real mother, wasn't really dead? What if she just switched me with a dead baby and faked her own death? . . .

Even I knew it sounded gothic. Like a mystery novel taken to extremes.

This conversation was making my head ache. I slipped the sunglasses back onto my face and closed the marriage license up in the little black box. Duhon patted my shoulder again, and I was suddenly too emotionally drained to care. The sun had broken through the clouds outside and every blade of grass and leaf glittered and steamed in the light.

'Listen, Bonnie, I know you want to find a mystery in your upbringing. It's natural. Perfectly natural.'

I tilted my head against the high wooden back of the seat. Closed my eyes. *It wasn't like that. I wasn't making anything up.* There *was* a mystery here. I was a mystery. But I didn't say it.

'Your mother was a single parent. Your father was an unknown. I don't think he even knew you existed.' Duhon paused. 'I'm not sure your mother even knew who your father was.'

I spoke without opening my eyes. 'You're saying my mother was a whore. Sleeping around with so many men that she couldn't keep them separated.'

'It's possible.'

I had waited patiently for answers from The Man. Waited for years. He knew *about* her, but he had never *known* her. And he thought she was dead. Dead!

I knew she was alive. I could feel her as surely as I could feel the breeze on my skin, smell the rain in the air.

I walked like her. Had eyes like her. Painted like her. She was part of the magic I had lived with for all these years. 'She isn't dead,' I wanted to scream.

And she had to have loved me to have provided for me, protected me for all these years. Protected me from whatever she feared so greatly.

A rage started deep in me. A fury so strong, so penetrating, I was surprised my skin didn't smoke and sparks didn't flare from my eyes. '*My mother wasn't a whore,*' I said softly.

'You don't know what your mother was.'

'No. And neither do you.'

Our conversation was over, choked to death on a lump of accusation, frustration, and my mother's deception. Duhon had never really known my mother. Only the Sarvaunts had known her. And I had learned long ago that they weren't talking. Not about the woman I believed to be my birth mother, the unknown woman known only as Marie DeVillier. And not about Elizabeth Sarvaunt.

Late, he took me home, rain again pouring around the bass boat, puddling in the bottom. The fifty-thousand-dollar check was safe in the folder of investment information I had insisted Duhon photocopy. Having stopped at one of the better hotels on the water he paid a small fortune to use their machine. And the rain couldn't touch the papers in the zippered leather cover I made him buy.

With the fortune Duhon made administering my trust fund, he could afford it. A few ancillary expenditures wouldn't break him.

By the time we got back to the Sarvaunt Shanty, the rain had died, but my dress was wet, the small yellow print clinging to my breasts and shoulders. Slowly, I stood in the flat-bottomed boat and stepped onto the dock, the boards creaking beneath my sandals. Duhon was staring at my breasts, his eyes lingering on my nipples, prominent through the transparent material. He flushed and turned away, pursing his lips like he'd sucked something sour. Like that disapproving maiden aunt I had compared him to.

Without speaking, I went inside, letting the door shut softly behind me. It was dark inside in the early evening light, the setting sun obscured by clouds. Tante Ilene's hurricane lamp did little to dispel the gloom in the small space. I dropped the Sarvaunts' fifty-thousand-dollar check into Tante Ilene's lap. It lay there, untouched.

Her eyes stared down at the envelope. Her hands, wrinkled like bird claws, clutched at the arms of her rocker. Once. Twice. She didn't seem to breathe at all. A cup of coffee steamed on the table beside her. Perhaps her twelfth cup of the day.

Tee Dom stepped into the room from the darkened space of the bedroom, his body short and squat and stiff as a corpse. They looked at each other a long moment, their eyes communicating something I couldn't follow. But then, that's how it had always been. Me on the outside.

Silently, I climbed the ladder to the black loft and lit my lamp, trimming the wick down for a soft glow. Moving quickly, I stripped down and stuffed my clothes into a small black canvas bag, balling up the damp dress so the moisture wouldn't soak the other clothes. The rest of my wardrobe, such as it was, I tucked in as well.

Changing into jeans, T-shirt and canvas sneakers – an off-brand constructed of thin fabric, poorly glued to even thinner rubber – I surveyed my private retreat. And dropped the old canvas duffel over the edge of the loft. It barely missed Tee Dom, who bellowed up at me Cajun curse phrases I had ignored all my life.

I laughed then. It was a strange sound filling the shanty, low and smooth. It wasn't a sound any of us had heard often. I had seldom had a reason to laugh, here in the shanty or in the trailer home. I had saved my laughter for my tutors and my art and my solitary trips up the bayou.

It occurred to me that perhaps Tee Dom and Tante Ilene might have been more giving to me about the secrets of my past, had I laughed more with them. If I had given more of myself to them. If I had . . . I pushed the thought away. I had tried to get them to tell me hundreds of times. Nothing I could do would have made a difference. Not a thing.

More gently, I eased down my canvases, leaving them leaning against the rocker, the table, the walls, trying to protect the ones still wet. In the humid heat of summer, that meant most of them.

My paints and brushes, the tripods for the old camera and the Nikon, the rolls of unused film and the photographs tacked to the rafters went into an old battered Pepsi container, a wooden crate which had once held a case of twelve-ounce glass bottles, each in its own small wooden section. Except for the unmade bed, makeshift easel, a half-dozen paperbacks, including the unfinished *Momo*, and a few toiletries I no longer needed, there was nothing else. The loft was empty.

I blew out the chipped lamp and tucked a cloth around the hot chimney, bringing it down with me, my feet finding the rungs easily in the dark. My footsteps had a steady finality as, for the last time, I climbed down the ladder.

Still without speaking, I loaded everything I owned into Tee Dom's johnboat. It was tied up at the dock, floating easily on the slow-moving water.

As an afterthought, I included the .20 gauge hanging on the wall. It wasn't mine, but I felt safer traveling at night while armed. Gators and floating logs, debris washed downstream by the recent rains could be dangerous. A shotgun blast both frightened off alligators and attracted a lot of attention if fired at night on the bayou.

'Wha' you think you doin', gir'?'

I didn't answer, letting the silence drift between us, like the deep water between bayou shores. I had always been 'girl' to them. A soft slow boil of anger started then. A simmer of long-repressed emotion. *Secrets*. Too many secrets.

When I got the last canvas positioned, I stood, one foot on the boat bottom, one on the dock. Tee Dom and Tante Ilene stood above me, silent and aged, as if any real feeling had long since been steamed out of them during their decades in the Louisiana swamp land. Yet, they were stiff and troubled, their bodies braced as if for a blow. Tante Ilene gripped Tee Dom's arm with both hands.

'If I understand what just happened here, your jobs are over. Duhon paid you for raising me. Right?'

Neither one answered. They stared with black eyes and tight lips, silent.

I shrugged my shoulders. 'So I'm leaving.'

'Dat's mah boat, gir'.' I had the feeling he had wanted to say something else, and the words wouldn't come, stopped by pride or the barrier of lifelong reticence. Tante Ilene's knuckles were white where they gripped Tee Dom's arm.

I laughed again. A short choppy sound. 'Elred can trailer it back to you tomorrow. I'll make it worth his while.'

When neither of the Sarvaunts had anything else to say, I turned and reached down for tie-off rope. A soft hand grabbed my upper arm and tugged, the indefinite pressure of nervous fingers. I turned, meeting Tante Ilene's black eyes, intense and watery, like the bayou after a rain. Unexpected tears pooled there. Her mouth hung open, her lips trembled, an anxious unsteady pulse beat in her wattled neck.

She stared into my eyes as if searching for something. A tear quivered and fell, tracing the uneven creases of her skin. Dropped from her jaw. She released my arm and stepped close, wrapping her arms around me in a hug made strong by long years of hard work. Tante Ilene was soft flesh over sinewy muscles. She smelled of onions and lavender and baby powder, and beneath it all, the scent of her homemade soap. I gripped her a moment, stunned to feel her body shake with a sob.

She pushed me away and moved quickly into the shadows of the doorway, sniffing once. Tee Dom spit a long stream into the black night, his eyes focused carefully for where it might land. His face was hard. His lips frowned as I watched, holding in . . . what?

I untied from the dock and pushed off. Not much of a farewell, but then, I didn't expect one.

It was dusk, the shadows cast by the dying sun long and dark and empty across the black water. My ability to see in the dark was better than average, and as a teen, I had attributed the night vision to my eye condition. To the fact that my pupils were larger under any type of illumination than a normal person's.

I learned only later that Physiological Mydriasis did not really result in better night vision. Instead, I had trained my eyes to see in the dark during all my night travel in the bayous. Like a successful hunter, I had trained my eyes to pick out horizontal shapes on a vertical landscape. Because most things in nature, like trees and buildings and even low shrubs, are vertical, hunters would study the land under faint illumination, searching for the things that went contrary to the usual up and down. Like the point where sky meets land. Or the motion of a moving animal. Or a man walking. I had taught myself to perceive what others could only guess at.

I made the trip through the bayou in the dark without mishap. There was no rain to damage my oils, the sky torn by fitful clouds, rushing ahead of the next front. The air was night-cool in my face, the mosquitoes too slow to bite and pinch, the moon bright against the fast-moving clouds.

I tied up at the public dock, paid Elred ten bucks to help me get my canvases home to the trailer in his van, and another ten to trailer the johnboat back to the Sarvaunts. He was helpful in the only way Elred knew how to be, offering to forego the payment if I was 'friendly' to him. Thanks, but no thanks.

Alone in the trailer, lying supine on the coverlet that rested on my twin bed, I watched the low ceiling through the long hours of the night. By 4 a.m. I had considered all the options open to me. Fifty thousand dollars had given me the freedom to live any way I chose. Go anywhere I wanted to go. Paint the things I had dreamed of painting. Do anything I wanted to do. And what I wanted was to know who I really was.

Dawn came slowly. And with it, a plan. Brazen and daring and so unlike me I could scarcely believe I would consider it.

In my cash box – the little black metal box The Man had given me so many years ago – I had 1700 dollars saved from my allowance. With that, I bought Elred's old '72 Chevy van.

Elred was delighted that I came to him with my transportation problem. He seemed to think that I would be back soon. That this trip away from home was only temporary, that when I returned I would sell the van back to him at a profit. His profit, not mine, of course.

Elred had always lived in his own little world.

I let him think anything he wanted, as long as he was agreeable. And as long as it kept his hands off me while we worked.

For a small fee, he installed wooden supports so my wet canvases could travel safely. I had him help me pack up the van with my few possessions, loading the contents of my trailer bedroom into the rickety space that was left.

I had him make a trip to the bait-and-tackle shop for ammunition for the .20-gauge shotgun and the .38 I was taking from the trailer. I didn't have permission, but I could send a check back soon enough. I had fifty thousand dollars to pay off Tee Dom and Tante Ilene for anything I took.

There wasn't much that I wanted. Only the guns and the stack of foreign art and fashion magazines filling the floor of my closet. A bolt of thin, loosely woven cloth which Tante Ilene had purchased to make drapes for my bedroom. My bed and frame, the chest of drawers, both of which I had bought with my allowance money long ago. My few clothes and books. Not much.

I cleaned out the bedroom and Elred loaded the van, his hands lingering on the things he touched. Although he was shifty, not exactly clean, and was clearly infatuated with me and my things, at least he was organized. It was a contradictory combination.

Once, while we worked, a car pulled up. A restored Jaguar with a dark red paint job, all sparkling, even in the limited sunlight. It was real old, built along more sophisticated lines than Elred's old '72 Chevy van.

A tall man in a cowboy hat got out and talked to Elred while I worked. I left Elred alone to conduct whatever business he was transacting, glancing out the window at the indistinct pair while I loaded boxes. I never got a good look at the stranger, but I hoped Elred didn't have a hire from one of his rich fishermen friends, the ones he was always guiding up the bayous to the best fishing holes. At least not until I got packed.

But it *was* a hire. I heard the stranger offer Elred fifty bucks to guide him up the Bayou Negre. I knew what that meant.

Elred would have headed up the Bayou Negre for my ten dollars. Now, it was sixty altogether. Elred had made a killing, all in tax-free income. You could always trust Elred to make an additional profit.

While we finished up, working fast so Elred could leave, he told me about his hire, the man with the expensive hat and gray ostrich-skin boots with silver tips at the toes. He was very impressed with the silver tips. I hadn't the heart to tell him that silver tips were real common these days; that 'silver' meant silver-colored. Money had always impressed Elred.

I wondered what he would do if I showed him the 50,000 dollar check in my pocket. Wisely, I decided that discretion was the better policy. The thought of a shotgun wedding to Elred – with Elred wielding the shotgun so he could get his hands on my money – was a too-real possibility. The local justice of the peace owed him big, or so the rumors went.

Half an hour later, I stood beside the van, Elred watching my face for any sign of tenderness. The trailer looked the same as it always did. Rusted. A bit forlorn. A lot like Elred. I shook Elred's hand, and stiffened only a little when he pulled me into his arms and kissed me on the mouth.

Not much to brag about for a first kiss. Nothing to take to dreamland at the end of a long day. Certainly nothing to stimulate passion.

His body smelled of grease and fish and onions. Nothing like Tante Ilene. I pushed away the thought of her face as I last saw it, and took off for New Orleans, the 50,000 dollar check hot against my skin.

CHAPTER 3

I had never seen ferns growing from the side of a building like these did. Big leafy healthy ferns, a couple dozen of them hanging from the pink stucco façade, roots buried in the fine cracks that spidered up the walls like a delicate web.

I eased my foot off the brake and maneuvered Elred's old van down the street, craning my neck at the wrought-iron Spanish-style balconies, old brick, and unsubtle hodgepodge of architectural styles given unbridled freedom in the Quarter. I had to keep moving.

Every time I stopped, or even slowed down, the interior of the van filled up with exhaust. The fumes filtered up through the rusted-out floorboards from the broken tail pipe. There was no muffler.

At any moment I expected to be pulled to the curb and ticketed for both noise and exhaust pollution, but so far I had avoided all the shiny black New Orleans patrol cars.

I felt like a rube, a river-rat, a real dyed-in-the-homespun bayou girl allowed into the big city for the first time. I rubbernecked at the downtown skyscrapers, gawked at the mish-mash of architecture, bemoaned the filth, had been intimidated by the snarls of traffic, and gotten lost at least twice.

By mid-afternoon, I had done the thing every tourist does the first time in town, toured the French Quarter. The Vieux Carré.

I loved the pastel two-story façades and the black wrought-iron railings, the working louvered storm shutters, the air of respectable yet shabby gentility, the slightly disheveled and worn aspect of the place. I loved the narrow streets and cobblestone alleys, the seedy bars and fancy restaurants.

I loved the bell-hop in his uniform standing on the sidewalk in front of an elegant old hotel, the faded livery of the horse-drawn carriage drivers, and the straw hats on their spavined steeds. The clip of horses' iron-shod hooves on cobbled streets.

I loved the sight of the Mississippi coiling through town, the paddle-wheel boat churning its muddy waters. I even loved the stench. The smell of rank water and rotten wood, old beer and dead fish, burnt cooking grease and coffee.

I felt I had been born here and removed in my infancy by some evil influence. I wanted to stay here forever. The desire to settle here was like a burning in me, as if only here would I be content. Only here could my questions be answered, my mystery solved.

I wasn't much schooled in the ways and means of living alone, and I figured I had several strikes against me and only one on my side. I was only twenty-one – but didn't look it – had no credit history, no job, no prospects, no real property and no assets. But I did have a fifty-thousand-dollar check in my pocket and a five-hundred-thousand-dollar trust fund which would come to me in three years. I figured money alone would somehow counteract all the negatives.

Leaving the van parked in a five-dollar-a-day parking lot – a narrow twisting paved piece of property that opened on to adjoining one-way streets – I found a pay phone and phone book, studied the yellow-page section under Investments. I made two collect calls back to LaRoque Parish before I walked to New Orleans's Royal Securities on Royal Street.

It was an old building, built in 1780, of concrete and brick and heavy plaster; inside, there were arches and columns and gilt over all. It was like a cathedral, a place to worship money.

It was cool and dark and elegant. It was also noisy in a refined sort of way, with cultured southern voices speaking softly into slim phones, computers printing beneath muffling hoods, the swish of fine fabrics as employees shifted in chairs or walked from office to office. It was just the place I would want to do business when I came into my inheritance.

I inquired at the receptionist's desk for the president, Claude Michau, feeling very adult and sincere until I glanced at the smoked-glass wall to the side and saw the weary image of a very young woman in a wrinkled dress, standing tiredly on the marble flagstones. She was me. Black circles beneath my eyes proved how little I had slept in the last few days. I looked my age or younger and when the receptionist informed me Mr Michau was unavailable, I knew I had to change tactics.

I had studied tactics. Tactics in politics, military history and the principles of revolution as taught by Dr Tammany Long, a distant cousin to *the* Louisiana Longs. An aging hippie even in the sixties, Dr Tammany, as he insisted that I call him, still grew his own pot and reminisced about the Beatles.

I knew I couldn't act like an assured and self-confident woman of means because I didn't look the part. Time to change tactics. It was a bit like the role-playing Dr Tammany and I had done for years as we assumed the parts of historical characters and playacted some vital turning point in history.

I sighed, sinking onto one of the straight-backed chairs in front of the desk and braced an elbow on the dark wood desk top, the smooth walnut cool beneath my arm. 'Oh dear.' I sighed again and rubbed my forehead, pushing my sunglasses back on my head. 'That does present me with quite a dilemma. You see, Mr Rufus Kirby of the LaRoque National Bank – you know – *the* Mr Kirby – said I should speak only with Mr Michau. And if Mr Michau wasn't available, then I should go to International Securities down on Poydras Street. But that was Mr Kirby's second choice, you understand . . .'

I stretched out the syllables in true, southern, damsel-in-distress fashion. Looked up from under my hand to see if she was following my story. She looked confused, like she didn't quite know what I was leading to.

'And I am so very tired. My transportation proved to be somewhat . . . unreliable. I do hate to make even the short drive over Poydras. And Mr Kirby will be so disappointed.'

Mr Kirby had made no such recommendations. Rather I had informed Mr Kirby what I intended when I called his office collect. I had chosen Royal Securities because I liked the building's façade when I had driven past. Understated and elegant. But Mr Michau didn't need to know that.

I tried to let my exhaustion work for me instead of against me. I tried to appear wan and a little bit lost as I unfolded my cashier's check and opened out my portfolio, pushing both toward the receptionist. She was a peroxide blonde with brown eyes and heavy pancake makeup. Her mascaraed baby browns opened up a good quarter-inch when she saw the check and the official-looking documents of the investment portfolio.

'Do you have any idea when Mr Michau might be available?' I asked.

The blonde blinked and said, 'Why don't you have a seat right over there and I'll check personally for you.' She pointed out a sofa and two chairs upholstered in a cream and mauve print on a matching oriental rug. A very civilized little nook beneath a framed New Orleans print.

I retrieved my check and closed up the portfolio, smiling like it was the last bit of energy I possessed and moved to the sofa. I sank slowly to the surface and down into the cushions, laying my head on the sofa back. With half-closed eyes I watched the receptionist enter the sanctum of the president's office and re-emerge moments later. She threw a furtive glance my way, returned to her post and the appointment book awaiting her. I managed not to smile.

Still watching beneath half-closed lids I waited. Ten minutes passed, allowing the tired act I was putting on to become fact instead of fantasy. I was suddenly exhausted, the last few days of little or no sleep catching up with me.

Michau stepped from his office and paused, studying me. I didn't open my eyes, but took in Mr Michau's appearance from beneath my lashes. He was a short, slender, pink-cheeked man in his fifties. A delicate little dwarf with spectacles and a bad hair piece. In the Hair Club for Men's Toupee Catalogue it was probably called the Lyle Lovett Look.

When he stood before me in his summer-weight wool finery – gray of course – with his silk tie and his charcoal wingtips, I allowed my eyes to flutter partially open. And hoped I wasn't overdoing it. And that if I was, the fifty thousand dollars would make him forgive me.

'May I help you? Miss . . .' Very elegant diction. Southern but . . . Yale or Harvard trained.

I took the hint and opened my eyes fully. 'Sarvaunt.' I extended my hand up to him and smiled, still wan and remote and a bit other-worldly, like a ghost tired of the haunting game. Michau's lips twitched.

'I'm so sorry to have intruded upon you . . . Mr Michau?' queried mid-sentence in my drawn-out southern accent. He lifted a brow and smiled down at me as I withdrew my hand from his bony paw. '. . . but Mr Kirby and Mr Duhon – my mother's executor or whatever you call them these days – insisted that I stop in and see you the minute I arrived in New Orleans.' I fluttered my lashes just a bit, not flirtatiously but like I couldn't hold my lids open a moment longer. 'And it was a most exhausting trip.' I smiled again. 'If you have a few moments . . .'

'Of course. Of course. Why don't we retire to my office and you can tell me what I can do for you. Right this way.'

Such a civilized word – *retire*. And Michau was good. His eyes never lit upon the portfolio case. Not once. I sighed and found my feet, one arm delicately extended for balance. A worn-out Grace Kelly, rescued and bedraggled, yet still elegant.

Michau's office was a power office filled with photographs of past glory. There was Michau and Bush. Michau and the Reagans. Michau and Jimmy Carter. Michau and Ford on a golf course. There was Michau and Glen Close, Michau and the Neville Brothers, Michau and a dozen popular Louisiana authors, a very young Michau and Huey Long. Michau was on every wall, bracketed by masculine frames, staring into the office and the future.

There were no recent photographs of Michau, however, as though the man had fallen on hard times at the same moment that Clinton had come to power. As if Michau had once been a dealer and a shaker, but was now in disgrace, hidden from the world in the small square of the French Quarter.

I settled into the navy leather chair, placed the cashier's check and portfolio before me on the desk top in the shadow of a computer, just out of reach of Michau's folded fingers. A calm and peaceful Pope, Michau looked like the spiritual advisor to a financial domain. I immediately liked his calm demeanor. However, I wasn't so certain how to respond to the amusement that lurked in the depths of his eyes.

'Mr Michau, I'm sure you're familiar with Rufus Kirby of the LaRoque National Bank?' I paused.

Michau nodded his head slowly. 'Rufus and I were on district-court jury duty a few years back. We're acquainted.'

That surprised me. Kirby, when I called him, had grudgingly admitted knowing of Claude Michau, but he had neglected to mention court . . . There was little that I could do about the happenstance, but I wondered what else I should know – and didn't – about the relationship.

'Well, Mr Kirby suggested that I come to you when I reached town and ask you to assist me in getting settled. I realize it is very short notice, but I had such a dreadful trip into town and without a credit card, I might not even be able to obtain a hotel room.'

I was amazed as words slipped off my tongue like Tante Ilene's hotcakes off the griddle. I sounded . . . competent. Assertive. And far more confident than the little lost girl image I had projected in the lobby. My former uncertainty began to slip away. I could do this. I could really do all this. I could travel to New Orleans alone. I could make decisions. And I could deal with professional people on a knowledgeable level. My mother's special training had prepared me well.

'With no credit history,' I continued, 'Mr Kirby said I would need the official backing of a financial institution to verify my respectability.'

Kirby had said no such thing, but he should have. My well-being should have at least occurred to the man when I called him collect. But I suppose the shotgun incident still played a part in Kirby's estimation of my ability to care for myself.

'Rufus knew I could help you, Miss Sarvaunt. We're here to serve.'

And make a profit and evict widows and orphans. I didn't say it, but the thought did make me smile. I pushed the check toward Michau. 'I'll need to open a brokerage account, please. I'd like to have access to twenty-five thousand for trading. I want ten thousand in a high-yield, secure investment. I realize that is a conflict of terms, but I'm asking for your best suggestion, perhaps a bond fund, or corporate bonds. Do you have a recommendation?' I was flushed and euphoric suddenly, using words I had only considered in theory, making plans I had studied for and prepared for all my life. Plans I had only imagined I might someday be able to make. I felt as if I were operating on some new and lofty level.

He started to speak and I interrupted, continuing as if I hadn't asked a question.

'In addition I'll need a money-market account, one that allows me to trade freely. Also I'll need a debit card available as soon as possible, so we may need to set up an account for that.

'I realize all this is very sudden, but I'll need a place to stay the night. Some place safe, here in the Quarter or nearby. Could I get your receptionist to make the reservation for me? I'm afraid I couldn't even get a room at the Holiday Inn on my own.'

Due to the damage of hotel rooms during Mardi Gras, when the city was filled with drunken and rampaging kids, teens and college-age party-goers, most hotels and hotel chains reserved the right to turn away anyone who looked like they might be under twenty-one. Even if they had cash. I sat back, expectantly.

I pushed over the portfolio, opening it up to a summary page for his perusal. 'I won't have control of my trust until I am twenty-four, but I'd like you to study over what I have invested at this time, make a few suggestions. Frankly, I feel Mr Duhon has been a bit too conservative and I would like to diversify a bit.' I paused, and Claude Michau sat silent, his eyes on the opened-out portfolio. 'Mr Michau?'

A strange smile stretched across Michau's face. Part shock, part pleasure. 'Of course, of course,' he drew out his words, real laughter on his lips now. Laughter I couldn't identify or categorize. It all seemed too easy, this appointment, this assistance from Michau. 'Now, let me get a few particulars.' Michau pulled a pad and pen to him and ripped off the top page, crumpling up the doodles and figures and numbers. 'I'll need your full name and social security number, Miss Sarvaunt. I'm sure we can have you set up and ready to go in no time.

'And, Miss Sarvaunt?'

I raised my brows.

'Two questions.'

I nodded, a bit uncertain, suddenly. It had been too easy. And the laughter in Michau's eyes was far too extreme for our conversation.

'You weren't really exhausted when you came in here, were you?'

I shook my head, watching his reactions to my words. 'Wired, more like it. Although I admit I haven't had much sleep in the last two or three days.'

'I thought so. And . . .' he paused a moment. 'Did you really attack Rufus with a sawed-off shotgun?'

I nearly choked. God. Michau had already talked with Kirby. That ten-minute wait . . .

'It wasn't a sawed-off. Only a twenty gauge . . .'

'How old are you?'

'How old do I look?'

'No gentleman would ever answer that question.'

'Fake it.'

He laughed delightedly, leaning back in his leather chair. The leather creaked slightly. 'Either an exhausted woman of twenty-five or a very sophisticated twelve.'

I paused for a moment, debating if I should tell Michau about the puzzle of my birth and the contents of the little black box. But the words of The Man still rang in my ears, the hint of pity in the depths of the syllables, when he told me that many orphans wanted some mystery to surround their origins. I wasn't ready to risk that kind of comment from Michau, even if the answer to his question depended on the mystery of my identity.

'Twenty-one.' I handed him my driver's license, and a photocopy of my birth certificate that was a part of my portfolio. If Michau noticed the slight hesitation before my answer, he gave no indication.

'Mr Michau, I also would like the name of a respectable private investigator. One who specializes in missing persons.'

Michau paused in the process of transferring data to the stack of forms in front of him. 'Do you want to tell me why you need a private investigator? Who you're looking for?'

'Not really. And the PI needs to be not too terribly expensive. I studied the yellow pages earlier and there are a zillion different companies. I'd like someone small. Low overhead,' I explained. 'And female.'

The last precondition surprised even me. Yet, all the people who mattered in my life were men. Kirby. Duhon. Michau. And in some way I was dependent on each of them. I wanted a female in my life.

The image of Tante Ilene's eyes, all watery and anguished as they looked into mine the day I left, appeared in my mind. I pushed it away.

'I may know someone you would like to work with.' There was a speculative look about Michau, as if he had an idea what I wanted a PI for, and the idea distressed him. 'Her name is R.T. Stocker. She's been in the business for some time, six years or so I believe, and works mostly alone. We've used her a few times and been very pleased with her services.' He smiled. It was a courtly smile, almost melancholy. 'I'm sure she would work well with you. She's very discrete. Would you like me to make an introductory call for you? At your age there might be a . . . ah . . . a credibility problem.'

'No kidding,' I said ruefully.

Michau laughed. 'I think you and I will work very well together, young lady. Rufus had some favorable things to say about your eye for the market. But, tell me, Miss Sarvaunt—'

'Yes?' I knew what he was going to say.

'Was the shotgun loaded?'

'Of course not. I was angry, not stupid.'

'Um.' Michau opened his mouth, closed it and returned to his form filling. But I could see he was dying to ask me.

'I came after him with the shotgun because he wouldn't keep his hands off me. He was like a perverted elderly uncle, all hugs and kisses and accidental touches. I didn't like it. I told him to stop, to keep his hands to himself or I'd shoot him. When he didn't, I came at him with Tee Dom's .20 gauge and threatened to shoot off his hands and any other body parts big enough to aim at.' I said the words slowly, watching Michau's face.

His reaction was minimal. His brows went up a fraction. His lips twitched. 'Of course you did,' he said, and went back to the forms again.

I could have sworn Michau was delighted.

'Yes. I think we will work very well together indeed,' he murmured again. A moment passed with only the scritch of pen on paper to keep me awake. 'Next time . . .' scritch, scritch, 'make sure the gun is loaded.' Scritch, scritch, scritch. 'If you ever make a threat, it should always be one you can carry out if necessary.'

The pen continued its satiny scrape across paper as I digested

Michau's soft-spoken advice. It seemed totally out of character for the dapper little man behind the big desk, but there was no doubt in my mind that he meant it. Every word.

'I'll keep that in mind.'

'Did you bring the shotgun with you to New Orleans?'

Such a casually spoken question. But Michau was smiling a small smile, his eyes on the forms. 'If so, I suggest you register it with the local police.'

'The handgun too?'

Michau looked up, the half-smile still in place. He didn't speak.

'It's a .38, and I need to send payment back home for both guns. I . . . ah, took them from the trailer when I left. They were my uncle's.'

'Yes.' There was a definite gleam in Michau's eyes. Almost approval. The same kind of look he might have awarded to a particularly intelligent pet. 'The handgun too. Tomorrow. I'll make the necessary phone calls to ease your way in.' He handed me a scrap of paper torn from the legal pad at his elbow. There was an address and a name on it. 'That's the name of the man to whom you should speak.

'Now. About accommodations. I'll have Belinda schedule a suite at the Ponchartrain which you may use for two nights at our expense. That should give you time to make other arrangements. Do you have transportation?'

'Sort of. It has four wheels but that's about all.'

Michau smiled again, that pleased little twitch I had spotted several times.

'You don't like Rufus Kirby, do you?' I asked.

'Despise the man,' he said smoothly. 'Is the vehicle a bit . . . disreputable?'

'A wreck. If I had any sense I would junk it in a minute.'

'How quaint. Now, Miss Sarvaunt—'

'Bonnie, please,' I said, laughing softly. I relaxed back in the chair and then sat up again, quickly. 'Any man that dislikes Kirby is a friend of mine.'

Michau inclined his head. 'And I would be pleased if you called me Claude.' He reached across the desk and we shook hands, two conspirators, both detesting Rufus Kirby. 'Now. To the forms.'

We spent a half-hour filling out forms and setting me up with counter checks until my personal ones would arrive, and discussing the weather in good southern tradition. Yes. I could live in New Orleans. I really could. It was a fact, not an empty desire. This strange town with its multicultural base, its rich history, its diverse peoples and fantastic old architecture could be my home. I left Michau and Royal Securities with satisfaction spreading over my face.

I didn't go directly to the hotel, but spent the next hours searching out the places my mother had frequented so long ago. According to the ticket stubs in the little black box, she had lived in the Quarter for some time, or visited often, and I wanted to go everywhere she had ever gone, to do everything she had ever done.

I ate oysters on the half-shell with custom-made hot sauce and a glass of dark beer recommended by the waiter in the long narrow confines of Felix's. My elbows rested on the bar with a stack of napkins to the side, as salty, slimy oysters slid down my throat with a full, satisfying feel. My mother had done this once, stood with her elbows on this bar and eaten this wonderful, almost sensual food.

I wandered by the Absinthe Bar with its wallpaper of dollar bills. Paused and watched through the windows as the patrons drank. They were a mixed lot, both tourists and locals. Yet, most were rough-and-ready types who gave the place a dangerous flavor. I walked through and sat at a little table, though I didn't stay long enough to order a drink. But I could have . . . My mother had.

As the sun set, I parked myself in Preservation Hall and listened to jazz. The pure stuff, not some modern rendition. Wonderful old tunes and newer melodies, all smooth and mellow, like the beer I drank as the evening wore on. I had three, and each one was better than the last. I could get used to this. Beer and music and people. Lots of people.

I imagined my mother walking these streets, eating and drinking and hearing these sounds. I loved the very idea of this city, its tastes and flavors and lush atmosphere, its laughing people. I loved it all, because of her.

And late that night, as the moon rose over the city, its dull light competing with the brighter and harsher city lights, I went to the famous old hotel. Had she slept here? Had she been in this elegant old lobby with its barrel-vaulted ceilings and beautiful decor? Had she studied the floral decorations hand-painted by Elizabeth Hadden and the priceless artworks of Charles Reinike that graced the walls? Had the old-world grandeur and opulence been an everyday joy to her, or was she overwhelmed by it all as I was?

I was escorted up the elevator to my room, a strange experience for one who had never been anywhere strange at all. And as the bellboy put away my meager things, I stood in the open doorway staring at the sumptuous suite and trying to keep my mouth from hanging open. The suite provided for me by Royal Securities was like something out of a home-fashion magazine, a three-room apartment with floral upholstery, antique tables, and a fully appointed kitchen. It was elegant and sophisticated and downright rich.

I finally managed to conquer my sense of awe and move into the room, out of the way of the bellboy. I tipped him a dollar and hoped it was enough. None of the magazines I had studied over the years had prepared me for the Ponchartrain.

And it wasn't lost on me that the reservations had been handled simply and easily. All Claude Michau had done was pick up the phone. There was power in the hand of a wealthy man, even if his wealth came from other people's money. Closing the door on the bellboy, I sealed myself into the silence of an air-conditioned environment and plush surroundings.

I put a can of tuna and a small jar of mayonnaise in the refrigerator, and a loaf of homemade French bread on the counter, things I had picked up on the way over in case I got hungry during the night. Closing the refrigerator door, I wandered slowly about the suite, touching the smooth varnish of an old table. Smelling the unfamiliar scent of a room that was different from my own room in Khoury. Public, yet mine. All because of money. And there wasn't a single mouse dropping anywhere. It was nothing like home.

I slept marvelously well on the unaccustomed mattress. Six full hours, waking long before five and lying in the darkened room, trying to plan out my day. I wasn't consciously excited. In fact

I felt quite logical about the entire move. Yet I knew I was in New Orleans. I knew I had made a break with the past. I knew I had only the future to face. And a soft sizzle of excitement raced down my arms and tingled on my fingers where they lay, laced across my stomach.

A craving for coffee forced me from the bed. I would drive back to the Quarter for café au lait and beignets at the Café du Monde. I would watch the sun come up over New Orleans. I would live the life I had only considered possible in my dreams. A life without swarms of mosquitoes, the stench of swamp, and the damp of bayou. A life with new people in it. People like Claude Michau. People who knew about the world and who practiced the gentle art of polite conversation on a regular basis.

I rose and dressed, choosing a loose cotton dress in a filmy weave and a soft pastel print, sneakers, and my ubiquitous sunglasses. The mesh bag I had once carried in the bayou, I filled with sunscreen, glasses case, film, and my wallet and the new check book from Royal Securities. I slung it over my left shoulder. My hair was French braided, and ended in the middle of my back, a long multicolored strand of brown and dark blonde and wisps of sun-bleached gold.

My cameras were too bulky for casual use and I decided that my first purchase of the day would be an inexpensive automatic 35mm camera. A brand-new one.

The sun was coming up as I tipped the sleepy-eyed bellboy for bringing my van around. He was a good-looking young man in his twenties, dark-haired and blue-eyed, with hearing aides in both ears. I figured he made more in tips than most people did in taxable salaries. Still, I tipped him only a dollar and he didn't seem disappointed.

I drove up near-empty streets, the sky a gray and pale peach confection of dumpling clouds above me. The rush hadn't started yet, the locals going to work, the tourists flocking to the sites like the egrets in my photographs. The streets were damp and vacant, just the sunrise and me.

I could have left the van at the Ponchartrain, taking the streetcar into the Quarter. Yet I wanted the freedom to come and go as I wished, independent of the whims of streetcar schedules.

I parked in the same lot as the day before, rousting the drowsy attendant and giving him a five-dollar bill to keep tabs on Elred's old van. It was still loaded with my belongings and the half-dried oils, and another day in the sweltering heat would not be good for the drying paint.

The scent of pigments was almost better than breakfast to me, and my hands twitched with the need to work on the unfinished canvases. To touch up the smears Elred's clumsy fingers had left. To bring something new to the process of my art. And from the aroma of overheated paint, I knew it needed to be soon.

But first, I parked the disreputable van and walked toward the water. Everything in New Orleans is toward the water or away from it, and the Café du Monde was right on the levee. My stomach growled, a *basso profundo* of need.

The crowd in the café was sparse at a bit after five, the tables in the open-air covered patio were empty. A waitress wearing a green and white striped apron to match the green and white striped awnings took my order. Two coffees – one black, one café au lait – and two orders of beignets, the steaming hot, fried pastries covered in powdered sugar, for which the café was famous the world over.

Six square doughnuts, crispy on the outside, full of calories and delicious fat were delivered to my table, and I ate them all, downing the black coffee first, for the caffeine jolt, and the sweet café au lait after. I burned my mouth on the coffee and my fingers on the beignets. Powdered sugar fell down the front of my pale pink dress, and was probably all over my face. And I didn't care. I was in New Orleans, the Crescent City, the Belle of the South, the Capitol of Bayou Country. And it was wonderful.

I tipped a street musician a dollar as I left the café and he stopped me with a surprised, 'But I ain't played nothing yet.'

'So play me something. Old fashioned. Like the jazz and blues they played here in the thirties and forties and fifties. Something so sad it'll tear my heart out.'

The white-haired, black-skinned man looked at me for a long moment before he put the polished brass of his sax to his lips. His eyes were strange, as he stared into mine. Black as Tante Ilene's, floating in yellowed gelatin. He blew a soft note, a clear 'C' into the quiet break of day, and segued into 'Are You Satisfied'. A haunting rendition so beautiful I left him another dollar, and walked away, my steps moving to the mellow beat of another decade.

The French Quarter was a treat by early light. Workers who earned their living in the ancient locale hurried to open up stores and restaurants. Drunks and drug addicts stumbled along, looking for a cool place to sleep through the heat of the day. Artists and musicians and mimes hurried to claim a wedge of sidewalk as their own. A priest, his rosary in his hands and his head bowed, counted the beads to the rhythm of his steps, walking toward St Louis Cathedral. Its sharp spires were dark against puffy gray clouds.

I walked along the wharf that topped the levee, staring down some thirty feet into the muddy waters of the Mississippi. I watched the sun tint the world with light behind the clouds, a soft diffuse glow, brightening the world with color. And then, before the heat could grow too intense, I went to work.

I found an apartment for rent on Royal Street at Conti, a second-floor walk-up above an antique store that specialized in green. Green jewelry, green crystal goblets, green depression glassware, green stones and gems.

The green 'For Rent' sign hung from a painted, wrought-iron railing on the porch. The phone number was printed in black magic marker.

The building, once a narrow private home, was centuries old. Its name – listed on a small plaque – had originally been called La Maison de Verdure. The greenhouse. Owned by the Greens from Natchez as a second home, the name had been a successful play on words then as now.

I stood beneath the sign and considered the location. All around me were antique shops, corner restaurants and boutiques. There were jewelry stores, crystal shops and even a shop which specialized in shot glasses. But the thing I loved best about the location was the sight of the art galleries. There were three within visual distance, one advertising African American Art, one advertising Cajun Art and Primitives, and one whose small brass sign claimed it handled only the finest estate art and restorations. There was a small Cassatt on an expensive old easel in the barred front windows.

I would be a full block from Bourbon and the night life I would want to avoid, a block from the New Orleans Jazz Museum, two blocks from the Old Absinthe House Bar, and a block or so from Le Petit Théâtre du Vieux Carré. Main tourist town.

I knew that no place in the French Quarter was really safe after dark for females traveling alone, but I figured that with the police down the street a bit on Royal, I was as safe here as anywhere.

There was also a two-story walk-up on Chartres available to let, but it was on further down, toward Barracks Street and I figured that if I was going to risk living in the Quarter, then I should rent in a prime location. The space above the small shop was exactly what I wanted.

On a whim, I looked up the phone number for the antiques store – La Demoiselle Verte, a name that could be translated The Green Dragonfly or The Green Young Girl. It was the same number printed on the little 'For Rent' sign. I felt that was fortuitous. The landlord would be available should a sink back up or something.

While I waited for the shop to open, I called the private investigator recommended by Michau. R.T. Stocker answered on the second ring, sounding initially as if she had a mouth full of beans. When her speech cleared almost instantly, I switched my mental image from beans to a pencil. I could picture this middle-aged Miss Marple or Agatha Christie, her hair in a neat bun, her fingers busy at an old Underwood typewriter, her yellow H2 pencil held firmly in her teeth. A vase of white mums on the desk beside her.

'Stocker and . . . Stocker,' she said. 'R.T. speaking.'

'Miz Stocker, I'm Bonnie Sarvaunt, and I . . . well, I . . .' I suddenly didn't know just what to say to the private investigator. It sounded a bit bald and brash to say I wanted to hire her to find *me*. And my mother.

'Claude called, Miss Sarvaunt, with a personal recommendation and a request for services at company rates.'

R.T. Stocker had a raspy voice with a slow southern drawl, from Georgia maybe, but not southern Louisiana. And my age expectations dropped drastically. A throaty mid-thirties, with a hint of a get-right-to-the-point attitude.

'You made quite a hit with Claude, Miss Sarvaunt. I got explicit orders to assist you as if I were assisting the securities firm itself. Missing person, is it?'

'Yes. Two actually. And it's rather . . . ah . . . complicated. I . . . Is there some place we could meet, maybe? I mean . . .' My voice trailed off. I wasn't changing my mind, and I wasn't nervous. But I did have a mental picture of the look on R.T. Stocker's face when I showed her the little black box and the clues I had from my past. A polite incredulity. A grown woman looking down her nose at an orphan's desire to find her past.

'Look,' I said before she could answer. 'I think that what I want might be stupid. You know. Like I'm making cloud pictures, seeing what I want just because I want to see it. I know that doesn't make any sense, but . . .' I stopped. For once I sounded like a teenager. Miss Taussig would have been delighted, but personally I hated sounding like a dithering pre-adult.

R.T. Stocker laughed. It was a low, soothing sound. The practiced sound that a doctor might make in the surgery department, just before he put you under. While he was sharpening his knives.

'Why don't I come to your place this evening and you can tell me what you want? There's no charge for a preliminary consultation, and if you change your mind, no hard feelings.'

I took a deep breath. 'I'm at the Ponchartrain.'

'Room 312, I know. Michau told me. Seven p.m.?'

'Fine. Coffee?'

'Thanks.'

The phone clicked off.

I replaced the hard black plastic receiver in the cradle and leaned against the pay phone. For the period effect, the phones in the Quarter are housed in ornate black iron boxes on slender poles. The protection from wind and flying hurricane debris wasn't incidental, however. Everything in New Orleans was designed for hurricane-damage prevention. Electric and phone lines are under ground, storm shutters are usually functional, and traffic signals are on poles at intersections. Efficient and sturdy. Dependable.

I couldn't figure out why I suddenly felt so bereft and disconnected, as if I would float away as if I let go of the heavy wrought-iron phone box. I rested my head against the black-painted iron surface. The same dark-as-pitch color as Tante Ilene's eyes.

Pushing away from the phone booth, I went in search of a new camera.

McCallum danced forward on perfectly balanced feet, swinging a long, deadly blade at his imaginary opponent. The dull blade flashed green fire as it moved, glowed green when still, reflections of the computer screen in the otherwise dark room.

For once, he was alone, the heavy carved bed empty. It wasn't often he found time to practice, as *she* didn't approve. His body, sheened with sweat, glistened in the dull light. His breathing was deep and regular, punctuated by deeper breaths with each lunge.

The blade never seemed to move with any speed. He never seemed hurried. Yet the blade seldom slowed, seldom paused in its intricate revolutions.

It was Kendo he practiced, an unorthodox form of the ritualistic Japanese sword fighting. And with him, it was martial arts elevated to poetry. The poetry of dance and history and war.

The computer beeped softly, alerting him to new information. With a single smooth motion, he sheathed the practice sword, finding the black leather case in the darkness with unerring accuracy. He had often been accused of having cat's eyes.

Taking up a towel, almost invisible in the dim room, he patted at his skin, striding barefoot across the wooden floor. Resting his left palm on the desk top, he bent over the computer screen, a slow smile lighting his face.

'Well, well, well. Look at this,' his said softly, his voice a satisfied purr. 'I have you now. You're mine.' With long, slender fingers, he lifted a pen and wrote down a series of identification numbers and an address. Then he deleted the information from the screen and entered new commands, changing the scope of his searches.

Quickly, he showered, dressed, and tossed a few pairs of jeans and T-shirts into a leather flight bag, added a sport jacket, underclothes and toiletries and zipped the bag closed. The entire process took less than ten minutes, and was accomplished completely in the dark. He liked the dark. It was useful.

Picking up his keys, he stepped into the hallway and locked his suite.

Stopping by the locked case at the front of the house, he added a short sword to his assortment of supplies and slipped out the front door. Twenty minutes following the warning beep of his computer, McCallum was on the road to New Orleans, the night wind ruffling his shoulder-length, blond hair.

Five minutes after his departure, his suite door opened, the lock turning smoothly. The light came on, revealing piles of dirty laundry, piles of books, trays of food, half-eaten and dried, empty wine bottles, scattered papers, and the huge black bed. Gray, wrinkled sheets were rumpled at the foot of the monstrous bed; the flat sheet was spotted with food stains and other, even more personal stains. There was even a small smear of what might have been blood at the head of the bed near an ancient, deflated pillow.

A man wearing boots with silver tips and tight jeans, and smelling strongly of horses, entered. Placing his feet carefully to avoid moving anything, he crossed the room to the computer. McCallum would notice the slightest change in the room. A second man, this one in a starched gray uniform, waited at the door, keeping watch.

His fingers moving on the keyboard, the booted man traced back through the last several screens, finding the one that had so interested McCallum. The computer beeped.

'He's got it,' he said, running his hand through his hair. 'He's found her.'

Backtracking through the commands and files, he restored the screen to its previous state. Unless McCallum was very, very good, and very, very careful, he would never know that his computer had been touched. Retracing his steps, the booted man returned to the doorway, checking behind him for the slightest change in the room. There was nothing he could do about the horse smell, of course, but McCallum's sense of smell had never been very acute.

'See to it that a bag is packed for me, Jenkins. I'll be in New Orleans for several days.'

'Very good, sir.'

CHAPTER 4

Renting an apartment in New Orleans was easier than I thought, mainly because I used Claude Michau as a reference. Apparently the dapper little man from Royal Securities was a fixture on the streets of the Quarter, well known to the local merchants as a reliable and credible arbiter of many financial disputes.

It seems Michau was a recognized expert on the value of estate antiquities, both art, jewelry and small *objets d'art*. Whether it was the going rate for an eighteenth-century Rococo portrait by François Boucher, an early Lalique vase, a Victorian pendant, or a small terracotta statuette by Clodion, Claude Michau was an unquestioned connoisseur. With his backing, I not only was permitted to inspect the apartment, I was offered a decrease in the security deposit.

I guess it paid to have important friends. It also helped that I spoke French. My second language wasn't Parisian French, but rather the broader, looser version of Southern France, the French of the countryside after the Second World War. The language spoken by farmers and vintners and merchants. The language I spoke every Thursday for twelve years with Madame Willoby. Mme Willoby was a French national who married an American soldier and followed him home after the war. She had six children and twenty grandchildren and raised pug dogs when she wasn't tutoring me or one of her other private students.

From her I learned deportment, court etiquette, world history, and an appreciation of foreign films. And French, of course.

Mme Willoby was a plump woman – plump arms, plump, rounded derrière, even plump ankles and dimpled fingers covered in rings. She wore a perpetual smile, and antique linen dresses, and I never once saw her un-stockinged legs. Not even the time her air-conditioner broke and we sweated through a deportment class in ninety-eight-degree heat. She had exacting standards, but Mme Willoby had also been my friend.

She died when I was in my senior year, just before Christmas. Her family came and sold off her belongings, her furniture and crystal, her china and books, her lace table-linens, her collection of hand-painted plates and her beloved pugs. I had purchased a few things at the estate sale, including a series of small charcoals of pre-world war Paris. Street scenes by night. Very elegant and delicate and carefully preserved. Like Marie Willoby's ancient French.

The owner of La Demoiselle Verte, Cee Cee Gaudet, reminded me of my old tutor. Cee Cee was in her eighties and although her French was the purer version of sophisticated Paris, we shared many idiomatic phrases no longer in use. Miss Cee Cee Gaudet was a short, slender pixie of a woman with flaming red hair, bright green eyes, and pale, finely wrinkled skin. She looked like a walking Christmas decoration, a Lucille Ball Christmas-tree angel in her green watered-silk dress with emeralds on every finger and a double stand of emeralds and pearls at her throat. She sparkled all over.

Cee Cee stood at the bottom of the stairs, only feet from the Royal Street traffic, shouting up comments as I climbed. '*Mon neveu a habité en haut, là.* My nephew, he lived up there. *Il a trouvé une position, il y a un mois il est allé à San Francisco. Lui et son bien aimé, si vous comprenez*. He got a job a month ago and moved to San Francisco. He and his boyfriend, if you know what I mean. *C'était un vrai amour. Si doux*. He was a darling boy. So sweet . . .'

Her words fell away as I stepped inside. I stood there just inside the entrance, not knowing what to expect. For 350 a month, probably some decrepit, run-down little place with fleas, no running water, and the plaster hanging off the walls in strips. Instead I nearly lost my breath.

The entrance was at the back left side of the apartment, with an added-on kitchenette beside the door, and the bath just down from there. The plumbing was from the 1950s, big chunky fixtures in kitchen and bath, heavy porcelain in gleaming white, with black and white ceramic tile on both floors. These rooms were just nooks, but were clean and shiny and smelled of pine oil. I couldn't fault Cee Cee's nephew for his house-cleaning ability. Even Tante Ilene, with her exacting standards, would have approved.

To the right of the entrance ran the body of the apartment, seven hundred square feet of space, divided into two main rooms at front and back. The ceilings were twelve feet high with wide, deep millwork at ceiling and floor. Carved rosettes and wooden swags draped along the joining of ceiling and wall. The wood roses and the moldings were painted a dark clotted cream, the color so rich I got hungry just looking at the paint. The walls . . . They were pale yellow-green with amber sponge painting . . . exactly the color of my eyes.

A strange frisson of *déjà vu* swept through me, as if I had seen the room in my dreams. As if it had been painted with me in mind and only waited for me to appear. I stood in the center of the huge room turning slowly in the dim light. And laughed softly. The sound was magnified by bare plaster walls and hardwood floor. A tranquil, lilting sound that really didn't sound like me at all. And when the laugh faded away, there was a peculiar emptiness in the big room. A sadness. A waiting silence.

The apartment had been constructed in the double-parlor style, one big, long room, from the street out front to the courtyard in back. It was divided in half midway along the width by a deep header which supported the roof. In some double-parlor-style apartments, the header was left open, in others, a door was inserted and walls came in from the sides to divide the big room in two. Here, there were three separate openings in the dividing wall with two ten-foot-tall, narrow louvered doors in each opening; they mirrored the three French windows opening onto the narrow balcony over the street and the functional shutters held closed with clips.

I walked into the front room, my footsteps a loud echo on the flooring, and opened the French doors inward, threw back the shutters. They banged solidly against the old-brick façade and vibrated gently. Brilliant light flooded the room, gleamed on the heart of pine floors, reflected on the enamel which coated the millwork, and moldings.

This room was done entirely in cream and honey tones; the plaster was sponge-painted in tri-color motif and accented with a heavy wallpaper border at the ceiling. Four long, narrow, floor-to-ceiling book shelves filled the scant wall-space on the dividing wall between the rooms. Empty, dust-free shelves awaited my art magazines and the few items I might wish to show the world. The ceiling was pressed tin, in a block-and-strip design with a central medallion in each, wired for fans or overhead lights.

There were drawbacks to the rental, I quickly discovered. There were no closets. Only a single large window-unit air-conditioner in the back of the apartment to cool the entire area. Only two small coal-grate gas-heaters to heat the space in winter. Almost no electrical outlets, no smoke detectors, no insulation. Water ran rust-brown from the old, worn faucets, and the old toilet tinkled constantly. All problems, true.

But I loved the apartment instantly. Like the city itself, the apartment seemed to have been waiting for me for all these years. It was as if I had come home. My mind made up, I closed the shutters and windows to the street and walked back down the stairs.

Cee Cee was waiting at the bottom, petting a dainty, long-haired dog, as flame bright as her own hair. They looked perfect together, the tiny little red-haired woman and the prissy little dog. Master and pet.

'I'll take it,' I said, long before I reached the bottom of the stairs. 'It's perfect. Can I move in today?'

'You like my nephew's little place? I don't go up very often, only at Christmas time and Thanksgiving to eat his delicious cooking. His boyfriend was a chef, you know.' Cee Cee spread a hand across her chest and sighed, a deep theatrical sound filled with pathos. She blinked her green eyes quickly, several times, a flutter more appropriate to a young girl, yet somehow perfect on the elderly woman. 'Such food. Ah well . . .' She seemed to put her memories of the gastronomic holidays aside as she smiled and waved her be-ringed fingers at me.

'Yes, my dear, you may move in anytime, and I'll prorate the first month's rent. All utilities are included in the monthly rent, did I mention that?' Cee Cee turned and went into the coolness of the shop as she talked, her fast-spoken French trailing out behind her.

I followed, stepping around the little dog. He yipped once and went up on his hind legs. A quick pirouette and he yipped again. Cee Cee shut the shop door on the dog, leaving him outside. 'Your dog—'

'Not my dog, Bonnie. But he's a cute little fellow, and I do love dogs. You know, in Paris, they let the pets eat right at the table in the restaurants . . .' And she was off again, telling me about Paris as it was the last time she was there, back in the seventies. Cee Cee had a pleasant lilting voice, and, like Mme Willoby, she never shut up.

Perhaps it was a trait of the French, although Tante Ilene had never been so voluble. Tante Ilene had seldom talked at all.

While Cee Cee chattered away, I wrote out a check on the counter checks from Royal Securities and accepted the key-ring for my first apartment. It was a dull brass ring with three keys hanging from it. A small, ornate key for the shutters on the balcony, a large old-fashioned brass key for the street-level gate, and a plain modern key for the deadbolt. The keys must have been charged with something, like electricity, or heat or magic. When they touched the skin of my palm, already warm and smelling like hot metal, something strange happened inside me. A bubbling up of . . . something. Something rich and heated and wild.

At the first possible break in conversation, I escaped from the shop into the fume-scented, pressure-heated August air, the keys like a brand in the palm of my hand. The door closed behind me, and I paused a moment, closed my eyes and rested against the door frame.

The little dog waited patiently beside the step, panting and bright-eyed. I paused and petted the small head, no bigger than my fist, and was surprised how soft the hair felt. My only experience with dogs was helping Tee Dom bury them, and the scrawny strays he shot with the .20 gauge were never so clean and furry. Most were mangy, starved, and sickly, abandoned on a deserted parish road by uncaring owners who no longer wanted the responsibility of a pet.

The little pink tongue licked my fingers, coating my hand between quick little pirouettes. I checked for a tag or collar, finding only a thin rhinestone band buried in the fur, with the word 'Perkins' spelled out in colored stones. He wore no other identification. Because he seemed lonely, I scratched his chest between his front legs, and smoothed his pointed ears. His fur was warm from the sun and smelled faintly of flea spray.

'Perkins, huh. You don't look like a Perkins.' The dog whirled again, his front paws held just below his jaw, his back feet dancing. 'I'll bet your owner isn't happy to have you loose. Did you slip out somebody's door and take off after a little lady dog? Are you lost? Hummm? Are you lost?'

He wore an expression on his small face that reminded me of the Precious Pup cartoon, the way the dog got all content and happy-faced after he was given a doggie treat. I half-expected Perkins to float up to the ceiling in ecstasy just from the attention.

Standing, I headed for my van. Perkins sat down on the doorstep to Cee Cee's shop and panted.

I pulled the van around and off-loaded my oils as the dog watched, seeming perplexed that one would move heavy furniture in the sweltering heat. It wasn't very bright, and to be sensible, I should have waited till dusk, but the drying oils couldn't wait, and I was too excited. I carried the wet canvases up the side steps two at a time, propping them against the walls in the front half of the big room. The dim light that seeped through the front shutters brought the night scenes to life.

My art had always looked its best in dim light. More alive. More vibrant. The lighting in this apartment was exactly what I needed.

Before locking up, I dragged the rest of my belongings, including the small mattress and box springs, up the stairs and into the front room as well, placing the simple bed frame at an angle to the windows and piling my clothes and magazines on the floor. My old bed would make a great sofa. All it needed was the right covering. Satisfied, I secured the deadbolt and went shopping. Perkins had vanished.

I had studied magazines for years. Magazines that displayed a better, finer way of living than I had ever known. I had studied and dreamed and hoped for a chance to own something other than the tired old primitives of a bayou shack. Based on figures gleaned from years of flipping through *Metropolitan Home*, *Architectural Digest*, and even Tante Ilene's *Better Homes and Gardens*, I had budgeted two thousand dollars for apartment furniture.

By day's end, I had upped the figure considerably. It might have been foolishness, or it might have been impetuous youth rearing its pimpled head, but when I got into the stores, I lost the ability to 'just say no' to the sales people. The Reagans would have been so disappointed.

On the advice of half a dozen satisfied sales people, I bought a king-sized bed and linens to fit, and a small wicker bedside table. For closet space, two old, Art Deco armoires with curved, rounded doors and beveled mirrors just begged to come home with me. The burled wood scrolled up the doors in fanciful fashion; the finish had softened over the years to an orangey glow.

I was familiar with Art Deco and its influence on the art world in years gone by, its power in the market then and now. The armoires were as beautiful in reality as any picture in one of my slick-paged magazines. To the amusement of the salesman, I spent nearly an hour just sliding my hands over the burled wood and peering into drawers and crevices.

Mme Willoby had loved Art Deco. When she died, I had wanted to purchase the beautiful Art Deco desk where we had studied French idioms for many years, but her daughter had claimed the desk. By the time the estate sale had rolled around, the desk was in Illinois. Having the armoires was like having a bit of Mme Willoby with me in New Orleans.

A small kitchen table and two chairs, a dozen small easels, two upholstered chairs for the front half of the apartment, and a dressing screen which was mirrored on one side and upholstered on the other, like something out of an old western movie, all came from a single junk shop. A tall chair and palette stand for painting completed my larger purchases.

I bought settings of mismatched china that an old saleswoman in a consignment shop just raved over, and old copper pots, dented and worn. For the table, I found crystal that matched nothing and tarnished, well-used, silver-plated tableware, the kind with the finish worn off in strategic places.

Almost everything I bought was old, used, or antique. Everything had its own character, its own aura, as if a bit of history emanated from the worn surfaces.

I bought linens and upholstered pillows and a covering that

would turn my old bed into a couch. I bought two worn rugs and mirrors and lamps. I bought two ceiling fans for the efficient use of the small AC unit, a radio and a small repossessed color TV.

I shopped at thrift shops and warehouses, Sears and art supply shops, arranging to have the heavier pieces delivered. Most of what I bought was on sale or marked down, yet I blew a small fortune to the unmistakable delight of a commissioned sales force across the city.

I was delighted to, and a bit bewildered by the things I bought, feeling something kindled deep inside me. It was as if I came alive for the first time as I shopped. As if each piece of furniture, each place setting of china, each sheet or pot was a part of the new life I hoped to create.

Eclectic. That was what *Met Home* would claim. That was me. No particular time period, no particular style. Just a medley of stuff which I hoped would compliment the apartment and each other and me.

I was constantly hassled for using the counter checks, and I was certain Michau was perturbed by repeated phone calls to verify my liquidity, but I enjoyed the day, the negotiating over price, and the freedom of choosing my own lifestyle. It was a heady experience. Almost as much fun as placing the new/old stuff in the apartment would be.

Near six, the van filled with portables and kitchen necessities and the used TV, I drove to the apartment. Cee Cee was long gone, the shop was a darkened hole, and the traffic almost bumper to bumper. Miraculously, I found a parking spot just two doors down from the apartment. It was an odd feeling to have so many things go right. As if I had a genie looking out for me, paving the way. I wondered how long it would last.

With a lamp in each hand and pillows beneath each arm, I climbed the stairs, fumbled for the key to the deadbolt, and found the keyhole by feel. When I finally pushed the thick oak door open, something furry flashed by my feet.

I almost screamed, until I caught a quick glimpse of red. *Perkins*. He must have followed me inside before lunch and been locked inside all day without food or water. Even if I had left the toilet lid up, he was too small to get a drink.

Standing on the landing, one floor up, I sniffed. Nothing rank inside, just the musty smell of closed-up house, my paintings, and air-conditioned air.

I deposited the lamps and pillows, and checked the apartment. No little surprises except for a few, long red hairs on my dirty jeans. They smelled faintly of dog.

Half an hour later, I had emptied the van. The apartment looked like the remains of a rummage sale, lamps on the floor, half-finished artwork on cheap easels, pillows and small tables all around. All mine. The glow with which I had started the day seemed to grow and expand, filling some of the empty places inside me. Places haunted occasionally by a vision of Tante Ilene's black-on-black eyes filled with tears.

Making sure no fuzzy little animals were trapped inside, I locked up and climbed into the van for the smoky, fumey ride to the Ponchartrain. Perkins was nowhere to be seen.

I made coffee in the Ponchartrain suite hoping that R.T. Stocker would be late. While it perked, filling the elegant apartment suite with a rich, strong, dark-roast smell, I showered and changed, pulling on a ragged jogging-suit and a pair of socks with multiple holes. I had no idea what the proper attire for meeting with an investigator might be – Mme Willoby hadn't covered that in my deportment training – so I opted for comfort over fashion. As it turned out, I made a wise move.

R.T. Stocker was not what I expected.

Neither a gray-haired Murder-She-Wrote image, nor a tough, chain-smoking dick, Stocker conformed to no image but her own. Tall, over six feet, and willowy, with long legs and wide hips, she looked like she had come directly from the barn. And smelled like it as well. Clad in jeans, brown cowboy boots, and T-shirt, she carried a briefcase in one hand, and a cowboy hat in the other.

She had Nordic features with blue eyes and a strong-jawed face, sun-bleached blonde hair worn braided, like mine, and perfect, white teeth. Transferring the hat to the briefcase hand, she shook mine. Her grip was calloused and firm. The horse-barn smell grew stronger with movement.

'R.T. Stocker, but call me Stocker. Everyone does. Sorry I'm late. I had a mare foaling all day and was just now able to get away.'

The excitement that had followed me like a shadow all day changed suddenly. An odd internal shift, a rough transition, like Elred's van trying to change gears. I was suddenly just me again. An inexperienced kid, an orphan with delusions of grandeur and visions of mystery.

The horse-smell followed Stocker into the suite, oddly comforting.

'Have you eaten?' I asked. 'I just got in and was going to make a tuna-fish sandwich.' Typical southerner. When uncertain take refuge in food.

'I'd love one. And some of that wonderful coffee.' Stocker sniffed, sighed as if the smell was pure heaven, and put her briefcase and hat on the small kitchen table. 'Mind if I pour?'

I shook my head, then buried it in the refrigerator, finding the remains of last night's tuna salad and mayonnaise, and smearing both thickly on bread. I heard the gurgles of coffee into cups, an intimate sound. One that reminded me of Tante Ilene, who had drunk two or three pots of strong chicory coffee daily. Coffee was a typical French Louisiana passion.

Stocker placed a cup of steaming liquid beside my hand, leaned a hip against the counter and started telling me about her horses.

She ran a Paso Fino breeding farm for an Argentinean conglomerate. A new business, only two years old, with twenty-seven mares and three young stallions who might be stud material some day, if they grew into their potential and did well at show.

I didn't ride, and knew next to nothing about horses, so I listened, said 'um' in the proper places and let the sound of her voice soothe me. By the time the small meal was over, I had a standing invitation to visit the farm anytime, and my nerves had settled a bit.

I had never been an emotional person. Was given to neither fits of anger nor bouts of ecstasy. I was, according to most of my tutors, well balanced, well adjusted, and possessed a modulated personality. I know. I stole peeks at my performance records on a regular basis. But ever since I saw the fifty-thousand-dollar checks, I had suffered swings of emotion, sensation and passion. Bliss, elation, fury, uncertainty. Anger. Sadness. I wasn't accustomed to it, this fluctuation, and I didn't like it. Not at all.

So I let Stocker talk till she ran out of words. I let her soothe me, knowing it was deliberate. She was trying to put me at ease and it worked. After half an hour and three cups of coffee apiece, Stocker pushed her cup away and sighed again. She had the thin lips of a Scandinavian ancestor, the blue eyes of a frozen North Sea. She smiled. 'So. You want to tell me about this missing person?'

'It really is dumb, you know,' I said slowly. 'I mean, I think I'm seeing it now. But I can't just . . . let it go. I really need to . . .' There was no way to explain it. I would have to show her. 'Wait here.' I padded through the kitchen into the bedroom, returning with the black metal box and the sheaf of papers.

As Stocker took notes, I laid everything out, the birth certificates, the death certificates, the marriage license, the photographs of gravestones and newborn babies, the ticket stubs. All the bits and pieces of the mystery of my two selves.

'You have a picture of your aunt and uncle somewhere? Something I could compare these baby pictures to?'

I brought back a closeup, one of several photographs I had taken when I was fourteen and trying my hand at charcoal. I had managed a few fairly good portraits of Tee Dom and Tante Ilene. The pictures hung in their trailer bedroom, in cheap, black, dime-store frames. Not bad likenesses for a fourteen-year-old artist working with a single stick of charcoal.

Stocker studied the photographs of the Sarvaunts, comparing the elderly couple to the baby pictures. While she studied, I told her about The Man, the financial arrangement set up for me, and the impressions Duhon had of the woman claiming to be Elizabeth Sarvaunt. Stocker took notes, made little 'hum', 'ah' and 'really' sounds. And when I finished, she tapped the pencil eraser against the pad.

'Well,' she said after a moment, 'there might be something here. And then again, there might not.' She smiled. 'Sufficiently evasive for you? I'd hate to take your money on a wild-goose chase, but there are a few things I could do. Preliminary things. Like check into the death certificates, see who identified the bodies, get descriptions of the bodies, talk to the coroner or medical examiner, if he's still around. Talk to the doctors who delivered the babies. If the mothers were regular patients, then the doctors might remember them and give us a description.

'We would need release forms, giving the doctors permission to talk to me. It would require a trip to Petit Chenier to accomplish, say, two or three days' work. But what I could learn should be enough to either put your mind at rest or prove at least the possibility of a switch.

'My fee for the security firm is two fifty per day plus expenses. Mileage, hotels, food, that sort of thing. If you say go ahead, I'll ask for a three-day deposit.' Stocker dropped the pencil and leaned back in her seat, lacing her fingers over her stomach.

'Good coffee. I'll never sleep tonight.'

'Is it stupid? To want to find out if I am who they say I am?'

'Nope. I only have one problem with it all. If your mother really was trying to hide you from someone, then there is the possibility of danger for you if you're found. Or the possibility of trouble – legal trouble – if you show up unexpectedly, some long missing heir, or the child of some long-missing criminal. We don't know where the money to set up your trust fund came from. Think about it. You might have to give it all back.'

That stopped me. My mother a criminal? It was only marginally better than Duhon's concept of my mother the whore. I rose, took the coffee cups to the sink and rinsed them in hot water. Rinsed out the coffeepot and turned it upside down to dry. The apartment was silent while I thought.

R.T. Stocker had no problems with silence. She didn't need to fill it in with chatter or inanities. She'd have been quite comfortable in the silence of the Sarvaunt household. She and Tante Ilene could drink coffee and listen to the crickets chirp. I smiled faintly, seeing my reflection in the warped plastic surface of the microwave.

I dried my hands on a towel and turned to face the private investigator. She was watching me, her face in half-shadow. The sun had set while we talked, and the room was lit only by the light on the stove. Too bright in some places, harsh shadows in others.

'I'd like you to go ahead. I'll write you a seven-hundred-fifty-dollar check.' The excitement was back. In a few days, I would at least know my name. Bonnibelle Sarvaunt or Carin Colleen DeVillier.

The paperwork took another half-hour – a standard contract, several release forms to sign and have witnessed, copies made of the photographs. The Ponchartrain had a notary and a photocopier in the office, saving us time. And after completing all the red tape, Stocker left, leaving behind the scent of hay and horse and an emptiness in the suite I hadn't noticed before.

Emptiness was a feeling I was becoming familiar with. An almost tactile experience. And I wasn't sure why. After all, I had always been alone. So why was the aloneness of New Orleans different?

The sun was setting as the woman stood over the headstones and contemplated the row that marked her family. A last rosy glow tinted the white marble vaults, shadows fluttered down over the angel's wings, darkened peaceful faces where they stood guard over the dead and rotten. Fifteen generations lay in the family plot. Five generations of them belonged to her. Four great-grandbabies were buried in the family plot. Five grandchildren. Her husband and his brother, and one of the children the two men had born on her body. And, of course, there was the grave of their father, the father of her husband and his brother. Royal DeLande. He was her father too, although she hadn't known that at the time the old man first seduced her.

But he had known. He had always known. She was eleven and beautiful even then, when he took her from her mother into his bed.

A bird called in the distance, the mournful sound announcing the end of day, the coming of night. She looked down, watching her feet where they touched the path. Her shadow seemed to leap along beside her, its steps meeting her own, its longer legs dancing over headstones.

And when she was thirteen years old and four months pregnant, he had given her to his sons to use. She shuddered a moment as the memories moved through her. Elegant hands, lean beautiful bodies. Pleasure and shame, as the boys used her. Shame greater because the man she had come to love watched the all-night scene, drinking and laughing and calling out lewd suggestions to his sons. Shame because she enjoyed it. Shame when he stood over them afterward, and told them of the relationship they all shared. Yet, she had survived.

Even when Royal DeLande had forced her to marry one of her half-brothers, she had managed to survive. Survive and conquer even through the shame.

And pain. There was always pain. Her eyes blinked several times as the shadows lengthened and the rosy sunset faded. The angels turned black and somber. Evil angels. The fallen ones. The shadows paused, standing still over the acres of marble and gardens.

Shame and pain. But she had won, then and now. She was still winning, with both of her goals at last in sight, just out of reach. Simple goals, really. She would create another like herself, breeding in the necessary characteristics. A Grande Dame to carry on the tradition of the DeLandes in the world. And she would destroy the family DeLande.

That her two goals were mutually exclusive had never occurred to her. That her destruction of her own family had led to seeds of self-destruction was equally obscure.

She had outlived the old man, poisoned one brother and lived in mortal sin with the other. Stolen the wealth and punished them all. Such an elegant punishment. She had stolen the idea from the old man. But she was so much better at it than he. So much more refined. So much more polished and proficient.

A cool wind blew as she walked through the graveyard, her fingers touching a name or a date in the sun-warmed marble. Pausing, she traced the single rose carved into her husband's tomb. She still missed him. Missed him with a passion. Even though she had arranged the scene that led to his death. Even though she had given the shotgun to her son and watched as the boy blew a hole in his father. Her husband. She had missed him as he lay dying, bleeding scarlet and gore all over an ancient and priceless Aubusson rug. Missed him as he gasped out his last breath. Missed him as she buried him beside his brother. In her own way, she had loved him as much as she had hated him.

The tomb of the old man loomed in the darkness. Huge and monstrous. A hulking crypt guarded by dark twin angels as tall at the shoulder as a man was high. Black marble devils standing over the black marble tomb, its surface polished and glossy. It was kept that way, as smooth as a mirror, so she could come here at night and see her reflection in the grave of Royal DeLande.

Slowly, she climbed the steps cut into the stone, and when she reached the top she stood over his feet and stared out over the burial plot. By far, this was the best, the most magnificent crypt on the grounds, towering over the others, lording it over the lesser dead.

She smiled as the moon began to rise, casting pale light and darker shadows over the city of dead. When the light was perfect, an optimal blend of silver light and stygian darkness, she stretched down and rested, putting her lips where his would be. Pressing her flesh to the still-warm slab.

'I hate you,' she whispered though the stone, completing the ritual. 'I hate you all.'

'I curse you. You and yours down through eternity. I curse you where you burn. I curse you where you suffer. I curse your children and your children's children. I will destroy them all. All.'

The words carried on the faint breeze. Electronically enhanced and recorded for later analysis. The scene was videotaped from three different angles, the cameras controlled by remote from a van more than a mile away. The private investigative firm hired to obtain the material had been warned to limit human presence, human involvement. They had been warned that she, the woman on the tomb, could sense them if they were too close. They hadn't believed the carnival mumbo-jumbo of course, but then, belief wasn't necessary. They were professionals, paid to do what the client wanted, the way the client wanted it done. Paid well. Well enough to follow orders and keep their mouths shut about what they learned, what they heard.

At midnight, the woman rose from the black marble tomb, moving stiffly and moaning slightly, as if her joints were old and worn, made rigid by contact with death and stone. For a moment she shuffled like a woman much older than her sixty-six years, infirm and ancient and doddering. Yet she seemed to loosen as she moved slowly down the stone steps, and by the time she reached the gravel path, she moved like a young woman. Lissome and supple and graceful. Following the path, she vanished in the darkness.

A mile away, a pair of hands deactivated the cameras and the recorders. Tomorrow a team would slip in and retrieve them, finishing a job which had been bizarre from the beginning.

It was early, just a bit after nine. Back home, in the shanty, I would be setting up my oils and photographs, listening to Tee Dom and Tante Ilene's soft Cajun phrases, too low to hear. The click of their Chinese Checkers – a game they played incessantly – or the soft shuffle of a worn deck of playing cards.

Here there was only silence. Propping myself on the big pillows, I flipped from channel to channel, enjoying the novelty of remote control and MTV, the A&E channel, Discover. I watched Madonna writhe across a stage, a dozen male hands on her body and remembered the apoplexy of Father Alcede when he talked about her and the profanity of the Holy Mother's name.

Poor Father Alcede. He'd have just died had cable and the availability of MTV stayed around. The old priest had considered it a personal spiritual victory when the cable company pulled out. Of course, to Father Alcede, most everything was a personal spiritual victory.

When the Free Will Baptist Church closed down after the preacher, Reverend Picarazzi, died, that was a victory. Heretics moved on or quit worshiping together. When the Picou Brothers' Bar and Grill was shut down for dealing dope and prostitution, the old Father had congratulated himself for weeks. And when the Walker boys got drunk and killed each other over a loose woman, Father Alcede went into raptures.

I flipped channels till after one, thinking about my new life and what I could do with it. Somehow, I hadn't really thought much beyond hiring a private investigator and getting my own place. The farther I got from home, the more I was acting and thinking my age. Little better than teenage tunnel vision. During the long hours of reruns and late-night talk shows, crime shows and comedy, I considered my options. And they weren't the same options to which I had limited myself while lying on my twin bed in the dark of night in Khoury.

I could live any way I wished now. The possibilities were limitless. The alternatives boundless. I could move to France or Spain and study art with the greats. I could move to New

York or the west coast or, if I was feeling real adventurous, Antarctica.

And yet, I found that there wasn't really all that much I wanted to do. Except paint. And I could have done that in Khoury . . . The truth of that was sobering.

I was up at daybreak, cleaned out the hotel suite and headed for the Quarter, Elred's old van making a horrendous sound. Sunrise over New Orleans wasn't much, pollution and haze obscuring the ball of sun, allowing, at best, a peachy glow or gold-tinted clouds. Today there wasn't even that much color. Just a gray mist, a dirty light.

After breakfast at the Café du Monde, watching the city wake up and peer groggily into the new day, I went to my apartment on Royal, unlocked the street gate and climbed the stairs. My stairs. At the top, curled into a tight furry ball sleeping on the landing, was Perkins. He looked tired, and the soft fur below his eyes was damp, as if he had cried himself to sleep. He woke up as I unlocked the oak door, stretched and yawned, blinking up at me. He followed me indoors.

I gave him water in a Royal Dalton saucer and part of a leftover beignet. As he ate – dainty little bites – little pink tongue lapping, I opened up the shutters at the front of the double parlor, letting the weak sun brighten the clutter.

I talked to the dog as I tried to bring some order to the chaos, my voice resonating from the bare walls and tall ceiling. 'I don't want a dog, Perkins. I have no idea how to take care of one, so you better not be planning on making this a permanent arrangement. I'm sure an owner somewhere is looking all over for you.'

Perkins looked up at the sound of his name, licked his mouth and nose and went back to the water bowl. The beignet was gone. Not even a speck of powdered sugar was left to mark its existence. Echoes of water lapped through the apartment as he drank.

I stacked my art magazines on the lower shelf of the wall that divided the front room from the sleeping area in back, making a mental note to change the mailing address. The old twin bed looked quite chic in its flame-stitched cover, and the huge upholstered pillows I piled all over its surface made it look like a lounging sofa. The TV went in the corner, on an old table, the wooden surface scarred and pitted. A bargain. By turning the

TV, the screen could be viewed from either room, though I had no desire at the moment to turn it on.

I stocked the kitchen, placing my mismatched treasures in the white enameled cabinets, tossing the empty packing boxes into the main room. And I continued talking to Perkins. I told him all about R.T. Stocker and her horse farm, her plan to hunt down my birth records, and her association with Michau. I told him about Claude Michau and Royal Securities too, and my plans for my investments. The little dog sat in the corner under a kitchen chair, safe and protected from flying boxes and my constantly moving feet, and listened. His ears and eyes followed me around the room.

It was soothing, talking to the little dog, watching his head tilt as he responded to the inflection of my voice. Because, naturally, he couldn't understand English, could he? If I hadn't been so certain that Perkins was someone's lost pet . . .

I put that thought away along with thoughts of Tante Ilene and Tee Dom. Yet when he went to the door and barked, requesting permission to leave, I felt an acute disappointment.

I watched him bound down the stairs, long-haired tail curled over his back. Perkins was only about eight inches high himself, barely taller that the risers, maybe six or eight pounds. And completely fearless. He squeezed through the curlicues of the wrought-iron fence at the bottom and disappeared around the corner. I closed the door with a soft, hollow thud, and went back to work.

The king-sized bed was delivered before eleven, followed shortly by the armoires and a few larger pieces. Before 1 p.m., a man from Sears came to hang my electric fans. They were cream-colored wood, modified by Victorian style, dependent light kits. With a cream-colored extension pipe, the fans dropped three feet from the ceiling before the blades turned. The air flow was an instant improvement over the meager cool air blown by the air-conditioner in the kitchen window.

I was starving, but instead of walking to the market after the last, sweaty delivery man left, I put brand-new sheets on the bed and stretched out diagonally across the vast surface. The bed alone was bigger than my trailer room in Khoury.

The fan blades made lazy shadows on the pressed-tin ceiling.

A soft whirr of fan motor and air filled the apartment. Traffic noises, muffled by the thick walls, intruded only occasionally. And for some strange reason I suddenly wanted to cry.

It was silly, futile, pointless, and adolescent to drop into a depression now. But telling myself all that didn't seem to help. I wanted . . . something. I wanted my mother. And I almost laughed through the tears when the thought settled into me. Talk about adolescent. Yet . . . Yet, what would she think of me, lying here in a New Orleans apartment? What would she think of my art, my paintings all displayed in the front room, in the section I already thought of as the studio? And what had she run from? Who had frightened her so much that she had hidden me away for so many years?

The sound of claws on the oak door interrupted a swift descent into depression, and I forced myself up from the huge bed to let Perkins into the apartment. He pranced in like he owned the place, got water from his bowl in the kitchen and then went exploring. I stood silently by the door, fingers pressed to my lips, and watched his progress.

He stuck his nose into every little nook and cranny, examining the new furniture with all five senses, tasting the tables, sniffing the armoires, following the scents of the different delivery men from door to furniture and back again, listening to the fans turning overhead. After a thorough survey he trotted back up to me and sat down beside my foot.

'I hope you don't have fleas.'

Perkins twitched his tail.

'If you had an owner, I don't think you would be permitted to roam the streets. And if you didn't have an owner, I think you wouldn't be so well behaved. And so well groomed.' Perkins had both long silky hair and short thick fluff. His coat was a combination of chow chow and Cousin It from the Addams Family. He needed a good brushing, but I wasn't volunteering my only hair brush to his vanity.

'I'm hungry. You want to go for a walk?'

Perkins did one of those quick, twirling pirouettes, then another. When I laughed, he whirled again.

'I don't have a leash, so if you run out in traffic and get killed, don't blame me, dog.' Perkins barked.

We walked down Royal, Perkins alert and excited, prancing by my left foot; together we turned toward the river and the market. The open-air market had been located in the same place along the wharf for so many years it had become a fixture, and if you looked hard enough, you could find almost anything for sale there. I bought fresh foodstuffs, rice, seasonings, and dog equipment, including a bowl, a leash, dog chow, and a collapsible rolling stand to haul it all back with me. I also bought a newspaper, a copy of the *Times Picayune*, so I could scan the lost and found section.

I stopped and ate at an open sidewalk café, stuffing myself with crawfish bisque and dark-roast coffee. Perkins got the French bread scraps soaked in leftover cream bisque. He was a dainty eater but there were no crumbs when he finished. Greedy little thing. He was so cute that no one said a word about bringing a dog on the premises. No one recognized him either.

We spent a short time at the apartment stowing food in cabinets and my badly wrinkled clothes in the armoires. I had rinsed out the damp dress – the one I had worn the day Duhon gave me 50,000 dollars. but the sour smell was still strong. It needed more attention than I knew how to provide, depleting my meager wardrobe by one.

Pitiful really. All that space and all those empty hangers. Well, I had money now. And places to wear all the clothes I had never cared about while growing up. Thinking of that, it was time to make a few investments, both in my wardrobe, and with Claude Michau.

Maybe I had no idea what to do with my life now that I had one, but money and clothing sounded like a good start. After a shower and change of clothes, Perkins and I took off for the streets.

Perkins on a leash was well mannered and prissy, walking with a little wiggle that screamed 'female'. Only the extra accessories dangling behind proved him male. He sniffed at everything along the way, tasted every puddle we passed, and marked every protuberance on the sidewalk with his scent. I hoped he wouldn't do that with my apartment. The sour dress was aromatic enough.

I left Perkins with the bleached blonde receptionist at Royal

Securities, quite certain that he would be ruined when I got back. Belinda cooed and baby-talked and offered him raisins from her desk drawer, and Perkins preened like a canine Casanova, pawing the air and sniffing her legs. Typical male.

I went into Claude Michau's office and invested twenty-five thousand dollars in wildly speculative stock options. As wild as stock options get, that is. Against Michau's advice, I bought call options on four different stocks that were in play. None here in the States, where he could advise me, but in France. And then I went shopping. Either I would be successful, or I wouldn't. I didn't worry about losing it all. I had done poor for years. It wasn't that hard.

CHAPTER 5

Perkins was an attention-getter wherever we went, stimulating conversation and then arousing pity in the listeners when they heard my lost-and-found story. Still, no one recognized him. No one. From the sales clerk at the consignment shop on Ursuline Street, to the owner of the Panama Hat and Bag shop on Burgundy near Iberville, to an antique costume-jewelry and ballgown boutique on Chartres, the Twice is Nice. Perkins and I covered most of the Quarter spending money on clothes, shoes and accessories, and looking for his owner. No luck. But my wardrobe was vastly improved.

Footsore and hungry, Perkins and I headed home trailing my two-wheeled shopping cart behind us. Shadows lengthened, casting a rosy glow across the Quarter as shop owners closed up, locking, bolting, and barring up their treasures. Tourists headed back to hotels and inns, crowding the trolley cars, congesting the narrow streets.

I bought a bottle of wine and some gourmet-flavored coffee from a tired clerk. He never asked to see my ID. He was too busy carrying on a conversation with Perkins. I should have bought a case.

It was dusk when we unlocked the ornate street gate and climbed the stairs. First thing, even before eating, I groomed Perkins, spraying him down with Adam's Flea and Tick Mist, brushing out his coat, and pouring some dried food and water into his new, double bowl. He ignored the dried food, literally turning up his nose, exactly like a gourmand might if offered up a plate of pork and beans. I laughed. And this time, the sound wasn't quite as hollow, not quite as empty and stark as earlier. It was as if the echoes had been muted, absorbed, diminished. It must have been the furniture.

I drew a bath in the antique tub, first letting the water run until it was no longer rusty-brown, then adding a generous portion of Caswell Massey pomegranate-scented bubble bath. I poured a glass of wine, opened a package of whole-wheat crackers, sliced some cheddar and warmed some brie in the open air. Finally, I put the food and drink on a tray, on the toilet seat in the bathroom within easy reaching distance of the tub.

I stripped down, tossing my dirty dress into a corner, and stepped into the deep porcelain tub. The water, hot as Tante Ilene's 5 a.m. pot of coffee, rose around me, steaming in the air-conditioned apartment, the scent of pomegranates wafting on the vapor.

Feeling decadent, I sipped the warm red wine, ate cheddar and brie on crackers, and soaked. I had no idea if the wine was any good – Tante Ilene had never served wine at meals – but like the moonshine she forced down me whenever I had a cold, the wine made me feel pleasantly drowsy and content.

Perkins, curled up on my dirty clothes, watched, clearly bored. His eyes were on the cheese and crackers instead of me. He looked hungry, and, relenting, I made him a cracker with a smear of brie on it. One obviously wasn't enough for the little pig-of-a-dog, but I had no idea what too much brie might do to a dog's digestive tract, and I didn't intend to find out. He ate every crumb and licked his lips after, a canine smile on his face.

He was a cute little dickens. Too cute. 'I'm going to have a hard time giving you up, dog.'

Perkins twitched his ears.

'But if I could trade you in for a "tall, dark and handsome" who could talk back, I'd do it. No offense.'

Perkins blinked, yawned, and rested his head on his paws.

I drank half a bottle of wine in the tub, and demolished the cheese, before the water grew too cold. And then, feeling pleasantly tipsy and festive, I drained the tub, dried off, and put on my new/old silk nightgown. It was a 1950s version, with heavy embroidery at the sweetheart neckline and along the straps, a 'find' I had picked up, used, for twenty dollars. It was cream with gold silk stitching, and fell to the floor in a full swing skirt. I had never slept in silk – had never worn silk at all – and I loved the rich swish of smooth fabric against my body. Perkins watched my hem as if it were a new toy, one he might pounce on and rip to shreds.

'Don't even think about it, dog.'

Perkins snorted.

I pulled on the matching gold silk kimono-style robe and went to the front part of the double-parlor-style apartment. I was a month behind in *Marie Claire* and *Paris Elle*, the French fashion magazines I loved best. I curled up on the sofa – my old twin bed – with the periodicals and read, catching up with the newest looks of the fashion world, and reading the articles about artists and designers.

The smell of drying oils filled the front room, but I was far too exhausted and inebriated to paint. Perkins jumped up and settled beside me on a tapestry-covered pillow. I decided he was too well mannered to sulk.

About 10 p.m. I came to a passage in *Elle* that caused me to sit up, dislodging Perkins from a sound sleep, sending him tumbling from the cushions. Taber Rhame, the artist, had relocated. The magazine had been speculating on his disappearance for many months, claiming that he had retired from art, or that he had lost his muse or gone on sabbatical, or that he was slowing down with age. Some commentators had been catty, some downright cruel. Now, the magazine's investigative reporters were claiming he had relocated. No longer in Paris, the half-French, half-Cajun expressionist had settled in New Orleans in the French Quarter.

I wasn't crazy about Rhame's later work. However, his early work, the quasi-political death series produced during his years in Spain, had always intrigued me. Rhame had a way of presenting the human body that simply screamed out torture, passion, dementia, ecstasy. Even his modern series, with its bold and vivid palette of colors and shapes, carried such intense emotion that his most vituperative political critics found it stimulating. And he was here, tonight, perhaps only blocks away.

I wondered if the move signified another shift in his art. Rhame had never specialized, preferring to throw himself intensely into a new spectrum every few years, discarding his old style and his old location in one grand gesture of a move. It had been reported that Rhame would walk into his studio one day after a period of intense work, and glare at his finished canvases or sculpture, make a few caustic comments and vanish. Leaving behind his art, his personal belongings, even his clothes and his apartment furnishings, he would disappear for months, reappearing half a world away with a new direction, reinventing himself and his art, taking both to new levels of eccentricity.

Taber Rhame went beyond the unconventional in a field where unconventionality was the norm. Rhame was intriguing, erratic, exotic and mysterious. Almost mystical. Exploring the unfamiliar in his life and his art. Fearless of both the insular art world, and the brutal public.

Taber Rhame was the man who had evaporated one spring day in 1987 and reappeared twelve months later with a violent series of works he called collectively, *Terror*. The paintings and small sculpture series were based on a year spent living underground in Beirut with a radical terrorist group called the Flaming Fist. How Rhame got out of the city alive was a mystery. That he was able to transport the paintings, as well, was a miracle.

The series had resulted in his greatest torment, as the public screamed out their disapproval of the violence and the sheer viciousness of the works. Yet, they had also been his most financially rewarding works to date, leaving him independently wealthy, able to thumb his nose at the world in general and the Bible Belt USA in particular.

And he was here. Only blocks away. New Orleans was the newest Mecca for artists, taking a share of the raw talent and artistic genius that used to reside only in New York and San Francisco. But Taber Rhame was the first European name to locate here.

The magazine was the July issue, which meant that Rhame had most likely been here for at least three months. Just blocks away.

The plans I had made to enroll in a few college-level art classes, or to take private lessons, were gone as if they had never been. I knew what I wanted. I wanted to be Taber Rhame's research and artistic assistant.

I spent the rest of the night scanning my collection of art magazines for any mention of the famous artist, and collected an impressive list of known facts about the man, his history, and his art. Toward 2 a.m., I finally calmed down enough to sleep for a few hours. But even in my dreams I was planning my assault on Rhame, determining the most effective way I could approach him and request a job.

He liked forthright people who spoke their minds and weren't afraid to state an opinion, right or wrong. In my dreams, I was forthright, brilliant in expression, and talented beyond Rhame's wildest dreams. I woke up at 8 a.m. to Perkins and his bathroom needs, my plans all mapped out.

As I dressed, I noticed the strange man for the first time. He rested a shoulder in a doorway across from Cee Cee's shop and my apartment, watching the passers-by. His eyes rested often on the stairway leading down from my apartment. And I realized I had seen the man twice before, always in the same location, loitering, one beefy shoulder against the wall, ankles crossed in what looked like a characteristic pose.

The pleasure that still drifted in my veins from the day of shopping seemed to change tenor and drain away, leaving me feeling . . . strange. I tried to analyze my feelings as I watched my watcher through the slats in the front shutters.

He had been there last night when I came home. He was here again now. Possibly a street person just spending the night in a dark doorway . . .

When I left the apartment, my sneakers moving briskly down the sidewalk, Perkins sniffing the morning air by my side, I pretended not to see him. He pretended not to stare at me. But I remembered his face, and it bothered me. I had no Tee Dom to chase off interlopers with his shotgun. No Tante Ilene to stare stonily through the door at a stranger who didn't seem quite right. No woman wanted to feel like prey – game to be stalked or a target waiting for the arrow.

Yet, my watcher didn't follow me. He didn't move, even after I turned the corner and looked back. And suddenly I felt the wariness and dread of the very alone. Understood the phobias and anxieties of my older tutors, single women who were prone to foolish fears and intense mistrust.

I was isolated from my past, my home, my people. The only family I had ever known, no matter that they were cold and silent. They had always been there for me. Always.

Now, I could vanish and no one would ever know. I walked faster.

Though he didn't follow, and I felt a bit ridiculous for my alarm, I couldn't seem to slow my heart rate or calm my breathing. Perkins, attuned to my feelings more closely than I had realized, whined and panted up at me.

'It's okay, boy. I'm just being silly.' But there was concern in his black eyes and he licked my ankle as it stepped past.

I glanced back again just before I turned down another side street. There was no one behind me. He was most likely a commuter, I told myself, waiting for a ride to work and then back home. It made sense in light of the unusual hours I had noticed him. It wasn't like he was there all the time.

And then I was out on Chartres, and the sun broke through a layer of clouds, tinting the Quarter a delicate pink. I laughed shakily and Perkins, sensing the strain in the sound, did a quick pirouette. My steps slowed as the street remained empty behind me.

Maybe Duhon was right. Maybe I was looking for a mystery where none existed. I took a deep breath and vowed not to look behind me again. I was proud when I succeeded, forcing the silly fear away, like putting a nightmare out of mind with the sunrise.

I ate at the Café du Monde again, feeding bits and pieces to Perkins as I scanned the *Picayune* for news of Rhame. What I found was profoundly disappointing. Taber Rhame had been auditioning for an assistant for the last week. If I had bothered to check out the art and leisure section of the paper instead of only the lost and found, I would have discovered that applicants had been waiting every day, lined up on the sidewalk, packed in the covered stairway leading to Rhame's second-floor walk-up. I had passed the line twice on my shopping spree and not known what it was for . . . and I hadn't asked.

Many applicants had flown in, and the reporter covering the story for the paper had interviewed a dozen of the hopefuls, some from France, England, Scandinavia, Germany. Several minor names in the art world had stood outside in the heat for several days, hoping for a job that would pay minimum wage and offer no benefits, but would allow the successful candidate to work with the famous artist, learn from him, and meet Rhame's clientele. Many a young artist got his start from such exposure.

As I read the interviews and discovered the attributes and abilities of the hopefuls, I knew I couldn't compete. At least, not on an artistic level. It was even rumored that Michelle Gray had applied for the job and was considered the front-runner for the position. Michelle Gray had been a fixture in the New Orleans are scene for years.

Considering the competition, I should have been crushed. Overcome with defeat. But I had been trained in strategy and tactics by Dr Tammany Long, a scholar of revolution. I had been shown evidences of lost battles suddenly won because an inventive commander had done the unexpected. Like Washington crossing the Delaware in mid-winter, leading starving troops on an impossible assault on a holiday. The unexpected.

Too, I considered the enemy – not the candidates, they were only obstacles – but Rhame himself. He was both prize to be won and the true competition. Rhame had a reputation as a decisive thinker. If he had discovered the applicant he wanted for the job, Rhame would have hired him and closed down the auditions. He hadn't. So I still had a chance. If I could find the right lever.

I finished the last beignet, brushed the crumbs off my plain white cotton T-shirt and considered myself. Dressed as I was, in jeans and worn-out sneakers, my hair in a ponytail, no makeup, and walking a dog, I didn't look like a candidate for a job as a famous painter's assistant. I looked like a teenager out for a stroll.

'Perfect,' I said. 'Hey, Perkins.' The dog looked up. 'You feel like bein' cute and charming?' I asked, using my very best ladylike southern drawl. It had worked on Claude Michau, so why not on Rhame?

Perkins wagged his tail, his black eyes on mine. 'Thought so. Come on, boy, we're going scouting.'

I stepped over the booted feet of the early riser who had settled two tables down. Beneath his jeans' hem peeked charcoal gray, ostrich-skin boots, tipped at the toes with silver. Expensive boots. Two-thousand-dollar boots. It was just a flash, but something bothered me about those boots. For an instant. And then the thought, half-formed and obscure, dissolved and was gone.

'Nice dog.'

I looked up from the boots to the man's black eyes. French-black. Black-on-black. Nice-looking man. Fair skinned, crinkles at his eyes when he smiled, ash-brown hair. And young. Maybe twenty-five. Maybe younger.

He was studying the front section of the *New York Times* and had a copy of *USA Today* on the table beside him. There were two empty coffee cups and a half-eaten beignet left from his breakfast. And a scattering of white-powered sugar down the front of his T-shirt. Not the reading material nor the breakfast of the typical rapist.

I smiled uncertainly. 'His name's Perkins.'

The man bent over and held his curled-under fingers out to the dog for sensory inspection. Perkins sniffed for a while, suspicious, his tail and ears down. Tentatively, Perkins tasted the man's skin and then bent to the fancy boots, sniffing all around as if there was a female buried beneath the heels, or better yet, something dead. His tail was wagging wildly in complete approval.

'He smells my horses,' the man said, as if he had heard my thought about the something dead. 'I come directly here every morning after I take care of exercising and feeding them. Dogs seem to love the smell of barns, or maybe it's the manure.' It was a pleasant voice, modulated Louisiana accent, elegant almost. Yet, that strange uncertainty touched me again.

'Awful fancy boots for wearing to the barn.' The words were out of my mouth before I consciously recognized the reason for my discomfort. No one wore two-thousand-dollar boots to work in a barn. 'Ostrich skin,' I said.

The corners of the man's black eyes crinkled into a smile. 'I change to work boots while I'm there. They're in the truck if you'd like to see. But no matter how careful I am, I always get *somethin'* on these before I change.'

His voice was mildly reproving, as if he sensed my unvoiced accusation. I blushed. I *had* been calling him a liar. Sort of. Something about him bothered me, and it must have showed.

'And yes. They're ostrich.' He held up his hand. 'Name's Miles.'

Feeling stupid and uncouth at my lapse of manners, I shook his hand. 'Bonnibelle.'

'I have breakfast here every morning, Bonnie. Perhaps you and Perkins would care to join me sometime.'

And then it hit me. Black-on-black eyes. I was reacting to the man's eyes. Eyes so much like Tee Dom's and Tante Ilene's. The feeling of 'something not quite right' evaporated. I felt churlish and gauche. And horribly embarrassed.

'We'd love to. Thanks.'

Miles smiled again, his lips full and yet sculptured. A sensuous mouth. 'Great. I hate eating alone.' And then he went back to his newspapers dismissing me entirely. Not exactly the gesture of a rapist or a mugger. Just a nice man striking up an acquaintance.

A *good-looking*, nice man. With no ring on his finger. Not that the absence of a ring signified Miles's marriage status.

Perkins and I headed back, away from the river, toward Conti Street. And I turned my thoughts back to Rhame, away from Miles and his black-on-black eyes.

As the sun was rising, gray against the clouds that carried overdue rain, I walked past Taber Rhame's two-story walk-up. It was on the corner of Conti and a narrow alley, beside which the covered stairs climbed steeply to the entrance at the back of the apartment.

At the end of the narrow alley was an open-air courtyard, full of bougainvillea and climbing rose, a tall, leafy banana tree, and an overarching, ancient live oak. Part of a bench showed beyond the edge of an old brick wall. The sound of water splashing, announced a fountain, out of sight.

Windows, ten feet tall, backed by shutters, marched across the front, over Conti and down the side of the apartment, overlooking the alley. The apartment was easily twice the size of my own.

Visions of the décor ran through my mind. Rhame had lived everywhere. Rome, Vienna, Bonn, Glasgow, Madrid, London, Stockholm, Geneva, and of course, Beirut. He was an avid collector. Virtually the only things Rhame sent for when he disappeared and re-conceived himself artistically, were his collections. He had amassed a collection of art, furnishings, and *objets d'art* worthy of many small museums.

But I put away visions of furnishings, and concentrated on possibilities. Possibilities of convincing Rhame he should hire me.

Rhame used his roof space. The apartment was flat roofed, like mine, with a tall wall around the periphery. In one corner I spotted an easel, a table and the arm of a tall chair. I wondered briefly if my apartment had roof access, and if so, where and how. Also like my apartment, Rhame's abode and studio was above a shop, a store specializing in antique and estate linens. Through the front window, I spotted thousands of tablecloths, sheets, slips, nightgowns, pieces of lace, yellowed and embroidered handkerchiefs. Beautiful workmanship, in a much bigger store than Cee Cee's small place.

An ivory silk baby blanket, embroidered all over with shamrocks and locked away in a glass case to protect it from the air and from thieves, gave the store its name. Le Trèfle d'Irlande. The Shamrock.

As I walked around, studying the visible portions of Rhame's newest home, the store-owner appeared, walking briskly down the street. I knew it was he, as the short but amply proportioned man carried an immense pile of folded cloth over one arm. Walking with bouncing energy, his belly moved up and down with each step. A balding, yet young Santa, all pink-cheeked and energetic, and very obviously gay.

I followed him into the store, lifting Perkins into my arms. The dog put his head beneath my chin and sighed, a lusty sound for such a small dog.

The oversized, yet diminutive man called back for me to 'Look around, dearie' while he went to the back and flipped on lights. His voice was a high-pitched Yat, his accent more reminiscent of Boston than the south, yet as native to the Crescent City as French or a slow southern drawl. The residual echoes of a post-Civil War Yankee invasion.

I had no intention of spending any more money, yet immediately my eyes landed upon an old lace tablecloth yellowed to honey tones, a fringed, white silk shawl in a jacquard fabric and an upholstered pillow in a white-on-cream stripe.

I carried my choices to the front without checking price tags, justifying an outlay of funds as 'investment money'. Linens for information. Seemed a fair trade to me. I only hoped the proprietor cooperated.

Perkins squirmed to get down, but I soothed him to be quiet, smoothing his long hair. The rotund owner was still opening up the store, rummaging in back, and the smell of dark-roast coffee wafted to the front as I looked around. Perkins and I sniffed appreciatively, and, leaving the articles at the cash register, followed the scent back to its source.

There was a tiny kitchenette tucked in the back, a bright and cheerful place, wallpapered with a fanciful tropical fruit print and decorated with exquisite antique linens and dark green wicker. The sort of place a Victorian grandmother might have loved, even down to the sterling silver samovar and matched china cups.

'Have a seat, miss. I'm worth absolutely *nothing* until I've had a cup of coffee. And with the rain coming, I need it more than ever. Arthritis, you know.'

I accepted a cup as I sat at the table, settling Perkins on my lap out of sight, and burning my tongue on his dark brew.

'Ah . . . ' He drew out the word and relaxed across the table from me, tilting his head back and closing his eyes in bliss. They popped open an instant later and focused on me.

'Charles Stuart, at your service.'

'Bonnibelle Sarvaunt, my lord. Forgive me if I don't curtsy.'

Charles roared with laughter, the high-pitched tones bouncing off the walls. 'A quick wit! Well come, Mistress Sarvaunt,' he said, pronouncing the words in the Old English manner, with an effeminate swish of his fingers.

Hiding a smile, I tilted my head in acknowledgment of the praise, and sipped more coffee over my burned tongue. It was strong, the way Tante Ilene liked it. Able to peel paint off the walls.

'I like your place. I picked out a few things to take with me. They're up front.'

Charles nodded, his cup to his lips, his blue eyes still merry. He had to be in his early sixties, but the few hairs that clung to his pate were still brown, and where wrinkles might have intruded on his face, the underlying fat kept age at bay.

'I'll bet you do considerable business here. Your selection is so wonderful, and the store itself so—' I stopped. Charles's eyes looked dark suddenly and he set down his coffee cup.

'I usually do *quite* a brisk business, but my new upstairs *tenant* and his blasted *ad* are *ruining* it. For the last week there's been a line running down the walk in front of my store, and *no one* wants to pass through a queue of side-show *freaks* to come and buy my linens.'

Charles suddenly realized he might not be making complete sense. 'Ever since the upstairs tenant ran that blasted ad, I've had almost *no* business at all. *Artistic* types with green *steaks* in their hair and *safety pins* through their *nipples*, wearing *torn-up* clothes and distressed *leather* have been *blocking* the entrance to the shop *ten hours* a day.' Charles poured himself a second cup and freshened mine.

'*Artistic, hell*. They're stoned out of their *minds* and engaging in *lively* discourse. Stuff that *sounds* like it should be English but makes no *sense what-so-ever*. Like "even the palette he chooses signifies the intense dichotomy between the fascist fundamentalists and neo-Nazis". I ask you, *what* does that mean? *What does it mean?* It's *ruining my business*.'

I was laughing, but his next words sobered me.

'I'd give *five hundred dollars* to find the right assistant for the man. That's what he wants, you know. Just some *practical, efficient* young person who wants to *work*. Someone clean, for God's sake . . .'

Listening with half an ear as Charles Stuart explained what I already knew, I considered his statement. Five hundred bucks to the right candidate. He really wanted Taber Rhame to choose an assistant, and soon. He wanted it enough to put his money where his mouth was. Probably enough to help the right person get the job.

At a break in Charles's complaints I said, 'So you really hate this Rhame guy, huh?'

'Taber? No, my dear, Taber's all right. We have coffee together after *lunch* most days. It's just the blasted *artistic* types who want to *work* for him.' Charles shuddered, a prolonged affair as the layers of fat carried the motion from skeleton to skin.

I took a deep breath, wondering how Charles would react to my interest in the assistant's position upstairs. 'So. You think

Mr Rhame might prefer someone practical and sensible instead of pathologically artistic.' I paused, 'Like, maybe me?' I toyed with my cup a moment before looking up at Charles. His blue eyes were twinkling.

'I *wondered* if that was why you were waiting out front for me to open up. My *usual* customer is a mid-forties *yuppie* type with too much money and not enough *taste*. Not that I'd ever *tell* them so, of course.'

I smiled slightly and petted Perkins beneath the table. 'I could use a job. And I'd rather work for an artist than wait tables or wash dishes. I'm not trained for much else.'

'Taber's rather *rough* on employees. It means long hours and . . . *unpredictable work* for minimum wage and *no benefits*, let me assure you.' When I didn't respond, he went on. 'I don't know what I could do to help you get the *position*, but I'll put in a good *word* for you if you like. Not that it would do you much *good*. I'm afraid Taber's got his *own idea* of what he's looking for. Says he'll know it when he sees it. And I have *no* idea what that might be.'

I took a deep breath. 'Actually, I was hoping you'd let me hang around this morning. I was thinking I might spot something he does or some place he goes that would give me a clue on how to present myself.'

'Better than *that*, I'll give you access to the *roof*. Taber paints up there most evenings, and practices his *martial arts* up there most mornings.' Charles tilted up his left wrist, checking his watch. 'He's probably there *now*. Come on, it's *quite a show*.' Charles sprang from his seat, a curiously quick motion for a man of his bulk.

'He won't mind?'

'The man gets so deeply into his movements he'll likely not even be *aware* of us. Just let me close up the shop. It's too early for *customers* yet anyway. I only came in early to put up and price some new *stock*. I went to an estate sale last night and you wouldn't *believe* the *magnificent selection*.' His voice floated up from the front of the shop, muted and mellowed by the stacks and shelves of linens.

'I see the pile of pretty things by the register. Did you hope to *bribe* me to get help with Taber?'

I nearly choked on hot coffee. That was exactly what I had hoped to do.

'If *so* you acted with more ingenuity than any of the *artsy* types. Come on.' Charles was huffing and excited, standing in the entrance to the kitchen.

I said, 'What'll I do with the dog?'

'Perkins? Oh, he's always a perfect gentleman. You tell him to stay in the kitchen and he will.'

I stopped. Not just the simple stop of halting as I rose from the chair, but an internal stop. As if my heart and lungs and nervous system, my muscles and bones stopped too. It was as if time itself was interrupted, and hung suspended. A cold dread washed through me. An abrupt freezing. 'You know Perkins?'

'Oh my, yes. Old Lady Freidham used to shop here *all the time*.' Charles, his back turned, was unlocking a door in the back of the kitchen. The jangle of keys and thud of hollow wood filled the kitchenette. 'It was such a *shame* when she went, you know. And the poor dear *never could decide* who to leave Perkins to. That was the reason she died intestate. *No will*, you understand.'

Time began to flow again. Sluggishly, with a lethargic pulse. 'Prissy Freidham had no family except that *stepson* up north and there was *no one* to take the dog.' The word stepson was uttered with loathing, as if the title was an insult. 'At the *estate sale*, I heard it whispered about that Perkins would probably go to the *pound*. Perkins *hated* Randall, you see. The stepson.' Charles Stuart pocketed the keys and crossed to my chair. 'I hear he even *bit* the cretin. Yes, I did. And that was a *good dog, yes it was*,' he added to the dog, scratching Perkins beneath the chin.

I realized I was squeezing Perkins in nerveless hands. He struggled silently and stared up at me with reproving eyes until I eased off the pressure. Intestate. No will. The pound. Perkins had no owner, no master, no home. None but me.

Standing, I placed the small dog on the floor where he shook out his over-long fur and jumped up into a chair. He settled himself instantly and I smoothed the fine hair over Perkins' skull.

Charles had gone through the open door, his voice echoing back to me, and I hastened after him, not wanting to miss a single word. It seemed I had stumbled on the answer to most of my questions and dilemmas. And that answer was busily climbing a set of spiral stairs to the roof.

'I got some *really fine* things at the Freidham *estate sale*, by the way. Remind me to show them to you later on.'

Unlike many fat men, Charles Stuart had good breath, not puffing or gasping as he trotted up two flights of ancient oak treads and wrought-iron supports. Talking all the way, he bounced up the tall stairs, past the second landing with its two doors, one that belonged to Taber and one that was a small storage space, he noted to me as we passed on and up to the roof.

It was deserted. I didn't know whether to be relieved or disappointed that the famous artist was not here.

With the coming rain, there was no canvas in the works, no brushes in water or thinner, no palette, nothing to show me the direction the artist was taking following his move to the States. Nothing but a plastic-wrapped easel and stool, a table with an umbrella hole in the center – the kind rich people used at pool side – and the skeletons of chairs and couches, stripped of cushions.

On the table was a crusted can of Campbell's chicken noodle soup, dried out and empty but for a gummy spoon, a cup with a half-dried smear of coffee lining the bottom, a bowl of milk with a few swollen Cheerios drowned and sunken, and a wine glass with a skin of red. Peculiar food for a gourmand.

Charles must have thought so as well. 'Tisk, tisk, tisk. He doesn't eat well at *all* when he paints, you know. Can't think well enough to prepare *anything* for himself. Too buried in his art. Just opens whatever's available and eats it *cold, directly from the can*.' The words sounded amazed, astounded, as if no one had ever done such a thing before. I took a shallow breath and held it, remembering the articles I had studied.

Taber Rhame's reputation as a gourmand was based on the well-publicized binges he went on following a successful show. Binges when he went to every three-star or better restaurant within driving distance and ate monumental piles of food. But no one had ever reported what he ate while he painted.

The seeds of an idea began to germinate as I released a pent-up breath. 'Where does Mr Rhame eat lunch, Charles?'

'Lunch? Why, up *here*. And then coffee with me afterward. The man *loves* his coffee.' Charles smiled then, glancing from my face to the still life of cans and dishes on the table. '*Bravo*, dear girl. Brav*o*.'

Suddenly I laughed, and kissed Charles Stuart square on the mouth. The look he gave me as I whirled for the stairs was half-shock, half-amusement, and I could hear his laughter as I whirled around and around to the street level.

When Charles caught up with me, I had written out a check for the amount of the pillow and linens and was busily scratching out a menu on the back of an envelope I grabbed from his garbage can. Perkins was sitting at my feet, licking a front paw.

'There's a little meat market on Market Street where you can pick up some andouille sausage or some green-onion-alligator sausage. Taber's mother was *Cajun*, you know,' he said.

I knew. I knew more about Taber Rhame than anyone of the artsy types who would gather out front this morning.

'You could cook some real Cajun dishes.'

I intended to.

'And I happen to know Taber really likes sticky buns. The kind with *lots* of pecans on top. You do the meal, and *I'll* provide the dessert, along with my Evangeline blend Community coffee. You ever had any? It's *simply* marvelous. Kenya double A and Santos Bourbon, *ahhhh*.' Quickly I scratched out dessert.

'And, Bonnie.'

I stopped scribbling ingredients and looked up. Charles was almost as excited as I.

'If you get the job, I'll tear up the check for the pillow and things. I haven't forgotten about my five-hundred-dollar *pledge*. How does that sound? Deal?'

'Deal. I'll be back by noon. Could you watch Perkins for me?'

'Of course. Of course. Perkins and I are *old friends*.'

With his promise, I flew out the door leaving behind the linens, the newspaper I had bought, and Perkins. *My dog*.

CHAPTER
6

Cooking had been part of my wintertime duties in the Sarvaunt household. The all-day chore of stirring, simmering, tasting, and adding to the day's dish was simply a part of life nine months a year, while we were trailer-bound. My only respite from the task came during the summer, when we lived on Tee Dom's vegetable garden and dried foodstuffs. These months it was too hot to cook, even with the propane cookstove outside, behind the shanty, under a lean-to.

But fall, winter, and spring, I cooked daily, all the handed-down recipes from generations of French women. Recipes for lean times, like red beans and rice with ham hocks, or crab gumbo made with crabs netted from the bayou, and recipes for times when money was more plentiful, like artichokes with Hollandaise sauce, or roasted goose with smoked-ham stuffing, and recipes for special occasions, like spiced fig gravy over roasted quail with crawfish cornbread stuffing and bread pudding with whiskey sauce.

Cooking wasn't the way I had thought to win the job with a world-famous artist . . . but the man had to eat. My feminist sisters the world over would probably be furious at my using a typical feminine wile to win a job, but then they didn't have the competition I did.

I ran back down Conti, took a quick turn down Chartres and reached the market breathless. I didn't have my rolling cart, so I kept my purchases to a minimum, moving quickly down the main aisle, picking out fresh onions and peppers, fresh vegetables and day-old bread.

I wanted to *wow* Taber Rhame with my culinary skills, but at the same time I wanted to be proficient. Not reach above myself and risk making a mistake on a dish I was less familiar with. While still in Charles Stuart's shop, I had decided on a simple meal of flounder stuffed with sauteed shrimp, andouille smoked sausage, with tasso, and smoked oyster Hollandaise, a potato salad with green-onion salad dressing (the recipe Tante Ilene had stolen from one of Paul Pudhomme's cook books, not that she would ever admit it), and bread pudding with whiskey sauce. I had scratched out dessert, but suddenly decided I would make the bread pudding after all. Rhame could choose his dessert – sticky buns or pudding. I bet he'd take the pudding.

I purchased the seafood from a little specialty shop on Orleans Street. They sold fresh seafood from one side of the shop, and Louisiana delicacies on the other. The oysters were already smoked, the flounder and shrimp fresh. The andouille and tasso, rich and potent. And in the back was a small selection of liquors. It would have been perfect, except that I had to show my ID and the cashier thought it might be fake and the proprietor had to come up front to verify the validity, and then they hassled me over the counter checks until I insisted they call Claude Michau and . . . I knew when I left the market that I'd find another place to buy meat. Perhaps the shop on Market Street that Charles was so fond of.

It was after ten when I reached the apartment, and I threw myself into the preparation of my interview meal. I started with the bread pudding because it had to bake for an hour or more at low temperature, but I could add the flounder in the last fifteen minutes and turn up the heat. I hoped it would work, and that the pudding didn't taste fishy . . .

In the rare moments when everything was either baking, waiting or cooling, I changed clothes, pulling on a simple navy dress and sandals, braided my hair in a tight French braid and pulled on a crisp white painting smock. When I first began experimenting with oils, Tante Ilene had stitched up three smocks out of an old white sheet, starched them and presented them to me as a gift. Although she never said so, I think the fact that I preferred to paint while wearing a worn-out T-shirt had hurt her feelings.

I'd have to write her if I got the job and tell her how the smock helped. It was the first time I had considered writing to her, and the thought cheered me immensely, as the scents from Tante Ilene's kitchen filled my own.

Just before I put the flounder into the oven, and simultaneously started on the whiskey sauce and the Hollandaise, I filled a basket with essentials. An old, starched tablecloth and napkins, a place setting of china, a worn set of sterling tableware with the ornate initial 'L' engraved on the handles, fresh butter – the real thing, not margarine – a crystal wine glass, candles and candlesticks and pot holders. It was a big basket and weighed a ton when loaded, but I didn't care. I just hoped Rhame liked late lunches and hadn't already eaten.

The hot dishes fit easily into a nest of pot holders, and the weight wasn't so bad once I got the basket up onto my right shoulder. In the mirror, I looked like a pink-cheeked version of an African woman, overloaded with firewood. All I needed to make it perfect was a turban. I tossed an antique bag over my left shoulder and went out the door.

August heat had descended in a wet, sweaty, hot-air sauna, the heat held in by low-lying clouds that threatened rain. By the time I had traversed the blocks to Rhame's studio, the navy dress was soaked through with sweat and I was grateful for the concealing fabric of the smock. My arms, held up high, ached with the strain of balancing the basket.

The line in front of the studio was half a block long, peopled with caricatures of artists. Long hair, lean lanky bodies, exotic dress, bell bottoms, tie-dyed T-shirts, leather portfolios and the scent of marijuana over all.

Even from a distance, the air was peppered with artsy phrases and lingo, long useless sentences containing words like fiberglass construction, photo mural, putatively illegal art, unsophisticated viewer, diptych, Kabakov and Bulatov, definitively unfinished, appoggiaturas, social processes, gelatin silver print, environmental art, fur and house paint, transformative actions, and performance sequence. English all right. Sort of. And the sound of it all, coming from the rouged mouths of young women and men, made me want to laugh. The businesslike portfolios kept me silent. That and the pain in my arms.

'Pardon me. Mr Rhame's lunch is here. Pardon me. Mr Rhame's lunch is here. Pardon me . . .' I made my way through the loose crowd, passed Charles Stuart's door. He had his face pressed against the window, grinning at me, his right hand open, displaying five fingers. 'Five hundred dollars,' he mouthed. I almost giggled. Beneath his left arm was Perkins, barking like a fool. 'Pardon me . . . lunch . . . Mr Rhame's . . .'

Somehow, I reached the bottom of the stairs aware that my voice had undergone an odd transformation. I sounded clipped and dignified, like Tante Ilene on Sunday at the Madonna church. I sounded French. And very busy. A 'don't get in my way, please' tone. And it worked. The artists and students, the talented and the desperate parted like the Red Sea. I could hear behind me scattered phrases. 'Smells wonderful . . . his own chef? . . . Cute ass . . . God, I'm hungry . . .' I hoped Taber Rhame was hungry too.

As I started up the stairs, my arms straining above my head, word seemed to pass ahead of me, and the hopefuls parted before I had to ask. Now it was *'Merci.* So kind. *Merci* . . .'

And suddenly I was at the landing. The man at the top of the line, the next applicant on Taber Rhame's list, opened the door for me. Half of his face was in shadow, a smile and straight teeth caught in the light. It should have made me feel guilty to sneak in this way. It didn't.

The apartment was bright with light from the ten-foot-tall, bare windows. Furnished with leather and Navaho blankets and lots of raw wood, the huge front room held no art. No paintings. No sculpture except a small bronze piece from his *Terror* series. Bare walls. Bare floors. And Taber Rhame and a horse-faced female sitting on a long blue-leather couch. The artist's mouth half open with surprise. Instead of speaking, I turned and stepped to the back of the apartment, looking for the added-on kitchen, which I hoped was located in the rear, like mine. It was.

Rhame's kitchen was three times the size of mine, with new white fixtures, new vinyl cabinets, a microwave, a high-tech Gaggia coffee-maker with a dozen settings, a full wine-rack and a bottled-water dispenser beside the refrigerator.

I settled my basket on the cabinet beside the stove, and shook out my arms. They tingled like they had the time I tested Tante Ilene's admonition about the electric-light sockets. I had stuck the tines of a fork into the elongated holes and been thrown across the room for my efforts. The blast of electricity had left me shaking and tingling for some time. Of course, now the nervous tingling might have been half fear.

As if I truly belonged in Taber Rhame's apartment, I began setting Rhame's dinette table. The starched cloth settled with a swish and a stiff drape over the wrought-iron and glass-topped table. The china tinkled softly as I placed it. And the aroma of seafood and whiskey sauce filled the apartment.

As if I were the sole arbiter of Rhame's time, I spooned up potato salad and dripped on the green-onion dressing. Beside it on the bone-china plate, I settled a stuffed flounder, placed four sauteed shrimp on top in a wave design and dipped on the smoked-oyster Hollandaise sauce. Water from the dispenser filled the crystal wine glass and finally I placed the silver to the sides of the plate. Snapping a napkin over my left arm, like a waiter in an old black and white movie, I stepped to the opening in the kitchen and interrupted.

'Mr Rhame. Your meal is prepared, sir. Miss,' I transferred my gaze to the horsey female. 'If you would be so kind as to wait outside, Mr Rhame will resume his interviews in half an hour.'

Rhame's brows went up. The horse-faced woman went out, closing the door softly behind her.

The sweat which had started on my walk over had chilled and an icy shiver crawled along my spine at the sight of Rhame's eyes. White-haired, with dark gray eyes in a swarthy face, Rhame looked like an offended godling, sitting cross-legged with arms outstretched along the back of the sofa. Slowly, so slowly I was afraid he would refuse me, Taber Rhame rose from the sofa and walked to the kitchen. His feet were bare and silent on the heart of pine floor. His body was encased in denim and chambray – jeans and a bleached-out work shirt with black stains on the rolled up cuffs.

He walked like a warrior, sleek and predatory. And I had no doubt that I had angered the man. My heart seemed to skip a beat as he passed me.

With the grace of an alley cat, Rhame settled into the chair, the sharp snapping of the starched napkin the only real indication of his displeasure. Still silent, the world-famous artist and gourmand picked up his fork and dipped it into the potato salad. A moment later he paused, his eyes on the food before him. Then he swallowed and tasted the flounder. Speared a shrimp. Drank his own water, and returned to the food.

Halfway through his meal he spoke, his voice a sudden thunder in the room. 'Do you speak French?'

'*Oui. Toute ma vie.*' All of my life.

Again he concentrated on the food. Then, in French, he said, 'The blending of peppers is perfect. Very few cooks can attain the proper proportions of white, red, and black.'

In the same language I answered, 'Thank you, sir. My Tante Ilene will be pleased that you like her recipe.'

'Do you paint?'

The question threw me a moment, then a fierce joy swept through me. 'All your applicants paint. But I cook. And I speak three languages and a smattering of a fourth.'

Rhame's eyes caught mine then, the intensity of his glance sending shivers along my chilled arms. I answered the question I saw in the gray depths. 'French and English, Spanish, and a smattering of Italian.'

'World traveler?' he asked in Spanish.

'Tutors,' I answered in Italian.

'Rich brat?' in Italian.

'It's a long story,' in Spanish.

'Did you really cook this?' in French.

'Yes. And if you hire me, I'll cook lunch for you every day,' in English.

Taber Rhame laughed, the sound resounding against the too-bare walls. 'I work demanding hours at times and demand a great deal of work,' he said again in French.

'I only sleep four hours a night and I want to learn.'

'The pay is low.'

'I know.'

'No benefits.'

'I'm covered.'

At his blank look I added, 'That means I have my own insurance, health and a small burial policy.'

'Ah. An American saying.'

I smiled with half a mouth. 'Correct.'

'What's for dessert?'

'Bread pudding with whiskey sauce or sticky buns, with Evangeline blend coffee downstairs in Charles Stuart's shop. He's waiting for us now.'

'Did he tell you to cook for me?'

'No, sir.'

Taber Rhame sat back in his chair and sipped his bottled water from my crystal, his eyes assessing me.

'How old are you? You look about seventeen.'

'I'm twenty-one and am accustomed to having to prove it.'

'Do you drive?'

'Yes.'

'Have a car?'

I smiled with my whole mouth this time. 'Of sorts. A van. It needs a muffler, and it leaks oil like a sieve, but it rolls.'

'You're hired. You may tell the others that the position has been taken.'

I swallowed, frozen on the spot of floor where I had stood, unmoving, for the last half-hour. With numb fingers, I unbuttoned the white smock and laid it on the nearest cabinet top, took a deep breath, and walked to the door.

A peculiar feeling possessed me as I moved through the apartment. A breathless tingling. A sense of electric heat like the long-ago aftereffects of the childhood electric shock. As if the air I inhaled was charged with energy, sharp and acerbic.

The door opened beneath my hand. Horse-face and the man who had opened the door for me looked up, their expressions changing instantly from expectancy to understanding. In the instant before I spoke, I realized just how beautiful the man was. With his face in full light instead of bisected by shadow, he was stunningly beautiful. 'Mr Rhame regrets to inform you that the position of assistant has been filled. Thank you for coming. Good day.'

I started to close the door, feeling faint. The beautiful man stopped me with a palm against the painted wood.

'You?'

'Yes.'

He smiled. 'Congratulations.'

'Thank you.' And quietly I shut the door. I stood at the tall windows watching the crowd disperse. There were various expressions below me on the applicants' faces. Disappointment, anger, shock, exhaustion. One lean, young man with dark, oily hair scanned the windows as he heard the bad news, and spotting my face, lifted his middle finger in a vulgar salute. I stepped back.

As I moved, I saw a shadow across the way, a quick shifting of darkness. My Watcher, his clothes blending into the shadows. He stood with another man, this one taller and black-skinned with kinky reddish hair. The men seemed to confer a moment before separating. My Watcher sauntered down the street. The black man took his place, leaning against the wall in the shadow of a boarded-up doorway. I realized I had seen *this* man more than once as well. So. Now there were two.

I stood there, hidden in the shadows, my hands clasped below my chin. My interlaced fingers were cold, as if the Watchers had reached up and sucked all the life out of my skin instead of merely . . . watching. My breath was hot and quick against my doubled fists.

I suppose I should simply have called the police. I could have. It wasn't like back at the shanty where we were isolated from an increasingly electronic world. Rhame had a phone. New Orleans had 911 emergency capability. An officer could have been here in minutes to handcuff my newest Watcher and take him away.

That is if the officers believed me. If I were right. If the man really was following me.

In Khoury, self-reliance was a way of life and the police seldom an accessible option. So although I could have called for help, I didn't.

As I watched the new man, warmth slowly returned to my chilled hands. My breath steadied. The police might not believe that I had a legitimate complaint, but at least I now knew that I wasn't imagining things.

I didn't doubt that they were following me. I simply didn't know why. R.T. Stocker would contact me soon. She could check into the situation. Talk to the men, maybe. Meantime, I had a .38 and a steady aim. I would begin carrying the weapon immediately.

The door to the landing opened behind me and I whirled, my heart in my throat. The beautiful young man who had congratulated me on winning the position stepped inside and closed the door. He placed a portfolio and leather travel-bag on the floor and headed for the kitchen. Making himself at home. I stepped forward to stop him, following him to the back of the apartment.

The Italian was rich and hearty from the kitchen, back-slapping and European body-hugs, kisses on the cheeks and mouth as Rhame welcomed the young man. And suddenly I felt terribly alone. I, who had never felt welcomed in my own home. Never been hugged by the people closest to me. Never been kissed. I pushed the unwelcome emotion aside and studied the young man.

He was in his early twenties, with chocolate-colored hair and honey-brown eyes, skin a delicate olive. He wasn't American. No American anywhere ever showed such emotion. He truly was beautiful. Tall and slender. And more than welcomed by Taber Rhame.

Suddenly I wondered about the security of my new job. My future as Rhame's assistant looked less than stable.

'Forgive me. I cannot even introduce you to my son. Roberto, this is my new assistant, Miss . . .' He paused expectantly, icy-gray eyes full of laughter.

'. . . *my son*.' I smiled slowly. 'Bonnibelle Sarvaunt.'

'Roberto Rhame. We've met.' He smiled a flash of bright teeth.

The beautiful young man and I shook hands. His was calloused along the outer edge, his grip firm and American.

'Don't worry, Bonnie. The job is yours. My son, he flies to me every time I hire an assistant, hoping I will hire him. But I taught him all I could years ago. You should see his oils. The boy's a photo-realist, and what he can do with light and shadow . . .'

Roberto smiled at his father, exposing perfect teeth. 'So. You won't hire me. But can you put me up for the night, Papa?'

'I can do better than that. I can offer you bread pudding and whiskey sauce, and good strong coffee downstairs. Come, Bonnie made the pudding.' With forceful, expansive gestures, Rhame waved us down the spiral staircase to Charles Stuart's kitchenette, his voice booming off the walls of the small tight space. Perkins, hearing the commotion of echoing footsteps, began a fierce barking.

My dog. My employer. My friends? A small voice at the back of my mind whispered, *But who were the men watching me? And what do they want?* I ignored the voice and followed the two exuberant men on down the stairs.

The dessert in Charles Stuart's kitchenette was a lively affair, the four of us laughing loudly enough to rattle the china on the open shelves, Perkins begging prettily and being fed bread pudding scraps and coffee, which I discovered he loved!

Strange dog. Very French. And all mine. He sat on my lap throughout the interlude, jumping to the floor to demand a treat from someone's plate, then returning to my knees.

I felt very full in those moments. For the first time taking part in a group conversation over food. Mme Willoby would have been proud, her lessons finding a home around Charles Stuart's table, where Continental mannerisms prevailed, and where protocol was both loose and formal at once. Where family, friends, acquaintances and employees came together at the same time, to form a cohesive whole.

Charles Stuart related my initial greeting to the small group, the witty comment about a curtsy withheld. So, upon demand, I lifted the long navy skirt and curtsied, a full-blown maneuver better suited to an eighteenth-century ballroom than a small kitchen in the late twentieth century.

Roberto, called Tito by his father, related my ingenious walk up the stairs, and how even he was fooled by the scent of food into thinking I was a delivery service. And how he opened the door for his own replacement. Taber, his eyes dancing over the rim of a delicate china cup, related how cool I looked when I informed the woman he was interviewing that it was lunch-time and how totally unemotional I appeared as he ate.

And I related how my knees knocked and my spine tingled as I did all the things they talked about. All the while my dog licked whiskey sauce off my fingers, and stared adoringly into my eyes, and I fell in love with this group of joyous men.

And even I, with my lack of experience about the opposite sex, saw how often Tito's soft brown eyes rested on me.

We called it a day at three o'clock. Taber to visit with his son. Tito to settle in upstairs, Charles to catch up on business, and me to take my kitchen supplies, my free linens, and my dog

124

home, reveling on the walk back in the sheer pleasure of the afternoon. Perkins and I passed winos and police cars, tourists and shopkeepers, speaking and smiling to each in good southern fashion, scarcely noticing the wet heat and the miserable crush of people.

Attached to the street-level gate was a three-page note from Cee Cee. Lime-green stationery with forest-green ink, clipped to the wrought iron with a plain wooden safety-pin, informed me to get a phone line and answering machine installed upstairs, and to check inside the shop for messages. It wasn't rude. It was simply classic Cee Cee, always one to waste words.

Inside the shop, surrounded by emeralds, jade and green stones of lesser value and quality, I shared a final cup of coffee with Cee Cee and related my day's activities. Cee Cee listened with unconcealed delight as I described climbing the stairs with a basket on my shoulder, and finagling my way inside. And her bright-green eyes glowed with amused speculation as I described Tito. Somehow I managed not to blush, and continued my tale through to the end.

Perhaps it would seem strange to another young woman, to share so freely with an octogenarian. To prop elbows on a table top and gossip for an hour as if with a girl of my own age. But I had never known another girl of my own age, and Cee Cee, with her inquisitive green eyes and animated, energetic movements, reminded me of my tutors, who had been my only friends.

To me it was natural to sit and chatter with an older woman. To tell her about Perkins and old Lady Freidham and Taber Rhame. To share and exchange news and details and to listen to Cee Cee's comments and slightly *risqué* innuendoes. It filled a void left vacant when I abandoned my life back in Khoury and Eloise. An emptiness in my life I had never seen nor recognized, like a vast, dark cavern buried deep within me. A void like the dull pangs of hunger when I had painted too long on too little food.

When the quiet hour of gossip was over, I returned my calls. R.T. Stocker was away from the phone, but her answering service said she had some news for me. She wanted to meet with me at Petunias, a restaurant in the Quarter, not far from my apartment. A pang of excitement coursed through me at the words. *News.* I agreed to the meeting, scheduled half an hour from now, and hung up. *News*. Claude Michau was next on my list. The brightness of my day began to pale with his first words.

'Are you all right?'

'Yes, of course. Why?'

'Well, perhaps it's nothing, but the strangest thing happened this afternoon. A man in a business-suit, bearing a subpoena, came by and demanded a look at your file. Of course, there was nothing much there, no address since you left the Ponchartrain, no phone number, no way he could trace you through me, and I certainly didn't volunteer any information.'

A cold chill settled in my stomach as I remembered R.T. Stocker's warnings about trouble should I continue my search for myself and my mother. 'Was he a . . .' I paused, uncertain what I might call the man. 'Was he a government type? Police? FBI?'

Claude Michau was silent on the other end of the phone for a long moment and when he finally spoke, it was with an awkward strain in his voice. 'Are you in any trouble, Bonnie? Was the check you deposited at Royal Securities obtained by . . . illicit means?'

I laughed, the sound tinny and apprehensive, uncertain. And as I tried to decide how much to tell Claude Michau, my second watcher crossed in front of Cee Cee's shop. The black man with ruddy hair and dark eyes sauntered slowly past as if window-shopping, his eyes raking the interior of the store, resting briefly on me before moving on. A sharp dread settled about my shoulders and my heart beat a rapid tattoo as I stared at the now-empty window.

'Mr Michau, to my knowledge, there was nothing strange or untoward regarding the check. Perhaps you might meet R.T. Stocker and me at Petunias in half an hour,' I added wondering if I sounded as ridiculously formal as I felt. Like I was inviting him to the cotillion or the prom. 'I must assume the investigation has . . . stirred up something . . . unexpected about my past or my family. And Mr Michau, I think I am being followed.'

There was a sharp pause, biting and quick, as if Michau's brain had taken a deep breath and gone into overdrive. 'Is there a courtyard behind Cee Cee's shop?' he asked.

'Yes. A small one,' I said, thinking the change of subject strange.

'Let me speak to Cee Cee, if you please.'

With numb fingers, I handed Cee Cee the phone and walked to the front of the shop. My second Watcher was across the street and down a bit. Perched on a ledge of old, crumbling brick, he kicked his heels and closed his eyes as if enjoying the light patter of rain that settled on his face.

Perkins, sensing my disquiet, raised up on his back feet and placed his front paws against my legs. A low whine escaped his throat. Without removing my eyes from the man across from me, I stooped and lifted the dog into my arms. His wet tongue touched my chin, and when I didn't make a fuss, Perkins began to groom my jaw and chin, and down along my neck. The gesture was oddly comforting.

Cee Cee touched my arm lightly, startling me from my reverie. 'Mr Michau is to meet with you and a Miss Stocker at Petunias,' she said, in her antique French. 'I have sketched out a small map.' She pressed a slip of paper into my hand, against Perkins' side. 'It shows where you will come out on Chartres if you take the back entrance from the store, and how to reach the restaurant.' Cee Cee's eyes were worried, following the direction of my gaze. 'Is that him? The man following you?'

'One of them. Cee Cee, do you have a Polaroid? One of those cameras that develops the picture while you wait?'

'Yes, dear girl. I do, but what . . .' The worry vanished from Cee Cee's eyes. 'What a marvelous idea. May I help? I could get his attention while you take his picture.' Without waiting for an answer, the bird-like woman whirled and went behind the counter, her copper curls disappearing behind the brass cash register. When she stood again, her emerald necklace hung crooked around her collar, a dust mote clung to the tip of her nose, and the Polaroid was clutched to her chest. The green sparkle was bright in her eyes. I held out my hand for the camera.

'You never said I could help.'

I smiled. 'What's the matter, Cee Cee? Not enough excitement in your life?'

She cocked a strawberry brow and waited.

'You can help. You can figure out how to get the guy closer to the shop so I can snap his picture. And then you can take care of Perkins while I meet with Michau and Stocker. She's a private investigator, you know.'

Cee Cee laughed, her perfect white dentures matching the pearls in her emerald necklace. 'I am so glad you rented my nephew's apartment. You are going to be such fun.' She handed over the Polaroid, taking Perkins in exchange, and setting the frisky little dog on his feet. 'Perkins and I are going to talk to the man across the street. Yes, we are,' she said, more to Perkins than to me. 'And then we are going for a nice long walk and distract the nasty man so your mother can make a getaway out the back. Yes, we are.'

I realized that the mother Cee Cee was referring to was me. I touched her arm to stop her from going out the door. 'Thanks, Cee Cee. I'll be back before you close up. Would you like to have supper with Perkins and me?'

'Absolutely. I shall bring the wine, and you will promise to tell me everything. Yes?'

'It's a deal.'

We grinned like two conspirators and parted, Cee Cee to cross the street with Perkins, me to look over the Polaroid and check its focus. I wanted R.T. Stocker to have a good clear picture of the man. It was too bad the other guy wasn't here too. I'd have liked to take shots of both men to Stocker.

I thought about the .38 upstairs in the bottom of my 1920 Art Deco armoire. But there was no way to reach the gun without being seen entering my apartment. I wanted a clean getaway out the back door while my Watcher was otherwise occupied.

Cee Cee was a regular flirt. She crossed the street, hips rolling from side to side, almost as prissy as Perkins. They looked like two flame-haired coquettes out for an afternoon stroll.

Perkins alone would have been enough to arouse the attention of my watcher, but with Cee Cee prancing by his side heading right to him, the man had no regard for passing traffic at all. He glanced once at the window of the shop, then Cee Cee was upon him.

Focusing through the window, I took half a dozen photographs of the two during the exchange, and, leaving my basket of kitchen supplies and the linens and pillow from Charles Stuart's shop on the counter beside the camera, I slipped out the back door. There was something refreshing about skulduggery. Escaping out the back was like winning a childhood race with the Boudreaux boys or outwitting Dr Tammany Long at chess, or bluffing a table full of poker players. Very satisfying.

The courtyard behind Cee Cee's was larger than it had looked from my apartment. Perhaps twenty-five by thirty-five feet, it was enclosed on all four sides by buildings except for the single, narrow opening beside the stairway to my apartment. Bricked-over archways proclaimed that the other entrances had been eliminated decades ago. The light rain I had noticed only moments before was gone, steamed into the atmosphere.

I unfolded Cee Cee's map, again on lime paper with darker green ink. It showed an 'X' at the entry to the building across the way. Crossing the cobblestoned courtyard with its ancient maple tree, profuse bougainvillea, oleander, and lushly blooming climbing rose, I glanced back at Cee Cee's.

There was a rusty fire escape leading from the roof to the ground, a sight that confirmed my apartment's access to the top of the building. Unfortunately, the fire-escape opening to my apartment had been obliterated when it was remodeled, adding on the kitchen and bath.

The doorway that should have given me access to the fire escape had been turned into a window. The same window in the kitchen that housed the air-conditioner.

I knocked on the door indicated on the map and waited. It was opened by a Rastafarian with long, ashy dreadlocks and topaz-colored eyes. The smell of marijuana – reminiscent of Elred's trailer home, behind the bait-and-tackle shop back in Khoury – wafted out along with the tinkling chords of New Age music.

I offered my hand, introduced myself and told him I was the new tenant across the back. He stared at my outstretched palm, blinked twice, slowly, and looked back up at me.

'Huh?'

I repeated myself, and this time the man seemed to understand. He shook my hand, blinked again and seemed to fall asleep before my eyes. His grip went slack, he yawned, leaned his head against the door and closed his bloodshot eyes. A deep sigh blew out through his nostrils.

I shrugged, slipped past him and through the shop out to the street. The Rastafarian ran a New Age store called La Lierre Veneneuse – Poison Ivy – specializing in crystals and 'healing herbs' and New Age sounds on tape and CD. I hoped the scent of marijuana wouldn't cling to my hair and clothes and get me arrested.

Petunias was only a short walk, and I arrived at the same time as Michau. He gallantly opened the door for me and allowed me to enter ahead of him.

The waiter knew him by name and showed us to a beautifully laid-out table in the back of the two-room restaurant. Petunias was decorated in shades of old rose and cream with china and crystal and heavy linens that Charles Stuart might have envied. A seventy-five-year-old Hunter fan turned lazily overhead, scarcely disturbing the cool air. Concert music, low enough to be appealing, whispered in the background, and Michau ordered three coffees and three slices of homemade pecan pie before we even sat down.

R.T. Stocker entered moments later, bringing with her the earthy perfume of a barn, her cowboy hat and briefcase, and *news*. She seemed unsurprised to see Michau, her boots clumping across the hardwood floors, her face set in thoughtful lines. Without explanation, she suggested we change tables to one in the corner where we could see both the front entrance and window, and the back entrance to the kitchen.

Stocker was worried. And perhaps a little frightened. And she turned my world upside down.

CHAPTER 7

'I don't know who *you* are, but Bonnibelle Sarvaunt – probably the dark-eyed baby in the picture you have – did indeed die on 7 September, twenty-one years ago this year. She had birth defects that were so severe there wasn't much anyone could do to save her, so the doctors in Petit Chenier remembered her case very well,' Stocker said by way of greeting. Her words came fast and staccato, as if they were bullets shot from a high-powered handgun.

'So we got some answers to some basic questions, but unfortunately, we've attracted some unwanted attention. Somebody is a little too interested in this investigation for my peace of mind.'

'It seems we all have news, but I fear I am the least informed,' Michau said in his oh-so-polite manner. 'Perhaps one of you would be so kind as to start at the beginning.'

Before I could respond, Stocker explained. 'Bonnie – or whoever she is – asked me to look into a small matter for her. She had some concern that, because she didn't physically resemble the Sarvaunt family, and because she was left a rather large inheritance, and some confusing papers by the woman claiming to be her mother, that she might not be the person she was brought up to think she was. Convoluted, I know. And frankly, at first, I didn't think I'd discover anything except that she was deluded. Sorry, Bonnie.'

Stocker paused, drank down half a cup of steaming dark-roast brew and scanned the room again. She waved the waiter over for a refill, taking the time to organize her thoughts. Stocker drank coffee like most people breathe air. I had thought only Tante Ilene ever drank as much coffee. I watched the coffee ritual with intense interest, ignoring my own coffee and the pie. I was on a caffeine and sugar overload as it was, my heart rate rapid and my breathing shallow. Michau, however, was unperturbed and composed. I had the feeling he would remain steady even in the face of hurricane, earthquake, or volcanic eruption, calmly awaiting salvation or destruction. He was a dramatically patient man.

'I'll provide you a complete report later, a detailed account of facts and expenditures. But for now, let me just summarize my findings.' Stocker set down her coffee cup and braced herself on her elbows, ticking off her discoveries on upraised fingers. 'Bonnibelle Sarvaunt died on 7 September, twenty-one years ago come next month. She was two months old. Her mother died four years later.' Stocker held three fingers in the air.

'Both mother and daughter are buried in Petit Chenier, Louisiana, in graves beneath headstones marked DeVillier. They accomplished that by saying the Sarvaunt girl finally married the baby's father, even though they did not have a marriage license to verify their claims. In these backwater towns, documentation of identity is haphazard at best.'

Two more fingers opened out to reveal Stocker's palm. It was heavily creased, the skin tough and calloused. I focused back on her eyes.

'The death certificate for the mother reads Marie L. Smith DeVillier. Her identity at the time of death was verified by a woman claiming to be her sister and by a middle-aged French couple who claimed to be her nearest living relatives. My guess is the couple was your Tante Ilene and Tee Dom, accompanied by your real mother. Although I can't begin to guess why your aunt and uncle would have deliberately misidentified the body of their own niece.' Two fingers of the detective's right hand joined the others pointing at the ceiling.

'The coroner had no trouble signing a death certificate because the woman had been living in a hospice for two months before she died, and everyone there knew her as DeVillier. But there's a problem with all this. I spoke with the man who prepared the bodies, and he insisted that when the woman buried her baby, she went by the name Elizabeth Sarvaunt. Not Marie L. Smith DeVillier.' Stocker dropped her eight fingers, sat back on her chair and drank down a second cup of coffee. When the cup was empty, she put it down with a smile that was positively approving.

'Whether your mother was involved or not, the wooden building holding the only copies of the cemetery records burned down a year after Elizabeth Sarvaunt was buried as Marie DeVillier. Effectively hiding the paper trail of the two individuals.' Stocker grinned approvingly. 'Your mother was crafty as hell.

'Oh, by the way, the woman who died in Gloree, under the identification of Elizabeth Sarvaunt, was red-headed, with blue eyes, and died of MS. I don't think she was really Elizabeth. I think she was another false trail laid down by your real mother. I think your mother found another young woman who was dying and switched identities with her. It worked once, so why not again? Crafty as hell.'

Michau settled to his pie, eating in tiny, quick bites like a bird at a feeder. Though I had known about the death certificate with my name typed neatly on the appropriate line, I couldn't quite decide how to respond to the confirmation of my own death at the age of two months.

I picked up my cup, took a sip, put down the cup. It was . . . unnerving. Part of me had always assumed that the death certificate was in error. Yet, I had always thought that I wasn't who I was raised to be. A contradiction within my own soul. I had always wanted to prove the fact that I was . . . someone else. But now that I had done so . . .

The silence around the table built, as the other two watched me absorb the information. I could feel their eyes on me. I could feel the cup in my fingers. But the rest of the world kept slipping away. Disjointed and displaced, the moment seemed to shift and slide past, then catch, as if the gears were stripped. As if my world moved like Elred's old van. Finally I spoke. 'So who am I?'

'I don't know yet. But I checked and no death certificate was ever filed for Carin Colleen DeVillier. At least not in Petit Chenier. I'd like to think that your mother left you all the clues you would need to find out who you are, but it's too soon to be certain.'

'Pardon me for showing my ignorance, but how could she masquerade as Bonnie when Bonnie was dead? Wouldn't the state discover the discrepancy?' Michau pushed away the empty pecan-pie plate, and sipped his coffee.

'Not necessarily. Remember, this was pre-computer days. Birth certificates and death certificates weren't correlated. Frankly, they still aren't in most parts of the state. So if the mother of a live child wanted to switch the identity of her child with a dead one, she could. It would have been easier to arrange a switch if the babies were both alive, of course, but the real Bonnie was dead eleven months before Carin was born. And in my opinion, you are Carin Colleen DeVillier.'

'What does this mean in regards to Bonnibelle Sarvaunt's trust fund?' Michau asked. Routine question for a man whose finger rested on the pulse of the financial world.

'Good question, and I don't know. A lawyer might be of some help, but again, you're dealing with a lot of unknown territory. My guess is, this could be tied up in the court system for years.'

My brain felt like molasses-soaked cotton. All sticky and tangled. But I knew the answer to that one. 'On 10 August, the year when I turn twenty-four – or Bonnibelle turns twenty-four – I can claim my trust fund by requesting a fingerprint analysis. If my fingerprints match the ones included in the trust fund, the money is mine. I don't have to provide any other identification.'

It all made sense now. My mother had arranged for me to claim my trust fund without regard to legal paperwork because she knew I might discover that I wasn't Bonnibelle Sarvaunt. Or the state might. Or, perhaps, someone else might . . .

My skin felt numb all over, icy and senseless. I licked my lips, tasting the residue of whiskey sauce from lunch. I couldn't think, couldn't feel. The mystery I had always suspected was real.

I pulled my antique navy satin bag forward and retrieved the six Polaroids, fanning the photographs out on the table. 'This man and one other man have been following me for several days. It looks like they usually work about two twelve-hour shifts, although I've seen them switch off at odd hours too. This one came on duty at about one this afternoon.'

Michau picked up two of the photographs and studied them, his mouth turned down in concentration. Stocker picked up a single shot, blinked and placed it back on the table. I was sure she recognized the man, but instead of commenting she lifted her fork and tasted the pecan pie.

'I don't recognize him, not that I would expect to,' Michau said.

'This is delicious. May I have more coffee, please? Bonnie, what does the other one look like? This guy's partner.' Stocker ate two more bites in quick succession.

'Average looking. Medium brown hair, medium height. About mid-twenties, I guess. He has a little beer belly and he stands like this.' I got up and demonstrated, leaning against a wall, crossing both my ankles and my arms. The waiter paused as I sat down, and leaned across me to fill our cups. I sipped at mine again and passed Stocker my pie. 'I'm sure it's wonderful, but I'm full. And I'm also sure you recognized the man. Who is he?'

Stocker pushed away her empty plate and tucked her fork into my pie. 'I know him as Cooter Bug, but I don't know his real name. He works part time for Jimmy MacAloon. MacAloon is an average guy with a beer belly who holds up walls when he's bored. Kinda like you demonstrated.'

Stocker smiled, took another bite of my pie, and chewed slowly, her eyes moving back and forth between Michau and me. Drawing out her moment of conversational control. 'This is very good pie.'

Michau rolled his eyes and sipped his coffee. I waited. Finally Stocker condescended to enlighten us.

'MacAloon runs MacAloon's Security Systems and Personal Protective Services.' She took a last bite of pie which did nothing to hide her grin. She swallowed. 'He's a bodyguard.'

Michau looked from Stocker to me and set his coffee cup down. He missed the saucer and coffee sloshed out of the cup over his hand. It should have burned, but Michau gave no indication of pain. 'A bodyguard. Like for famous people, to protect the privileged from the riff-raff.'

Stocker, almost giddy with amusement, tapped the air with her fork. 'Give the man a cigar.'

I laughed, a sudden blurt of sound like a horn accidentally jostled by an elbow.

'Miss Sarvaunt, have you hired a body—'

'No, Mr Michau. I haven't hired anybody,' I interrupted. 'And no one from Khoury even knows where I am to hire a bodyguard for me.' A faint shiver started low along my spine. It could have been too much caffeine, or it could have been the beginning of fear. *Why had my mother tried so hard to hide me? How much danger were we both still in?*

My shiver spread outward as the obvious became apparent. 'In fact, the only way I could be traced is through the check deposited at Royal Securities.'

Michau blinked, opened his mouth and closed it. Finally, he said, 'Then perhaps we should contact the man who handles your trust in LaRoque parish – Mr Duhon?' he queried mid-sentence, recalling the name from my portfolio. I nodded. '– and determine if he knows what is going on here.' Michau lifted his finger for the waiter and requested permission to use the phone. In his unhurried style, he called Belinda at his office for Alex Duhon's business and home phone numbers. Then, using his calling card, he dialed Duhon's office.

I sipped coffee; Stocker guzzled it while we waited. Petunias advertised bottomless coffee cups. It looked like Stocker was trying to drain the restaurant dry.

Duhon was in his office, closing up for the day, his last client long gone. There was no wait. Michau identified himself, put me on for a moment so that Duhon would be willing to discuss what might prove to be confidential matters, and proceeded to question my mother's attorney.

Michau learned less about my background and my mother than I already knew. But he did learn that Duhon's office had been broken into the day he was out of the office to deliver the cashier's checks to me.

Although nothing was taken, the files were ransacked and dozens of copies were made on the office copier. Duhon's secretary always kept an accurate tally of copies made, and it was evident someone had photocopied at least one file.

There were no fingerprints, no evidence. But it was conceivable that someone had copied my file. Duhon speculated that someone had kept a watch on one of my mother's trust-fund accounts and when checks were issued, drawn on that account, they were able to track down Duhon. And through him, me.

When Michau and Duhon had exchanged all the information they could, Michau returned the phone to the waiter and requested fresh coffee. I decided that Stocker and he could out-drink even Tee Dom and Tante Ilene . . . who were not really my aunt and uncle. Never had been.

Orphans, when they first discover they aren't who they thought they were, typically experience a feeling of disassociation. I knew that. I knew it was normal. But I still wanted to cry.

'If you can stand a bit more bad news, I need to offer some.' Stocker pushed away the second pie plate and drained her coffee cup, her eyes on mine. I nodded and she continued. 'Someone tried to get into my apartment.'

Michau sat forward in his chair again. The cold chill up my spine thickened, like condensation on a cold glass. I realized I was sweating.

'I live over the main barn in a renovated apartment. There's only one entry, which happens to be visible from my trainer's cottage. The guy's drunk half the time, but last night Mick was sober enough to hear the dogs barking and went out to look around. He saw someone at the top of the stairs and heard glass breaking. Whoever it was took off when Mick fired his shotgun into the air. Scared hell outta my horses, but then my trainer's not wrapped too tight. As soon as I find sufficient reason I'm firing the guy, but that's neither here nor there.'

'Are you working on any other cases at this juncture, R.T.?'

'No, sir. Only this one.'

'So it is safe to assume any interest in your office is related to Bonnie.'

'Well, it could have been a simple robbery attempt, but we've never had a break-in. The dogs make too much noise and scare off any would-be burglars. Considering the . . . peculiarities . . . surrounding this case, my guess is that the break-in was related to you.' She nodded at me. 'Bonnie, do you have . . . any protection?'

'A dog, a .38 and a .20-gauge shotgun.'

Stocker's eyes widened.

I smiled and quoted Tee Dom to her. 'No one bu' fool go into de swamp or deep into de bayou wi'ou' a shotgun to scare of' de alligator. Rule number one be, Gator got *biiig* teeth! Rule number two be, Gator is real dumb! Rule number three be, "In matin' season, even a fla' bottom boa' look good to a horny gator."'

They both laughed, and so did the waiter who replenished our cups. I put a hand over mine, blinking back tears that sprang up at my mention of Tee Dom. 'No, thank you.'

'I take it you can use both weapons.'

'Yes,' I said simply. I didn't tell her about the hours Tee Dom spent teaching me the care and use of the guns. I didn't tell her about killing raiding nutria or a dog with distemper who danced on his hind legs, mindless with pain. I didn't tell her about the year I brought home a goose for Christmas dinner.

I had been twelve and still young enough to go hunting with the Boudreaux boys, the half-black young men who lived as relative outcasts in Khoury. They had been my friends for nearly a year, until Louise Gastineau turned up pregnant and I was no longer permitted to associate with males. But that summer, they had honed my shooting skills, teaching me to be a fine shot with either shotgun or handgun. A fine shot.

I didn't say any of that. Just swallowed hard and tried not to think about the fact that Tee Dom and Tante Ilene were no longer mine. No wonder Duhon had been forced to pay them fifty thousand dollars to raise me.

I sipped my cold coffee to hide the prickles beneath my lids.

'Bonnie.' Stocker's hand covered mine. 'Do you want me to continue with this investigation?'

'You have to. I have to know now. Because whoever my mother was hiding me from, it looks like they've found me.'

'Can you pay for this?'

It was a strictly business question, the kind of thing I was comfortable with. I had spent years learning from Rufus Kirby how to handle myself in business situations, so I didn't blush or feel uncomfortable. I smiled again, realizing only after I did so, that my face was betraying some of my grief.

'If Mr Michau waves his magic wand and lets my investments triple, I could pay for your services indefinitely. As it is, I have enough to carry this a while longer. Besides. I got a job today,' I said, trying for a light tone while Tante Ilene's dark eyes swam with tears in my memory.

'Oh? Doing what?' Stocker asked.

'I'm Taber Rhame's assistant.'

Michau sat forward again. 'You don't say.'

I nodded. 'I start in the morning.'

'I'd love to hear the details, but I have horses to feed. Bonnie, I think you should go back to Khoury. More correctly, I think we should go back to Khoury together, so I could ask your aunt and uncle some pointed questions.'

'They aren't my aunt and uncle.' I hadn't meant to sound so woebegone, and again sipped my cold coffee.

Stocker leaned forward, again touching the back of my hand. 'I was raised by my uncle. My real uncle, but he was more of a father to me than most fathers know how to be.' She paused and waited for me to look up at her. 'My point is, bloodlines don't amount to much. It's the dedication and the love that matter.

'Your aunt and uncle stood by you for twenty years or so, for only fifty thousand dollars. That comes to two thousand five hundred dollars a year. No interest. I think the money was a secondary consideration for them when they agreed to raise you. Which means there must have been another reason for them to spend twenty years of their lives on you. Think about it.

'And while you're thinking, plan a trip to Khoury. When you get a day off, leave a message with my service. And I'll work on finding Marie L. DeVillier's husband. Okay?'

'Yes. I . . . Thank you. I'll . . . call.'

Stocker took her hat and her briefcase, and departed Petunias, her boots clomping on the wooden floors. The scent of hay and horses followed in her wake.

'Mr Michau, would you care to join Cee Cee and me for supper? She's bringing the wine, I'm providing the meal, and we'd love to have you. I could tell you about my new job then, if you like,' I said, my voice thick with emotion.

'I'd be delighted. Would seven be an acceptable time? I need to tie together a few loose ends at the office.'

I checked my watch and agreed on seven. We parted with no fanfare, no fuss, Michau paying for our snack and staying a moment to talk to one of the restaurant owners. I slipped away and walked slowly home, my emotions like a roller coaster. Stocker's comment sounded in my brain, as clear as if she walked beside me. *'There must have been another reason for them to spend twenty years of their lives on you . . .'*

I stepped out of Petunias into a hot rain, air so wet my dress instantly clung to my body like something from a wet T-shirt contest. The kind they had back in Khoury before the Picou Brothers' Bar and Grill closed down.

I hadn't noticed it until now, but the heat in the city was different from the bayou. More cloying. Both were a damp sticky heat, but in New Orleans the air felt different, heavy and dirty. Perhaps because of the concentrated exhaust fumes, or because the low, tightly built structures in the Quarter stopped most breezes long before they could clear or cool the air. Or perhaps because of the levee that cut the city off from the air flow generated by the Mississippi River. What the city gained in safety from floods, it lost in cooling drafts of air.

Glancing behind me into the deluge, and into store front windows, I determined that neither of my Watchers had managed to find me. For the moment at least, my back door escape route was safe. As safe as I could expect.

By the time I walked back to the New Age shop, I was so soaked that my dress looked like navy skin, and the contents of my second-hand bag were swimming in an inch of water. The proprietor of the store never noticed when I entered, so stoned only his snores proved that anyone was even there. I found him in the office, his head on a desk, cradled in his arms. In his open palm were the keys to the shop, and after a moment's hesitation, I lifted them and locked up the front door.

I figured I was just being a good neighbor and careful to boot. Of course, there was nothing I could do about the puddles that marked my passage. I don't think the floor had been mopped in ages and there was no mop to be seen. Perhaps the puddles would simply evaporate before the Rastafarian woke.

Cee Cee was watching, and let me into the shop before I could even knock. She was waiting with a half-dozen frayed terry-cloth towels to dry me down, and practically smothered me with them when I stepped through the door. Perkins did his part by licking my ankles. When I was sufficiently dry for Cee Cee to allow me into her immaculate shop, we gathered all my things – the basket of clean dishes from Taber Rhame's lunch and my linens from Charles Stuart's shop, Perkins' leash and Cee Cee's umbrella – and went out the front door and up to my apartment.

My Watcher waited across the street, sodden and dripping, his face protected by the brim of a baseball hat I hadn't seen before. I resisted the urge to wave.

Clean and dry and dressed in my favorite holey jogging suit, I related the conversation from Petunias to Cee Cee, fed Perkins, and set the table for three. When Cee Cee heard we were being joined by a gentleman for supper, she tried to send me to change into 'Proper Attire', and when I refused, she combed her own hair and put on fresh lipstick, primping while I steamed fresh vegetables and carefully reheated the remains of Rhame's lunch. Cee Cee and Mme Willoby would have loved one another. Deportment and appearance were paramount to both.

I didn't know how to cook for one, being accustomed to preparing heavy meals for three people, twice a day. I hoped Cee Cee and Michau were ravenously hungry, as I had managed to prepare a week's worth of food for Rhame and I didn't really care to eat leftovers for the next six or seven days.

Cee Cee and I were halfway through with the bottle of wine when Michau knocked, standing in a faint rain, thoughtfully bringing a fresh bottle to the little party. I figured even the rain catered to Michau, letting up the downpour in respect of the man's perfectly tailored suits and high-piled Lyle Lovett hair. Me and my ruined navy dress were another matter entirely, although Cee Cee insisted that she knew a cleaner's who could save the second-hand dress. Of course, Cee Cee was two sheets to the wind when she made the claim.

It was a pleasant party, with conversation ranging from history, to politics both local and national, to recipes, to investments. True southern conversation, all cordial and decorous with disagreements glossed over and sugar-coated. Although I understand many rednecks often conclude conversations with a fist fight or shotgun, the true southern way was a polite sort of pretending not to notice the difference of opinion or education, no matter how glaring.

The meal was a tremendous success, mainly because I whipped up fresh Hollandaise for the seafood. Actually, the meal tasted better reheated than it had fresh. Either the spices and herbs had time to blend, or the wine I drank made everything taste more satisfying.

Under the pretext of allowing the damp, cooler air in to freshen the apartment, I had set up the table in the front room, before the open French doors leading out onto the balcony. The main reason for the arrangement was so I could keep an eye on my watcher. He stood in the pouring rain, looking morose and watery.

The sound of rain beating steadily down was better music than any CD could have provided. A pleasant background to the meal, but not very pleasant for my watcher.

This occasion was the first time an outsider had viewed my oils. As the sun set behind the lowering clouds, and the room fell into near darkness, the paintings seemed to come alive, to whisper tenebrous secrets and somber mysteries. Twice during the bread-pudding dessert, as the light changed and shifted, Michau excused himself and went to peer at one painting or another.

The third time he rose, he forgot the verbal courtesy in his preoccupation with *Empty Nests*. I had just lit the candles as full darkness settled into the corners of the room, folding down with furtive stealth. The wavering light illuminated the canvas.

'My God,' he breathed. Even Cee Cee seemed transformed, following behind him, for once with nothing to say.

'I'm almost finished with it. It lacks only a final touch-up,' I said from my place at the table.

'No wonder the artist hired you. They're magnificent. But they looked so dull and lifeless by daylight. You're positively gifted,' Michau said, his voice still hushed.

I laughed, the alcohol in my system making the sound waver like the light. 'Taber Rhame never saw my work. I was hired because of the smoked oyster Hollandaise sauce, not my art. But thank you. I have a wall-sized work in mind, a day to night scene of an egret rookery. More of a triptych, really, with the center painting the largest, at sunset when the birds return.'

I sipped more wine, trying to remember where I put the photographs of the rookery. I had picked them up from Boddie on the way out of Khoury, and vaguely remembered stuffing them beside the van seat.

'I wish to purchase this.'

It would be a real hoot if the photographs had fallen through the rusted-out floor of Elred's van. I could picture the expensive prints scattered – The thought stopped in mid-image.

'I beg your pardon?'

'I said I wish to purchase this painting,' said Michau.

'Why?' as soon as the word left my mouth I knew it was dumb. I'll bet Taber Rhame had handled his first sale with a bit more panache than a dumfounded 'Why?' I definitely had no head for alcohol.

'Because it's extraordinary.' Michau was laughing. 'Because I think this painting will be an exceptional buy and because I believe your work will increase in value tremendously over the next few years. Would you accept five hundred dollars for it?'

'But it isn't finished yet.' Oh God. I really had too much wine. Talk about a klutz. I blinked and tried to pull my mind together. 'You really want to buy *Empty Nests*?'

'Yes. I really want to buy *Empty Nests*.' Michau crossed the room and placed a hand on my shoulder, as if to keep me from rising. Or maybe I was wobbling in my chair and he was protecting me from a concussion.

'But I've never sold a painting before,' I giggled. Oh God, I had always hated women who giggled. Mme Willoby used to say that it made them sound empty headed. I gripped the table-edge with one hand, trying for some semblance of sobriety.

'I can have it finished by morning,' I heard myself say. Finally, I sounded like an artist instead of a silly twit. 'But it'll need to dry a few more days.'

'May I pick it up a week from today, after work?' Michau was signing a check. The ripping sound loud in the apartment as he tore it from his checkbook. The rain had eased up, the gutters on the side of the building still gurgling. The hard splat of sound as drops collected on the iron railing and fell to the sidewalk below. I picked up the check, surprised that Michau used regular checks, just like ordinary people. Not embossed and oversized and printed with Old English letters.

Five hundred dollars, written in Michau's neat script. My first sale.

'Yes. A week from tonight will be fine.' I sounded woozy, as drunk as a skunk, as Tante Ilene used to say whenever Tee Dom came home from Mishu Pilchard's Place. Or snookered. I always wondered where she got that term. Snookered. It sounded English, not French.

Suddenly Cee Cee was talking, her chirping French running all over the place, words tripping all over one another. But what she said, in essence, was that I could put the rest of my paintings in her shop, on commission. She had a dark corner that would bring out the subtleties of light and shadow, and she would take a ten percent commission . . . and the dear woman was off again coming up with ideas for frames and display techniques and . . .

Michau said softly, underneath Cee Cee's chatter, 'You are marvelously talented, Bonnie. And I'm honored to be your first customer. Are you sober enough to write out a receipt?'

I nodded, and stood slowly, heading for the bedroom to find the pad in the little black box. It was just blank paper, but I figured I could write out an acceptable receipt. If I wasn't too drunk to write . . .

'And, Bonnie?'

I paused, one hand on the open doorway closest to my armoires, and looked back. There were two Michaus . . . I wondered if that meant I would need two receipts. The awful giggle escaped again. Michau seemed not to notice. The perfect gentleman.

'I'd like to see a sketch of the triptych you mentioned. For the firm. We're redecorating next spring, and we have a twenty-foot-long plaster wall that will need something special.' He smiled. 'And the firm pays much better than I do.'

I nodded, not knowing what to reply. Terrified that my giggles would somehow erupt if I tried to speak and that I'd never gain control of them again. Definitely not sophisticated behavior. Mme Willoby would have been appalled.

My guests left by ten, and I washed dishes, thinking over the evening and the success of my oils. Not so long ago I had wondered what a meal with real conversation might be like. Already today I had enjoyed two such experiences – the dessert at Charles Stuart's linen shop, and supper here. I would have to be careful what I wished for in the future. It might not be long before the fate gods decided to make me pay for enjoying so much good fortune. The answer to my next wishes might take a bizarre turn. Superstitious thoughts. Or the wine talking.

I changed into a long T-shirt as wet breezes blew through the apartment, and Perkins curled up on the new pillow. He looked like burnished copper even in the dull light, his coat flame bright against the pale two-toned fabric.

I watched him sleep as I mixed up the new shade of paint I had discovered my last night in the shanty, preparing enough to finish up the painting I had just sold. The dog made a pretty picture himself in the half-light, and before I put up the brushes for the evening, I sketched out an oil of him on a small, irregular-shaped canvas.

I always bought my canvases prepared and ready for brush, so all I needed to start was a tube of paint and the small brush with which I always sketched. Some artists sketched with pencil or charcoal, but I preferred to use the oils I would paint with. It gave me a feel for the way the color would move against the surface, how well it would accept color and what depth of paint it would require to achieve the luminous quality I preferred.

Finally, exhausted, I cleaned my brushes and readied myself for bed. At two, I slid between the sheets and drifted off, leaving the French doors open to the balcony and the breeze.

At five thirty the sound of sirens and the flash of blue lights woke me. Perkins, his long hair bristling, and a growl grinding low in his throat, stood on the balcony, guarding and ready to attack. Throwing back the covers, I walked to the windows and stared down at the street level.

Directly across from me, his body sprawled in a pool of black blood, his dark skin and clothes still wet from rain, his hair ruddy against the sidewalk, lay my watcher. Cooter Bug.

CHAPTER 8

McCallum, his blond hair plastered by the rain, wiped down his blade with a soaked scrap of newspaper lying in the gutter. The police lights flashed, reflecting blue on the rain-splattered windows, blue in the water that ran down the sides of the streets, blue on the people gathering around the body. He laughed, the sound too soft to carry.

The bodyguard had been a surprise. And when the man got too close – close enough to make an identification – it had become necessary to eliminate him. It was his first human kill. And like the stray dogs he had practiced on in the past, little sport. Yet, adrenaline coursed in his veins, and when he laughed, the sound was shaky. His first human kill.

Cal sheathed the blade and walked down the alley, away from the commotion in front of the girl's apartment. He had expected her to be unprotected, but someone had known she might be in danger. Either the girl herself, or the Eldest . . .

McCallum unlocked the door to his Aston Martin, placed the sword on the floor behind the driver's seat, and climbed behind the wheel. The presence of the bodyguard – and his death – changed things. McCallum drummed his fingers on the leather-wrapped wheel. He would have to rethink his plans.

Starting the 1960 classic car, he pulled into the street. Behind him, another police cruiser appeared, siren wailing. The car pulled around him and disappeared, moving toward Royal Street. Cal smiled. And his smile was angelic as he considered the man lying in the street.

Stocker handled the unpleasantness with the police. The questions for which I had no answers. The innuendo. The confusion.

In the watcher's pocket was a Polaroid of Perkins, Cee Cee, and me, taken the day I first looked at the apartment. Stapled to the back was a typed description of me, my name, address, and Cee Cee's description. There was a small spiral notebook chronicling my every action since just after noon the day before, when I had seen the two watchers change places. Cooter Bug also had two Polaroids of Michau, one taken as he climbed the stairs to my apartment, the other taken as he waited at my landing to be let inside. There was a question mark on the white edging of the first shot of Michau, followed by two times: 7 p.m.–10 p.m. The hours Michau was inside my apartment.

The police wanted to know who the dead man was, as he carried no personal identification. They wanted to know who had hired him, and why I was being watched. From whom I was being protected. They wanted to know why the man had been killed outside my apartment, and who might have committed the crime.

Stocker told them what we knew, but wasn't able to shield me from everything. And the police weren't satisfied with my repetitious 'I don't know's. However, short of charging me with a crime, there was little the police could do to hold me.

A witness appeared on the scene, claiming to have seen a scuffle and heard a muffled scream. He then saw a man run to the back of a building down the street. The witness was drunk, but was certain the suspect was tall, male, blond, and may have worn a beard. Not a description that fit me.

Based on the witness's statement, the police had to let me go, but they weren't happy about it. I was the best lead they had.

Stocker followed the police to MacAloon's home, and stood in a corner while they asked him questions. Unfortunately MacAloon had no answers for the officers either.

The man who hired him was a new customer, tall, dressed in an expensive double-breasted suit. Paid cash. Called himself Mr Jenkins. MacAloon had no reason not to take the money. He wasn't being paid to do anything illegal. He was being paid to protect the man's niece. Perfectly legit. And it might have been legitimate, except that Mr Jenkins looked nothing like Tee Dom, the only uncle I knew.

No one went back to bed that morning and no one went away satisfied. Least of all me.

Three and a half hours was enough sleep for me, but not enough for Perkins. I left the little dog snoozing on the new pillow, trying to catch up on his beauty sleep. Walking alone through the wet streets, I kept my hand on the gun in my pocketbook. It was paranoid, but I didn't care. Perhaps the killing of Cooter was just a random thing, some junkie needing his cocaine, mugging a solitary mark for the funds to buy his next fix. But the fact that Cooter had been wearing his gun made me question that theory. The police said he hadn't even gone for his weapon. And the gun wasn't taken. On the streets, the police told me, a gun like Cooter's .38 policeman's special would have kept the average junkie in crack for several days. The only thing missing was the dead man's camera. An odd thing to steal when the gun was so readily available.

I ate my breakfast at the Café du Monde, two coffees and three pastries, but this time there was no Perkins to share my meal. Not even the appearance of Miles, the nice-looking man who liked dogs and wore expensive boots. Just the waiters and the rain.

I was accustomed to being alone. I had been alone all my life, even when living with Tee Dom and Tante Ilene. But somehow, today's aloneness was more acute.

I took a quart of hot coffee with me to Rhame's studio, and a pound of Community coffee, sold at the café. A quick glimpse inside Rhame's cabinets and pantry the day before had proved their barrenness. Rhame liked to eat, but didn't know how to shop. Stocking his shelves to cook his meals would take some time. I woke the artist and his beautiful son, both robed men greeting me at the door with bleary eyes and dark morning beards. They fell on the coffee like winos to a bottle of Mad Dog, greedily downing the black concoction with soft sighs and groans. I made a fresh pot on Rhame's Gaggia coffee-maker with bottled water and the fresh-ground beans.

Although at the Sarvaunts' I used a plain, old-fashioned tin percolator that Tante Ilene had referred to as a drip pot to make our coffee, I had used coffee-machines before at one tutor's or another, and also at the Ponchartrain. And the Gaggia wasn't so different that I couldn't figure it out. And it did seem to provide a particularly smooth drink, proving its maker's claim to superior quality.

In the refrigerator was milk, eggs, cheese, English muffins, olives, butter, and lemon juice. In the cabinet over the stove were some spices, never opened. It was obvious that Rhame didn't know spices retained their freshness longer if refrigerated. There was no meat and nothing fresh. While the men drank coffee, and tried to wake up, I poached some eggs, toasted some buns in the oven and made up a quick Hollandaise sauce with butter, three egg yolks, the lemon juice, salt and a pinch of cayenne. With the black olives sliced thin on top, I served a meatless version of eggs Benedict. No one complained and the men started the meal in silence, Rhame doodling on a paper napkin.

'Bonnie,' Rhame said, halfway through the meal, 'where have you been all my life?' It was said in Italian, my poorest language, but I could follow most of the words, smiling and shrugging at the teasing question.

'Careful, Bonnie. That's the line he uses on all his new conquests. I think even my mother fell for that one.'

'Your mother paid a bellboy to let her into my suite, and then proceeded to seduce me. I was innocent,' Rhame protested – his hand over his heart.

'That's not the way she tells the story.'

'Your mother always had an active imagination, which was mostly a burden. But it was a useful thing in the bedroom.'

'Papa! For shame!' All in Italian. I had a feeling my fourth language was going to improve quickly.

The men were laughing, sharing the closeness of father and son. Again, the feeling of aloneness that had touched me at the café seemed to hover nearby. Like a ghost, insubstantial, yet compelling.

'Bonnie, are you ready to go to work for this old man?'

'I'm not so old that I could not best you on the mat, Tito. Remember the last time.'

'Yes, but then you had not eaten a meal full of fat and cholesterol. That is the American word, yes?' Tito asked me, his liquid brown eyes laughing. 'Cholesterol?'

I nodded, smiling slightly, pleased to be a part of the light-hearted banter. The ghost of loneliness faded a bit.

'As soon as the rain clears, I will show you who is the better man. Age is unimportant on the mat. There is only style and fluidity. You will see,' Rhame promised us both. 'This boy, he thinks he is so all grown up. I will show him a thing or two.'

'Well, Papa, why wait for the rain? We could push the furniture apart and settle this right now. I have learned a few things since we last had a practice session. So why wait? Unless your old bones are too stiff yet.'

'Old bones! Come. Now. We will see what you have learned, you impudent pup.'

Still bantering in Italian, the men left the dirty dishes. As I cleaned the mess, I could hear the sound of furniture being moved, and the silence as they went to change clothes. Beside Rhame's plate was the napkin he had doodled on during the first, silent part of the meal.

It was a rough sketch of me, a nude, my back to the men, my hands busy at the coffee-maker, my clothes puddled on the floor, a tattoo curling up my body. Below the sketch was a list of things Rhame wanted done today. For an artist, it was remarkably detailed. There were phone numbers and names of individuals and companies. Where supplies needed to be ordered, even the shipping companies were specified on the list. Taber Rhame was a very organized man.

From my bag I pulled a small notebook I had brought for the purpose, transcribed the list and information in its neatly ruled pages, and went to work. The sketch I carefully folded and placed in my bag next to the gun. I would frame it and hang it on my bedroom wall. That seemed the best place to hang such a fanciful nude.

The men grunted and fell for two hours, cursed in Italian and challenged one another to feats of prowess, proving mastery of one technique or another. They tossed their bodies around, the thumps through the mattress on the wooden floor like some huge bass drum. I wondered how Charles Stuart's customers liked the ruckus. Meanwhile I worked, losing myself in the business of the day.

It took four hours to make all the phone calls and order all the supplies Rhame needed. Among other things, I ordered wax from Italy, terracotta from Mexico, an electric oxidation kiln from Norway and wooden boxes he wanted made to his specifications here in the city. I worked in the kitchen, stopping only once to make a quick trip to the market and to two specialty food shops for lunch fixings. It was to be simple today. French bread, grilled with garlic and heavy with butter, red wine, and turkey carcass gumbo made with turkey bones, whole ham, and hot sausage, served with a better quality red wine to drink than the cheap one I bought to cook with. And dessert downstairs with Charles, flavored coffee and leftover sticky buns.

By the end of lunch, as we three trooped back up the spiral staircase at the back of the apartment, I knew my position as Taber Rhame's personal assistant and cook was secure. The meal was a success, and he was pleased that I had accomplished so much by phone. So pleased that he gave me the next two days off, time he wanted to spend showing New Orleans to his son . . . time I could use to further the investigation into my past.

Before I left Rhame's for the day, I called Stocker and made plans. We would leave for Khoury at eight the next morning. I tried to ignore the sense of anticipation I felt stirring at the thought of going home. I tried not to think of the shanty as home; unpainted wood, mildewed pilings, mud, mosquitoes by the millions, the stink of swamp. No one wanted to call that sort of place home.

But the memory of Tante Ilene's eyes, brimming over with tears, trembled at the edges of my consciousness, roused by Stocker's words in the restaurant yesterday. '*Two thousand five hundred dollars a year. There must have been another reason for them to spend twenty years of their lives with you.*' Must there be another reason? And if so, what? And why had Tante Ilene cried when I left home?

I walked to my apartment, my hand again on the .38 in my pocketbook, but no one seemed to be following me. Even my Watcher, MacAloon, the man with the beer belly, wasn't there. Perhaps the death of his partner had convinced him to work somewhere else. Somewhere safer.

Perkins yipped once and tore down the stairs when I opened my door, so desperate to relieve himself that he didn't bother with a hello. He did his private business out back now, depositing his leavings on the courtyard soil. So far he had marked all four corners and was working on the patio furniture legs. I hoped no one complained at the stench. And I was glad he didn't mark my apartment similarly.

We had a quiet evening, Perkins and I, watching TV, painting, taking naps and eating leftovers. Just before dusk, I glanced out the front windows at the street. MacAloon was leaning against the wall of the shop across the street, his arms crossed, his beer belly straining the seams of his T-shirt. He was clearly unsettled, watching the street, the sidewalk, the dark openings of the shops all around, transferring his attention in jerky little twitches.

He could no longer pass for a loiterer, a street person looking for a place to hang. Now he was a man with a mission, a job to do. And when his eyes landed on mine, standing in the shadows, he paused and nodded, his eyes hooded and still for a moment. He knew I knew now, and he didn't bother to ignore me. Then he returned to the duty of watching the street. Watching the passers-by. Protecting me, if that could be believed. But protecting me from what? From whom?

I was comforted by his presence. Yet, when I turned off the lights at 2 a.m., I put the shotgun beside the bed, within easy reach. Placed Perkins on the bed beside me, his chosen pillow as his mattress. If I was awakened in the night, I didn't want to shoot the dog instead of an intruder. This way, I'd know if the dog moved. With my Watcher, my fierce attack dog and my gun, I felt reasonably safe, and slept well, all things considered.

The Grande Dame stared down the long table, over the low centerpiece, the glistening china, the sparkling crystal. Glanced around the faces gathered for the meal. Hers. All hers, in one way or another. All gathered for this, the last meal.

It wasn't a formal setting, with menus at each plate and footmen stationed about the room. Only the two, dressed in service whites rather than the more formal gray uniforms to serve the twenty gathered here. Only two. Not quite the most elegant meal she could envision for her plan, but . . . It would do. It would do.

She smiled down the long length of table and nodded to Jenkins, standing by the kitchen door. Regally. Royally. 'You may begin, Jenkins.'

'Yes, ma'am.'

The first course appeared, followed by the second, served with smooth and effortless precision. The footmen were unctuous, the meal perfect. And then, with the main course, came the tea.

Only recently had she allowed tea to be served, insisting that water and wine were the only two liquids she would allow at table. White-trash might serve iced tea at meal, but never a DeLande. Never until last week when *he* insisted on the change.

He had taken everything else from her, and now he was taking over her duties as Grande Dame as well. Removing the tasks that were under her domain as mistress of the estate.

She had bowed to this singular demand, that iced tea be served at meal. She had been gracious and kind. Until today. And today would be the last time.

She smiled at him, sitting at the head of the table, in the Eldest's place. Smiled a bit wider when he took his first sip of tea. His second. Drained his glass, and drank from the refill.

Excellent service. She'd have to commend the footmen.

'You're not eating, ma'am,' he said from the far end of the room, his brows lifted in concern. 'Are you well?'

She laughed then. She couldn't help it. 'Yes, Eldest. I'm quite well.'

'And your tea. I notice you haven't touched it at all. If you fear for your safety, let me assure you the rumors were entirely false.' And he smiled then, an amused, slightly taunting smile. The room fell silent.

'Rumors?' Her hands started shaking. Just a minor tremor, controlled when she clasped them in her lap.

'Yes. The rumors about the tea and its . . . peculiar taste. The cook complained about the flavor. Thought it might have . . . gone bad. So he poured it out. Made fresh. I assure you it's quite delicious.' He sipped again, smiling over the rim of the glass. Someone coughed. No one else moved. And they were all staring at her. Staring.

From the other end of the table, McCallum watched her, a gleam of untamed violence in his eyes. He was amused and entertained by her small failure. At her expense, he chuckled, his voice carrying softly.

Slowly, so slowly, she lifted a finger and scratched at her scalp. The one itchy spot that . . . bothered her lately. It just . . . itched.

It was one hair that caused the discomfort. A single strand buried in the mass of silver hair. If only she could find it . . . McCallum watched, his eyes, so like Royal DeLande's, narrowed. His gaze filled up her world.

With one perfectly manicured nail, she teased among the hair, testing for the sensitive root until she found it. The one that suddenly burned. Suddenly itched almost violently. Gently she eased the strand loose, pulling it from the smooth twist of hair piled on her head, up high like a crown.

And jerked it out.

Smiling, she placed the single silver strand beside her plate. Lined it up between two silver spoons, sharp and flush.

And drank down her tea. All of it.

Miles was at the café the next morning, wearing his old boots, the fancy, silver-tipped ones resting on the chair seat next to him. Though he never brought them up, the boots he wore today were proof of his former assertion about the horses. I was embarrassed, but since he didn't mention the boots, neither did I. I was just happy to have company for breakfast this morning, not wanting to repeat the solitary experience of the morning of the murder. Loneliness was new to me, and I found I didn't like it at all.

Miles was reading a *Times Picayune*, concentrating on the financial section, a section of the newspaper I particularly enjoyed. With Perkins at our feet, digging like mad into the seams of Miles's old boots, we shared breakfast and the paper, talking softly as the sun rose and the café filled with tourists.

Partway through the meal, when I set down the New York Stock Exchange section for the NASDEQ section and my attention was diverted, Miles said, 'Did you hear about the murder a few blocks over? Rotten times when a man isn't safe to walk the streets at night.' He was reading the headline story about the Royal Street murder. I was looking for my French Stock Market investments. I had a feeling that Stocker was going to cost me plenty in the next few weeks and money was going to get tight.

Yet, at the mention of the death, a strange whisper of excitement or warning flickered through my nerves. A man had died outside my apartment. A man hired to protect me. The sudden reaction was intense. Chilling. A man had *died* because of me . . . I looked up, studying Miles's face, intent on the paper.

'Yeah. It happened right outside my apartment,' I said. 'Perkins and the siren woke me up.'

Miles put down the paper and picked up Perkins, settling the dog on his lap, his eyes on his own hand as he stroked the long hair. A silly smile touched his face, the kind of smile displayed by an animal lover whose free hand was being bathed by a loving pink tongue. 'Really? Did you know the guy?' It was an offhand question. The kind one acquaintance might ask another, casual concern being the polite thing to express. If the concern cloaked a bit of ambulance-chasing thrill that was only normal.

I told him part of the story. About how I had hired a private investigator to research my background, and how the bodyguards had appeared out of nowhere, but even the security firm didn't know who had hired them to protect me. I gave Miles no details, telling him only that I was looking for my mother, but he seemed quite taken with the story, asking questions about my history and my people.

It was a particularly southern peculiarity, the tracing of family lines and history, elaborating on the aristocratic connections while ignoring the more mundane or low-class pedigree. A part of the furthering of any acquaintance always involved bloodlines and breeding, as if people were no better than their sires or dames. Like thoroughbred horses or breeding stock on a cattle ranch.

'I have a branch of Sarvaunts in my family,' Miles said, at one point, his black eyes sparkling, his long-fingered hands stroking Perkins. The little traitor sighed and closed his eyes in what looked like ecstasy beneath the tranquilizing strokes.

'My uncle's name is Robert James Sarvaunt,' I volunteered, 'And my aunt is the former Ilene Sarvaunt. They were second or third cousins, so they had the same last name before they were married.' I wasn't a Sarvaunt. Elizabeth Sarvaunt wasn't my mother. But not having any other name to offer, I stuck with the familiar.

'My mother's mother was a Sarvaunt. Perhaps we are related several generations back. I'll have to ask.'

'Perhaps,' I said. 'Wouldn't that be a coincidence.' Not that it really would be, of course. Back a few generations, everyone was related to everyone else somewhere along the line, either on one side of the sheets or the other. But it was the proper thing to say, and mouthing the words was second nature to me after Mme Willoby's deportment classes.

Miles and I discussed the financial pages next, discussing the latest happenings in the EC and the changes in European social life likely to affect the world as France, England, and Germany adopted a common market. He was well versed in the trading practices of most of the smaller markets entering the EC as well, and it was fun talking with someone my own age who understood the world situation. I had feared that most young people I might meet in New Orleans would be attuned to MTV and Hollywood and the latest sports.

We talked too long, as the café filled up with tourists and the noise level rose around us. Over an hour later, it occurred to me that I had plans for the day, and I literally gasped as I looked at my watch. Standing too quickly, I sloshed cold coffee out of a cup. 'Well, if I can pry my dog off your lap, we'll be going. Perkins and I are going to LaRoque and Khoury today.'

'A family visit?'

Something twisted deep inside me and my enjoyment of the morning faded. Family. That was one thing I didn't have.

'Something like that,' I said, putting aside my disquiet, and pasting a smile on my face. Miles stood, placing a pacified Perkins on the tiled floor of the café. We gathered our respective belongings, Miles offering me the paper, claiming to have finished it. I accepted the gift and we parted amicably, me with the gifted paper beneath my arm, Miles with his fancy boots beneath his.

I glanced back once, watching the slim man walk toward a parked car. It was an old one, with gleaming new paint in a raspberry red, a silver jaguar leaping from the front hood. A classic car, one even I knew to be very expensive, one that triggered some half-buried memory. But it wasn't the car that held my attention. It was the man. There was something familiar in his walk. Something elegant and fluid about the way he placed his feet, the smooth, sleek gait. It bothered me to watch him move. Bothered me more that he got into the car and drove away without a backward glance or wave. When the old Jaguar pulled around the corner and thrummed down the street, I walked on, moving quickly. I was dissatisfied and uneasy but not able to specify why.

At the next block, MacAloon waited, his stance for once not remotely relaxed. He stood, hands fisted at his sides, his face furious. 'I thought that private dick said you didn't know who hired me.' A drunk, sitting on a low stoop, looked up, bleary eyed, but interested.

I looked at MacAloon in surprise. 'Huh?' Scintillating repartee. Mme Willoby would have swallowed her tongue.

'Night before last, when the cops came to tell me Cooter Bug was dead. That Stocker woman told me you didn't know who hired us to watch over you.' Perkins bristled, growling low, placing himself in front of my feet to protect me. If the man pulled a gun with his big toe, I was safe. Any threat from higher up, and I was in trouble.

'Yes. I mean no. I don't know who—'

'Don't give me that bullshit.'

The gun. It was in my purse, available, but not ready to hand. Already I had neglected the common sense of having the gun at all times ready to use. I took a step back, then braced myself. It was broad daylight, and he was paid to guard me, not hurt me. Right? 'I beg your pardon?'

'That man. That man you was eatin' with. That's Jenkins. The man who hired me to watch you.' The drunk hiccuped and settled himself for the show.

I jerked my head around, but the shiny red car was long gone. 'Miles? Miles hired . . .'

Perkins barked, jerking to the end of the leash, trying to decapitate MacAloon at the kneecaps. His angry little yips sounded like he was being stepped on instead of playing guard dog. I pulled the leash back and lifted Perkins in my arms. He struggled there, his teeth bared, lips contracted in a fierce snarl. Low growls warned MacAloon to stay back. In another situation it would have been amusing.

'Miles?'

'Is the same Mr Jenkins who hired me to watch you.' He peered at my face. 'You din' know.' It wasn't a question. More a surprised statement of fact.

'No. I didn't know.' I blinked. Suddenly I felt more woozy than I had during my dinner party two nights past when the wine had overcome my usual sense of decorum. I had the same uncontrollable desire to giggle. The same dizzy feeling. I took a deep breath, not able to fill my lungs. I tried again, and a tingling started in my fingertips. 'I hate to be a bother . . .' my voice sounded breathy and weak, '. . . but I do believe that I'm about to pass out.'

MacAloon shoved the drunk to the sidewalk with a thump and, gripping me by the shoulders, sat me down in his place. My teeth slammed shut, with a pained grunt Perkins went silent, and I found my head thrust between my knees. MacAloon held it there while Perkins – who was crushed against my knees – and I struggled to breathe. Most unladylike posture, but perhaps better than lying sprawled in the street.

The thought crossed my mind again, as I came to my senses, that I might have been safe had I never cashed the 50,000 dollar check, and stayed in Khoury with Tee Dom and Tante Ilene.

Somewhere in the faint recesses of my mind, another part of me disagreed. This intrigue, whatever it was, had been put into motion before I was even born. I might have delayed being found, but my discovery was inevitable.

I ignored both parts of my inner argument and concentrated on not passing out. Perkins crawled from his tight perch and jumped to the ground at my feet. The sidewalk was bare. I wondered where the drunk had gone.

When I had my wits about me again, MacAloon walked me the rest of the way home. It was after eight, and Stocker was waiting at the curb in front of Cee Cee's store. MacAloon climbed into the passenger seat to confer with my investigator while Perkins and I climbed the stairs and packed a small bag. Dog food and flea spray for him, my little black box, clean underwear and a change of clothes for me. By the time I reached the street again, MacAloon and Stocker had concluded their professional business. I took his place in the front seat of Stocker's 4 × 4 dual-wheel Chevy truck, settled Perkins on the seat beside me, and we pulled onto Royal.

Traffic was light, and I realized it must be Saturday. No incoming suburbanites, no school buses or garbage trucks, no city vehicles at all. Just a clearing sky and a fresh heat and Khoury by noon.

Stocker pulled onto 12 heading west, then took the 90 South Exit. When we were moving safely in the right direction, Stocker handed me a gallon thermos of coffee and two Styrofoam cups.

'Got enough coffee here, Stocker?'

'It'll last me till noon.'

I took that as a joke and the jug as a hint, pouring us both a cup, black. Half a minute later she shoved her cup back for more. Okay. So maybe it hadn't been a joke. I poured her another cup and this time she drank only half before setting the cup into a plastic holder in the dash.

'So. Tell me about Miles or Mr Jenkins or whoever he is.'

I gave her a description of Miles, his car, his boots, his clothing preferences, and a quick run-down on how we met and what we had talked about. When I finished, she drank down the rest of her coffee and returned her cup for thirds. I poured as she spoke.

'So. Let me get this right. You essentially told this good-looking guy all about yourself, where you live, who you work for, and all about your search for your mother, yet you neglected to find out his last name, his occupation, his address, or any other pertinent facts about him.'

I placed the Styrofoam cup in her waiting fingers, concentrating on not spilling any of the steaming liquid and hoping she wouldn't notice my blush. Hearing it stated so baldly, it really did make me sound incredibly naïve. The teenaged blind spots I thought I had somehow avoided altogether. 'That about sums it up, I suppose.'

Stocker laughed. 'I should have brought my dog Cassie. She's a miniature pinscher, a little large for the small breed, a throwback really, but I'll bet she and Perkins would have had a ball.' She talked on about her dog and the farm, but never again mentioned my big mouth. Later, as we drove through the outskirts of New Orleans, I referred back to Miles.

'So. What are we going to do about the man who paid for my bodyguards?'

'Nothing. Not a thing. But MacAloon is going to run his license plate number on Monday and we should have an ID on the guy by Monday night.' She glanced at me out of the corner of her eyes, a gleam of amusement lurking in their depths. 'Gotcha.'

I laughed at Stocker and she joined in. She had a musical voice, low-pitched and soothing. Part of that slow-moving quality I had noticed. Horse sense. It probably didn't pay to laugh loud around a jittery half-ton of reactive flesh.

In fact, as I thought about Stocker, I realized that everything about her was slow and easy, as if the years of working with horses had squeezed out of her all quick and sudden movements. I had a feeling that if Stocker was startled, she would flinch in slow motion.

We chatted quietly, until a silence settled and Stocker tuned in a country station to fill the void. Clint Black's soothing mellow voice filled the cab.

The terrain changed as we drove, from the quaint enduring style of the Quarter, to the dirt and despair of uptown's urban failings, to the poorly planned outskirts of New Orleans's sprawling growth. And suddenly, with a single exit off the main road, my old world returned. The world of my childhood, the world of my art, the world of darkness and solitude that I had left behind.

Cypress knees rising from black water, egrets fishing and old men crabbing in the bayou that snaked along beside the two-lane road, unpainted shacks and worn women hanging laundry, half-naked children playing in the mud. Spanish moss draped over the twisted arms of ancient cheniers. The green of live oaks spread dark, sinuous branches against the clear blue sky. A family of raccoons scampered across the road. A buzzard, ugly and greasy as the lump of road-kill at which he pecked, lifted his head, perhaps catching his reflection in the finish of the truck.

On high land, property that had been cleared and back-filled to make pasture, cattle trotted or drowsed. Cattle birds – the white birds that groomed parasites from the coats and ears of lazy steers – settled in for the day's first insectoid meal. Horses rolled in soft sand, kicking their long legs in the air, or pranced in the morning light, sun-dried mud on their coats.

And on each side of the road was black water. Black water, smooth and slow, maundering through the bayous. Or black water, stagnant and still, slimed over with green algae. Stumps lifted above the water, sun-warmed stools for frogs, snakes, and turtles by the dozen.

The sun came out, brightening the world, and I pulled my sunglasses from my bag to protect my sensitive eyes, which suddenly wanted to tear up against the glare. Stocker asked directions, diverting my thoughts and, as if sensing my misery, she began a story about the way she got her dog Cassie. I managed to blink away my tears and make the necessary responses, but I don't think I fooled her for a moment. Going home was hard.

As we drove, the cities and towns grew smaller, older, separated by wider and more desolate stretches of land. Sugar-cane fields patched the flat landscape. A huge piece of farm machinery slowed the scant traffic, trundling down the road. Its driver was a black kid, perhaps fifteen years old, wearing a Nike baseball hat, driving the massive, red-painted steel monstrosity with one hand, directing traffic around himself with the other.

In some states a fifteen-year-old kid couldn't even drive a car, but responsibility comes early in rural America. A teenager's bid for independence often resulted in more work, not necessarily more freedom. Perkins, napping on the seat beside me, was awakened by the tractor's roar. Jumping upon my lap he lunged, barking through the closed window as we drove around the tractor.

Firmly, I put him back in his place and told him to be still. Surprisingly he obeyed, settling in quickly for another snooze.

By the time we entered LaRoque Parish, I was nervous. As jumpy as a cat with two tails in a rocking-chair showroom, as Tante Ilene used to say, the phrase gently mangled by her Cajun dialect.

We drove past La Farge Refinery, the rusty metal buildings and stained petroleum-holding tanks standing stark in the too-bright sun. Beyond the ten-foot-tall, chain-link fence, the pavement was cracked and pitted, weed filled, home to rabbits and possums and oversized rats. A faded-out 'Welcome to Khoury' sign flew past. Someone had used the sign for target practice recently; the 'K' was now a hole the size of my palm.

We drove past the closed First Baptist Church, its 'For Sale' sign tilted over in the weeds. We passed the old school house, deserted since desegregation and a falling tax base had made busing preferable to the expense of building a new school.

The tingling I had experienced that morning when I discovered that Miles was the man who hired my bodyguards returned, along with the breathless sensation of suffocation. Without taking her eyes from the road, Stocker said, 'You're breathing too fast. Slow it down or you might work yourself up to a panic attack. It's called hyperventilation and it'll make you tingle, and nervous, and your heart race. If your decide to hurl, kindly open the window.'

I laughed, the sharp sound waking Perkins. The word *hurl*, coming from Stocker, seemed to do the trick as I fought for control. Miss Taussig's yoga techniques did the rest. My breathing slowed, my heart rate descended to normal and resumed a regular rhythm. The tingling diminished. Perkins stretched and yawned, climbing back to my lap to view Khoury. He looked unimpressed.

'Hurl,' I murmured under my breath.

'I saw *Wayne's World*, and I watch *Beevis and Butthead* occasionally to keep up on my lingo. That and the high-school girls I hire to help at the farm keep me current. Where to now?'

We were stopped at Khoury's only traffic signal on the corner of Main and Khoury Avenue. A minuscule branch of the LaRoque National Bank stood on one corner, the condemned Center theater opposite, with a Texaco station and the Main Street Bar and Grill on the remaining corners squared up like a foursome at a country dance.

'Left, then four blocks and take a right on Meaves Street.' I talked her through town – what there was of it – and out to the trailer park on the south side.

Once there had been over thirty trailers in Reedy Trailer Park. Now there were fewer than ten, with the single-wides scattered over seven acres, separated by trees, shrubs which had never felt the sharp side of a gardener's hedge-clippers, and the empty concrete pads that once supported Khoury's financially disadvantaged families.

The dirt road meandered through the trailer park, dried out and dusty, even after yesterday's rain. Stocker's 4 × 4 sent billows of white powder into the hot air as we pulled around to the front of the Sarvaunts' winter home.

There was a 'For Sale' sign on the front stoop.

I hadn't expected them to be here. Not until the end of the month. But the sign . . .

Before Stocker cut the engine, I had abandoned the cab and Perkins, bounding up the three steps to the stoop, key in hand. The lock was stiff and the door creaked as it opened. Inside, there was only empty space. No furniture. No rugs.

I stood in the empty front room, not bothering to fight the hyperventilation that strained my heart and lungs. Not bothering to hide the tears that fell.

They were gone.

CHAPTER 9

To call Eloise's bosom ample was to do the lady a disservice. Overabundant, graciously generous, even mountainous were more appropriate terms. I know. I was crushed to her chest the instant I walked into the washerette. Stocker, following me inside, viewed the scene with amusement.

'You poor dear. It must have been awful. Just awful. You must have been scared to death. But you didn't have to run away; you could have come to me. I'd have protected you. Dr Boddie and I talked about it all last week, and we had it all figured out, how you could have hidden out at my place at night and stayed in the photography studio during the day and we'd have put you a TV in there and everything. You poor dear, you poor dear.'

Eloise rocked back and forth with each 'poor dear', nearly throwing me from my feet with the motion. Stocker snickered. My private detective had a warped sense of humor.

'Eloise,' I finally interrupted, 'what are you talking about?' I pushed away, my hand against her midriff. Padded steel met my palm, startling me, but perhaps it took the world's strongest metal to hold in Eloise's girth.

'What do you mean, what am I talking about? I'm referrin' to the man who came to town to steal you away. I'm referrin' to the man who threatened your aunt and uncle. I'm referrin' to the forces of evil from the outside world tryin' to gain a foothold here in Khoury.' Eloise was quoting Father Alcede. I figured I had been the topic of last Sunday's sermon. 'That's what I'm talkin' about. Who's this?'

It sounded like an accusation, and Eloise shoved me behind her for protection. It seemed a pretty safe place too. Steel-piercing bullets might have made their way to me, but little else.

'This is R.T. Stocker, Eloise. A private investigator I hired. And my friend.'

'Oh.' I was jerked back in front, feeling very much like a rag doll two children were fighting over. Stocker was enjoying the show so much I doubt she'd have lifted a finger in my defense. She stuck out a palm.

'My friends call me Stocker. Any friend of Bonnie's here is a friend of mine. We've all been worried about her up in New Orleans too. It's a real pleasure to discover she has such fine allies back here in Khoury.'

It was my turn to roll my eyes. Stocker's lips twitched before she continued with her little speech. She'd have made a great politician with that line.

'There's been some problems in New Orleans, people following Bonnie, that sort of thing, and I'd really appreciate it if you'd enlighten me about the problems here in Khoury. I'm sure they would help me to protect Bonnie here from the, ah, the forces of evil, and that's what we all want. Right? For Bonnie to be safe and happy.'

Eloise, who had been folding clothes when we appeared, trudged her way to the washerette's front window and turned over the sign hanging there. It went from 'Full Service' to 'Self Service' with the flick of her hand. 'Come on in back, you two. We got some serious talking to do.' Eloise turned serious eyes to me, slits of blue pinched between puffy lids. 'Are you sure you can take this, Bonnie? Are you ready to hear the unvarnished truth?'

'Yes, ma'am. I am.' I had no idea what Eloise was talking about, but if it suited her sense of melodrama, then I'd agree. I'd agree to most anything to discover the truth about myself.

'Come on, you two. I'll start a pot of coffee in the back.' We followed Eloise to the office, a dark, windowless cubicle in the back of the washerette, housing a small color TV, a bedraggled sofa, an apartment-sized refrigerator and a microwave. A Mr Coffee was on a two-drawer file cabinet beside the TV, with a stack of Styrofoam cups to the side. I had often been to this nook of a room, lunching with Eloise, sharing her favorite soap on TV with her, listening to gossip. It was familiar, like the trailer should have been, but wasn't.

Stocker, the coffee addict, made herself at home with the

Mr Coffee, while Eloise pushed me to the worn-out sofa. It had once been a red, mauve and pale green floral. Now it was a dirty, frayed, sun-bleached thing with cording showing through at the seams and the foam peeking through the cushions. It looked like something one might see abandoned on the side of the road, or tossed into the bayou at a favorite fishing hole, a useful item on which catfish might attach eggs. I sank deeply into one corner. Any springs the sofa might once have boasted were now long gone, prey to Eloise's weight.

She closed the office door and stood in the center of the small space, her fists on her hips, jaw out thrust. 'You sure you can trust this woman?'

'Stocker?' I grinned when the PI turned around, brows lifted. 'She comes with the highest recommendations.' Stocker went back to the coffee machine, measuring out grounds.

'Well, the day after you left – and God knows I've missed you, child,' she fell to the sofa beside me, gathering me up in one of her wonderful hugs. I realized, as I breathed in the scent of hairspray and Wind Song, that I hadn't really been touched since Eloise's last hug. The day I left home. Eloise pushed me away and wiped her eyes.

'Anyway. The day you left, a man came to town asking questions all about how to find you. He stopped at the City Hall and asked Miriam Moncada – you know, she works there as a clerk – anyway, he asked Miriam how to find you, and she told him he'd have to go by boat, to the Sarvaunt Place on the Bayou Negre. So she directs this man – he's real young and good-looking and she says he could have charmed the pants off a saint. Of course, Miriam's head's always been easily turned.

'Anyway, she sends him to Elred out to the landing, but Elred was helping you pack so he went to the trailer and spoke to Elred and Elred told him he'd be along directly to the landing to rent him a boat. Never knowing at the time that the man wanted to find you. And there you were, inside the trailer all the time, packing up your things and I didn't know, and, oh, child, I've missed you so. Are you all right? Are you safe in that big city? Father Alcede prayed the longest prayer last Sunday for your protection and the safety of your soul too, of course. And he was saying as how evil that city is, and how easy it is for a young girl like yourself all alone with no family to guide and protect you, to fall into prostitution or naked dancing or pornography or some such thing and we were all just so worried and . . .'

Finally I took a deep breath and interrupted. 'Eloise!'

She stopped, her pink lips held open, moist from the volume of words and worry. 'Yes?'

I patted her hand. Stocker crossed the small room and leaned against the door jamb as hot water sputtered in the coffee-maker. A bulge showed beneath her loose shirt.

I realized she was carrying a gun.

'Yes?' Eloise repeated.

'Ah. Oh. Tell me what happened the day I left.'

'Well, there's what I saw happen, and what I heard happen, and, ah . . . well, then, there's the rest of it,' Eloise finished with a blush. A blush was an amazing phenomenon on Eloise, starting at her pudgy bare ankles and rolling up over the swells of fat, past her heaving bosom and vast cleavage to tint her apple cheeks even redder and finally disappear into her hairline. A blush meant only one thing. Eloise was guilty of something.

'Just start at the beginning, Miss Eloise,' Stocker said from the door.

Eloise averted her eyes. 'Well, I suppose.' Her blush deepened.

'Well, after you left – and I do appreciate you coming by, child, when you were in so much danger, and I din't even know it and all – Elred and that young man took off up the bayou. He, the man, asked Elred to take him to the Sarvaunt Place, and you can imagine Elred's surprise. But you know Elred. He didn't ask why the man wanted to go. So considerate is that boy. Never lookin' into anybody's business.'

Elred never had a considerate moment in his life. If he kept his mouth shut it was because the stranger overpaid Elred to take him up the bayou and Elred wanted the money. I was sure he had taken the time to trailer Tee Dom's boat back on the same trip, making a fine profit. But I didn't say so. A noncommittal 'mmmm' sufficed.

'So when they got to your folks' place and the man stepped up onto the dock things started to get strange. While Elred was tying up the johnboat he could hear them all inside talking, and everything seemed to be going fine until the man said your name and your uncle went crazy. Just crazy.

'Your Tee Dom took a shotgun off the wall and chased that man out of the house and off the dock. And he stood there hollering at Elred and the man in French and firing off that shotgun over their heads all the way back down the bayou. Elred said the man was mad as hell and white as a sheet.' Her head bobbed emphatically, creating extra double chins and then causing them to disappear between nods.

'He didn't say much on the ride back to the landing, but when Elred got the boat docked, this man started asking him questions all about you, like where you were and what you looked like and all.'

'Of course, Elred – well, you know he's always had a tendre for you – he got mad. He din't say a thing. Just picked up the phone and called the sheriff. And when the man drove off, Elred followed him.' Eloise was working herself up to a real passion, her chest heaving, her face as red as the sofa's faded upholstery. 'Followed him all through town. And that . . . that . . . that man finally left town because Elred wouldn't let him ask anyone about you. Every time the man parked that fancy car and tried to talk to someone about you, Elred would tell them not to answer because your uncle chased him off with a shotgun.'

Stocker served us all cups filled with black coffee as Eloise patted down her face and cleavage with a tissue she pulled from her pocket. 'You poor child.' She sipped her coffee. Stocker drank hers. I put my cup aside.

'Eloise, you talked about his fancy car. What kind of fancy car?'

'It was a red Jaguar.' A cold dread settled across my shoulders. *A red Jaguar*. 'An old one, according to Elred. He got the license number. I have it with the letter I got from your family before they left town the next morning. Here. Let me get all that stuff, honey.'

And I remembered then why I reacted so strongly to the sight of the Jaguar when Miles drove away only hours ago. I had seen the same car parked in front of the trailer the day I packed up and left Khary. The very same car.

Eloise set down her coffee cup and levered herself up from the sofa. Air sucked back into the sofa cushion, as if the furniture were taking a relieved breath. Eloise stalked to the file-cabinet beneath the Mr Coffee and bent over from the hips, presenting us with a fine view of a capacious polka-dot dress stuffed with huge hips and an immense derrière.

When she turned around, Eloise was holding her bottom lip in her teeth and an envelope in her hand. Her fingers were shaking and the blush was back across her face. Focusing on the envelope, I understood why. It had been torn open along the side seam. Eloise had opened it and read the letter.

Eloise had always been a gossip, sticking her pudgy nose into everybody's business. What she couldn't learn about someone from listening in on her customers' conversation, or by direct questioning, she put together by inference and a close study of their laundry. This was, however, the first time I had known her to tamper with the mail.

I tried to decide if I should be angry, but a laugh bubbled up around the anger and drowned out its energy. Eloise looked so woebegone, like an overfed puppy caught piddling on the rug. The laugh bubbled out. Eloise's blush deepened as she handed over the letter. I caught my breath. The letter was addressed to Carin Colleen DeVillier.

The tingling I had fought all day long swept back with a vengeance, overwhelming me. *Shock*, the calmer part of me reasoned. This time I resisted the effects of hyperventilation and panic, drawing on Miss Taussig's years of teaching, to steady and control the panic that wanted to control me. I could hear her voice, her delicate French accent so different from the harsh backwater Cajun sound of my aunt and uncle. It was as clear as if she were in the room with me.

'Now, Bonnie. It is easy in young girls for the body to panic, to take over the control and run away, carrying the spirit and the intellect along with hysteria. This you wish always to avoid, striving for balance in emotion and in the thoughts.' Here she had tapped my head to drive her point home. 'The breathing restores control. Slow, deep-relaxation breathing. Slow and deep.'

Her voice in my memory carried me to a deeper place within, a quiet place where I found a semblance of calm. Surprisingly, it was a place I recognized. The egret rookery, dark and peaceful, silvered by a gibbous moon. 'See?' her voice seemed to ask. 'See? It was always there inside you, this wonderful place. Waiting.'

Carin Colleen DeVillier.

I opened the torn envelope and pulled out the folded pages. They had been ripped from a small spiral notebook, the mutilated edges rough and crushed. Tante Ilene's stiff script stared up at me from the sheets. She had never finished the seventh grade, having left school to care for her mother who died young of some undiagnosed wasting disease. Hence her penmanship was poor. Most words were spelled phonetically. I touched the greeting with cold fingers.

Dear Bonnie,

You alway wan to know bout you name. Carin Colleen DeVillier what you mother name you. But she be chasin by her mama. That old woman done some bad thing to her. You mama say to hide you. Elizabeth done lost her baby, so they just give you her dead baby name. Elizabeth died when you was little, and you mama took her name. She promise us money to keep you safe, and you such a pretty, fine little thing so big eyes and sof hair. You Tee Dom and I love you.

The house on the bayou is belong to you. You mama buy it before Elizabeth die, and you three live there. Then, when Elizabeth die, you mama say is danger again, so she leave. She never come back.

Somehow they fin you again now. You mamas mama done sen a man to fin you. Tee Dom and I, we run him away. But we leave now. We plan to leave soon anyway, but go now soon. Tee Dom, he got a sister. We go stay with her. You be safe. We love you.

Tante Ilene

I smoothed the small pages in my hand. Perhaps I should have cried. Perhaps I should have felt some sense of release or happiness at finally having confirmed the story of my past. Perhaps a lot of things.

The calm place, the egret rookery by night, faded away. The panic I had carried somewhere inside me for days also faded away. I felt only a little empty. A little sad. I had known for days that Bonnibelle Sarvaunt was dead. This was only one more confirmation.

The only new bit of information was my name. Carin Colleen DeVillier. I had been right all these years. The scenario I had envisioned so many years ago when I first saw the death certificate for Bonnibelle Sarvaunt hadn't been far from the simple truth.

A sister. I had never known Tee Dom had a sister. I had never known Tee Dom at all. And now they were gone.

A chill crawled over me. When Tante Ilene would experience a chill unrelated to the weather, she used to say, 'Someone walk over mah grave, yes.' And she'd nod slowly in consternation and primitive alarm before going back to her crocheting. I knew what she meant now. This chill was like that. A small whisper of death.

I handed the pages to Stocker, watching a moment to make sure she could read Tante Ilene's writing. Then I slipped from the small office to the unisex bathroom.

There was a round, antique mirror over the lavatory, clean, but spotted with black where the silvering was tarnishing through. I stared at my face, familiar yet suddenly strange. I reached out and touched my face. The mirror was cool to the touch, like a corpse at one of Father Alcede's funeral services. Bonnibelle Sarvaunt was dead.

I had known it, of course, since I was fifteen. And all the information uncovered by Stocker over the course of her investigation had only confirmed this knowledge. Yet, hearing it from Tante Ilene made it real. I wasn't Bonnibelle. Never had been.

'Carin Colleen DeVillier.' The words were foreign, acerbic on my tongue. 'I am Carin Colleen DeVillier.'

Tears gathered at the corners of my eyes. Strange tears. I stared at them dispassionately as they pooled up, catching the light. Slowly they faded.

Bonnibelle Sarvaunt was dead. Tee Dom and Tante Ilene were gone.

I was now truly alone. My whole life was a lie.

Dry-eyed, I walked from the bathroom back to the office.

The Grande Dame bent forward and eased the silver strand of hair back into the chignon. This close to the mirror, the rare wrinkle could be detected at the edges of dark eyes and around her full lips. And the faint scar in the hairline . . . She frowned as her eyes found the imperfections, but then she was over sixty. Perhaps it was time to show a little age.

She had perfect skin, a delicate olive as fine as a newborn's, and eyes like black diamonds. She was one of those exceptional women who seem never to age, the kind whose photographs vary not even a little from decade to decade. If she had dyed her hair when it began to gray, she could have easily passed for a female in her thirties. Even now, she could have passed for forty-five but that would have been unnecessary vanity. She would much rather have power than beauty. She was, after all, the Grande Dame.

Clipping a heavy platinum bracelet around her left wrist, she stood and smoothed out the silk of her skirt. It's color perfectly matched the bracelet and her hair, leaving only the black eyes and the pale pink mouth to draw a viewer's attention.

She felt him before he reached her door. A clipped aura, wavering and incomplete, dulled by pain and the drugs he took to control it. Further inhibited by the liquor he drank to sleep. A cripple in body, mind, and soul. But he was all she had left to work with.

He was capable. The last corrective surgery had given him that back at least. His weren't the genes she had wanted to use, but, denied a better specimen, she would have to make do. And she had other plans for McCallum. Other uses for his special talents and his unique genes. No, there was no choice but Marcus.

Quickly she opened the door, startling him. He drew back his knuckles from the aborted knock, his eyes wide. She smiled. The beautiful smile. The one that had earned her a place in Louisiana history. The one she had used to win wealth and power and create a dynasty. The one which had given her power in a man's world. The one which had seduced generations. He hadn't seen it from her in years, and blinked several times, finally focusing on her lips. When he spoke, the words were breathy with liquor and something that sounded like longing.

'Mother.'

'Marcus.'

'May I escort you to dinner?' The same phrase he had uttered for months. Usually she didn't bother to answer, just moving past him at a steady speed that left his motorized-chair behind. But now that she had a new use for him she paused.

'Yes, Marcus. I think that would be delightful.'

Marcus pulled his brows together as her words penetrated the drugged haze clouding his mind. 'You do?' Uncertainty, distrust rang in the words.

'Yes.' She slipped a hand to his shoulder and pulled the door closed as he maneuvered back, his puzzled eyes on her face. 'Come along, Marcus.' Together they moved sedately down the hall, the elegant woman matching her stride to the wheelchair. Carpet, woven by hand in Shanghai in 1930, muffled her steps and the rubber wheels. She waited as Marcus entered the elevator, a brass forties version, and clanged the doors shut, before she spoke again. She understood about timing and its importance. If one wanted power, one had to understand timing. And use it.

'Marcus?'

'Yes, ma'am?'

He was confused. That was good. And slightly drunk. Even better. A slightly drunk Marcus wouldn't likely doubt her change of heart. The elevator began to move down, its motor jerky. She leaned close to his head so her breath would be warm on his ear as she whispered.

'I have a gift for you.' She hesitated, letting the phrase sink in. Letting the ancient words work their mystery on her malleable son. He swallowed. 'She's young, Marcus. And special.'

He sucked in a quick breath, suddenly almost sober.

'But Mi—'

'He isn't here, Marcus,' she whispered into his hair. It was faintly scented with shampoo and cigar and fresh liquor fumes. 'Just you and me. And your present. A little something to make up for ignoring you.'

Marcus caught her hand, a desperate look on his face. Desperate and disbelieving. 'Young?'

'Very. You'll like her, Marcus. She's Richard's youngest off a pretty little colored girl. The child has his green eyes and kinky ash-brown hair.' A sweat started on Marcus's skin. A slight sheen. 'I want you to break her in before He gets home. That doesn't leave you a lot of time.'

Marcus smiled, a baring of teeth more vulpine than joyous, and placed a kiss in the palm of her hand, his lips lingering a moment on the scented skin, moving there as he spoke. His eyes met hers. 'I may need your help. This chair.'

'When the moment is right, I'll handle things, you know I will. Don't I always? She'll be conscious but there will be no fight left. I promise you.'

'I wish I had time to do it right for you.' His eyes were soft and liquid as he released her hand. The elevator reached bottom with a soft jar. 'I wish—'

'The next time you can do it right. That would please me. But this time, I just need it done. I want a child off her in nine months. Just after Mardi Gras. I've checked the stars, Marcus, and there isn't time to do it right.'

Marcus kissed her hand again before opening the brass cage and letting them free. 'Whatever you want, Mother.'

'Marcus?' His eyes again met hers. 'Don't call me Mother.' She swept away, leaving him to follow at his mechanical speed.

Stocker was fascinated with Elred. I don't know if it was the repulsed fascination of a sophisticated, ethical, civilized being for a rude, uncivilized, uncultured, surly, insolent redneck, or if she simply had never met a man who had a total aversion to soap. It wasn't that Elred didn't bathe. It was just that water alone had little power over the stink of the fish Elred cleaned for the fishermen tourists, and the stench of boat exhaust combined with the reek of human body.

I had long ago learned to disregard Elred's scent and the sight of the large flakes that drifted steadily out of his scalp to his shoulders. It was diverting, seeing the man through her eyes.

And Elred was at his finest, self-satisfied and gloating. Elred had wanted the entire town to know that he had defended the safety and honor of his intended lady-love. Me. Even more important to the man was that I should know it. With little prompting, Stocker and I heard the entire slow, painstaking story twice, each minute detail carefully engraved on Elred's usually inert brain.

He relished telling the story and, for emphasis, spit long streams of tobacco juice out the window on the pathway beside the bait shop. It was probably the first time in years he had squandered his brain for anything other than remembering the locations of the best fishing holes, so there was plenty of room for specifics and particulars.

Sitting in a lawn chair, my feet propped up on the bait-shop counter-top, I listened to the story with mixed reactions. Uncertain emotions. I didn't know what to feel anymore. What to think. Bonnibelle was dead. I was Carin Colleen. I didn't belong here in Khoury. Never had.

Elred gave a graphic and vivid description of the man who had wanted to find me, his car, and the route he took while trying to question the town's people. He remembered every overheard question, every casual query.

Not that Miles had managed to complete many of his questions with an outraged Elred on his tail. And it was Miles. There was no doubt.

'So. Basically, this man wanted to know where Bonnie was, how long she had lived here, who her parents were, who the Sarvaunts were, and how to contact Bonnie,' Stocker said, shifting to the side to avoid a stream of brown juice.

Elred opened a bag of Red Man, uncrinkling the paper with slow steady movements. He was staring at the bulges in Stocker's shirt. All three.

"At about covers it. You a cop?'

'No. I'm not a cop.'

'You a private detective?'

'Yes. I am. I—'

"At other one was a private detective too, I reckon.'

Stocker paused. Her face intent, icy eyes narrowed. 'What other one?'

'The other man what come looking for Bonnie. Two days after I run off the first one.'

The tingling was back, but different this time. Now it was hot anticipation. Stocker's eyes narrowed further, like a snake's eyes when he spots a fat, juicy frog.

'Why do you say that? That he must have been an investigator?'

'Wore a gun.' Elred spit the well-chewed glob of tobacco into a foul, brown-stained, Styrofoam cup, rinsed his mouth with Mello Yellow and packed in a fresh pinch, maneuvering the soft, flavored leaves around inside his mouth with two dirty fingertips. Stocker waited. 'Drove a plain brown Dodge with one of them cellular phones, not a reg'lar police radio. Dressed better 'n a cop. But acted like one, know what I mean?'

'Could you describe him?'

'Better 'n that. I got a picture.' He pronounced it pick-chure as if it were two words. Without prompting, Elred leaned over, picked up a small stack of Polaroids behind the bait-counter, and handed them to Stocker. They were greasy, and the once-white boarders were spotted with oily fingerprints, as if Elred had studied them for hours.

'I'd a got a picture of the first one too if I'd a had a camera. Paid a t'ur'st to take these. Skinned his fish for free. Seven a the littlest catfish you ever did see. Mostly bone. Waste a time to cook.' Elred stuck a finger back into his mouth and poked at the tobacco.

'What did he want?'

'Same's the first one. But he weren't right.'

'What do you mean, he wasn't right?' Stocker asked, her eyes on a shot of the man's car. The license plate was plainly visible.

'First man, he was just plain folks, nosy and all. But 'at second one, he was mean. Cold. Tried to give me money to take him to the Sarvaunt Place.'

'Tried to?' I asked.

'Ain't never turned down no guide job before. But this un,' he touched a damp finger to the man's face on one of the photos, 'this un was bad.'

'How do you know?' Stocker persisted.

Elred crossed his arms and stared harder at Stocker's shirt front, his eyes higher than the gun bulge at her waist. 'I seen all kinds come through here. Them Yankee bizness men wantin' fish. Them oil men wanting oil. Trappers. Moonshiners. Drug traffickers. Even one time a killer. I knowed it when he come back with blood on his clothes and the boat windshield shot out and his fishin' partner gone. I know what to look for in a man's eyes. And this un was a bad un.'

'And you didn't take him to see Bonnie's Tee Dom and Tante Ilene?'

'Nope. Told him they'd moved. All three. Sent him to Baton Rouge, to 150 State Street.'

'What's there? At 150 State Street?'

'Don't know. May not even be a State Street. Ain't never been to Baton Rouge.' Elred grinned, exposing dark brown teeth in puffy red gums. He thought it was clever, sending the man off to chase his tail. Perhaps it was. 'He ain't come back.'

'May we have these?' Stocker asked, tapping the greasy photos with her finger.

Elred held out his hand for them, paged through them and removed one. It was a shot of the rear of the brown Dodge and the man himself, walking toward the driver's side. 'I'll keep this un. For the sheriff. Just in case he comes back.'

The look in Elred's eyes was pure mean, as if he had figured out a way to stop the man from looking for me. Elred had worked for some unsavory types off and on over the years. Rumors of smuggling, everything from moonshine to drugs to illegal aliens, had followed him for years. I could envision Elred planting some sort of contraband on the man or his car, then high-tailing it to the nearest phone. Elred D. McArdle, concerned citizen.

He spat a long stream of brown, shooting squarely out the window onto the pathway outside. Elred was mean, but he had a great aim.

'Is Tee Dom's boat still here, Elred? I want to go to the shanty.' The words surprised me. I had wanted to get away from the shanty for as long as I could remember, hating the smells, the mold, the nutria and the water roaches with a passion. The only thing good about the shanty had been its location, so close to all the dark themes in my art.

But my mother had bought the shanty. It was mine. Whose name was on the deed, I wondered? Who had paid taxes on the land all these years?

'Your uncle left it for you. Said the boat's yours.' Another surprise. I nodded. 'Got gas in it?'

'Yup.'

I dropped my feet from the counter-top to the floor and stood. 'Thanks, Elred.' Stocker's boots followed me to the door. I shoved my sunglasses onto the bridge of my nose to protect both my eyes and my privacy.

'I'll come back to LaRoque Parish on Monday and see what the records say about this property you own,' Stocker said, her voice carefully toneless. I nodded again and headed for the dock.

The johnboat was just as I had left it. Old and worn and difficult to crank. It spluttered to life on the third pull.

I fought the desire to cry, most all the way to the shanty, my ragged breathing hidden beneath the roar of the small motor. Stocker alternately studied the landscape and my face, but she didn't try to talk over the noise.

It seemed a longer trip than usual, the scenery changing too slowly from developed property, to abandoned property, to wild, untouched nature, trees bending over black water as if paying homage to the bayous. We motored past the widely scattered homes, the Holy Ghost Church of the Madonna with Father Alcede fishing lazily from the dock. He lifted a hand as we sped past. And then, suddenly, we were turning up the Bayou Negre and the tears I thought I had conquered threatened again.

The shutters were locked over the windows and the heavy wooden front door was closed. The door was never closed, except twice a year when we opened it up for the first time come spring and closed it up in the fall. It looked strange, like a coffin sealed too soon, before the grieving could even begin.

I slowed the johnboat to a crawl, docked it with scarcely a bump, and tied up. Common things. Ordinary things. Bitter, solitary things. I had a key to the door, although I had never used it. And although the lock worked well, the door had swollen shut with recent rains. Once before it had done the same thing, and Tee Dom and I had put our shoulders against the wood and shoved. Together.

I touched the wood of the door, feeling strangely disconnected. A long time ago the door had been painted a dark green; traces of the faded paint were still faintly visible in the grain of wood. Stocker put her shoulder where Tee Dom's had once been and we shoved. The door opened with a groan and shriek of tortured wood. Heat, bottled for days, rolled out and over us like steamy waves.

Inside, we opened two shutters and the back door, so air could flow through, but it did little to cool the place. Stocker leaned a shoulder against the wall and waited for her eyes to adjust. I removed my sunglasses and moved slowly about in the gloom.

Every piece of furniture was in its place. The pie-safe. The long table and benches. The soft upholstered chair Tee Dom had claimed as his own. Tante Ilene's rocking chair. The cupboards. The humpbacked trunk that sat beneath the front window. The rugs, old braided things Tante Ilene had carried outside twice a week and beat with an oar, were rolled up in a corner, just the way we always left them when we closed up in the fall.

I touched Tee Dom's chair, feeling for the first time how worn the upholstery was. Ran my fingers along the arm of Tante Ilene's rocker. Sent it rocking slowly across the uneven floorboards, the soft thump sounding familiar and hollow. Empty.

As my eyes adjusted I saw that a few things were gone. The linens from the bed in their room. The blanket stand. The shotgun from its rack. Tee Dom's prize .30 gauge.

Only one thing had been added. A book sat squarely in the center of the long table. Its cover was worn, cloth over paper. Inexpensive when new, the pages were still amazingly intact now that it was old. Not made of cheap, modern, acidic paper that would disintegrate in a matter of years, its pages were only slightly yellowed. And covered from margin to margin in a tiny, neat script.

I paged through it slowly, noting the dates at the top of each page. A diary. With a feeling of suppressed excitement I turned to the front of the diary and smoothed down the first page. On the center of the page, in the neat scrawl, was a name.

Elizabeth Diane Sarvaunt.

My excitement faded. It wasn't my mother's diary. It wasn't DeVillier.

Without a word, I closed the diary and shut up the shanty, sealing out the light and trapping the heat. I handed the diary to Stocker, untied the johnboat and pushed into the faint current. The tears were gone now. Just as in the tiny unisex bathroom at the washerette. Faded away.

Bonnibelle Sarvaunt was dead. And Carin Colleen DeVillier was alone.

CHAPTER 10

The sun was a golden-yellow orb hanging on the tree tops by the time Stocker and I climbed into her 4 × 4 for the last time that evening. Perkins, who had stayed all day at the washerette with Eloise and shared her supper, was lazy and sated with round-bellied contentment. He stretched out on the seat beside me, yawned, scratched and burped with satisfied abandon. Just like Tee Dom used to do after a rare lazy day and a good meal.

I stroked Perkins' head and his small pointed ears, rubbed his too-tight stomach when he rolled over a bit and presented it to me. His hair was softer than usual, as if Eloise had groomed him. He licked my fingers as if to say, 'Wasn't today a wonderful day?' I didn't have the heart to refute him.

I stretched a bit myself and relaxed against the seat belt, allowing the wide straps to hold me in place. The radio was off, the silence in the cab hidden beneath the roar of the mud tires against the pavement. Earlier in the day, I hadn't noticed the tire sound, my mind too concerned with thoughts of home. Seeing Eloise. Eating Tante Ilene's cooking. Perhaps convincing her – finally – to tell me about my mother.

Now, none of those half-acknowledged dreams had taken place, my whole life, my very identity was changed by the things I had learned. Now that I noticed it, the tire sound was both too loud, and soothing at the same time.

We made it to Houma, gassed up the Chevy, picked up barbecue platters from a honkytonk, found a hotel and ate, sitting at the room's little table. We showered, taking turns in the minuscule bathroom, and got ready for bed. We lay in the light of the single lamp between the beds. And still we hadn't spoken.

Stocker read the Gideon's Bible and did paperwork on her bed. I lay in the center of mine, Elizabeth Diane Sarvaunt's diary at my side. Occasionally, I stroked its cover. Perkins slept on the pillow beside me, satiated with rich food, too much attention and adventure.

At 10 p.m. Stocker closed the Bible and turned off the light. We lay in the shadows, the hum of the room's air-conditioner filling the room with sound and cool air.

Finally Stocker spoke into the darkness.

'You really should read it, you know. She may be the only person in the world who knew your mother.'

'Yeah,' I said softly. There didn't seem to be anything else to say.

A long moment later Stocker spoke again, her words measured.

'The woman in the coffin in Petit Chenier was most likely Elizabeth Sarvaunt.'

I said nothing.

'That means your mother, whoever she is now, may very well still be alive.'

Those words were echoing in my mind when I woke the next morning at 4 a.m. The sky was still velvety dark when Perkins and I slipped from the room. The world was still slumbering, except for the all-nighters, the exhausted eighteen-wheelers making a fast run on diesel fumes and caffeine, the police and EMTs, city-workers and graveyard-shifters who kept the city safe and the state's economy running along.

Traffic whizzed by on the highway beyond the chain-link fence. A siren sounded somewhere. A cool wind blew in storm clouds that steadily erased the stars overhead. A front moving in, for once from the north instead of from the Gulf of Mexico or the hot Texas plains. Perkins sniffed the breeze, his little black nose twitching, ears at attention in the half-light of early dawn and the pools of artificial brightness cast by the hotel's security lights.

He did his business, marking several of the stunted, ornamental nandinas before he was finished. I hoped dog pee didn't kill plants. We took a second turn around the parking lot, this time moving faster as we both woke up, me lengthening my stride, Perkins cantering at my side. Warmed up and awake, we headed back, stopping at a coffee-machine tucked into a nook of the hotel walkway for two paper cups of a hot, but tasteless concoction. I sipped mine once, instantly burning my tongue as I turned the corner toward the room.

A form lunged toward me from the shadows. Blacker than the night.

It seemed to move slowly, as if the world had slowed down or as if the figure flew in, blown by a breeze. I had the instant impression of Count Dracula, his cape furled, sweeping in on a victim.

His body collided with mine, forcing the air out of my lungs, shoving me back against the rough brick. Cool steel instead of fangs, pressed into my neck beneath my jaw.

I reacted instantly, without thinking, throwing up my hands. Tossing the cups into his face.

He screamed, fell back, and was gone, his footsteps slapping the concrete walkway back along the blackness.

It was so fast. He was there one moment, gone the next.

I stood, my back against the brick side of the hotel, and remembered to breathe. Perkins was barking furiously, attacking the sidewalk where the man – Man? – had stood. There was a gun there, visible in the faint early dawn. The steel that had pressed against my neck. I stared at it a long moment, blinking.

And then I ran, Perkins jerked along behind. Our room was only two doors down. Too far. Forever away. I fell against it, banging my fist on the painted steel surface. The world moved again at its normal rate of speed. Unexpected, that strange shift of time. Even more unexpected was the intense need to vomit. The burning in the back of my throat.

Stocker jerked open the door, a gun in one hand, and pulled me inside, slamming it shut. I don't know what she understood from my babble, but she pushed me to the phone with one hand and a command to call the police, and re-opened the door. She stood there, protected behind the frame, the gun held in her hands, pointed to the ceiling beside her face. She studied the shadows a long moment before darting outside and returning with the gun my mugger had dropped. She held it by the tip of the barrel, away from her body.

Calmly, Stocker placed the gun on the bedside table and

relocked the door. She took the phone from my hands and straightened out the mess I had made with the police.

She was utterly unruffled, standing before me in a pair of silk pajamas, her feet bare on the industrial-weave carpet, her gun still in one hand. Talking to a police dispatch officer and giving our room number. She might have been holding a glass of wine talking to a pizza delivery man. So damn calm.

I giggled. It had a rough hysterical edge to it.

Perkins, his leash trailing behind, trotted the boundaries of the room, sniffing. Sticking his nose beneath the beds, into the suitcases, up onto chair cushions. Making sure our shelter was safe.

The need to vomit swelled and rose and suddenly I was face down in the hotel-room toilet, retching over and over. The sour liquid coated my teeth and burned the length of my throat like acid. Stocker put a cold towel on the back of my neck and, when I calmed, she half-carried me back to my unmade bed and tossed the thin covers over me.

The police arrived, two cars, lights flashing. My teeth started chattering. Stocker holstered her weapon and let the cops into the room. Hotel security followed the officers in, filling up the too-small space. Perkins jumped up on the bed, burrowing his head beneath my arm, his body twitching and warm on my lap.

I was shaking. Stocker covered me with another blanket, playing mother hen, now that her role as gun-toting guardian was no longer required.

As coherently as possible, I told my story, offering the gun and my burned hands as proof. As I threw the cups into the attacker's face, the coffee had sloshed back onto me; my hands and wrists were blistered a fiery red.

The officers asked a dozen questions, about the time, where I was standing, what I was doing outside. They asked me to recount exactly the way the attack happened. They conferred with the security guard and split up, the male officer going outside to search the grounds.

'Can you give us a description?' the female officer asked, although she was the only cop in the room. She was short and stocky with full black hair and soft features. A baby face on a power lifter's body.

I closed my eyes, forcing myself to remember the instant of time when the steel was pressed against my neck. He hadn't been a vampire. No Count Dracula out for a midnight snack before turning in. Just a man.

I was an artist. Anything I could see, I could remember, couldn't I?

In memory, the brick scraped though my T-shirt at my back. Perkins cowered against my ankles.

'The gun was under my right jawbone.' I touched the place on my neck. 'That means he was holding it in his left hand. He was two inches taller than me, the end of his nose coming to about here.' I indicated the bridge of my own nose, seeing it in my mind's eye. My artist's eye for detail.

The urge to vomit returned, and I pressed my mouth with my balled fist. Lips and fingers both trembled. I didn't know why I was so upset. It wasn't like I had been injured or anything . . . Yet, my body didn't respond to the logic.

'But his knees were bent a bit, so add maybe two more inches.'

I bit my lip, my eyes still closed. I wanted desperately to brush my teeth. To wake up from this ugly dream.

'He was dark-haired, average build. Had a mustache. A thin one. And acne scars on his cheeks. I couldn't tell his eye color, but maybe dark.'

I envisioned him as he ran, screaming. 'He was young. His voice broke as he screamed. Wore jeans with something light-colored on his . . . left buttock. Maybe a worn place or a tear. And a dark T-shirt. Sneakers. No hat.'

I opened my eyes to find Perkins' face in mine, his head cocked. 'Sorry, boy. I can't tell them how he smelled. All I could smell was the coffee.'

The officer was writing on a tablet, filling out a form. Standard bureaucratic procedure.

'Will you fingerprint the gun?' Stocker asking sensible questions.

'Yes, ma'am,' the officer said, not looking up.

'Because this may not have been a simple attempted mugging.'

The officer and I stared at Stocker. 'Why?' we both asked, the words a half-second apart.

I looked at her name-tag below her badge. Officer Tamporello. 'Cigar? Cigarette? Tamporellos?' I fought off the mindless giggle.

'Because. One of her bodyguards was killed in an apparent mugging a few days ago. But nothing was taken. Not even his gun.'

My eyes grew big as I put the attack on Cooter Bug together with the attack on me. I pulled the blanket tighter, enclosing Perkins and me within its comforting folds. He settled more securely on my lap and sighed, a big lusty doggie sigh from his small mouth. I stroked him, finding comfort in the action. Stocker was still talking, telling the officer specifics about the killing.

'. . . you might want to talk to New Orleans homicide about this guy, if you're able to ID him. Find out if he was in New Orleans the night her bodyguard was killed.'

'Give me a minute. My partner ought to hear this.'

Tamporello pulled a radio hanging on her black leather belt and called her partner back in. Together they listened again to Stocker's story, then they called in an investigator. While we waited, I brushed my teeth and changed into clean clothes so the officers could have my coffee-stained ones. While I dressed, Stocker conferred softly with Tamporello, their voices too low to hear.

Clean clothes seemed to help, and my shaking slowed. I found I could breathe normally. I thought with longing of the wasted coffee. Thank God it had been so hot.

The rest of the day passed in a whirl of uniformed officers, questions, and calls to the New Orleans PD. The gun dropped by my assailant was taken into custody, along with the coffee cups, my clothes, and what must have been a two-inch stack of paperwork.

It wasn't likely that the man who attacked me was the same one who killed Cooter Bug. But what if . . . Stocker's words. What if.

The officers ran the tag numbers on Miles's car and the car belonging to the man Elred sent to Baton Rouge. Miles's tags came back registered to Mousseau Collections, Inc. The brown Dodge was registered to Aucoin Investigations, a one-man PI outfit in Remy, a small town in St James Parish. He didn't answer when the police tried his number, and no one answered the knock when the local police paid him a visit.

Anthony Aucoin had an answering machine. His voice was deep and resonant, demanding that the caller leave a message. Stocker called it twice, allowing me to hear the voice. It was no more familiar than his face had been in the photographs.

I watched Stocker's blue eyes shine as the day progressed. She was working on a fascinating puzzle with lots of twists and turns and sharp, disconnected angles. She was having fun. I needed a vacation.

And I needed her to find Tante Ilene and Tee Dom. The urgency I felt for my aunt and uncle was surprising. After all, they weren't my real family. They had kept me in Khoury, isolated from the rest of the world, living in near-poverty conditions. But safe, whispered some small rational part of my brain. I had always been safe.

So, during the course of the day, I found time to add Tante Ilene and Tee Dom to the list of people I wanted Stocker to find. She didn't seem surprised, and I think it secretly pleased her to have a bigger puzzle to solve.

I felt better after I had her promise to look for them. Calmer. Able to sit and listen to Stocker and the police talk about my life as if it were some stranger they were discussing. Perhaps the stranger I had become.

We got back to New Orleans to find MacAloon waiting in front of my apartment and the streets filled with revelers. It was one of New Orleans's many festivals, with street musicians on every corner and booths serving food, beer and col' drinks. MacAloon looked worried as we drove up to the curb and parked. He was walking stiffly back and forth in front of Cee Cee's store, watching the celebrants with suspicious eyes. Instead of 'Hello, how was the trip?' his first words were, 'Bonnie's place has been ransacked.'

'My paintings!' I was out of the truck and running, taking the stairs two at a time, Perkins at my feet. But the door was locked, showing no signs of being forced. MacAloon and Stocker climbed more slowly, their heads together, voices low, as I fumbled for keys and pushed open the heavy door.

'They got in through the back,' MacAloon said. The two

followed me though the door and into the apartments. 'Took out the air-conditioner and crawled through. Doesn't look like a typical burglary, though. They left the TV and the radio.' The place was a shambles, with my clothes, magazines, and art supplies scattered across the floor. The linens had been stripped from the bed. The kitchen looked like a post-hurricane scene, with cans tossed from the cabinets and dishes on the floor. Surprisingly nothing was broken. But it was a mess.

'I called the police. You just missed them. They want you to make a list of anything stolen and give it to this guy.' MacAloon gave me a card with an officer's name on the front in black letters. I tucked it into my back pocket. I had a feeling nothing was taken. I had a feeling I knew what they were looking for. My little black box, which was still sitting on the floorboards of Stocker's truck.

The mystery of my identity. The mystery of my mother and the people from whom she had hidden me all these years. That was what they were looking for. The answers in the little black box. Cold chills lifted the fine hairs on the back of my neck.

'Where are you? Where are you hiding?' I wanted to ask. For I was certain now that she was alive. Though I couldn't have explained my certainty, I was sure that someone had found me. That I was in danger. The same danger from which my mother had tried to protect me for so many years. And I wondered if my actions had somehow placed her in danger as well.

In the front room, the studio, my paintings were fine. Untouched, dull and lifeless in the bright afternoon sun. Amateur work. I closed my eyes. I hated people to see my work by sunlight.

'Don't look at the paintings yet.' Okay. Maybe it was vain in light of all the horror of the last forty-eight hours, but I wanted my art seen only in its proper milieu.

Stepping over the things on the floor, I opened the window to the balcony and stepped out, then pulled the shutters closed and latched them. I repeated the process at the other two windows, casting the front part of the apartment into shadow. Closing the three doors that separated the front half of the apartment from the back completed the effect. It wasn't the same thing as full night and candlelight, but it was enough to begin the process. My palms were sweating. Foolish, but after all, it was my art.

'Okay. Now.'

But Stocker and MacAloon were already moving from easel to easel slowly.

'Shit.' Stocker stared at the scene of the chenier behind the shanty, surrounded on three sides by black water. I had painted it though my bedroom window on a hot mosquito-ridden night. It was mystical and soft, moving with shadow and odd twists of perspective. The angle of looking into a tree from two-thirds up almost made you dizzy. It glittered as you stared down through the limbs at the still water, clear night sky and sickle moon caught in its branches, reflected from the bayou. 'Shit,' she said again, but the expletive was intended as a complement.

I wiped my palms down my thighs.

'And that artist you work for hasn't seen these?' Stocker asked.

'No.' Whispered.

'My ex-mother-in-law would have a fit if she saw this one. She fancies herself not only a collector but a – what do you call it? – a person who discovers and subsidizes new artists. Anyway, she would really love this one.'

'A patron.'

'Yeah. Patron.' Stocker moved and viewed the canvas from another angle. Almost to herself she added, 'I love this one.'

I opened one of the sets of shutters, flooding the canvas with sunlight.

'Jeez. You killed it.'

I laughed, finding it interesting that someone else used the living/dead analogy for my work. Because that's the way I always saw it. In the dark they were alive, breathing. In the light, they died, became empty.

'Where do you show?' MacAloon asked.

'Downstairs. In Cee Cee Gaudet's shop. Well, I will show there as soon as the lighting is worked out.' I vaguely remembered Cee Cee promising to set up a back corner in the dark for my work, and hoped I wasn't claiming something not true. Something half-remembered through an alcohol-enhanced haze.

'You should make sure your employer sees these. Invite him over to dinner or something.'

It wasn't anything I hadn't considered before. Sneaky. But perhaps effective. I opened the rest of the shutters, killing the remaining paintings and exposing the wreckage of the apartment.

Stocker checked her watch. 'I hate to leave you with this mess, but I didn't make arrangements to have the horses fed tonight.'

'Go on. I'll get it all cleaned up.' Charitable words. But inside I was appalled at the thought of cleaning such a mess, and horrified at the thought of being alone.

'I'll stay and make sure the air-conditioner is securely in place. A few half-inch screws should do the trick,' MacAloon said.

I took a deep breath, feeling relieved. And that was even more foolish, because all I had was MacAloon's word that he had my best interests at heart. After all, it wasn't like I had paid him to protect me.

The same thought must have occurred to Stocker. She was halfway to the door, her boots clomping across the wooden floor, when she stopped and turned. The sunlight caught in her blonde braid. 'MacAloon, who's the guy paying you to take care of Bonnie? You ever find out?'

'Nope. But I got a cashier's check in the mail yesterday and a typed set of instructions.' He looked up at Stocker and grinned. 'It's in my glove compartment in case you're worried.' He tossed her a set of keys that she caught one-handed. 'Accommodate your suspicions, ma'am. Then toss my keys up to the balcony. I have strict orders not to let anyone near her. And I've hired Josh Campos to pull the night shift.'

'Campos. Indian guy? Ponytail? The one who took a bullet for that judge, what was her name? Cortinez?'

'One and the same.'

'I'll toss up the keys.' She turned partway for the door and paused, turned back. 'And I'll give Campos a call. Just to verify his employment.'

'Wise move.'

MacAloon's eyes were glinting blue with laughter by the end of the exchange. He looked at me, standing in the glare of the setting sun, my shadow stripping the floor. 'Stocker's a good PI. Suspicious of everybody.'

I nodded, waiting. I was growing distrustful myself, it seemed.

'Hey, Bonnie.' The voice was flat, muted by the French windows. I opened one and walked out. Stocker tossed the set of keys up to me. I missed the catch in the glare and they landed at my feet. 'He's okay. Tell him about Aucoin Investigations and Mousseau Collections and the attack on you this morning. I'll see you later. Soon as I have something to tell you.'

'Thanks, Stocker.' Perkins pranced out to the balcony and stood with me, his tail wagging slightly.

'You forgot your bag,' she yelled.

I saw her unzip the battered case I had packed for travel, slide the diary and little black box inside and zip it closed. One-handed, she levered herself up, and jumped into the back of the dual-wheel truck. Winding up like a pitcher in a major league game, she tossed the bag up to me. This, I caught. And then she was gone.

It was a long night, once MacAloon left. Long and lonely.

I was utterly dependent on Perkins for company, while outside my balcony windows, it was celebration and party time. And then, later, the sounds of successful entrepreneurs closing up for the day. Human voices, human sounds.

Inside, I cleaned up my apartment, which wasn't as bad as it had looked. The trespassers weren't vicious, only thorough. The magazines were still in order, my clothes not torn, even my mattress was not slit open like the bad guys always do in the movies. In three hours it was dark outside and silent. And my mess was cleaned up. Perkins, unimpressed with the disarray, spent the hours chewing on a calf-hoof, a gift from Stocker I had found in my duffel beside the diary.

Standing in one of the openings between the bedroom and the studio, I turned slowly around, checking the apartment for anything I might have missed. The floor was clear again. The kitchen clean. And I was hungry.

I bathed quickly, brushed my hair, and clipped Perkins to the leash. In the mirrored screen at the door we made an unlikely duo. Me in a shapeless, calf-length dress, my hair in fashionable disarray, my eyes dark and bruised-looking. Perkins – an effete little toy – looked snobbish and wimpy. Perfect victims.

I smeared on lipstick, tossed my bag over my shoulder. It was heavy and chunky, a 1960s style with fringe and gaudy paintings on the leather, weighed down by my .38. Okay. Not exactly a victim. Not anymore. Not ever again.

We walked into the night, the sissy little dog and I. One hand on his leash, one on the gun in my pocketbook. I wouldn't be able to pull it and shoot, but that wouldn't stop me from firing. So what if I ruined a perfectly good bag? I locked the apartment door behind us.

As we descended the stairs, there was movement in the shadows across the street. A man emerged, faintly visible. Tall. White T-shirt and jeans. Western boots. Miles? No, not Miles. Just a man in boots. Half the state wears western boots. It was the south, after all. He had black hair pulled back into a ponytail. Stocker's description of Josh Campos.

But she never mentioned gorgeous. He had a long face with hollowed cheeks, black eyes, full lips, and a lean, whip-cord body. A gun bulged out slightly at his waist. I descended to street level, almost awed.

I had thought Tito was beautiful. And he was, in a soft, untested way. Young. That was Tito. Juvenile. Adolescent. Green.

Not this man.

I crossed the street, holding my dog and my gun. Watching the way he moved as I approached. He was alert, studying the street. Muscles taut. There was nothing passive about him, yet he didn't appear to be overtly aggressive. He was composed, collected and observant. I realized I was staring, and had no idea what to say to my new bodyguard. I opened my mouth hoping something intelligent would emerge.

'I'm hungry and lonely and I want supper.' *Oh, how awful. Why not just say 'I'm a virgin. Would you like to correct the situation?'* I plunged on, my mouth working independently of my brain. 'And I'm buying. You have any idea what's open?' That was better. I think. I took a deep breath.

Josh grinned, exposing a wide expanse of teeth, whiter than white. 'Yes, ma'am. Houston's on St Charles.'

I nodded once, glad the light was behind me so he couldn't

see my blush. 'You driving or am I? I have to warn you, my van is a pile of rust held together with twine, paper-clips, and bubble gum.'

'In that case, I'm driving. But don't you even want to ask my name? It's normal under these circumstances, I believe.'

His mouth quirked up on the right. My stomach took a dive, and I had trouble thinking of a reply. I surprised myself when I answered, 'Not really. I don't think these are normal circumstances, Josh. And frankly I'm too hungry to care.'

He blinked once. He had incredibly long lashes. 'Well, you may have a point, Bonnie. Let's go eat.'

He took my arm, the one holding the gun. I figured I was safe with Josh Campos, so I released the grip and walked along beside him.

'How did you know who I was?' A casual question. Amused. I looked up at him. Up. He had to be six foot four in his boots. Up was a fairly novel experience for me, the average-sized bayou-dweller being my size or smaller. A smile hovered on his lips. His eyes moved back and forth across the street.

I realized he held my elbow not lovingly, but firmly, as if he might at any moment shove me behind him, to the ground, and pull his weapon.

'Huh?'

'How did you know who I was?' More amusement. He flicked his eyes my way and back to the street. Left. Right. Glance into the windows across the way.

I felt gauche and naïve and terribly inexperienced. I tried to think of Josh as a seventy-year-old tutor with liver spots on his bald head, hoping it would settle my thoughts and let me speak freely. It didn't work. The mental picture just made me want to smile. 'MacAloon told me.'

'Ah.'

A block from my apartment was a sleek, classic sports car. A 1965 Corvette, dark blue with polished chrome. Josh led me around to the passenger side, opened the door and eased me in. If Josh Campos was other than he seemed, then I was putting myself in danger.

Smart move, Waldo. The words thrummed in my head, unheard for three years. Dr Tammany Long, half-stoned, half-drunk, and completely rational, berating me for a stupid move, putting my queen in danger by his knight, or my king at risk by his bishop, some three plays down the road. Smart move, Waldo.

But Josh was sliding into the driver's seat and gunning the motor. He pulled away from the curb, his eyes flicking into the rear-view mirror, into the street ahead and to me. My breath was a bit fast, my pulse fluttering.

'Nice car.' Scintillating conversation.

'Nineteen sixty-five Fastback,' he said, companionably. 'She has four hundred twenty-five horsepower, close-ratio four-speed transmission, front louvers, air scoops, knock-off wheels, and a three hundred ninety-six big block engine.' He rattled off the numbers with ease and precision, almost as if he expected me to be interested. 'Her top speed is one thirty-eight.'

'Oh. Right.' My impression of Josh Campos did a nose-dive. The guy was car crazy. All I knew about cars was how to turn on the ignition and how to drive to the nearest repair shop when anything went wrong. And that was all I wanted to know. However, hearing the description of the car seemed to settle me somehow. I took a deep breath – one that actually reached my lungs, this time – and relaxed back against the seat.

'Not that I'm a car nut or anything.'

'Uh huh,' I said, smoothing my wrinkled skirt. 'Just like if I described my paintings by size, medium, and content, tossed out a couple hundred fancy, arty words and stroked my canvas like you're stroking the steering wheel, I wouldn't be an art nut.'

That was better. My mouth and brain were back on speaking terms again. I just wished I had taken a bit of time with my appearance. He might be a car nut, but he was nice looking. Devastating, actually. And men who fit that description were a rarity in my life.

Josh laughed. 'Point taken. I love my car. It saved my life a year ago. What can you expect?'

He pulled straight down Royal and suddenly we were on Lee Circle on St Charles Avenue. The acceleration pressed me back into my seat as Josh put on a CD. It was something old, turned down low. I thought it might have been Carol King, singing a seventies hit. Perkins, usually so protective, was curled around my feet, staring adoringly into Josh's face.

I wanted to ask him how a car saved his life, but the thought escaped me, lost in hunger pangs. Houston's neon sign was suddenly in front of the car, then it swept past and we were parked.

'What about the dog?' he asked, glancing down at Perkins.

'He won't piddle in your precious car,' I said with a half-smile. 'He'll wait.'

Josh laughed, a deep baritone, cut his eyes at me and got out. It was a nice laugh and my heart did a little dance. I had heard of people's hearts doing that in the books I read, but thought the writers were speaking metaphorically. I was thankful for the car's dark interior as a flush heated my face.

When he reached my door, I defended Perkins, 'Besides. He may look like a stuffed toy, but Perkins barked and growled the night Cooter Bug, your predecessor, died. He probably saw the murderer.' I climbed out of the car, glad I had at least worn a dress. 'Stay, Perkins.'

I glanced up at the chiseled profile of Josh Campos and tried for a bit of levity. 'Guard the car, boy. Guard. We don't want a broken-hearted bodyguard watching over us.'

Perkins tilted his head as if he thought I had lost my marbles. Josh laughed and bent down into my face. 'I said, point taken! I'll admit I love the car.'

I placed his accent. Texas. Slow and drawling.

'And I wasn't insulting your pretty little dog. I'm sure he's perfectly well behaved. And a fierce guard dog too, of course.'

I was being teased. An unfamiliar circumstance for me. I laughed and my blush spread just as my stomach rumbled with hunger. Embarrassed, I strode ahead of my bodyguard into the restaurant, hoping he hadn't heard.

Inside, Houston's was dark and noisy and smelled heavenly of blackened meat and seared onions and chili. There was no waiting, which Josh said was rare, and the service was fast. One waiter took our order, a second brought us drinks, a third brought the appetizer and a fourth the meal. Fast. Mouth-watering delicious beefburgers with hot, thick chili and my first cola since I left home. A hundred times better than typical fast food. A gastronomic delight. And food in my system helped to diminish the case of nerves I had developed when I first saw Josh Campos. It was odd how my body had reacted, when my mind had not been interested at all . . .

Surprisingly, my thoughts turned to Taber Rhame. The artist would love Houston's. I could bring him here some day when I didn't want to cook.

I remembered the nude Rhame had sketched of me. I had found it on my bedside table where I'd left it, untouched by the vandal. The snake and rose tattoo climbed my left buttock and up my back, the bloom below my right shoulder blade, the snake's tail wrapped around my left thigh. Very fanciful nude. The thought of the portrait heated my face again. I owed Rhame a meal for the portrait.

We managed to carry on a conversation throughout the meal, Josh talking about cars, me listening. I remembered my comment to Perkins about being willing to exchange him for a tall, dark, and handsome. It seemed the kindly genie who watched over me had heard and delivered. Too bad I hadn't added compatible to my list of prerequisites.

After consuming massive quantities of red meat, carbohydrates and fats, I sat back, totally unrepentant and satisfied, sipping my Coke, and thinking not at all. With Josh, it wasn't necessary.

We skipped dessert and drove home, little to say and less in common. My social skills with drop-dead-gorgeous car jocks left a lot to be desired. I wondered if I ought to be upset about that defect in my education.

Perkins made the only sounds on the ride home, eating scraps out of a piece of tinfoil at my feet. I was careful to protect the carpeting.

Josh checked out the apartment when we got back, pronounced it safe and looked like he'd be willing to protect my body from close proximity. Blushing, I shooed him out the door much like I'd shoo out a pesky housefly and relaxed against the door jamb.

For the first time all evening, my face cooled. Josh might be a car jock, and of no interest to me intellectually, but he did strange things to the rest of me. I sighed and smiled down at Perkins.

The little dog curled up on his pillow in the middle of my bed, his coat flame-bright against the two-tone white of the fabric. Canine contentment was clear on his furry face. His attention was riveted on his front paws, which he was cleaning with his tongue.

Changing into my long T-shirt, I opened the shutters and turned out the lights. By the flame of a single candle, I painted.

The impact of all the emotional reversals in my life – the attack, the ransacking of my apartment, the disappearance of Tante Ilene and Tee Dom, and my reactions to Josh – should have hit me tonight. Should have swamped over me like an emotional storm surge, flooding me with uncontrolled and chaotic feelings. And perhaps that all happened as I painted. Perhaps all the shock, all the anger, all the fear and disappointment did rush through me. If so, it was transmuted by my art. Mutated by the scent of oils and the hypnotic movement of the brush on canvas. Commuted from something awful into something good by the magic of the bayou I painted.

By 4 a.m. all thoughts of Josh Campos and my lacking social skills were washed from my mind. All the worries and fears sluiced away. I had completed every last one of my existing canvases, including the newest of Perkins, and had them all ready to be displayed in La Demoiselle Verte. Of course they'd need to be framed . . .

Exhausted, surrounded by the smell of onions and garlic from my meal, and paint thinner from the studio, I fell into bed.

CHAPTER 11

I woke early to the sound of rain sliding down my windows and gurgling in the gutters. I loved late-summer rains. In Louisiana, where there was a whole season of late summer, with its long, sweltering days and heavy pollution, it was often difficult to force one's lungs to inhale the air. Except when it rained. Then there were dark skies, cool breezes, and the air smelled so clean and fresh. As if you were really supposed to breathe it into your lungs after all.

Perkins, sensing I was awake, stretched, yawned, shook himself and climbed from his pillow to stare sleepily into my face.

'You need to go out?'

He wagged his tail slightly.

'Okay. Let's go, dog.' I levered myself out of bed and walked to the door. Perkins wasn't crazy about going out into the rain, so I pushed him with my foot, thinking of it as encouragement rather than animal cruelty. When he bounded back up the stairs, five minutes later, bedraggled and sopping, I was waiting with a towel.

Quick as greased lighting, as Tee Dom would have said, Perkins evaded my arms and the drying cloth to leap onto the bed and shake the rain off. Even in the dark I could see droplets spread throughout the room. Then, to complete his toilet, Perkins burrowed beneath my pillow. Mine. Not his. In fact, his pillow was totally dry. He peered at me from beneath my pillow, his black eyes dancing, his mouth open in a big doggie grin.

'Got me back, did ya? Well, good. You can stay home today as punishment. Looks like I have laundry to do anyway.' I dressed in jeans, T-shirt, oversized big-shirt, sneakers, and my yellow rain slicker. The loud snaps of its ancient metal clips brought back memories of Tee Dom and rainy days on the bayou.

I remembered the day the eight-foot gator surprised one of Tante Ilene's chickens. The gator sat right on shore in a pouring rain finishing his meal, instead of pulling the pullet beneath the water in typical alligator fashion. There were white feathers scattered all over the muddy bank. He was a very self-satisfied gator till Tee Dom blew his brains out with a shotgun. We had gator steaks and gator sausage for weeks afterward, storing the excess meat in Mishu Pilchard's freezer. No one turned Tee Dom over to the state boys for poaching. Bayou indigens looked out for one another.

The dog, staring back at me from the bed, had eyes like that gator. I grinned back at the dog. 'Good thing for you I'm not Tee Dom. To him the only good dog is a dead dog.'

I stripped off the wet, dog-scented sheets, gathered all the bath towels and dish rags, and stuffed everything into the duffel bag I still used for dirty clothes. It was time to find out if Cee Cee's cleaners were as good as she claimed. They'd had my sour dress (the one transported from the bayou in my old duffel) and the rain-damaged navy dress for days. If the dresses could be salvaged, they should be ready by now.

Perkins was peeved at being left behind, sitting on his pillow on the mattress cover, sulking. 'Don' you look at me in dat tone of voice,' I said, quoting Tee Dom again. Perkins tilted his head. 'You make dumb mis-take in de bayou, yo' die. Yo' punishmen', sit 'ere all day, yes.'

I grinned at the dog, pulled the slicker hood over my ponytail and stepped into the rain, locking the door behind me. It was barely light, the downpour a steady drumming on my hood. The duffel wasn't waterproof, and just like the last time I took Eloise my dirty clothes, this batch of laundry would be soaked.

Waggling my fingers at Josh, I trudged through the rain for the parking lot and Elred's van.

'Need a lift?' It was Josh, the living embodiment of the American adolescent girl's dream. Perfect face, spectacular hard body, classic 'Vette. Everything to turn a girl's head.

'No, thanks. I'm going to run some errands. Be back in a couple of hours,' I shouted over the deluge. Turning the corner, I noted

Josh hot-footing it for his car. By the time I pulled Elred's old van out of the parking lot, Josh was idling at the curb, a sour look on his face. I didn't know if his expression was one of displeasure at getting his car seat wet, or disgust at the vision of Elred's van. Both, maybe.

Josh and his 'Vette followed in Elred's fumes, exhaust pouring from the muffler connection, as I made the trip to the cleaners. Jones Specialty Cleaners lived up to its reputation; the dress I pulled back through the drive-up window was the same dress I had bought originally. Crisp, sharp, the navy linen unfaded.

I left them the rest of my clothes and tooled on down to Midas for a new muffler. I was first in line, and provided the mechanic with his first laugh of the day. I could hear him chuckling the whole time I waited for the replacement, and once heard him say, 'Hey, Charlie, look at this. The passenger seat is held in place with a two-by-four and wire. You can see right up into the cab!' Charlie's reply was unintelligible, but I determined never to ride as a passenger in Elred's van.

I found my photographs of the egret rookery beside the driver's seat, wedged between the rusty seat-support and the side wall. While I waited, I went through the shots and mentally composed the triptych Claude Michau had mentioned for the securities firm. It wasn't a promise I would let him forget. When the firm commissioned work for the main room, I intended to be among the finalists.

The shots of the egrets were stunning, especially the ones with the sun sitting on the bayou, a huge vermillion ball bleeding into the scarlet water, with rose-tinted birds settling for the night. Several were suitable for framing, and would look great on the wall between the kitchen and bath.

Café du Monde was too far away to satisfy my craving for coffee, so I stopped in at La Pomme Verte for apple turnovers and a cup of dark-roast Community coffee. La Pomme Verte – the Sour Apple – specialized in everything to do with apples. Apple doughnuts, apple croissants, apple pie, apple tea, apple cider, apple juice, apple wine, even crisp apples with caramel sauce for dunking. I bought a supply of pastries to take to Rhame's and ate the sticky turnover as I drove. Marvelous breakfast.

The art-supply store on Market Street was open at seven and I bought two new brushes, some thinner, and asked about framing prices. They sold most frames by the foot, the method making it easy for me to guesstimate my expenses. I chose a simple black wood frame, and made an appointment with the framer to bring back my works. There were an awful lot of them and it made sense to deal directly with the craftsman himself.

Josh was still in attendance, waiting in his car, the windows steamed up. Taking pity on the guy, I took him one of Rhame's pastries, a rich confection with almonds and glaze on top, and slid it through the window to him.

He took one look at it and curled up his nose. 'No, thanks, lady. You got any idea about the sugar and fat content of this stuff? It's murder on muscles and skin tone and even your hair.'

The anger that flushed through me was as unexpected as it was combative. 'That's the purpose, you dweeb,' I said before I could stop myself. 'It's not supposed to be good for you. It's supposed to be a treat.' I pulled the pastry back and marched through the rain back to Elred's van.

I had no idea why the guy's remarks had made me so mad, but I was. Really, really mad. Fat and sugar content were not good reasons to turn down a great pastry.

Elred's van roared to life and I pulled out into the dreary world. Out of spite, I ate Josh's pastry too. It was delicious.

After my errands, I parked in the five-dollar-a-day lot again and paid my bill. I really needed to find cheaper long-term parking. Maybe Claude Michau would know of one. I'd have to ask when I stopped in later in the day.

Josh pulled in next to the curb and watched me climb the stairs. I was a bit ashamed of my outburst, but I didn't go over and apologize. I didn't know why he had such a strong effect on me. But I did know that I was still angry.

Rhame was up, his door unlocked, a note thumb-tacked to the center at eye-level. Standing in the rain, I read the list of 'to do's' for the day before pushing my way inside.

The apartment was cold, the dreary cold of a winter rain, and dark as the inside of a storm cloud. The air-conditioner was going full blast, chilling the air even further. I turned the thermostat up and switched on the lights, giving the kitchen the artificial, barren brilliance of a carnival after the crowd goes home.

The scent of coffee perking soon enlivened the apartment and I put together a tray of pastries and a vacuum-thermos cup I discovered on a shelf above the sink. Unironed linen napkins made of rough plaid fabric enhanced the ensemble, one dampened so excess sugar wouldn't make fingers too gummy to hold instruments. I held the thermos cup beneath the hot tap to warm it, dried it with a towel and filled it to the brim with coffee. The sugar and creamer, and a single, small, silver spoon completed the arrangement. It was a perfect vignette.

Silently, I carried the tray into the front room, past the leather couch and into the room beyond. I hadn't seen the studio on my previous visits. I had seen little beyond the kitchen.

The studio was stark white walls and industrial lighting, natural wood floors and drop sheets, tall windows and shutters thrown open to the rain. And Taber Rhame, wearing jeans and nothing else, stood in the center of empty space, his bare toes splayed on the floorboards, his bare chest sheened with a light sweat. An easel – a baroque monstrosity with curlicues and gilt and mother-of-pearl insets – held a larger-than-life canvas. A dark, despondent work that seemed to suck the life out of the room the way light seemed to suck the life from my art.

My tray had legs. Careful to avoid scattering my culinary masterpiece onto the floor, I lowered the legs, secured them and stepped away. Before slipping out of the room, I opened the thermos cup so the scent of coffee could mingle with the scent of rain and the faint hint of acrylic paint.

Rhame hadn't noticed me. He was focused too deeply on the canvas before him, his face like carved stone, his eyes blazing like bright flames in the harsh setting. His gray eyes were dark and the skin beneath hollowed and bruised. It looked as if he hadn't moved away from the canvas in hours. Perhaps days.

In the living room, stacked beside the leather couch, were unopened packing boxes. Some were from Italy, others from Mexico. A few were from here in the city. Following my list of 'to do's', I opened the boxes, compared the contents to the packing slips, checked them off from the master list I found on the kitchen table. The empty boxes went beside the back door leading to the spiral stair.

Locating Taber Rhame's ancient Brother electric typewriter,

I dove into the correspondence piled beside the list. So began my first full day as Taber Rhame's assistant. Cook, secretary, errand girl. Girl Friday.

Toward 2 p.m., the smell of lunch brought him out of his artistic fugue long enough to eat a bowl of seafood stew, half a loaf of French bread, and drink down three cups of coffee. During that time, we didn't speak. I knew better than to interrupt an artistic focus.

I worked through the day, trying not to think about the strange things that had been happening to me. Trying not to worry about Tante Ilene and Tee Dom. Trying not to wonder about my mother and the danger I might have led to her. Did her danger increase as the investigation progressed? Would it stop if I called off the investigation, or was it already too late?

At 5 p.m., when I left for the day, he was still painting, his dark and brooding creation changing from moment to moment. Points of brightness had begun to appear as if they had been birthed from the chaotic womb of the morose and brutal background. Modern impressionism. Shapes and color communicating emotion and message. I had little appreciation for this style as a general rule, but I could see the beauty of this work. It was a passionate and fervent evolution.

Trailed by MacAloon through the wet streets, I made it to Claude Michau's office just before he left for the day. Belinda, her face inches from a compact, waved me on through the reception area. 'He's waiting for you. Go right on in.'

Waiting for me?

His door was open, the interior of the office lit by a single desk lamp. Shadows, like gray cats, sat unmoving in the corners, curled lazily on the book shelves, obscured the faces in the photographs with teasing paws, toyed with the keyboard, the pen set, the files on the desk. The painting Michau had purchased from me would look perfect in this darkened setting.

Claude Michau was standing before the single window in his office, staring out into the courtyard behind the firm. The twelve-foot-tall window was covered inside with dark-stained wood blinds, the slats tilted to allow a bit of dreary light. Thin, diffused slits of almost-brightness covered the carpeted floor.

Michau, his hands in his pants pockets, was a shadow in

silhouette, appearing even more diminutive than usual, his hair even taller, when measured against the length of the window. When he turned his face to profile, it was obvious he suffered with an excess of curl due to the dampness. It suddenly occurred to me that the ungainly hairstyle might not be a toupee, but an unkind act of nature. Like a platypus's flat, horizontal bill, or the giraffe's too-long neck.

'Bonnie. You could have called. No need to come back out in the weather. Cee Cee would have allowed you to use the phone, I'm sure.' He didn't turn from his wet window view, but spoke with his back to me, his voice musing and pensive.

'I haven't been home. I came by after work to tell you your painting was ready. And to ask if I should have it framed.' I was back to speaking formally again. As stilted and proper as Emily Post. Claude Michau seemed not to notice. He nodded thoughtfully.

'I've chosen a simple black frame for my other canvases.' The silence after my words was too long, almost uncomfortable. Finally, Michau spoke.

'That would be most appreciated. Please bring the framer's bill to me and I'll reimburse you.' Michau took his hands from his pockets and looked at them, as if trying to decide if it was time for a manicure. 'Have a seat, Bonnie. We need to talk.'

I had been about to say that there was no need to reimburse me when Michau suggested I sit. I followed his invitation, the leather chair making a whooshing noise as I sat. Michau's voice had a curious sound, as uncomfortable and stilted as I had felt only moments earlier.

A sense of dread settled over my shoulders. But then, lately, dread had rested itself often upon me, as dark and shifting as the shadows in the corners of Michau's office.

He sat in his leather chair, the tall back a frame for his too-tall hair. The leather was soft, yet creaking as it conformed to his weight.

'Bonnie, I would like for you to tell me something.'

He opened a folder on his desk, the pool of light just beyond the margin of the papers. Carefully, he removed two pages and slid them across the slick, wood desk. 'Why did you choose to invest in these two companies?'

Each sheet of paper was a computer printout of financial activity, showing the fiscal wealth of a company. All the investments I had made were in France, none in the United States, and it had been several days since I had checked the financial pages. The feeling of dread nestled more closely about me.

'Bonnie?'

'I study . . . well . . . really . . . I read a lot of French magazines. They come . . . they came to Khoury. I subscribe, you know.' Great. My mouth had developed a case of dysentery, spewing all over the place, like it had the night before when I met Josh.

I took a deep breath and started over. 'I subscribe to, and read, quite a few foreign magazines. The four companies I invested in have been increasing their advertising as well as showing steady growth in the European stock market. That's how I chose all four of the companies in which I invested.'

'See . . .' I leaned forward, finding Michau's eyes in the darkness. Rain suddenly battered the window-panes outside, but I kept my eyes on the president of Royal Securities. '. . . There's a German company, I can't pronounce its name, but it means Aura of Loveliness. And they've been buying all the small cosmetic firms and perfumers on the market in Spain, Portugal and France. And these four companies looked like the type of enterprises in which they had previously shown an interest. Small, developed and expanded by single individuals or small family units, whose products were environmentally clean and yet elegant. I even studied the packaging and advertising styles of the companies previously taken over by Aura of Loveliness. These four companies fit the criteria.'

I took a deep breath. 'Did I lose my shirt?'

Michau was quiet a moment, his face hidden by unvarying shadows. 'Yes. You'll be lucky to recoup half of your original investment in these two companies. And that is if you leave your funds with them a few years and allow them time to rebound. Some scandal about products purchased on the black market from the illegal slaughter of whales in the Pacific?' The question hung in the air.

I studied the two printouts. 'Maybe . . . ambergris,' I said, drawing out the word. 'Both companies were heavily into perfumes. Ambergris, which is obtained from whales, might have been involved. I've heard it's one ingredient which can't be synthesized well. And certain Oriental fisheries still specialize in the illegal slaughter of whales.'

Michau's hair nodded slowly back and forth. With great deliberation he covered the two sheets with two more. 'These companies, however, are a different matter.' His left index finger tapped a page. 'Your capital invested with this company doubled in value overnight.' He tapped a second page, now with his right index finger, the tip moving up into shadow and down into the light with a small tattoo of sound that was almost lost in the roar of rain.

'This investment did a bit better.'

I watched his fingertip, mesmerized, scarcely breathing.

'Your original six-thousand-two-hundred-fifty-dollar investment is now worth over seventy thousand dollars.' The tapping ceased. Thunder rumbled in the distance. Lightning flicked through the slitted shutters.

Over seventy thousand dollars . . .

'It was purchased by a German cosmetics company this morning in a hostile takeover. By the end of the week, you will be worth perhaps an additional ten thousand.'

The dread that had pursued me was gone, replaced with a complicated mix of emotions. I couldn't have told Michau what I was feeling. Can one be both numb and elated at once? Ice-cold and yet sizzling with heat? Empty and too full?

I had played the stock market for years, winning and losing fortunes of play money. Once I had amassed a treasure of three million dollars. Fake treasure. Fake assets.

But this was real.

I had done what I had always known I could do. I had made money. Real money.

'Sell on Friday afternoon,' I said, my voice a whisper. 'All four companies. I'll have a new list for you on Friday morning.' I clenched my hands in my lap. 'I want twenty-five thousand put into my personal account to reimburse my original twenty-five-thousand-dollar investment.' I sat forward suddenly. 'I'll re-invest the rest. I'll . . . I'll . . .'

Michau chuckled in the darkness, his face lit momentarily by lightning. 'Congratulations, Bonnie.'

I swallowed, sitting there in the false night, the sudden storm beating against the thick walls and old glass panes. 'Thank you, Mr Michau. Thank you.' Over seventy thousand dollars . . .

'May I drive you someplace, Bonnie?'

Michau was standing, and I realized I had been lost in thought as he gathered up his briefcase, umbrella, and raincoat. He was a dark shadow in a lightless room. I stood with all the grace of an overzealous adolescent, nearly tipping over the chair. Not my usual self. Not at all.

Over seventy thousand dollars . . .

'Thank you, Mr Michau,' I said again. 'Yes. I'd appreciate a ride. And while you're at it, a suggestion as to long-term parking. At five dollars a day, I'm getting eaten alive.'

Michau chuckled again. 'You can afford it, Bonnie. You can afford it.'

He was right, I could. I could afford many things now.

Michau drove me home through the rain, covering the few blocks to my apartment in only moments. I arrived dry and unwrinkled, while MacAloon, jogging the same distance, was wet through, his jeans dark to mid-thigh, and his hair running rivulets. I should have given the man a hot drink and a plate of supper, but the tub beckoned. Rather than being charitable, I was hedonistic. A bubble bath with wine and cheese and fresh fruit on a tray on the toilet top. Vivaldi on PBS, Perkins on his pillow. And later, with the wine still warming my blood stream, the diary of Elizabeth Diane Sarvaunt. My mother's friend.

Although I covered only the two-page introduction and three months of her life that night – and learned nothing of my own origins – I discovered a great deal about the people who raised me. Tee Dom and Tante Ilene had been the bearers of secrets even then.

Beth Sarvaunt had been an unpretty, dark-haired child with a tight, curvaceous script and a gift for melodrama. Her diary opened simply.

'My name is Elizabeth Diane Sarvaunt. My mother was a whore and I am a bastard. I know this because my aunt and uncle told me so.'

In the introduction to her diary, Beth Sarvaunt told her mother's story. The story of an affair with a married man, a pregnancy and a child born out of wedlock. Common. Nothing unusual in the tale, although sad. Until two months after the birth of the 'bastard child', as Beth referred to herself. The mother died of a massive stroke, leaving Beth to be raised by her aunt and uncle. Tee Dom and Tante Ilene.

My Tee Dom and Tante Ilene.

The young girl opened her eyes slowly. As slowly as the man in the wheelchair lifted himself from the bed and back to his seat.

He grunted. Different grunts from when he had hurt her. No rhythm to these grunts. Just strain, as he used his arms to push his legs into place, lifting the useless limbs and placing one leg here, then here, then finally into the chair.

She watched, as always. And as always she prayed that God would make him slip. Make him fall. Make him die. So far God hadn't done any of those things. So far. She figured God had something even meaner worked out to punish the man. Because God always punished the wicked. The Bible said so.

The man finally got settled in his chair, his pants zipped, his shirt buttoned, covering the plastic shit bag on his side. She had never seen a plastic bag attached to a person. It was kinda like an extra part, like the six-million-dollar man had, only uglier. No. She had never seen a shit bag before. But she had seen shit before. And that's what was in the bag.

The man sighed and reached over, slipping the cord off the bedpost. The cord was tied to the bedpost to keep her from fighting. The other end of the cord was tied to her left wrist. There were similar cords tied to her feet and her right wrist. Holding her still while the man hurt her.

But God would punish him. She was certain of that.

The man pushed the stick on the arm of his chair, and the motor between the big, back wheels hummed, pushing him from the room. At the doorway, he paused, opened the door with the key from his pocket and rolled into the hall.

All she could see was carpet and hallway wall on the other side. But she knew it meant escape. Freedom. Safety.

Again he paused and reached back, stretched, leaned and pulled the door to. It closed behind him with a soft thud. A heavy door. She knew. She had tried to escape more than once. And failed.

She kicked free of the remaining three ropes, and bounded from the bed. Naked. They kept her naked.

She ran to the bathroom and turned on the shower. Hot. Scalding hot. Steam billowed up around her. She stepped inside.

She scrubbed clean every part of her, especially the parts he touched. The parts he used. Hot water. Hours of hot water. At home, the hot water had run out after a while, cutting her shower short. But here, it just went on forever. Hot water. Maybe they were closer to hell here than at home and water stayed hot easier.

Later, staring at herself in the mirror, green eyes in a dusky face, light, kinky brown hair crowning her head, she considered again the way the man had wheeled himself out of the room. It was important. She knew that. God had told her so. She just didn't know why it was important. And she had to figure it out. She had to. Soon.

And finally the tears started to fall. Just this once. She'd let herself cry just this once. After all. Today it was her birthday. Today she was sixteen.

CHAPTER 12

My life fell into a rhythm in the following weeks. Up early for breakfast at the Café du Monde with a short walk to work with Perkins on a leash. Prepare a breakfast for Taber Rhame, complete correspondence, put away supplies, organize his store room, shop for lunch, then prepare it. And more of the same for the afternoon.

My greatest delight in my job was unpacking Rhame's store of art, sculpture, and photography, and placing them about the apartment, hanging them on the walls. My greatest challenge came from an unexpected sector, however. Protecting Taber Rhame from the adoring or hostile public. People came to the door at all hours of the day requesting interviews, wanting to steal a glimpse of Rhame's latest work, asking favors. The constant parade of visitors was especially annoying for MacAloon. He ended up anchoring himself in the shade outside the door, screening every person who entered the apartment.

Between visitors, he tilted back a chair against the wrought-iron railing and dipped Skoal. Whenever a visitor would approach, he'd stand, waiting as they climbed the stairs, probably looking huge and menacing to the arriving supplicant. MacAloon was good at that. Looking mean. His presence kept out the riffraff. As thanks, I kept MacAloon in coffee, Cokes and fed him lunch. It seemed the least Rhame could provide for the unofficial security.

In the evenings I would walk home, MacAloon on my heels, Perkins at my side. And though I never again asked Josh out, I was aware of him. And aware of his interest in me. Back at my apartment, I locked myself in for a long evening of painting, knowing I was protected by Josh Campos, only yards away.

The silence of the apartment was luxurious, muted sounds of traffic or rain or tourists from outside, the enclosing darkness, the way my work seemed to come alive, resurrecting itself at dusk each night, waiting for my brush. It might have sounded boring to anyone else, but to me it was heaven.

I had put all my finished paintings, simply framed and elegantly displayed on easels, in Cee Cee's shop. She hadn't forgotten her suggestion, even going so far as to pay an electrician to install the proper lighting in the back corner of her store, so my work appeared at its best.

Although most artists didn't bother with the expense of framing, I thought my paintings needed the boundary. Without it, the dark, elusive tints seemed to bleed off into the surrounding shadows.

I hadn't sold anything yet, but there had been a positive response from walk-in traffic.

With the appearance of *Empty Nests* in the president's office of Royal Securities, interest in my work was growing. I had been formally requested to submit a preliminary drawing for the twenty-foot wall in the firm's main chamber. I had provided a written description of the proposed work, as well as a scaled-down oil sketch of the painting on three small, cast-off canvases. In a month or so, I'd know what the board of directors had decided. Meanwhile, I painted.

Using the two hundred photos of the egret rookery, I had begun a series of work different from my usual paintings. A bit more surreal. A bit more mysterious. Gators eating, pulling innocent creatures beneath the black water. Egrets in agony. Bizarre stuff. Dark and bitter, reflecting my inner self. And strangely, all of the dying egrets had Tee Dom's eyes or Tante Ilene's tears.

Stocker had been unable to find Tee Dom and Tante Ilene. Stocker had been unable to find my mother. Stocker had been successful only in proving my ownership of the shanty and all its contents, and in locating the man we thought might be my father.

William Marc DeVillier – whose name was on the marriage license to Marie L. Smith – was a bit of low-life scum. An unclever convict, serving time in state prison for assault with intent to kill, breaking and entering, and a host of lesser charges.

The charges were the result of a botched burglary attempt. Drunk to the point that he no longer could stand up straight, and fresh out of malt liquor, he had thrown a brick through the front window of a grocery store, catapulting his body in afterward. Cut, spraying blood all over the display cases, he had tried to escape with three quart-sized bottles of Schlitz beneath his arms and a case of Bud Light cradled against his chest.

When a passing police cruiser had stopped him in the parking lot, my resourceful father had then dropped the Bud Light and dazzled the cops with his marksmanship. He managed to shoot out another store window, put a hole in the cruiser's radiator, and blow off his right big toe. Clever, clever man.

Stocker was making a trip to visit the intellectual genius who may have contributed a single sperm to my genetic makeup. I only hoped he had enough brain cells left to recall my mother.

I had stopped carrying my .38 around in my pocketbook, trusting MacAloon and Josh to protect me. I didn't want to follow in my illustrious father's footprints and shoot off a toe. I did, however, still sleep with the shotgun beside the bed. It was only prudent, I reasoned, in light of the identity of my mugger from Houma.

Identified by the fingerprints on the gun he had dropped, the man was Richard Smitts, a very young, very inept, small-time hood with a bad heroin problem and overdue child-support payments. He claimed he had been paid a thousand dollars to kidnap me and bring me to the outskirts of Houma.

On a hunch, Stocker had shown Mr Smitts one of Elred's photos. The man in the photo with the brown Dodge, Anthony Aucoin, was the same man who had offered Smitts the money for the kidnapping. There was a warrant out for Aucoin now, but so far he hadn't reappeared. It was obvious that he hadn't spent much time looking for me in Baton Rouge. He could be waiting just down the street.

Like I said. A shotgun by the bed was prudent, not phobic.

Toward the middle of September, on the same day Stocker was in a prison interview-room matching wits with my father, Taber Rhame and I had a visitor. The rich, the fashionable, and the wealthy had tried before to interrupt my employer, to force his concentration away from the series of canvases in his studio. Tried and seldom been successful.

Only if Rhame was taking a rare break, relaxing on his leather sofa, eating a meal, or climbing out of the shower would I allow an interruption. And then only if the visitor's name was on Rhame's Master List. The Master List was a rolodex of names, addresses and phone numbers for people from all over the world. Fabulously wealthy clients and art patrons had cards marked with a red diamond in the right-hand corner of the rolodex. Critics and politicians were marked with a black spade, friends with clubs, and old lovers, children, and wives with red hearts.

I had strict orders to interrupt Rhame's work only for the red hearts.

The day Stocker was at the prison, a heart came to the door.

MacAloon tapped respectfully on the door, an unparalleled event in itself, alerting me to the unique. The woman on the stoop, standing beside MacAloon, was indeed unparalleled. She was about sixty, beautiful in the way that Elizabeth Taylor and Sophia Loren are beautiful. Agelessly, exquisitely, and gloriously.

She was black-eyed and platinum-haired, dressed in an elegant Italian design, a watered-silk dress in a soft floral print, rose-tinted pastels on an antique background. Gucci leather pumps, a matching bag, and a gold rope sparkling with diamonds completed her ensemble.

She extended her hand and took mine in a gesture that was more blessing than greeting, squeezing gently with her fingers. Americans tend to greet one another with a pumping grip, half-assessment, half-challenge, exerting pressure with the muscles of forearm and bicep. This woman took my hand like the Queen of England might have, squeezing with a faint pressure. It was a curiously Continental gesture.

MacAloon, his mouth free of snuff for once – he must have spit it over the railing when she started up the stairs – said, 'The Grande Dame DeLande.'

She was royalty. At least she was royalty as far as Louisiana was concerned. The DeLande name was illustrious and infamous, reaching back into history for more than two centuries, and, until lately, had been a controlling influence in politics and finances.

Legal problems, scandal and the recent deaths of three DeLande heirs had complicated an already-tangled corporate hierarchy and temporarily bruised their dominance in financial circles. Socially, the family had taken a tumble as well, I recalled, but with their money, any social ostracism wouldn't last long.

At the center of the rumors, gossip, and inter-familial legal maneuvering was the Grande Dame. Her picture had graced the society pages for fifty years. She was an icon. A symbol of both grace and debauchery. I realized I was staring.

She smiled. It was like watching the sun rise, warming, dazzling.

'Come in.' I was rather pleased that my voice didn't squeak.

She swept past me and moved toward Rhame's studio with unerring accuracy, dropping her bag on the leather sofa and kicking off her shoes as she went. It was totally unexpected, the sight of her stockinged feet. And then she did the most amazing thing. Glancing back over her shoulder, she said, 'I'm a heart, in Taber's rolodex. He is still using that old rolodex, isn't he?'

I nodded like a mute child. And stared as she let down her hair. Long silver waves, like spun crystal over sterling. She laughed, and goose bumps raised up along my arms. It wasn't a lovely sound, her laugh. It was the sound of power. Of a woman absolutely certain of her beauty and her allure, captivating, almost mesmerizing. She had been the Queen of England one moment, Madame Pompadour the next. Royalty superimposed over sensuality. Elegance over carnality. Without knocking, she opened the door to the studio and slipped within. And the room seemed to go dark.

MacAloon, standing in the open doorway, kept his silence until the door to Rhame's studio closed behind the Grande Dame. Heat roiled in on the September air, dense and cloying.

'Jeeeezus.'

'My sentiments exactly,' I managed softly. 'You want some coffee or something?' I asked. I didn't want coffee, but making it would give me something familiar to do with my hands. I often took solace in the pouring of grounds, the soft sound of water perking, and the fresh-coffee scent. When I painted at home in the shanty, I had been known to descend to the ground floor in the middle of the night to make a pot. On the rare night when the painting didn't go well, making coffee seemed to settle my hands, and calm my mind.

MacAloon nodded. His shadow, cast across the room, nodded too, bigger than life.

'You know who that is?'

I turned, heading for the kitchen. 'Yes. I know who that is.' One of history's most ravishing and wanton women. And she was in Taber Rhame's studio . . . doing . . . what? It wasn't hard to visualize Rhame, who painted always in bare feet and jeans and nothing else, tossing down his brush and enfolding that lush body and . . .

I ground fresh beans, poured water, and found a filter by feel, enjoying the orderly process and the quiet that descended on me. I had worked for Taber Rhame for weeks, watching him eat and paint and, once, I had even seen him emerge from the bathroom clad in only a towel draped over his hips, his lean body damp, his strong legs striding to his nearest canvas. The artist, taken in a surge of inspiration, forced back to the canvas, his shower forgotten.

I remembered the way the hair on his chest tapered to a thin line and disappeared beneath the low-slung terry cloth. The way his chest muscles pulled tight, as if to contain the artistic image he had seen. The way his footprints left damp places on the wood floor. The way the light caught splatters of water when he shook his head, showering everything in range. The way he cursed in French, softly, under his breath, when he realized a droplet had landed on his painting. I shivered.

I had thought about Rhame in a purely professional way for weeks now, ignoring the occasional twinges of something else coiling deep inside. But like water snakes brought out of hibernation early, that something else arched and curled, spiraling upwards to the heat as I envisioned Taber and that woman back there. She was old enough to be a grandmother, for God's sake.

Silently, MacAloon and I shared a pot of coffee. Even more silently, we shared the noon-day meal. Taber and the Grande Dame never appeared. At five o'clock I left, locking up for the day and pocketing the key, passing the limo on the street. A limo, for Pete's sake. Elegant and old-fashioned.

A limo from the early sixties. And they were still inside the apartment.

What could make a man and woman disappear for hours, ignoring mealtime and coffee? I knew the answer. And the half-formed images of my imagination impressed themselves upon me for the long silent hours of the night, creating an unaccustomed restlessness. A peculiar heat that the air-conditioner and whirling fans couldn't blow away. An inner warmth that even my painting couldn't assuage.

The next morning at the Café du Monde I looked for Miles. It was childish perhaps to seek his company. I suddenly wanted to take someone – Miles? – to Houston's and to Petunias and sightseeing and to the theatre and the symphony.

I tried to talk to Josh Campos, but he had only two topics of conversation. Cars and the human body. I had no interest at all in carburetors, struts and chrome. Even less interest in dietary requirements and the evils of pastries. Two minutes after he opened his mouth, I knew it was a mistake. I ended up spending my breakfast time watching him drink three glasses of orange juice while he pontificated about vitamin supplements.

At least with Miles I had been able to talk finances. Politics. The world situation in terms of both money and power. And with him I could have found some answers to the questions that haunted me. I could have asked him why he hired MacAloon . . .

With Taber Rhame I could have talked art and technique, trade secrets, mediums and meaning, the interpretation of art in light of the human spirit and political history. Could have. But never had.

As Josh ran on – something about fat burners and metabolic rates – I thought of all the things I could have done, could have said to Taber Rhame over the course of the past weeks. I thought about the nude that now hung beside my bed. And without conscious thought, I doodled on the napkin, pressing against the tabletop in the café.

A man's body took shape on the rough paper. The long length of thigh, muscles taut. The curve of calf, arch of foot. Round, high buttocks and lean torso. Chest hair tapering to a draped towel. I crumpled the napkin.

'I'm gonna be late.' I stood, startling Perkins at my feet. Silencing Campos. Thank God.

Again I looked around. No Miles. No one I knew except Josh Campos. Lucky me.

The limo was still parked at the curb in front of Rhame's studio. I say 'still' because the driver was wrinkled and sleepy-eyed. As if he'd slept in the car.

The coffee from the café settled uneasily against the beignets in my stomach. Stupid. Really stupid. I don't know if I was accusing myself or describing the Grande Dame. But before I could analyze it, the door at the top of the stairs opened. The Grande Dame herself stepped out, as beautifully dressed as the morning before. Just as fresh. Just as elegant. Not a hair out of place in the upswept hairstyle. She smiled as she descended the steps. I nodded to her as I climbed. Midway up and down we met and she paused. Reluctantly, so did I.

'Where do you show your work?'

Not 'Do you paint?' but 'Where do you show your work?' And it occurred to me that Taber Rhame had never shown an interest in my art.

'Cee Cee Gaudet's shop, on Royal. The—'

'La Demoiselle Verte. I know it. I purchased the Emberville pearls there some ten years ago.' She flashed that fabulous smile, bright and glittering. 'I will drop by before I leave today.'

I didn't know how to answer that, so I nodded.

'You have most unusual eyes,' she said.

The sun was hidden behind clouds this morning, the light diffuse enough that I had my sunglasses pushed up on top of my head. My strange eyes, the pupils far too large, were exposed to her probing stare.

'My mother had eyes like that. Large pupils. And so did two of my daughters,' she added, as if sharing a confidence. Just like a young girl, gossiping in a stairway before work in the morning.

'Physiological Mydriasis,' I said, a bit stiffly.

'Yes. That's it.' Brightly she smiled again. 'Taber will be so happy you brought him coffee. He's never been a morning person.'

I dropped my eyes to the large Styrofoam cup I carried. Shielding my all-too-large pupils. Shielding my thoughts.

She chuckled softly. 'So that's the way of it. Should I have asked permission then?'

'I'm sure I haven't the least idea what you might mean.'

'Um. Well. At least you're polite about it. Thirty years ago I had a young woman threaten to tear my eyes out for sleeping with him.'

My gaze lifted from the capped cup to her beautiful eyes and back down again. Thirty years?

'Go on up, little girl. Offer to rub his shoulders. They bother him when he paints too long. And he's been painting nonstop for some twenty hours now. I'm sure he's very tired.'

Twenty hours? She hadn't been here much more than that time. Had Taber Rhame, world-renowned womanizer and skirt-chaser, spent the last day and night alone with a beauty like the Grande Dame . . . painting?

As if she could read my thoughts, she chuckled again, and moved on down the stairs.

Quietly, feeling very gauche and very young, I went into the apartment and locked the door behind me.

As usual, I made up a tray of coffee and pastry for Rhame. Carried it to the studio, my sneakers almost silent on the wood floor. I had made a point to wear soft-soled shoes for weeks, afraid the tapping of harder heels might disturb his work. Had he noticed?

There were six canvases at various stages of completion placed about the room on massive easels. The sturdy wood-frame supports were necessary to buttress the immense paintings. Rhame, wearing his usual worn, denim jeans, the top button undone, was standing in the center of the room, turning slowly, three brushes in his left hand, his right hand resting on one hip. He didn't look pained, as if his shoulders ached. He looked the way he often did following a sequence of those flowing exercises he performed daily. Negligent. Relaxed. Exhausted. Euphoric.

'I'm thinking of calling the series *Homecoming*, something like that,' he said.

I placed the tray on its four legs near the table holding his paints and brushes. Opened the coffee and carried it to him.

Without a glance he handed me the brushes and took the Styrofoam cup. His fingers were cold when they brushed mine.

I could hear the sound his throat made as the still-hot coffee went down.

'I'll finish them tonight. All of them. And next month they will be shown at the DeLande Estate. The Grande Dame—' He drank again to lubricate his throat. It was raspy with fatigue. 'Wonderful woman. Did you know she discovered me in Paris when I was broke? A starving artist quite literally.' He laughed softly and drank again. The coffee was half-gone. 'The Grande Dame is going to throw a party for the series. I'm planning for twelve in all. She'll invite the entire art world, I don't doubt, and although it's the end of the world out there on her estate, they'll come. Just to see her, they'll come.'

He strode around the room, drinking from the cup, talking. His bare feet totally silent on the floor, his rough voice thrown back from the stark walls. A hollow sound.

'She was my first patron, and she feels a certain responsibility for me.

'Do you like this,' he continued, 'the way the light seems to stop just here and then reappear again over here?' With the cup, he indicated two places on a dark, menacing canvas. 'Some stupid critic will say it signifies hope and the conquering triumph of the human spirit.' He grinned at me. 'I see a child's mobile from beneath, with the sun bouncing off the geometric shape.'

He was right, and I smiled back at him.

Rhame paused at the pastry tray and picked up a cold beignet, eating it as he moved his eyes across the canvases.

'How is your wardrobe?'

The shift caught me by surprise. 'My wardrobe?'

'Um.' He chewed and swallowed. 'For the showing. As my assistant you will be expected to attend. Perhaps show some of those wonderful paintings your friend Claude Michau raves on about.' Taber Rhame laughed, his eyes sparkling, bright orbs above the dark circles of weariness.

I closed my mouth with a snap.

'I didn't think you knew he called me.' Rhame waggled a half-eaten beignet at me, his eyes sparkling with laughter. Powdered sugar plopped onto the floor at his bare feet. 'It was to obtain a recommendation on your work. Some small matter of a commissioned painting for the lobby of his firm?'

I didn't know what I was feeling at that moment. I hadn't known what I was feeling from the moment I saw the Grande Dame DeLande step out of the apartment. Perhaps just a sort of emptiness waiting to be filled. Perhaps nothing. All I knew was that my eyes filled with tears too quickly to blink them away. Taber laughed again and drank the rest of the coffee. He put the empty cup on the pastry tray and licked his fingers slowly.

'Now, Bonnie. Today I need a break from all this.' He waved his fingers – still wet from his lips – lazily about the room. 'So. We shall go peruse these wonderful paintings and you will take me to lunch. Yes?'

I nodded and caught a tear on the back of my hand.

'And then we will consider your wardrobe. A day off, what is the American term?'

'Play hooky?'

'Yes. Exactly. Now. Let me shower and shave. I smell like a goat.' And with that, Taber Rhame, world-renowned artist and womanizer, padded off to the bath.

Twenty minutes later he shouted and I ran back to the studio, Perkins at my heels. Usually the little dog sat beneath my chair gnawing on the calf-hoof he liked so much, and staying out of the way of my roving feet while I cooked. The sound of Rhame's raised voice excited Perkins and he abandoned the chew to investigate.

Rhame, his hair damp, his face freshly shaved, hung out from the bedroom, supported at an angle by the door frame. Naked to the hips, the rest of him was hidden in the next room. 'What do I wear to lunch?' His eyes were laughing, as if he knew what seeing him in that position did to my breathing.

'Jeans and sneakers,' I said. Or I thought I said.

'Good. How soon can we eat?'

'Not until eleven.'

'Um.' And he disappeared back into the bedroom.

While he dressed I finished up a bit of paperwork, writing up checks to pay for the supplies which had arrived in the last month. Only, I found myself doodling again, fanciful nudes of Taber Rhame. One of these I left at the table. Rhame at his canvas, again draped in a towel, a half-dozen cats curled at his feet. It was good. Catching the intense, controlled expression he habitually wore when painting. I put it at the bottom of the stack of checks awaiting his signature.

Rhame, looking fifteen years younger than his forty-nine years, strode from the studio, catching up Perkins in his arms. 'Good dog. Good boy.' He ruffled Perkins' long hair, his eyes on me. 'I ate another of those cold beignets. I think I can survive until eleven. Shall we go look at your work?'

A sudden nervousness slithered up my arms, resting against my skin like an itchy wool sweater. The morning coffee roiled again. 'Sure.' A lighthearted enough reply, but my palms were damp and as I turned, I scrubbed them against my jeans.

Rhame whistled tunelessly through his teeth as we walked, two fingers of each hand hanging from his pockets, his steps jaunty. He seemed to be studying the façades of the buildings we passed, the deep-set windows and stuccoed walls, the pastel shades of paint, the jewelry, clothing, hats, soaps, perfumes, and antiques gathered in the window displays.

'You don't have to be anxious, you know. I don't bite.'

'I'm not anxious.' And I wasn't. I was terrified. It was too much in one day. Taber Rhame and the Grande Dame DeLande were both going to view my work. And then Rhame and I were going out to lunch. Together. Too, too much.

Perkins, sensing my disquiet, walked close to my ankle, his body a shield between Rhame and me. MacAloon trailed along behind. Unobtrusive. Earning his pay. The sun, hidden behind clouds for hours, peeked through, allowing a bit of silky blue sky to show, like a seductress, exposing a hint of undergarment, a promise of the heat to come.

At La Demoiselle Verte, Cee Cee Gaudet was in a flutter of excitement. Her eyes were open wide, her hair in flame-bright disarray like a camp fire that has been fed too much dry wood, too fast.

'Oh. Oh. Oh. *Alors*. La Grande Dame. La Grande Dame DeLande. *Alors*.' She fanned herself with a jade-handled fan, an expensive little trinket from her stock. '*Alors*. *Alors*.'

The Grande Dame, it seemed, had just left, perhaps only moments before we entered, although the limo was nowhere to be seen. Cee Cee fluttered a check in my face.

'She bought it. She bought them both,' Cee Cee chirped in French. 'Oh my. Oh my. I need to sit down. Oh my.'

And when I looked at the check, I needed to sit down as well. It was written for a bit over twelve thousand dollars.

'She bought one of the Chinese pieces. It was over-priced and it was in stock forever. Do you remember the little gold and jade pin? The one shaped like a horse's head? It went right here,' she pointed to a spot on the display shelf, 'and now it's gone. She bought it.' Cee Cee clasped her wrinkled hands below her wrinkled neck and sighed, then plucked the check back to stare at the signature again.

'And of course, she bought one of your paintings.'

My heart did a strange little flutter, like the check in Cee Cee's hands. The Grande Dame was known in artistic circles as a patron to starving artists. Her interest in obscure painters and sculptors had often been enough to launch an entire career. 'She did what?' My voice was breathy and I thought for a moment that Cee Cee wouldn't hear me.

'She took it with her. The one of the chenier and the water. She just ooohed and aaahed over it and then she offered me two thousand dollars for it. And you know we hadn't priced them and so I said yes. The Grande Dame DeLande herself. It's been ages since she was in here, you know. Just ages. And she bought my pin. The one I thought would never sell. Never.'

She glanced up, following Rhame's retreating back. With that quick, bird-like change of subject that was so typically old-world European, she whispered, 'So. Is that your artist?' Her green eyes sparkling with speculation.

'Yes,' I whispered back.

'Bonnie.' Taber's voice, a note of amusement in its depths, called me from the back of the shop. From the corner where my canvases were displayed.

Cee Cee waved me on toward the back before folding the check and tucking it into her bra.

'Go on, then. Go. Go.'

My heart in my throat, I went. Rhame, his silver head tilted to one side, his feet spread and arms akimbo was studying one of my night scenes. A watery composition of moonlit bayou, a drifting pirogue, and a curious alligator. I stopped behind him, scarcely breathing.

He turned and looked at me. But it was more than a simple look. It was far more than that. His eyes were sharp, hard, the same intense blaze as when he painted.

'You never brought me any of your works. I never saw these.' It was curiously like an accusation. As if I had hidden my work from him deliberately. My chin went up and I crossed my arms, suddenly angry.

'Your studio would have killed them. It's too light. Too bright. They have to be viewed in almost darkness. Like here. Or at night. I paint at night.' So what if he didn't like the paintings. So what if he hated them. I didn't care. But I felt a flush start deep within me and rise to the roots of my hair as I spoke. I was glad the shop was dark, so Rhame wouldn't see the color in my cheeks.

Rhame turned his eyes back to the canvases, and I clenched my jaw, refusing to say the hundreds of things that filtered through my mind as he looked at the paintings. His eyes, when he glared, were the eyes of an angry prophet. The eyes of a jealous god. Too piercing, too penetrating. Almost savage.

Minutes ticked by. My flush faded as did my anger. And I really wanted to know what he thought. Still he was silent.

'She asked me about you,' he said finally, his voice softer, almost musing. 'About your work.'

And I knew he meant the Grande Dame. It was in the almost caressing way he said 'she'.

'She asked if you might be good enough to show with me next month. It is a peculiarity of her showings. The ballroom is set up for the premier artist, but the hallways, the parlors, the music room display young, up-and-coming artists.' His voice, still rough from lack of sleep, had softened. Its vibrato quivered up my arms. 'Very effective. She has launched the careers of several young talents over the years.'

He moved on, to better view another painting. This one was a desolate scene of open sky and marsh and dead trees, limned around by faint, silvery light.

'Many artists can paint things,' he said, still in that musing tone. His words were measured and slow, deeply accented. 'Or the human form. Or perspective. And they can grasp concept and convey meaning by use of shape and texture and the juxtaposition of one object to another. But very few artists can paint . . . light.'

He paused and then moved on, his feet making a soft scuffing in the quiet shop. I followed, twisting my fingers together hard.

'And only a few very great ones can paint shadow. The average person would be surprised how difficult it is to paint shadow with its twisted bands of broken light. Its effect on perspective and tone.' Rhame's lips curled up on one side, forming a deep crease along his face, running from nose to chin. 'And though your work lacks maturity and passion, it's possible you fall into this last category of artists.'

I put my fingers over my mouth and pressed, forcing my lips against my teeth cruelly. Tears sparkled against the dim light.

'I envision the hallway leading to the ballroom, lit only by candles in the wall sconces, the light flickering in the breeze, and your paintings like soldiers lined up its length.'

My hands went limp, falling bonelessly to my sides. His words roared in my ears. '. . . a few great ones . . . last category . . .' He was . . . Taber Rhame was . . . I swallowed, unable even to think what I thought he might be saying about my work. A choked sound forced its way past my frozen throat, half-whimper, half-sob.

He looked at me then, a trace of a smile in his eyes at last. 'I'll recommend that she put your works there. Congratulations, Bonnie Sarvaunt. You're about to become a Name.'

His words made me smile at last, and a tingling ran down my arms. A jolted, peppery feeling like heat. A name was the one thing I had never been able to call my own. And now that I had discovered the one I used wasn't mine, it appeared to be attached to me forever. Bonnibelle Sarvaunt. Artist and corpse. My smile broadened.

I wondered if Stocker would find Tee Dom and Tante Ilene before the showing. I wondered if they would come.

'Versace, I think.'

Rhame was looking at me, speculation in his eyes. Suddenly I knew what he was thinking. He was dressing me for the showing. I laughed out loud.

Versace was an Italian designer who sold creations all over the world, and many were so elaborate that they were artworks in themselves. They were often showcased in the French fashion magazines I read and dreamed over. Rhame's steps were like a dancer's as he moved around me, viewing me from every angle, lips slightly pursed. 'Versace, in a lemon yellow and verbena, I think.'

'I can't afford Versace,' I said, laughing, turning with him in a spiral, my toes *en pointe* and my heart light as a feather. 'I'll have to find someone closer to home to dress me for the showing. A local designer.'

'No, I don't suppose you could afford Versace on what I pay you,' he said simply, and held out a hand. 'But I can.'

I placed my palm into his, warm now, and strong. It was the first time he had consciously touched me. My heart beat an unsteady rhythm for a moment, as it so often did, like a toddler banging an overturned kettle with a wooden spoon.

Fleetingly, I considered telling him it would not be appropriate for him to purchase clothing for me. Mme Willoby would have insisted it simply wasn't done. But I kept my old tutor's counsel, and my own mouth shut.

'We have a busy day before us, I think,' Rhame said. Turning to Cee Cee, who had been hiding behind a display case listening, her green eyes sparkling like jewels, he nodded his head and wished her a good day.

Perkins, angry at being left behind with Cee Cee, stood on his back legs, front paws against the window in the door, barking. He seemed to know we were going to Houston's and that he was being left out of all the fun. Cee Cee, the check still crinkling in her bra, waved us on.

Rhame, his stride long, tucked my hand into the crook of his arm. And took me on a whirlwind day.

Leaving the van parked in various lots, we shopped at Passe-Partout, Madaline Couture, Mettre à la Mode Limited, and at Carrefour, buying silk under-things in one shop, a nubby flax jacket in another, shoes in a third, and over my protestations, Rhame ordered two dresses made up to his specification. We bought silk, wide-legged pants and two form-fitting sweaters, a shawl, fringed all around. Almost everything he chose was in pale shades of yellow, oat, wheat, beer, and lemon. And in one shop on St Charles Avenue, Rhame found the Versace.

The boutique was going out of business, everything at half-price, everything discounted at far below market value. Rhame held up the dress against my body, the skirt flared open, his arms passed through mine, our bodies barely touching back to front. His face was clinical as he pulled and adjusted, considering. I might have been a mannequin for all of his awareness of me as a woman. He was an artist now. Not a man.

But my heart was beating far too fast, like a johnboat motor running on too rich fuel. Burning up. Racing. About to explode.

'Put this on. I'll get the shoes from the van, and the shawl.' He tossed the dress over me with one hand and pushed me gently toward the dressing-room with the other. Again I stripped off jeans and T-shirt, socks and sneakers and with the help of the sales lady, pulled Versace's creation over my head.

It was silk next to my skin, silk and latex, a luxurious fusion of textures, the silk soft and subtle, the latex clinging and form-fitting. The sales lady secured the dress, pulling the hidden zipper up beneath my left arm.

I'd never worn anything that zipped up the side. More than anything else, that seemed to proclaim the dress a designer piece.

The sleeves were long, coming to a point below my wrist, the neckline high and rounded, the sleeves and bodice like a second skin beaded all over in a yellow-hued multicolored, free-flowing design, like an artist's palette gone wild. The skirt was a long, full circle of flowing saffron silk. Out in the main alcove again, I bent and turned, dipped and grinned at my reflection.

Rhame, his face a study in concentration, knelt beside me on the floor, and slipped the gold leather pumps onto my feet.

'Cinderella,' I murmured.

He looked up and grinned. 'Exactly.'

Standing behind me, he draped the shawl, removed it. Tied it about my waist, removed it. Tried it several other ways, and finally gave up, leaving the shawl draped over his own shoulder. It looked incongruous hanging there, and I laughed in sheer delight.

'Exactly,' he said again. With nimble fingers he unbound my braid, raking the tight curls loose, pulling the pads of his fingertips over my scalp, arranging my hair in a tangled mass. Hands moving slowly. Almost sensuously.

My heart skipped a beat, and my nipples tightened suddenly, as a shock traveled through my body. In the mirror his eyes lingered there a moment, while his hands lay buried in my hair, and then rose to meet my gaze.

'Exactly.' His breath was a soft whisper at my ear. 'Look.' Rhame stepped back, moving out of the triple mirror, his eyes on mine. 'Look.' And then he was gone and it was just me reflected there.

Me. Not me.

A gypsy in colors gaudy, yet elegant. Flushed, breath too rapid. Hair wild and disheveled. Eyes wide and somehow mysterious, cat-yellow above the beaded dress. A gypsy princess after some reckless dance, unrestrained and barbaric, fierce and aroused. Erotic.

Me. Not me.

'Exactly,' came the word again, whispered from the corner of the room.

CHAPTER 13

We ate at Houston's, a late lunch, stomachs growling, two jeans-clad shoppers, ordinary, common, mundane. Except for the memory of Rhame's hands in my hair and the picture of me in that dress. For me, it was a revelation.

All my life I had wanted to know who I was. What I was. Where I came from. And suddenly, that day, at some point in the long, glorious day, I realized it no longer mattered. Rhame, without saying a word, taught me that it had never mattered who or what I was. And it never would.

This man, this strange enigmatic man that the whole world watched and emulated, had resurrected himself, redirected himself, recreated himself again and again. Always evolving, always growing, always seeing himself and the world around him in a new light, with a new focus. And that, he somehow taught me, is the nature of art. Real art. True art. The art of the brush or the pen or the potter's wheel. The art of the stonemason or the carpenter or welder. The art of being alive.

All through the late afternoon, we toured the Quarter together, riding the streetcars, stopping in bars, shopping in small shops, and trying the wares of street vendors. I even had the opportunity to use the new camera purchased when I first arrived in New Orleans. We danced on the wharf overlooking the Mississippi, a riverboat churning its traditionally muddy waters. The sun set rosy and golden, fading at last to plum-colored clouds.

And when the saxophonist would have put away his horn and left us without music for our dancing, Rhame tossed him a fifty to stay a while longer. The old black man opened up his case again, licked his tired lips, moistened the reed, and played some big-band melodies.

Taber Rhame, womanizer extraordinaire, guided me through the steps, pleased that I could rumba, foxtrot, jitterbug and cha-cha with the best of them. My tango, on the other hand, he pronounced pitiful. And of course he was right. The tango is the carnal experience in dance. I had been taught the steps by a retired spinster and had practiced neither the dance nor the carnal experience. Pitiful indeed.

We ate tacos from a street vendor, heavy on the jalapeños and sour cream, bought Rhame a hat from a shopkeeper, a floppy down-under hat, imported from Australia, and forced a clerk to stay open late so he could peruse the imported coffees in tall glass jars. We ate pralines and ice-cream and drank too much beer, joining the tourists in the square in cheering on a duo of aged musicians playing the blues on ancient horns. And we danced again, our bodies pressed together, moving in tempting, tantalizing rhythms, the alcohol in my blood making me soft and warm and . . . passionate.

We passed transvestites and call girls, strippers and dancers, and Rhame, his mouth at my ear, made lascivious comments, verbally undressing each and describing their surgically altered attributes. His arm tightened around my waist each time I laughed, holding me close.

And at midnight, when the tips of my breasts were so tender from contact with my shirt and the pressure of his chest that I thought I might die from the sensations in those delicate, sensual points, Taber Rhame took me home, followed me up the steps, and left me there.

Alone.

Perkins and I stood in the doorway, the dog sleepy and stretching, me, just a bit stunned, listening as the man I had assumed would take me to bed, clattered down the steps and disappeared. Whistling. I closed the door, locked it, and laughed, standing there with my arms full of the packages we had picked up from the van on our walk home. More packages were on the floor at my feet, dumped there by Rhame before he turned and left. Perkins was now scratching at the door to be let out.

Again, I opened the door and watched the little dog disappear into darkness. Josh Campos, sitting propped against his fender, nodded at me. We didn't speak. For weeks we had merely nodded or waved from a distance, though I felt his eyes on me often.

And so, on this night when I might have discovered the stirring passions of the body and soul, I painted instead. Something new and provocative, the palette in yellows and ocher, and deep earth tones. A woman standing in a three-way mirror, naked and aroused, and a man's hands coming from behind, touching her. A different pose in each of the three mirrors. The man's hands in different places on her body. Touching. Caressing. Faceless bodies in nameless arousal, the man's lips in her hair. My hair. My desire.

I finished it at 4 a.m., having painted in a frenzy and a rage, a fury of seared nerve endings and need. I called it *My Hair*. And I loved it, positioning the canvas in my bedroom on an easel, angled so that I might see it upon first waking.

Exhausted, still tasting the tacos on my tongue, I slept, fully clothed, paint beneath my nails and my hair tangled upon the pillow. My breath was sour with the taste of onion, garlic and beer the next morning, and I woke with an unaccustomed headache. But when my eyes fell upon the erotic painting of Taber Rhame's hands on the woman, my blood seemed to sizzle with need and I knew. I knew how good it was.

'Oh God,' I whispered from the knotted sheets. 'Oh God . . .'

In one night my work had changed. Evolved. Been reborn. The man's hands – Tabor Rhame's strong, beautiful hands – were alive, moving, as aroused as if they had been a frontal nude in the act of sex. The sunlight poured through the shutters, touching those hands. The nails, the veins, the texture of the skin so alive in the sunlight.

'Oh God . . .'

I threw off the covers and let Perkins outside, wishing for the first time in my life that I had a phone. To call him. To wake him. To make him come to me. To show him what he'd given me. Feelings I did not understand, I had somehow been able to use.

'If the mountain won't come to Mohammed . . .' And I laughed, rushing through my toilet. Laughed as I combed my hair and tossed it into a ponytail; laughed as I brushed my teeth, blowing bubbles of Crest into the sink; laughed as I pulled on wrinkled jeans from the night before and a clean tuxedo shirt, the cuffs rolled up my forearms; laughed as I hung up the clothes I had left by the door in the wrappings, my fingers touching the Versace. The beads were cold.

'Josh,' I yelled. It was late, MacAloon should have been here, but the blue 'Vette was still parked out front. The man appeared, his right hand on his gun butt at his waist. Prepared. I wondered if he'd ever had to use it. 'I need a favor. I need a wet canvas taken to Rhame's place.'

'Will it fit in Lori?'

Somehow, I wasn't surprised that Josh had named his car. Probably had a sexual experience every time he climbed inside. 'I don't think so,' I yelled back. 'But how about on top, on a quilt to protect it?'

'I guess a quilt would keep the finish safe. You got one up there?'

I meant the painting, but Josh understood me to mean that we would be protecting his car. I didn't rectify his impression. Perkins barked, sticking his snout out and peering down the stairs.

'Several of them.'

'Fine. Need help to get it down the stairs?'

'Thanks, yes. Come on up.'

The bed wasn't made. But since there wasn't a car snuggled up on the pillows, I didn't think he'd notice. Tight jeans straining at the crotch, he bounded up the stairs. And stopped dead. Eyes on *My Hair*.

'Jesus. Shit, girl.'

I grinned. 'Yeah.' There didn't seem to be anything else to say.

I skipped the café and breakfast, and still arrived late at Rhame's studio. I could smell coffee perking through the door and felt a stab of guilt. Guilt that simply dissipated as *My Hair* climbed the stairs held gingerly in Josh Campos's blunt-fingered hands.

I pushed open the door and preceded the painting inside. Rhame, in the act of walking from kitchen to studio, stopped and stared at the light pouring in through the front door. He was wearing jeans, his bare feet firmly planted, his chest naked and muscled. Oh God. Please let him like it. It was as close to prayer as I'd come in years. Please . . .

Josh Campos followed me through the doorway, the canvas throwing a rectangular shadow across the bare wood.

'Thanks, Josh. You can put it right here.' He set the canvas on the floor, still moving slowly to avoid getting the wet oil on his hands. Ignoring both men and the measuring glances they leveled at one another, I repositioned the painting so the light from the open front shutters fell just right.

'Josh. Thanks again. Hope we didn't get any paint on Lori. I'll see you tonight. Okay?' It was an awfully broad hint, but after all, it was time for him to go. Time for MacAloon to take over as my guardian angel. And I wanted to be alone with Taber Rhame.

Josh's eyes moved from the painting to Rhame, measuring, considering, and then finally to me. 'Yeah. Right. Tonight, Bonnie.' And he laughed a low, intentionally sexy sound. Poor boy. He must have thought I liked cars. Sauntering almost, he left the apartment, closing the door behind him.

I watched Rhame's face. He looked rested. And perturbed. His eyes moved over me much like Josh's had. Measuring and evaluating. And . . . jealous? I studied his reactions.

Rhame was jealous, the way older men often are of younger, more virile men. The way the older, white men in Khoury had been jealous of the Boudreaux boys as they grew to a bronzed and beautiful manhood. Jealous and frightened of someone new and different and younger, who walked with pride and assurance and who might not look upon the old men with honor and respect.

Jealous of that empty-headed, brain-dead, car-jock with a vitamin complex. Who also happened to be a beautiful physical specimen. Sexy. Deep voice. Tough. And thirty years Rhame's junior.

It was an artwork in action, the interplay of emotion on Rhame's face, coupled with Josh's almost strutting vitality.

'What do you think?'

'He seems like a nice young man,' Rhame snapped.

'About the painting,' I said gently, biting my lip in amusement. 'The painting?'

Rhame turned and considered. Outrage wafted from every pore in his body. He was . . . offended. This, the man who had left my apartment last night whistling. *Whistling*. Was offended. I tasted blood in my effort to keep a straight face.

And suddenly, Rhame changed. The outrage thinned and faded, flowing from his body like water from a sieve. He moved closer to *My Hair*. Adjusted the angle of the canvas to the light, and studied. Silently.

Perkins, his nails too long, clicked through the apartment, checking the place out. I had forgotten all about the dog. He must have gotten out of Lori and followed me up the stairs.

My palms began to sweat as the seconds became minutes. My skin began to burn. To itch. I moved so I could see his eyes. But for once they were inscrutable. Almost cold.

'I don't know if I got the hands right,' I said. 'But the Versace in the background and the hair . . . and your mouth . . . I think all those are . . . right.' Whispering. Could he hear the pleading? I hoped not. But please. Please like it.

Rhame looked at his hands then, and back to the canvas. And at his hands, turning them. Looking. Studying. Still silent. Still inscrutable.

He looked at me, his eyes expressionless. And slowly he lifted his right hand, extended it to me, like the dancers we had been the night before.

I don't know why I wasn't embarrassed to have him see the canvas. To see my need and my response to him so fully. Perhaps only because it was art. And in art there is no embarrassment. No shame. Only beauty and need and the glory of human expression.

I took his hand.

He pulled me to him. Turned me so I was staring at *My Hair*.

His hands moving slowly, he pulled up the loose T-shirt I wore, slipped his hands beneath, to my skin. Caressed my stomach with a feather-light touch. My breasts hardened, like those in the painting. Tight buds. Aching.

Moving slowly, as slowly as a light snow falling and melting on warm leaves, he lifted the shirt and pulled it over my head. Dropped it at my feet. Oh God. Oh God.

He unzipped my jeans, the sound going on forever, bouncing off the plaster walls. Slowly, he pushed my jeans from my hips. Exposing the hollows, the roundness. The nylon print panties I wore. Pushing down, allowing the jeans to finally fall, pooling at my feet with a soft cloth-thud. And then the panties slowly pushed, slipped, fell.

His fingers traced the hollows of my hips, feather-light. Touched a bud of breast. Lighter still. Again I thought of snow, which I had so seldom seen. Burning cold. And I shivered.

The pads of his fingers pulled at the rubber band holding my hair. Slipped it loose with a soft twang and threaded his fingers into my hair. Massaging my scalp. Moving over the hollows and protuberances of bone and flesh, lifting my hair. Teasing it out. I closed my eyes and rested back against him, weak and powerless to oppose the sensations.

Rhame's mouth parted. I felt the faint motion of his lips in my hair. The fanning of his breath, so slight. Breezy warm.

'This is art, Bonnibelle Sarvaunt,' he said slowly. 'This is passion. This need that is so strong it pounds through your veins like a savage drum and raging bonfire. This heat beneath your skin, captured in the point of breast, the curve of waist and hollow of shoulder blade. The tender nape.' His fingers followed his voice, touching, barely, the surface of my skin.

'Use it. Use it all. And paint. For without passion, there is no art. Without passion, the artist has no power. His works lack life and fire and he might as well give up his art and teach three-year-old children to fingerpaint.'

And with those words, Taber Rhame, artist and womanizer, world-renowned rake and cad, left me and returned to his studio.

'Get dressed,' he called back. 'I will make you a place in here today. Bring the painting. We will paint together.'

Paint together? *Paint together?*

A ridiculous laugh surged up inside me. A silly, uncontrolled, unrestrained giggle that tinkled through the apartment. Taber Rhame wanted to paint with me.

I suppose I could have been insulted. Angry. Affronted and embarrassed. Perhaps I should have been. Instead, I considered what he was trying to say. Taber Rhame was an artist before he was a man, I knew that from my studies of him. And for the artist, there was only passion. Without passion, there was no art. With passion, art reached new levels, new heights . . . That was what he was trying to show me. And suddenly I understood.

I pulled on my clothes and lifted the painting. Carried it to the studio where Rhame had moved his finished canvases out of the way and set up an easel for me. A blank canvas, roughly the size of *My Hair*, was centered on the support.

Together, as the day flew by, we painted, pausing only twice, to eat leftovers from the fridge and for coffee. We talked as we painted and Rhame offered suggestions, pointing out refinements in technique, things I had never known or forgotten. Rhame tossed out anecdotes and spun yarns about famous names in the art world, making faces and sharing ribald jokes. I listened and painted and laughed, my blood pounding through my veins.

At five o'clock, exhausted and aching between my shoulder blades and down the length of my back from holding a brush for so many hours, I started home. MacAloon made the trip to the parking lot for my van, and helped me load *My Hair* and the new, partially painted canvas in the back.

Inside my apartment, the door safely closed and locked on the outside world, my body submerged in the deep, claw-footed tub, I soaked away the strain of unaccustomed activity. And I remembered the way Rhame's hands had imitated the placement of his hands in my painting. Remembered passion. The passion of art. Remembered every moment as the steam rose up around me and PBS radio played a long somber melody, something by Bach.

It should have been wild gypsy music, to echo the strains I could almost hear in my soul. Music put there by Taber Rhame's hands and the sheer joy of painting.

I began work on the new series that night, a sequence of near-erotic art. Nudes in fanciful places touching and sharing long, sensual glances, or thinking about making love, or remembering making love. Two black women in a sauna, faces dreamy, bodies lethargic. A man and woman dancing on a wharf, naked, a black sax player in the background, eyes closed as he belts out a tune. A young girl, belly swollen with pregnancy, wearing a down-under hat and nothing else, eating tacos, smiling in the obvious aftermath of passion. Other scenes, equally passionate.

They went fast, these almost erotic oils, the work churning out of me as if I were only reproducing the scenes, instead of painting them for the first time. They were bright, sensuous scenes, revealing a new part of me. Although the emotions that were pouring from me were untested, and the passion I painted was never really experienced, these paintings were full of life and energy.

Though I never again painted with Rhame – was, in fact, never invited into his studio except as a part of my duties – my painting went fast. And the days folded into weeks as the long summer drew to a hot and steamy close.

Moving slowly, so his footsteps couldn't be heard in the shop below, McCallum lifted the scarred black metal box and carried it to the front room. It had taken him a slow silent hour of searching to find it.

A mewling sound brought a half-smile to his lips. Hidden beneath the bed, the little dog scratched and whimpered and licked at himself. Cal didn't think the dog would ever again be so bold as to attack him. Animals learned fast. Pain was an excellent motivator.

There was light in the room she used as a studio, thin slits stripping the wooden floor. Squatting, he used the illumination to pick the lock on the box. His smile spread as it finally clicked open.

He paged through the contents of the box, finding the papers with the names he sought. 'Marie L. Smith DeVillier,' he whispered. 'Carin Colleen . . . pretty.' Bending into the light, he studied the dates, putting together Marie's duplicity. The girl had been good, even at sixteen years of age, covering her tracks well enough to hide from the DeLandes for two decades. Considering the scope of DeLande influence, vanishing was an impressive feat.

Carefully, he replaced the papers in their original order and closed the box. The lock clicked.

Before he left, he walked slowly about the studio, stopping before each of the paintings. He supposed they were good, but he had always preferred sculpture to canvas. The tactile sensations of cool bronze, or warm wood, or smooth stone were what satisfied his artistic soul, not color and paint. But to each his own.

Shrugging, he returned the box to its spot in the bottom of

the armoire. With sensitive fingers, he adjusted its angle until it perfectly matched its original position.

Pocketing the key he had stolen from Cee Cee Gaudet's bedside table, McCallum let himself from the apartment.

There was a strange scent in the apartment, delicate and sweet, scarcely detectable beneath the stronger smells of paint and thinner. Perfume. Vaguely masculine.

I stood in the doorway a long moment before the wrongness of it all hit me. The smell. And the absence of Perkins. Someone had been in my apartment.

A shudder quaked through me and I gripped the door jamb, dropping my bag to the porch. Inside it, a small mirror cracked and split apart, the small sound sharp on the silence. Perkins wasn't here.

I took two quick steps backward, toward the railing. 'MacAloon!' I shouted, though the sound was too breathy to carry far. 'MacAloon! Someone's been in my apartment.'

He must have been watching, waiting for me to enter and close the door, because his footsteps on the stairs followed instantly on my words. Unceremoniously, he pushed me aside and entered the apartment, his gun held in one hand, pointing downward. Tears started then, and my lips trembled.

Flipping on the lamp, MacAloon moved into the apartment while I waited, frozen to the porch. I was too much a coward to follow. Afraid of what he would find. My imagination sent vivid pictures of Perkins, dead on the kitchen floor, his blood dark beneath him. My shivers increased.

'It's clear, Bonnie. Come on in.'

'Perkins?' I was crying big silent tears, and MacAloon looked up at me from beside the bed. He was bent over, one arm beneath the bed, pulling. Perkins followed the arm's slow withdrawal, his small black eyes wide in the lamplight.

I buried my face in Perkins' fur and gave way to tears. A good old-fashioned sobbing, like a relieved child. I had lost Tee Dom and Tante Ilene and even my own identity. I didn't think I could stand losing Perkins too. His pink tongue lapped once at my wet cheeks.

'Let me have him, Bonnie. I think he's hurt.'

I gave Perkins over to MacAloon's capable hands and watched as the bodyguard checked over the small dog. Perkins was stretched out on my bed, trembling, but curiously still. A flame about to flicker out. He whimpered as MacAloon pressed on his front legs, and I whimpered with him.

'They aren't broken, but I think he should be checked out. Who's your vet?'

I sniffed. 'I don't have a vet yet.'

'Come on. I have a friend who'll see him.'

MacAloon lifted Perkins from my mattress and cradled the small body in his arms. I suppose it was obvious that, in my present state, I would drop the dog within two steps. I was so relieved at finding Perkins alive that I was weak all over, my knees trembling as much as Perkins'.

I had left him alone because of the rain. But the rain had stopped just after lunch and the sun had come out. I should have taken him with me . . .

Perkins rested on my lap all the way across town, his tail wagging only rarely. The visit to the vet was a drawn-out affair with blood drawn and X-rays and even a small tube inserted up into Perkins' bladder. An hour and half after we walked in the door, MacAloon, Perkins and I went back home.

Perkins was bruised as if he had been kicked, with a small amount of blood in his urine from traumatized kidneys. But the vet thought he would be fine in a day or two. He sent us out the door with instructions to return in forty-eight hours for a check-up, giving me a small vial of liquid medication, and a list of symptoms to watch for should Perkins take a turn for the worse.

I didn't sleep that night, lying curled on the bed beside the small dog, watching him breathe. I cried off and on all night, unable to regain the control I lost when I thought Perkins was gone or dead. I knew my tears were as much for Tante Ilene and Tee Dom as for my dog. And for myself. For the changes I had created in my own life and the identity I had lost.

I had never really believed that I was Bonnibelle Sarvaunt, yet I had never mourned her passing. During the long hours of the night, I cried for them all. All the people I had lost.

And now, there was also fear. Even though MacAloon had

changed the lock on my door before he left me alone in the apartment, I knew I was vulnerable. I was being hunted like a doe in the woods. Stalked by someone who had somehow gotten a key to my home. MacAloon said the lock had not – could not have – been picked. I was prey. I was afraid.

After that night, Perkins was never left alone. He stayed with Cee Cee or Charles Stuart if I couldn't take him with me. And when I painted, he lay curled up at my feet, wanting to be close to me, his eyes on my face. He was the best kind of critic. He loved everything I did, everything I painted. And the painting continued to flow from me, the erotic oils and the bayou scenes I had loved all my life.

During the weeks that followed the attack on Perkins, I also worked on the triptych for Royal Securities. The sunset-to-moonlight nesting scene of the egrets coming home to roost. And when I wasn't working for Rhame or painting in my apartment, I was visiting galleries and museums and studios of other artists, most of them native Louisianians, painting Louisiana scenes. Picked up suggestions, absorbed technique, listened to the egotistical authorities, the self-proclaimed virtuosos speechify, vocalize and articulate. In other words, brag.

I decided that boasting wasn't for me. If anyone asked me about my work, I'd just shrug and say 'I don't know where it comes from'. And, in truth, I didn't. Then the painting just poured out of me like dreams, like sweat from the pores, like sexual desire. Like the passion Taber Rhame had taught me.

Besides my painting and Perkins, the other bright spot in my days was the Grande Dame. She loved my work, buying *My Hair* for ten thousand dollars and calling it a steal, her eyes glistening and wide as she stared at the canvas.

There was something in her eyes as she stared at *My Hair* for the first time. Some emotion I couldn't name. Her lids seemed to grow heavy, and her fingers languorous as they stroked the long column of her throat. Her skin flushed a soft and delicate pink, and her breathing became unsteady. Her reaction, while gratifying, was so bizarre, that I almost wished someone else had purchased the painting. Or that I had never sold it.

Yet, my growing relationship with the Grande Dame was the kind of association that any young artist would kill for. She took me to lunch twice and to supper three times. We ate at Felix's, and Mike's on the Avenue, Tujagues, Delmonicos, and the Napoleon House. Elegant places. Places where I could wear my new clothes, break in my new shoes. Places where she introduced me as a new and talented artist. Her protégé. The attention was heady as wine.

She bought me small gifts, including a priceless amber piece that looked stunning with the Versace. Perhaps I shouldn't have accepted it, but it was perfect with the dress and far more expensive than anything I could have afforded alone. Taber advised, 'Take it. Enjoy.'

And I continued to make money. Not a fortune, as in the seventy-thousand-dollar bonanza, but a steady yield as the European market took an upward turn and the dollar continued to fall. I was getting good at making money. Twice, Claude Michau followed my lead with positive results. The ultimate acclaim.

The only darkness in those weeks was with Stocker and the things she learned about my past. William Marc DeVillier was a scrawny, wasted, pale imitation of a man. HIV positive from repeated jailhouse rapes, vacant-eyed and haggard, he had stared silently at Stocker across an interview table as she questioned him. She had tried a dozen different ways to get him to respond, but the most he would do was suck on a molar as if it pained him.

The guard, watching her efforts, just laughed. 'He's always like this. A real magpie, that boy. Chatters away like a gossipin' girl.' After fifteen minutes Stocker was ready to give up, gathering her bag, her clipboard, reaching for the tape-player to shut it off, when Billy Marc suddenly looked up.

I listened to his words on tape, again and again, following the transcript Stocker had provided. Visualizing the scene, the conversation, the body language. I could almost see the burnt-out, sickly man, old before his time, balding, weak-chinned, with watery eyes and a thin moustache. It was so clear, I might have been there.

'Who?'

'Marie Lisette. Your wife.'

Billy Marc stuck a finger into his mouth, and palpated the sore gum. 'Ain't got no wife.'

Stocker slipped a crisp sheet of paper across the table to Billy Marc. 'According to this, you do.'

Billy Marc studied the photocopy of his marriage license, brows pinched together, blinking slowly. Finally he nodded, his wet lips almost smiling. 'She give me a thousand dollars fer that. Cash money.' His spit-damp fingers rubbed against his thumb in the universal sign for currency. 'Said she needed a new name and mine would do. A real looker, that gal. Even if she was knocked up. Did I tell you she paid me a thousand dollars? Cash money.' There was a long pause as Billy shook his head. 'Never saw her again. Figured we was divorced by now.' Again the pause.

'You say she was pregnant when you married her? Big pregnant?' Stocker prompted.

But Billy Marc was no longer paying attention, sucking gently on the back tooth. His eyes blank.

'In my professional opinion, the man's mind is gone, either because of the HIV or the years of living in a bottle,' Stocker said in our post-interview conference. 'And I don't know how much significance you can attach to anything he said during the interview. But we know your mother was trying to hide herself and you from someone. It would seem to be in character for her to pay a man to marry her, change her name, maybe more than once. She could have married several men during her pregnancy, changed her name each time. There's no way of knowing.

'My suggestion is to concentrate on the man paying MacAloon to protect you, and keep looking for your aunt and uncle. That is, if you want to continue the investigation. Do you?'

I didn't know if I wanted to find my mother anymore. I wasn't sure if it really mattered. But I did want to find Tee Dom and Tante Ilene, and my need for them continued to confuse me. We had been estranged for so many years. Like strangers who share a piece of real estate yet aren't on speaking terms. Yet, at times I was almost paralyzed with worry about them. Unable to paint. Unable to think clearly. And I would sit and stroke Perkins for hours, letting the little dog lick my face and hands for the comfort he gave me.

Their welfare and unknown whereabouts pulled at me continually. Their eyes haunted me from the half-finished canvases, cried out to me as the swamp dwellers pulled them beneath the surface.

They were in trouble. Somehow I knew it. They were in trouble because of me.

Because of the secrets in my past. In my mother's past. Secrets so terrible that my mother had hidden me away for my whole life. Secrets that somehow had been unlocked by someone. Secrets that had cost Cooter Bug his life . . .

The Grande Dame divided her time between the estate, the plans for the showing, and New Orleans. She never asked about my past, who I was, where I came from. My past seemed unimportant to her. But my plans, my dreams, my hopes . . . These she probed and prodded. Cultivated. She encouraged me to go to Paris to paint. Encouraged me to travel. Encouraged me to live a free and independent lifestyle, see the world, taste new things, experience cultural diversity. Live, as Taber Rhame had lived so widely and well, and then paint what I felt, what I saw and smelled and heard, touched and tasted. She was cheerleader, sponsor, champion and friend. She was an adventure in herself.

Although Cee Cee and Perkins had reservations about the Grande Dame, both remaining aloof and distant, I liked her. Because she liked me. Doted on me. Lavished attention and money and effort on me. I loved it. I was susceptible to the blandishments of wealth and power and beauty. I admitted it. And if a small, quiet voice questioned my good fortune, I stifled it.

The invitation to the showing arrived in the mail, an embossed card on heavy paper, a family crest on both invitation, RSVP, and the envelopes. I ran my fingers over the raised crest, which looked like some kind of bird of prey.

The excitement bubbled up again like bubbles in champagne, and I felt almost giddy. Not a very adult response to success, but who cared? I stroked the invitation. Sniffed its woodsy scent, overlaid with the sharper fragrance of printer's ink. I'd have to buy a scrap book soon to keep a record of it all. Press releases, blurbs in the society pages.

And underneath the excitement ran a storm-surge of fear. I had read so many unkind reviews of an artist's first work. What if they hated my paintings, the amorphous 'they' who controlled the public appreciation of art and artists.

I practiced my yoga often after that, finding a sort of serenity in the stretching, the slow pull of muscles, the controlled, steady breathing. I had forgotten to exercise in the days and weeks in New Orleans, replacing the mastery of my body with the exhilaration of new sensation, new people, new perceptions, and a new lifestyle. On a small scale, I had lived the adventure the Grande Dame had recommended. And been swamped by it. Taking control of my body again helped me to see my world and my self with greater clarity and a bit less narcissism. Besides, the weeks in New Orleans had made me flabby.

Rhame scarcely noticed me at all, communicating with me by notes left tacked to the front door. Ignoring the meals I cooked by day, devouring the cold leftovers late at night, alone, and leaving the dirty dishes in the sink for me the next day.

He painted twenty hours a day, pouring himself into his art. Losing weight. Forgetting to shower or shave. The few times I saw him, he looked and smelled like a hermit living in a cave somewhere far from civilization.

It was just as well that he was too busy for me, I thought. I needed the time to paint. But I missed the human touch – Taber's amused glance over coffee, his exuberant laughter, the stories he had previously shared with Charles Stuart and me in the kitchen downstairs after lunch.

Now, I heard his voice only in his studio, whispering to his canvases as if they could hear. Murmuring endearments.

At some point I came to realize that Taber Rhame was a self-absorbed man whose ego had cost him numerous marriages and relationships. And since the day Perkins was hurt, I no longer wanted to be among the list of women he had loved. What the dog's injury had to do with Rhame, I didn't know. But since my all-night cry, I simply felt nothing for the artist at all, as if my tears had flooded out all extraneous emotion.

All I wanted was to be left alone. Perkins was good company, affectionate and loyal, unlike Rhame. And though his conversational skills left a lot to be desired, he was markedly more interesting than Josh Campos had ever been.

However, I had begun to change following my brief contact with human touch. I began to want . . . something. To need something new and different in my life. Something . . . exciting?

Perhaps only that indefinable 'more' that so many people search for all their lives.

Strange things were happening deep inside me, changes simmering with slow heat. Things that woke me from restless slumber. Things that left me feeling dangerously empty. And that emptiness I poured into my art.

Preparing for the showing altered me in a thousand small ways. And yet, ten days before the showing, I discovered a catalyst that redirected my focus.

I was perusing a little gallery on Chartres, a cool, dark, closet-of-a-place, so small I could view half of all the canvases from a single spot. It was all modern work, Cubists and Impressionists standing cheek-to-jowl with Louisiana landscapes and photo-realists. Some of it was very good. Some mediocre. And one which was riveting.

It was a bayou scene. An oil about twenty-four by thirty-six inches, all bright and airy and somehow full of promise.

In the foreground was the bark of an old oak, the texture so rough and coarse I could almost feel its roots all gnarled and twisted, sunk deep in black water.

A single egret, standing on one leg, stood poised, his gaze directed into the water. Fishing. And in the background – its front porch the dock, its foundation huge pilings green with mold – was a house.

It could have been any house on any bayou, weathered, beaten, rugged, and plain. And any old oak.

But the oak had a silver boat-tie forced deep in its side. The kind you screw in with hand power alone, like screwing in a corkscrew. It was anodized metal. Triangular in shape. It was the boat-tie screwed into the bark of the fallen chenier on Bayou Negre. The one that was now under water. And the house . . . was the Sarvaunt Shanty . . . closed up for winter.

My jaw ached. A blinding pain shot through my eyes. Forcing a breath deep into my laboring lungs, I fought for calm. For the peace promised in the painting. But I found neither. Even behind closed lids I could see the triangular tie. The empty house.

'Interesting piece, isn't it?'

The voice, a low melodious tone, spoke from my shoulder level. Female. The kind of voice you hear in a darkened hospital room, or from a nighttime FM channel. Easy listening. I just wanted her to go away.

'It's one of the artist's earlier works and one of the finest we've ever carried.'

I heard the sentence again. *It's one of the artist's earlier works, and one of the finest we've ever carried.* Slowly, so she wouldn't vanish like a character in a dream, I opened my eyes.

'One of her earlier works?' I took a deep breath, shuddering.

'Yes. Are you familiar with LaVay's work?'

'No. I'm not. Tell . . . Tell me about her.'

Tell me. Tell me about my mother. Because I knew, beyond any doubt, that I had found my mother. My real mother. The one who gave me her genetic history, but denied me her life history. The one who secreted me in a backwater spot, and left me to be raised by a loveless couple.

They didn't love me. They didn't. They couldn't have loved me all those years and yet never touched me. Never talked to me. Never told me about my mother and my past and . . .

Then why had Tante Ilene cried when I left home?

'She's been around for years, at least fifteen, and I understand that she lives in Milan now.'

Milan? Italy?

'She comes to the States once a year or so, to show her work. We've been friends for about five years. She's quite mysterious and exotic, but for some reason, she likes me. That's how we are able to offer her work on a regular basis.'

'How much?'

'Five thousand. Of course, a more recent work would go for five times that. But these early works are beginning to sell well too. LaVay is about thirty-five now, I think, and this one was painted about twenty years ago before she developed her present technique. You can see the adolescent hand in the perspective and the light. You can see the occasional flaw here and there, and yet you can also see flashes of pure brilliance in the way the light touches the feathers of the bird and flashes on the water.'

'I'll pay four thousand. On condition I get to talk to the artist.' The words surprised me. I hadn't known I was going to say that.

'I don't know . . . I—'

'Look. Here's the check.' I drew out my checkbook and quickly wrote one for four thousand dollars. 'You contact the artist, okay? Tell her that I have to talk to her. I can be reached here most days.' I scribbled a phone number on the bottom of the check. 'I work for Taber Rhame. This is his business number. Have her call me. Please. I . . . I really like the work.'

'Well, I'm sure you do, and I would love to sell it to you, but, only four thousand . . . I don't see how I could let it go for that.'

I looked at the store-owner then, wanting to know what kind of woman my mother would like. She was portly, with shiny skin and too much eye makeup. An unattractive woman with a flat nose and exposed nostril openings. She dressed well and there was a kindness in her eyes that I liked. But none of the guile so necessary to the born salesman.

'You'll take the four thousand,' I said with a certainty in my voice I didn't really feel. 'And you'll call this LaVay because you're curious. And because she'll know my name. And because you want to meet Taber Rhame.'

I took a deep steadying breath. The blood was pounding in my head, and the pain was spreading down, into my neck and back. 'And I can arrange for you to meet him.' The sentences came out clipped. Short. Like my breathing.

I was suddenly lightheaded and dizzy. And then I realized I had been lightheaded and dizzy from the moment I saw the silver anodized boat-tie. And I might very well pass out. I took a deep breath. Another. Fighting the pain and the shock and the vertigo that flooded over me.

'Can you?'

'Pass out? Yes. Very likely,' I wanted to say. A titter gurgled at the back of my throat. Because I didn't answer, she asked again. And I knew I had her. I knew I had the painting.

'Can you introduce me to Taber Rhame?'

'Better than that,' I said, my voice all breathy and slow. 'I can get you an invitation to the private showing of his newest series at the DeLande Estate next week.'

The shop-owner looked at the check, the canvas on the wall, and back to me. 'I'll hold the check until I have the invitation.'

'I'll tell the bank to hold the check until I get the call.'

The store-owner laughed. It was a melodious tinkling sound, like wind chimes in a light breeze. 'I can't guarantee she'll want to call you.'

'Look. You tell her my name, give her my number, and if she calls, fine. If she doesn't, fine. Four thousand for the painting and the attempt on your part.'

'How do you know I'll even try to reach her?'

'I don't. I'm gambling four thousand dollars that you will.'

'Sold. To the deal-maker in the sneakers and the rayon dress who might pass for twelve on a good day.'

I laughed, and so did she. And I knew why my mother liked her so much. I knew.

CHAPTER 14

Royal Securities had narrowed the field of artists from a dozen down to three, and my name made the cut. The story was being followed by an art lover on the local news, and I actually heard my name, along with the two other finalists, mentioned on the late news.

It was a slow news day, and the reporters were having a hard time showing excitement about anything not involving an AK 47 or handgun violence. But the announcement was exciting to me. Buoyed by the rush, I slept even less than usual after that night.

And because there were no more problems related to my security, no more unexpected visitors to my apartment, nothing unusual in my life at all, I was able to enjoy the excitement. Perhaps it was simply my youth, something about being able to put problems out of mind, or perhaps it was the constant presence of MacAloon and Josh, but I found I was able to throw myself into my work and forget the danger to myself and my mother.

I turned the excitement, the elation, the unfulfilled passionate energy into my art. It wasn't usual for an artist to divide her concentration between two such disparate series of works, but I had no difficulty working on the bayou series and the carnal series at the same time.

The bayou series – which was dark and mysterious, haunting even – I called *Genesis*. The earthy, sensual series, I called *Wanton Dreams*. And it was as if I turned on one half of myself to paint *Genesis*, then – like flipping a switch – ignited the other half of myself to paint *Wanton Dreams*. Through my art, I was living out the two sides of myself, Bonnibelle Sarvaunt, the girl raised in backwater bayou territory, and Carin Colleen DeVillier, unknown artist, and untried hedonist.

Somewhere, between working as Tabor Rhame's mostly ignored assistant, painting, and handling my growing investment portfolio, I found the time to read the diary of Beth Sarvaunt. It was the classic story of a young girl following in the footsteps of her fallen mother. Meeting a married man – her supervisor at work in the refinery – and indulging in a clandestine affair. And when she became pregnant, she ran away to hide her condition and her disgrace from her family and her world. It wasn't until she met an even younger unwed mother, long after the birth and tragic death of her child, that Beth Sarvaunt's story became so riveting.

In the last few days before the showing at the DeLande Estate everything seemed to come together. The paintings were drying, both series completed except for framing. Taber Rhame was sending me home early every day. The gallery owner had left my message with LaVay, and although I hadn't heard from her, I knew that soon I would . . . I just knew it.

Stocker had a line on the mysterious Miles Jenkins who was still paying MacAloon for protecting me. It wasn't anything that she would discuss with me until she could provide some documentation to support the hearsay. Miles Jenkins, who was apparently out of the country, was expected back in the next two weeks. At that time, she would be able to confirm or deny the stories she had unearthed.

Tante Ilene and Tee Dom had not been located. The only thing Stocker had proven about my aunt and uncle was that they had not gone to Tee Dom's sister, as my letter from them claimed.

Stocker had found the elderly woman living in a small clapboard house in Lafayette. She was worried sick about the brother who had not arrived as planned, and who had not contacted her to explain. She promised to call Stocker when – if – Tee Dom called her.

At loose ends, just a bit bored, and worried about the elderly couple I now thought of as having abandoned when I left Khoury, I walked with Perkins through the Vieux Carré, shopped, cooked solitary meals, and read Beth Sarvaunt's diary. She was a lonely, desolate woman. I read how she loved the one friend she had ever made: Mary. My mother.

Nowhere in the diary was she identified other than as Mary, except once when Beth wrote, 'I was wrong. Her name isn't Mary. It's Marie, but pronounced like the French do. So – Mary. Such a pretty name. Such a pretty girl. So tall. And beautiful eyes. Really beautiful eyes.'

And in another place, 'She took me to dinner tonight at the Tearoom. I had never eaten at a place like that before. It was so great. And even when she was bigger than a watermelon, Mary was so cool. So elegant. I wish I could be half so classy.'

It was at 2 a.m. during a rain storm, when I found the first glimmer of truth about my mother. Beth Sarvaunt had written,

Mary is really my cousin, like my second or third cousin or something. She explained it all over supper tonight. We went to Bascomb's and had fried seafood platters and she paid as usual and she told me about how she had been looking for me.

She eats like she's starving, but even though she's five months along, she never gains any weight. Weird. Anyway, she had found Tee Dom and Tante Ilene, and stayed with them a few days and they asked her to find me. They had my letters, after all, and she went to the place of the postmark and finally tracked me down. They want me to come home. Me and the baby. But my baby Bonnie's dead. I have to think about this. I have to decide. My best friend turns out to be my cousin, and they want me back home. They really want me.

Beth Sarvaunt had been in awe of Mary. So much so that when Mary eventually proposed giving her baby Bonnibelle's name in order to protect her daughter's life, Beth agreed. What a tangle my mother had created to hide me away. Why? What had been so terrible to a sixteen-year-old girl? What had been so bad, that she married a stranger – at least one stranger, perhaps more – and exchanged her child's identity for that of a dead baby? What had she feared? Or whom? By the time we left for the showing none of my questions had been answered.

The day finally arrived when Taber Rhame and I loaded up our canvases in a rented van, each canvas secured by a padded frame. Behind the canvases, we stacked our luggage, mine in my new-old Louis Vuitton travel cases.

I had picked the cases up in a sixties retro shop, a place where everything was well used, at least fifteen years old, and some considerably older. But you can't hide quality. The cases cleaned up very nicely.

Rhame's things went south in a World War II packing crate. One the French had once used to store uniforms. And then the Germans had used to send stolen antiquities back to the Fatherland. And we rode down together with MacAloon and Josh Campos trailing along behind in Lori.

Josh had a hard time keeping the fast car at the sedate speed I drove. For Josh, the fifty-five-mile-an-hour speed limit was more in the line of a casual suggestion instead of the law. I supposed he would bite his fingernails to the quick and wear out his brakes long before we reached the DeLande Estate. The roar and screech style of driving wasn't characteristic of Josh, and had to be making MacAloon half-crazy. But I had to drive in a leisurely fashion to protect the canvases riding in the back.

For me it was a wonderful trip thanks to the air-conditioning. The state's one cool spell had long ago burned off in the heat of Louisiana's extended summer. Residents of Louisiana were always parboiled or steamed from April through October, but at least the winters were mild and easy. Many homes in Khoury didn't even have central heating, making do with electric blankets and kerosene heaters on the few really cold days.

We stopped twice for Rhame to check the canvases and to pick up snacks. Boudin balls – highly spiced meat and rice, fried to a crisp – and cracklins, Cokes and red beans and rice, a dietary staple in the state. My red beans were better than the ones we purchased, but then, I didn't have to cook these. And the boudin was really good. As good as anything Tante Ilene ever served.

Rhame talked as I drove, telling me about his Cajun mother and the stories she told about Louisiana, entertaining him in the years of his extreme youth. It was the first time in weeks he had even noticed that I was alive, and it was gratifying to see the sparkle in his eyes and know that I had put it there. I wasn't naïve enough to think that he was interested in me. But his conversation did make for a pleasant trip.

Rhame's mother had been born in a two-room shanty in the middle of a hurricane, raised to be self-sufficient, educated as a nurse, and then moved to Lafayette to work in a hospital. At the start of World War II, she had enlisted, served in two hospitals in the States, one in England. After the war, she was transferred to France, her native tongue securing her the plum assignment of a station in Paris. There she had met and married Rhame's father, a wounded resistance fighter.

Taber had been raised on stories of alligators and catfish, shrimp and crabs, poisonous snakes and swamp land. He had known and loved the wet abundant landscape vicariously all these years. But he had never visited it. I offered him use of the Sarvaunt Shanty anytime, and his eyes sparkled at the thought of living for a while as his mother had.

But first – the showing.

Taber Rhame, world-renowned artist, could be nonchalant about a small showing in the middle of nowhere. Even a showing as exclusive and elegant as this one would be. But for me it was a beginning. A first.

My level of excitement climbed as I drove, and my giddy chatter kept Rhame entertained for much of the ride. When we weren't discussing his mother, I was babbling away in disjointed phrases, pointing out the first of the sugarcane fields, the old tidewater homes, a dark hirsute man in loose boxer shorts crabbing from a pirogue. We saw green fields of purple water-hyacinth covering the bayous, obscuring the dark water, an alligator cooling himself in the deeps, only his eyes visible. Buzzards, raccoons, and once, an armadillo.

We drove past mansions no union general had torched, palatial homes restored to pre-Civil War grandeur. Horse farms were everywhere. Huge modern barns and expensive homes on acres of rolling green pastures stood neck-and-jowls with small, rundown mom-and-pop spreads. Minuscule places of five or ten acres where any single horse was valued higher than the unpainted family home.

The land was rich and lush in the late summer months, muddy, yet clean. Seldom did we see trash on the side of the road, and then only because it floated on top of the green algae that coated the still, stagnant swamp water. I'll admit I took the scenic route, following the map through back roads and detours, meandering across the landscape. But Rhame enjoyed it as much as I.

Our arrival at the DeLande Estate went unheralded by trumpets and ceremony. For miles we passed cultivated fields and sugarcane, hay barns and outbuildings, and of course pasture. Acres of it, all part of the DeLande holdings. The horseflesh visible in the fields off the road were thoroughbred racing stock, even to my untutored eyes. Huge animals, silky-coated and rambunctious, strong-willed and high-spirited, grazed or played or were worked on longue line or under saddle. The smell of hay and fresh growing things and manure wafted into the truck cab through the air-conditioning system.

And the main house itself was simply magnificent.

Set off the road on the top of a slight rise, a double row of old oaks banded the drive. To the left was pasture, to the right, a pecan grove, and all around the house were gardens. It was too late in the season to see the thousands of azaleas in bloom, but I could imagine the sight, the riotous color, the frenzy of intense hues bracketing that splendid house. The huge, beautiful house.

It was two stories of sparkling white-wood frame, built to withstand hurricanes and time. From the front it appeared to be shaped like an 'E', the longest wing facing the drive. It had a wrap-around, two-story porch with circular stairs at each corner, and tall windows from ceiling to floor, as well as a perfectly stunning number of rockers and chairs and small lounges and tables and wicker sofas tucked against the house wall.

A circular porch with a pointed roof like a witch's hat was to the left of the entry, leaving the house unbalanced. Yet the effect was quaint. The front door was massive, ebony wood centered with an astonishing plaque of the DeLande symbol.

It wasn't a family crest in the traditional sense, but more of a trademark. A ferocious, warlike bird of prey with blood-ied talons.

I knew a bit about birds and this one had no basis in reality. Dr Tammany was a bird lover of the highest order. When we weren't discussing history, we were watching birds through the back windows of his house or from a secret place in the woodland, binoculars pressed to our eyes. The DeLande bird had talons and the correct number of toes, two wings, feathers and a beak. But it wasn't a falcon or a hawk, an eagle or an owl. It was the product of someone's imagination. Vicious and feral. Utterly lovely. Something about it reminded me of the Grande Dame, and the comparison made me shiver.

The only blight on the beautiful postcard-perfect setting was a bare patch of earth to the left of the front door in front of the witch's capped porch. Mounded earth and piles of sawdust proved that a great tree had once stood on the spot, shadowing the little porch that now glistened in the too-bright sun.

The tree had been removed only recently. The stripped raw earth was peeled open, marked by tire tracks and footprints and small twigs. Sprays of wilted wisteria lay among the debris, broken and crushed, the vine shriveled from the heat. Wisteria was a two-faced plant. Looking fragile and weak and boasting of large purple blooms, it was a beautiful vine in early spring. Yet it slowly strangled any tree or bush it climbed.

Odd that such a destructive vine had been allowed to grow unchecked in the cultivated southern garden. Somehow I knew it had, however. And it had killed its host tree.

As the rented U-Haul truck pulled up, the front door opened, revealing a dark maw centered with a formally dressed man of about fifty. Closing the door behind him, the man walked to the top of the porch steps and paused, his hands clasped behind his back, his brows lifted in inquiry. A disdainful and patronizing pose.

Rhame opened the door of the cab and heat roiled in. Before he could open his mouth, the man spoke.

'Mr Rhame, I presume?' His speech was stilted and nasal, and as he spoke, his lips thinned with distaste. I instantly disliked the butler.

'Yes. I am he. And—'

'And may I assume that Miss Sarvaunt is accompanying you?' Apparently Rhame didn't talk fast enough to suit the butler. His whole attitude said that he considered us artistic trash, little better than traveling gypsies. Rhame's gray eyes narrowed.

'Yes. You may assume that. You may also assume that our canvases and luggage are in the back, and our bodyguards are in the car behind us.' Rhame stepped from the truck cab and climbed the steps as he spoke, each foot landing perfectly balanced and smooth. 'We will need three chambers, one for Miss Sarvaunt with an adjoining suite for her bodyguards, and a larger one nearby for me.' The butler's brows rose and he took a step back before he stopped and squared his already blade-sharp shoulders.

Rhame had reached the porch, standing a single step below the butler. Taber Rhame wasn't a particularly tall or menacing character, unlike MacAloon who was climbing the stairs to Rhame's left, yet the artist somehow seemed bigger suddenly. Ruthless and almost dangerous.

I laughed softly, hidden in the cab. Taber Rhame had dealt with haughty underlings for years. His own conceit with them was legendary.

'You, my good man, may go and inform your mistress and the head butler that we have arrived, prepare our rooms, and then send some servants to assist in off-loading the canvases.' Before the butler could speak, he added, 'Well, go on. Don't dawdle about in the heat, man.' Then, with great disdain, Rhame turned his back on the butler and started down the stairs, his head bent to MacAloon as if in conversation. Two seconds later, Rhame paused and looked back. 'And by the by, what is your name?'

'It's Jenkins, sir. The *head butler*.' Jenkins' eyes were glacial, in counterpoint to his color which was over-warm.

'Really?' Rhame started back down the stairs again. 'Even the Grande Dame must have difficulty in obtaining good help these days. Surprising. Her standards were always so high, you know.' This last to MacAloon, whose lips were quirked up in a grin.

The butler huffed off. I predicted we would have poor service and problems with the help during our entire stay, but it was worth it to see Jenkins' expression just before he stomped off. There was even a damp stain darkening the starched armpits of his formal coat. Probably the first time in years he had broken a sweat.

The servants Rhame had demanded never appeared and the four of us ended up toting the canvases through the hallways to the ballroom without assistance. From blinding sunlight and wet heat, into mercifully cool, dry air and darkness we trudged again and again, carrying Rhame's twelve canvases and my ten.

The ballroom was down the main hallway which ran the length

of the house, then to the right, down another hallway, then left and down still another hallway that ran the length of the ballroom.

The elegant old chamber had been restored to its pre-Civil War perfection, with heavy painted plaster scrollwork at the ceiling moldings and above windows and doors. The floor was inlaid parquetry with multi-hued woods, the long boards at the periphery a uniform fourteen-inch-wide cypress. The long space of persimmon-painted wall was broken by old masters wired for security and tall, gilt-edged mirrors. The moldings were a two-tone shrimp and pale peach with the rosettes tinted a darker peach with green leaves.

The focal point, the highlight, the very heart of the room, was the ceiling. Designed in a parody of Michelangelo's Sistine Chapel, it rose eighteen feet above the floor in arches that came together in the center of the room. The arches divided the ceiling into four sections, and in each section was a scene of Rubenesque nudes cavorting with satyrs and fiends. An erotic playground.

I couldn't imagine any mother allowing her virginal daughters to dance beneath the painted scenes, at least not back during the days of the ballroom's heyday, the days of pre-Civil War pomp and circumstance. The scenes practically thumbed their noses at Victorian propriety. Anyone who could have given successful parties in this room would have proven their power with little else said or done. And perhaps that was the point, after all. The mighty DeLandes had answered to no one back then. And things hadn't changed much since.

With the help of Josh and MacAloon, Rhame and I placed twelve easels along the back wall of the room, and rested each of Rhame's canvases on them. The Grande Dame's display easels were antique and probably cost more than twenty thousand dollars apiece. Some were matched Spanish pieces of ebony wood inlaid with mother-of-pearl. Others were of rosewood or cherry, inlaid with other precious woods or strips of silver. Two were gilt – the real thing, not an imitation. Wood overlaid with beaten twenty-four-karat gold.

It was an eclectic setting for the modern paintings, yet, somehow, instead of looking out of place, the canvases looked perfect. When Rhame was pleased with the placement of each easel and painting, we worked on the hallway out front, locating the more mundane easels with my canvases.

At the beginning of the hallway, where shadow was strongest, we placed *Genesis*, making sure the wall sconces had fresh candles, and unscrewing the lamps that would have cast too much light and wounded the bayou scenes. Further along the hallway, where the tall French doors let in light and the view of the pool, we displayed *Wanton Dreams*, with *My Hair* prominently located at the wide double doors of the ballroom. There was a discrete 'sold' tab on the corner.

During the time we moved heavy canvases and easels and worked up a sweat, we saw no other members of the household, though I had understood that the estate was home to four generations of DeLandes. Even the servants had vanished. The work of the irate Jenkins, no doubt.

When we were finished, Rhame took me on a tour of the ground floor of the main wing. Talking in loud tones, he described the grandeur of the building itself, gave me an art appreciation course along the way, and led me through the parlors, the music room, the dining room which was big enough to hold my entire apartment without straining at the seams, and the family room.

It was a curious house, stuffed with a mish-mash of treasures from the last three hundred years, all placed in unbalanced combinations. It was almost unnerving, yet the décor was held together throughout the main floor by the use of dark forest-green moldings and wood-carved trim.

The ballroom was on the end of the bottom of the 'E'-shaped house, with the drive along the long front of the upright. The music room was in the bottom corner of the house, graced with a grouping of antique violins and a cello, all stringless, an old Steinway – out of tune. There were two dark green Art Deco-style chairs positioned to view two Monets.

On the parlor walls to the right of the entrance hung a collection of Picasso drawings, the modern shapes a sharp contrast to the ornate turn-of-the-century furniture. Everywhere were old rugs, priceless art, family heirlooms, and collections that rivaled those of most museums.

The dining room, to the left of the entrance and behind the locked library, on a wing that paralleled the ballroom, was my favorite room. It boasted twenty-six, tall-backed Frank Lloyd Wright chairs grouped around an ornate Louis XIV table. A collection of antique swords graced one wall, the steel polished and sharpened, sealed behind a locked glass door. On the opposite wall was a glass-fronted modern Scandinavian armoire some twenty feet long and eleven feet high, exhibiting elegant Oriental vases and the family china.

The walls in this room were painted a matte black, textured with a sponge dipped in dark green enamel, the same shade that shadowed the woodwork. Matching green drapes fell twelve feet from the ceiling to puddle on the dark wood flooring. A funeral parlor of a room. It would have been dark and dreary, but one whole wall had been replaced with tall French doors, through which the afternoon light filtered.

Rhame walked slowly down the length of the room, his fingers tucked into his back jeans pockets, mouthing a tuneless whistle, until he stood before the sword collection. I was more interested in the vases locked in the Scandinavian armoire. Two of the vases appeared to be Ming, and there was a bronze horse that looked Tibetan. It was old. Very old.

'Bonnie, come here, please.'

'Um?' I turned and looked at Rhame; his shoulders were tense.

'I need you to verify something for me.'

I walked the length of the room, following his gaze to an Oriental sword hung below its scabbard. It was a beautiful piece, like everything else in the house. But unlike the other swords, which were well cared for and gleaming, this one was rusted in spots.

'Tell me. Do you think that is blood?'

It was a perfectly innocuous question. Almost casual. Yet the hairs on the back of my arms lifted. An ominous, restive feeling settled upon me, the way a cat settles slowly onto a limb, draped and watchful.

The rust spots ran along the blade, coating the cutting edge, and were smeared into the tracery on the blunt edge, obscuring what might have been a dragon. There was more rust coating the curved guard and the grip, as if the rust had flowed down and puddled in the grooves. In places it was flaking. Blood. Not rust.

I wrapped my arms around myself, cold fingers against my cold upper arms. 'Yes,' I said softly, my voice sounding as formal and peculiar as the room itself. 'I'd say it's . . . most likely blood.'

'Blood could ruin a fine blade like that,' Rhame said musingly. 'I'll have to tell Jenkins to clean it.'

'Clean what, sir?'

Jenkins stood behind us, his eyes steely, his face a forbidding plaster cast. When Rhame turned, Jenkins' left eyebrow crooked up. A contemptuous gesture. Again Rhame turned, for the second time presenting the butler with his back. If there hadn't been a bloody sword hanging on the wall, I'd have chuckled.

'The sword, Jenkins. I do believe it's been used to kill some . . . thing. And put up dirty.'

Jenkins blanched. I had never actually seen anyone blanch, and it was an unusual process. First Jenkins stopped breathing altogether, then the blood faded from his florid face like a drain had been pulled in his nether regions; he turned white from the top of his head on down. His lips thinned even more than ordinary, practically disappearing into his mouth, and his eyes went all glassy.

I had the distinct impression that Jenkins knew or suspected a great deal about the bloody sword's significance. At any rate, Jenkins underwent an immediate attitude adjustment. Still white as a beached fish, he actually attempted a smile, another feat he probably hadn't accomplished in years.

'Children. Always playing pranks. Of course, I'll handle it posthaste, sir.' Flapping his hands like a dish towel, Jenkins shooed us toward the main entrance. 'I have your rooms prepared, sir, miss, and I hope they are to your satisfaction. Would you like to inspect them before I have your luggage brought up? I was just informed the house boys never showed up to assist with the paintings. Marvelous pieces of work, if I may be so bold, sir, miss.'

Yeah. Right.

'I have placed you both, and Miss Sarvaunt's protection of course, in the East Wing. That's the newest section of the main house, constructed in 1952 and remodeled in the early eighties. Although it lacks a bit of the post-war charm of the rest of the house, it does have a private bath for each room. I thought that would be appropriate. And your room, sir, as the Guest of Honor,' he pronounced it in capitals, as if it were a title, 'would best be called a suite, as it has the most delightful little sitting room . . .'

Jenkins prattled on as he led us through the house, back to the main entrance, up the curving staircase and east, to our quarters. He was clearly rattled, glancing back at the sword once as he ushered us from the room. Taber seemed amused by the butler's unease, while I was . . . wary. Apprehensive.

Blood on an antique sword? *The butler did it*. A cliché. Wasn't it?

Taber approved of our rooms, ordered the suddenly servile Jenkins to send up our baggage and park the cars . . . posthaste. The term was lost on Jenkins, who seemed interested only in dumping us and scurrying back to his little hole. He had gone from pretentious to subservient in the space of a heartbeat. Mouse-like. Very mouse-like. And all because of the bloody sword . . .

I spent the next hour in a Jacuzzi whirling my worries away, soaping down with a bar of homemade chamomile soap. It was as smooth and gentle on my skin as any Tante Ilene and I had ever made, and left me feeling just as sleek and clean.

I loved what the steam rising from the Jacuzzi did for my hair, curling the little tendrils into uneven corkscrews, kinking it up all over my head. I used the effect when I dressed for dinner, spraying the curls into place before I swept my hair up and secured it with two Oriental-style hairpins I found on the vanity. Rhame had warned me that the DeLandes dressed for dinner. Even he was wearing a suit, and I had steamed out my brown silk pants, a silk tunic in peach, and the fringed shawl Taber had bought me. The outfit was vaguely Oriental, like a Chinese peasant of the last century.

With my hair up, I looked older. I could have passed for maybe eighteen. Better than my usual too tall gawky twelve. I liked the effect, and hoped I was formal enough for the DeLandes.

She walked back through the house, touching things. Moving gracefully, ostensibly checking for dust, overseeing the efforts of the cleaning staff. She repositioned a jade figurine behind a vase. Sometimes the Chinese could be so gaudy.

She paused at a mirror, and bent forward, inspecting her face – flawless as usual – and her hairline. It itched again.

With one perfect nail she slid apart the hairs, making a part back an inch from her face. There it was. The offending strand. With delicate movements, she teased out the single offending hair, sliding it loose, pulling it through the chignon she wore.

With a quick tug, she removed the solitary silver strand, pulling the root from her scalp. The itching ceased.

Serenely, she proceeded to the kitchen. The tea hadn't worked. But perhaps the wine would do. Or the coffee. Did they all drink coffee? Yes. Coffee. Perfect.

CHAPTER 15

At precisely seven minutes before seven, while the polish was still tacky on my nails, a knock sounded at my door. I managed to get the raised paneled door open without smudging my polish, but nearly ruined the effect by biting my knuckles when I saw my escorts.

Taber Rhame stood there, silver hair brushed back, gray eyes crinkled up at the corners. He was wearing a tuxedo, a very conservative, almost severe cut, with black cummerbund and black bow tie. Like a godling, or a prince out of a black and white 1940s movie. I had never seen him in anything but jeans or a towel, and it was true what they said . . . clothes do make the man.

MacAloon and Campos were standing behind him, similarly attired, except that MacAloon's tux was a dark brown 1970s leisure style. Campos looked good enough to eat. He smiled a slow sexy smile and let his eyes travel down my body and up again in approval. I wouldn't have thought it possible, but he looked even better than Rhame, standing behind the older man in the hallway, one hand on his hip in a negligent pose.

I wondered if I was finally going boy-crazy. I had missed the stage while growing up; not having a boy around to stimulate the phase can do that to a girl. But I certainly understood the hormone-crazed reaction now. Rhame and Campos. And MacAloon of course. No need to be rude. The man couldn't help it if he looked like Archie Bunker in an old-fashioned tux.

Rhame stepped into the room, turned me around slowly, looking me over with a critical eye before smiling. 'Almost perfect. All you lack are these.' 'These' were a pair of perfectly matched, pink pearl earrings. The kind that pick up any warm shade a woman might wear nearby, like my peach tunic.

I don't know what I said. I know it wasn't 'Thank you.' It might have been a garbled version of 'They're perfect' or 'They're beautiful' or even a squealed 'For me?' Whatever I said, all three men laughed as Rhame stepped into the room and secured the earrings through the holes in my ears. With wet nails, it was something I couldn't have done. The pearls were warm from his hand, and seemed to pick up the earthy tint of the tunic instantly, as if they were made for one another.

Campos nodded at the effect, his eyes almost hot. The only way I would get a stronger reaction from the man was if I had myself chrome-plated and put on wheels.

Trailed by MacAloon and Campos, my arm drawn through Rhame's, I descended to the main level, arriving at the dining room just as an under-maid – a maid in training – rang the supper bell. She was standing in front of the main intercom, dressed in navy and white, her hair a bit frowzy, her lipstick a bit uneven. When she set eyes on Josh Campos, the bell stilled and the little maid said simply, 'Oh my . . .'

My sentiments exactly, but at least I managed to keep my mouth closed. I glanced at her, snapping her from her reverie, and she clanged the little silver bell into the intercom. I had a feeling it wasn't the soft tinkle the DeLandes usually anticipated.

The meal was more formal than I expected, with a full complement of silver and three footmen at each end of the table. Footmen, for Pete's sake! Just like something out of a nineteenth-century etiquette book. Just like the old-fashioned court etiquette taught to me for so many years by Mme Willoby. My mother had prepared me for this, making certain that my education would cover every eventuality, every possibility.

MacAloon and Campos took their places, standing, arms clasped behind their backs, at the entrance. The bloody sword was missing from its place on the wall, leaving the arrangement out of balance. Skewed.

Rhame and I wandered about the room – nervously, if the truth be known – our eyes drawn to the empty place on the wall – until the family began arriving. My anxiety and apprehension, until now carefully banked and repressed like water behind a logjam, began to slip loose, to trickle down around me in tiny little rivulet's of alarm.

I shouldn't be here. Here in this huge house with this family of legend. I should be at home in Khoury, standing in a bayou in mud up to my knees, working loose a fishing line from the sunken branch that tangled it. I should be cooking supper on an outdoor flame, sweat dripping off my elbows. I should be anywhere but here.

The girl watched through half-lidded eyes as the crippled man – Marcus – although she never used his name, eased from her body, lifting one bony leg, then the other with his hands. His legs were getting better, stronger. Some doctors had cut him open and fixed something inside and he could move his toes some. And he could feel with them a little bit. She knew this because the beautiful woman talked to Marcus sometimes, here in this room.

She – the woman with the silver hair – would follow him into the room and sit on the edge of the bed and they would talk. It was like she wasn't even in the room with them then. She'd be strapped down the way Kirby, Marcus's manservant, always left her and they'd come in and sit and talk and never even look at her there, beside them, tied to the bed.

He was getting better. Stronger. More agile. But the shit bag was still there, all full of shit. At first she was afraid it might bust open and spill on her. And maybe that might have been better than what the man did to her. At least shit would wash off.

I had never seen people like these DeLandes. Elegant. Graceful. They seemed to float when they moved. I met Bella Cecile, Anna Linette, Angelique, and their young adult children. They all moved with a fluid balance, a smooth elegance, a poetry of movement it took years of dance lessons to achieve. And yet, I'm certain it was all natural. Something bred into the genes, something innate, instinctive, an unconscious reflex of motion as natural as the tides or the wind or the movement of the bayou. Watching them, I knew what it meant to be a DeLande.

They were beautiful people in every interpretation of the word. Perfect physical specimens. Tall, all of them. Classic, long faces, the kind of hairstyles created in Parisian salons, with clothing to match. I felt like an outcast, gauche, rude, and awkward, and I understood suddenly Jenkins' superior attitude. He had served perfection. Anyone else would be inferior.

I met McCallum DeLande, a slender boy two years my junior with blond hair and topaz-colored eyes. Cat-brown with yellow flecks. Tiger-yellow. They seemed to grow more yellow as he took my hand, riveting eyes that changed tint with his emotion. And a smile so perfect it rivaled Mona Lisa's.

He bent over my hand, pressing those perfect lips against my wrist in a gesture that was so schooled it looked natural. There was nothing of the affected about Cal DeLande. Nothing at all. Yet, I had the strangest urge to snatch back my hand and wipe off the skin . . .

'A pleasure, Miss Sarvaunt. I feel that I know you already, from the paintings in the ballroom promenade. The Grande Dame has been raving about you for weeks, promising that I would be enchanted. And I see she was right, as usual.' He smiled into my eyes and stepped away.

On the note of such fulsome praise, I met the wives of the deceased DeLande heirs, Priscilla DeLande – Cal's mother – Pamela and Janine, and their children, names that came and went in a current of sound as fluid as the bodies. They all had beautiful names, even the half-black Glorianna DesOrmeaux who was the mistress of two of the deceased sons. Without discrimination, her presence was accepted at the table. An unusual family this, all gathered together regardless of legitimacy, regardless of race or educational background. And then the Grande Dame herself arrived, taking the head of the table with Taber Rhame to her right and me to her left and we all suddenly seemed to fit somehow. Because the legendary Grande Dame DeLande made it so.

There was a second odd note, when the Grand Dame greeted McCallum. She was standing at the head of the table in the hostess's place, her palm on the back of her chair, when McCallum stepped up and kissed her on the cheek. The Grande Dame lifted a perfectly manicured hand and gently stroked the side of the boy's face. It was a slow caress, her fingertips resting finally on his perfect lips.

It was always acceptable for a woman to pat her grandson's face. Perfectly fitting. Yet, there was something inappropriate about the Grande Dame's action. Something sensual. And Priscilla, who stood watching, lifted her hand, seemed about to speak, to interfere. Yet, she stopped. And then McCallum stepped away, and the moment was gone. I wasn't sure what it was that I had seen, but the discomfort lingered.

Before we sat, Rhame and I were formally introduced to the family, and I realized that although several of the assembled lived on the DeLande Estate permanently, many were here solely to meet us and for the showing tomorrow night. My nervousness increased.

Taber Rhame was asked to return grace, and if the request startled him he didn't show it. Rather, he smiled, kissed the Grande Dame's hand, tucked it between his own and bowed his head. And prayed.

I admit I didn't pray. I didn't even bow. It wasn't that I wasn't grateful for all the blessings He had sent my way. I was, though not in the way Father Alcede might prefer. It was that I couldn't take my eyes off the DeLandes. These mysterious, baffling people. They were subtle and elusive and, in some way, incomprehensible. Yet, almost familiar. Very, strangely familiar, like a dream half-remembered and confused. Like a sense of *déjà vu*.

I missed most of the first two courses, scarcely tasting the caviar and the chicken broth, my eyes too busy on the proceedings to concentrate. I just hoped I was using the correct silver, and didn't embarrass myself.

No one served seven-course meals these days. No one. Mme Willoby and Amy Vanderbilt insisted that thirty-four guests be served when seven courses were offered, with at least one footman serving each four guests. The Grande Dame could easily have seated thirty-four at her table, but perhaps a DeLande – especially *this* DeLande – could make her own rules. For her, the official etiquette books didn't count.

Emily Post listed only four courses. Soup, main course, salad, and dessert. But the DeLandes lived by another standard. One devised in the eighteenth century and not deviated from since.

So – seven courses. Two through which I may as well have slept, watching this marvelous family.

Behind me, standing with their backs against the wall, were MacAloon and Josh, who had not been asked to join the party. They stood silent and watchful at their places by the door, ignored by everyone there except the boy beside me. McCallum turned several times, watching the bodyguards, his yellow eyes inspecting each man in turn. He seemed fascinated. And when he wasn't staring at my bodyguards, he was staring at me.

I remembered the way the Grande Dame had touched his face. The discomfort of that moment lingered beneath the pressure of McCallum's eyes. But nothing could lessen the effect of such delectable food.

The third course was broiled bay scallops and rock shrimp, seasoned with a delightful blend of spices, few of which I could identify. It was a rather crass thought, but by the end of the seafood course, I was wondering what the DeLandes paid their chef. His cuisine was exquisite. *Everything* was exquisite. Including the service – Jenkins' department. I had to hand it to the butler. He really did a bang-up job. Even Mme Willoby would have been impressed.

The footman who served me was red-headed, slender and short, about five foot six, the average height of each footman. He kept my wine glass at least half-full and my water glass topped off, appearing so often at my side, that I ceased to be startled when he added to my drink or replaced the dishes.

The Grande Dame, as if cognizant of my preoccupation, directed most of her comments to Rhame during the first two courses, turning to me only after I came back to earth during the seafood course. With her amazing eyes sparkling, and what looked to be honest interest, she queried me about my family, my upbringing, and my art, drawing me out about subjects she had heretofore avoided, and including McCallum in the conversation. It was a heady experience, made more so by the wine, a different kind served with each course.

It was a perfect meal. The kind Mme Willoby might have dreamed about. Perfect service, perfect food, perfect conversation and too much good wine. Until the end of the third course.

The red-headed footman was removing my dish with its silver

'supreme' glass and china 'liner' when a shadow, cast by the last rays of the late summer sun, fell across the table. Perhaps it was the three glasses of wine I had consumed, but the room seemed to pause for a long, slow moment. The twenty-six of us and all the servants registered the shadow, grew still, and looked to the French doors.

The shadow was long, tall, topped with a stretched-out cowboy hat, its shape distorted by the centerpiece and the chandelier above. For an instant I stared at the shadow, then raised my eyes to the windows, a half-beat after the other eyes at the table turned or looked up.

McCallum swore softly. The Grande Dame dropped her silver, her fork landing with an undignified clatter upon her main-course china.

The diners whose backs were turned to the French doors whirled, a chair scraping. And there was dead silence in the formal room, the echoes of the dropped fork rebounding from the green-on-black walls.

A man stood there, as long and lean as his shadow. And I knew who he was long before he stepped away from the glare. Before he removed the dusty hat. Before my eyes adjusted and he smiled. Miles.

The crippled man settled into his wheelchair and pulled his clothes together. Buttons. Zipper. Smoothed his hair. And then he did the one thing she waited for. He slipped off the tie from her left hand and started for the door, the wheelchair motor whirring.

With her free hand, she quickly loosed her right wrist. *Heart pounding. Could he hear it?*

The crippled man was one-third of the way to the door. His back was turned, the soft hum of the motorized chair the only sound in the quiet room.

Like lightning, she sat up and pulled off both foot bindings. The left ankle freed by the left hand, the right ankle freed by the right. Heart pounding a drum in her ears. Could he hear it?

She'd practiced for hours until she could do both feet with a single hand. Twice as fast as one foot with both hands, and then the other foot. Twice as fast. He was two-thirds of the way there.

Azalea bounded from the bed. Quietly. Tossing the sheets to

the floor. Stepping forward on the worn, braided rug. Gasping now. Too loud. *He'd hear*. She knew he'd hear.

The man's chair had reached the door. He unlocked it with his key, whirred over the threshold and turned the wheelchair to the right. He never looked back. Never.

Azalea ran, hands outstretched. Eyes on the padded black handles protruding from the back of the chair. Gasping. And he never heard.

My subconscious mind smiled back. And I knew somehow that I had expected him. He belonged here, with these graceful, elegant people. He was like them in the way he moved, the way he smiled.

With slow deliberation, he lifted his left arm and removed the cowboy hat, his shadow drifting across the table, the centerpiece, the diners, like a blessing or a curse. Boots rang hollowly, reminding me of Stocker's footfalls, but these were smoother in placement, more graceful, more . . . more elegant . . . than Stocker's. More perfect than anyone's. More . . . And I knew I was slightly drunk and I knew my face was flaming, and my mouth hung open just a bit.

With the light behind him he looked like a denim-clad dark angel, a shadow of vengeance. I wondered briefly why I thought I knew this man so well, this man I had met only twice or three times over coffee and beignets.

He moved around the silent, still table, speaking softly to each diner he passed. 'Anabelle, you look lovely with your hair up. Grace, you've always looked so pretty in blue. Josie, I like the new hair color. Very Hollywood. Pris, I see they're letting you eat with the family again. Does it make you yearn for the joys and peace of the nunnery?'

And on around the table, he greeted each of them by name, touching a chair back, a chin, stroking a head of hair. Anabelle smiled and ducked her head, touching her neat bun. Grace touched the blue collar of her blouse, her eyes downcast. Josie smirked. Pris laughed outright. To every member of the family he spoke and offered some personal comment. Charming them all. Until he reached the head of the table.

His smile changed then, grew more formal, less personal. Less caressing. He extended his hand to Rhame. 'Mr Rhame. I've admired your work for years. Especially the *Sanctuary* series. I saw it displayed in Geneva in eighty-three, I believe it was, just before they dispersed the paintings to the buyers. Very powerful.'

If Taber had been a little boy offered a chocolate bar, his face could not have lit up more. From the mouth of Miles, the most mundane comment took on style, charisma, and import. Rhame stood, his chair a soft scrape on the floor.

'I'm pleased you liked the work. It was a real challenge to obtain it. But I'm afraid you have the advantage, young man.'

Miles smiled. A flash of white, white teeth. 'Miles Justin DeLande, sir. And we have met. In Geneva. I was with my . . . with the Grande Dame.'

The shock washed through me, leaving me confused. *Miles Justin DeLande?* I felt I had just been offered the solution to all the puzzles that had beset me since I moved to New Orleans, if I could put all the pieces together. And then I remembered the way he moved. So languid and sensual. Of course he was a DeLande. But why would a DeLande pay for my protection?

'Ah yes. You stayed in my hotel suite.' There was an uncomfortable silence then, as if Rhame had uttered a gaffe. A slight blush stained his cheeks. The silence lasted a painful moment longer while Rhame stared at Miles, and Miles stared at the Grande Dame.

Miles laughed. 'Indeed. And a most comfortable couch it was, Mr Rhame.' The tension eased a fraction. I wasn't stupid. I realized that there was something going on in the dining room. Something happening below the surface. Something exposed and yet hidden by the words.

The Grande Dame sipped her wine. Replaced her glass. Again china and silver clinked into the silent room.

Miles turned to McCallum and nodded. 'Cal.' It was only one syllable, but the word was imbued with insult. Insult I didn't understand. Miles laughing at the boy and McCallum's hands fisted in his lap. He nodded, his movements jerky.

Miles turned to me and moved around behind the head of the table, '*Carin*. I see you found your way home at last.'

The Grand Dame laughed. A low, throaty sound, part growl, part victory.

The words penetrated the haze of wine and the world sped up again. *Carin?*

Miles's face changed, as if moving into focus.

Carin?

Concern replaced the welcome on his features.

Carin? No one here, except MacAloon, knew about Carin.

Slowly, Miles knelt beside me. Took my icy hand. 'Carin? She hasn't told you yet, then? I'm sorry. I thought she would have told you weeks ago. MacAloon's reports indicated she spent a great deal of time with you. I see I was mistaken.'

'You are mistaken about a great many things, Miles,' the Grande Dame said, growling her throaty laugh. My confusion grew.

Miles ignored her. 'I'm Miles Justin, the Eldest. You'll understand what that means later. But for now, I'm your uncle. Sort of. Your mother, Marie Lisette, was my sister.'

'Was?' Out of all the unexpected things he said, my mind separated out a single verb. The only verb that really mattered to me. His thumbs stroked the backs of my hands.

'Yes. She died three years ago. In Houston. I'm sorry.'

I laughed, a bruised sound in the quiet room. Disbelieving. 'What name did she use?'

'When she died?'

I nodded, my eyes watching his.

'Victoria Robicheaux. She died in an apartment fire. I'm sorry.'

Wrong. My mother had pulled another fast one. She was always one step ahead. But I didn't say it. I nodded again, mute. *One step ahead of these people. Her family. Right? Or perhaps one step ahead of my father.*

'Who was my father?'

A tremor passed through his fingers, telegraphed to me. He hadn't expected that question. Not yet.

The crippled man started to turn his head.

'What—'

She grasped the padded black handles of his chair and pushed.

With all her strength, she pushed, forcing the chair toward the for doorway and the darkness beyond.

'No! You . . .'

Digging her heels into the hall carpet, she grunted with effort, strained and shoved. The man's arms flapped, one shoulder bumping her nose. The wheelchair made a noise, grinding. Head down, she pushed, grunting with the strain. The darkness was there. Just as she'd known it would be.

'No!' the man screamed.

'Yes,' she hissed back with the last of her breath. 'Yesss.'

Then the wheelchair tilted. Tilted. And was jerked from her hands.

She caught herself on a doorway. One foot out over the darkness. She hung, partially suspended.

The man and his chair tumbled slowly down into the darkness. The noise was terrible. His screams worse. Mostly drowned by the roaring in her ears. Down. Straight to hell. Falling forever. The noise stopped and there was silence. Complete silence.

The screams stopped. I was standing. We all were. Miles still holding my hand. And before any of us could move, Miles had crossed the space to a small, narrow door in the wall behind my chair. I hadn't even noticed it. Flush with the wall, painted green on black. Camouflaged. A servants' door.

Miles jerked it open.

And something silver and bloody fell out into the room.

No one screamed. No one moved. Not a sound at all in the too-quiet, too-still room. It seemed the assembled scarcely breathed, yet the shock and horror was almost palpable.

The taste of blood filled my mouth, salty and warm. I released my lip from between my teeth.

Why didn't someone say something? Why didn't someone move? I couldn't take my eyes away.

It was a man. Dead. His head tilted back beneath his body. His legs were tangled in a twisted wheelchair. A bone protruded, jagged edges caught on cloth.

Josh and MacAloon were beside me and slightly back. A solid wall of protection, as if they feared that the body might jump up and do me damage.

'Say hello to your Uncle Marcus, Carin. And welcome to the family,' the Grande Dame said, laughing again. Her voice was sharp and yet hollow, a tight irrational pitch I had never noticed before. The sound of her laughter bounced off the black walls.

I looked up the stairs. The long, narrow flight of worn-out wooden stairs. At the top stood a child, in silhouette. She was naked. Arms spread. Legs together. Like a crucifix. Hair haloed by the faint light behind her.

'Vengeance is mine, says God.' The words floated down the stairs. A child's voice. Lyrical. Silent footsteps. And then she was gone. And again, behind me, I heard the Grande Dame laugh.

Miles grabbed the banisters on either side of the dead man and swung himself up, over the body, onto the second step. Boots beating every third tread, he rushed to the top and disappeared. Following the child only the two of us had seen.

The room remained preternaturally still, an awful silence descending over the diners. Except for the Grande Dame. She ate, heavy silver chinking and clinking, crystal wine glass raised and lowered. Slipping her fork into the main course. Wild rice and new peas, julienned carrots, and buttered pearl onions. Slices from what looked like a game bird. Grouse perhaps. I had never looked at the printed menu beside my water glass.

And Uncle Marcus's blood trailed across the wood floor toward my feet. A slow, red river, bright and sticky-looking.

Miles reappeared at the top of the stairs. Again he was back-lit. Hatless this time. Slowly he moved down through the dark, narrow stairway, boots a hollow sound. Rhythmic and smooth.

Watching him descend, I suddenly realized why he had always seemed so familiar. Why this family seemed so familiar. All the DeLandes moved like Miles moved. Smooth and fluid, a seemingly effortless shifting of muscle, a graceful balance and poise. A DeLande trait. One I shared.

My throat moved as my dinner tried to rise. A hot, biting taste filled my mouth. I swallowed it down.

Miles reached bottom. Using his arms, he swung himself over the body. His boots landed before me, narrowly missing the puddle of blood. I stepped back to allow him into the dining room. And to avoid the trickle of blood still moving toward me.

'Jenkins,' the Grande Dame said pleasantly. 'Set a place for the Eldest. I'm sure he's famished, and the *rôti* is delicious. My complements to Delasbour. Everything is wonderful, as usual.'

Jenkins looked to Miles, who shook his head infinitesimally. Miles Justin. Miles Jenkins. Of course. He'd used the *butler's* name when he hired my bodyguards.

Miles glanced at me, as if he'd heard the sarcastic tone in my mind. Returning his attention to the butler, he said softly, 'Nine one one.'

'Very good, sir. So glad to have you home, sir.'

Miles smiled a half-smile as Jenkins turned and walked toward the kitchens. 'Everyone please stay here. MacAloon, would you have your associate wait at the front entrance for the coroner and the police? My brother has had an accident.'

Accident? All this blood from an accident? Accident, my left foot! The thoughts hit me simultaneously. Hysteria threatened.

'Breathe, Carin.' Miles touched my cheek, Dark eyes soft. Concerned. 'Breathe, girl, before you turn blue.'

I took a deep breath. The air rasped like water against sand. My panic leveled out. I breathed again, in and out. I had stopped breathing when Marcus fell into the room.

Miss Taussig would be quite disgusted with me for falling into a panic over so little a thing as a dead man. A riot of giggles burbled at the back of my throat. An unsuitable reaction to the blood slithering across the floor.

Miles leaned close, his lips secret against my ear. 'Don't mention the girl. Trust me. Please.'

Trust him. Trust him? 'Who was my father?' The question came from nowhere again, startling Miles. Startling me.

Miles opened his mouth, closed it.

'Later, Carin.'

'No. Now.' It seemed important. It *was* important. I knew now that my mother hadn't run from Billy Marc, the man I had thought to be my father. Had she run from these people? Her family? Tante Ilene's letter had claimed that my real mother was running from her own mother . . . The Grande Dame? I looked over at the legendary woman and caught her stuffing a pearl onion into her mouth with her finger. She licked it clean.

'Now, Miles,' I said pointedly.

Miles ran a hand through his hair, ruffling the fine strands.

For a long moment, he watched his mother eating her meal. Looked down the length of the table. The massed DeLandes looked away. Looked uncomfortable. Pris drank her wine in a single gulp. No one else moved. McCallum's place was empty. I hadn't noticed him leave.

Miles blew out the breath he'd held and took my arm. His fingers were warm on my cold skin through the colder silk. He led me behind the Grande Dame to the French doors, opened one and escorted me outside to the patio. Heat enveloped me; I shivered in the delicious warmth.

Behind me, Miles paused. Jenkins was entering the dining room, the connecting door swinging in on silent hinges. 'Jenks, would you set a small table in the family room? A buffet from the leftovers perhaps. And escort the family there. And Jenks, have someone stay with the Grande Dame, please.'

'Of course, sir. Right away.'

Again Miles paused. 'Jenks?'

'Yes, sir.'

'Would you please clean the room at the top of the stairs?' His voice held an odd tone, warning and bitter all at once. 'Personally.'

'Of course, sir.'

Miles closed the door to the dining room and his – my? – very strange family. The late-day glare on glass cut off the sight of Marcus and Rhame and the Grande Dame. He led me to a cushioned seat and pushed me down into it. Pulled up a second one. Knee to knee we sat a moment, Miles's eyes on his hands, my eyes on Miles.

'Carin—'

'Call me Bonnie. I don't know who Carin is.'

He smiled at his hands, clasped them together.

'Bonnie, then. It suits you somehow.' He paused, and I was afraid he wouldn't continue. He looked up, met my eyes. His were troubled.

'What do you know about the DeLandes and the scandal that hit us last winter?'

'There was a court case,' I said slowly, forcing my mind to think, remembering the sensational headlines. 'With accusations of incest and child abuse, followed by the deaths of your uncles under . . . suspicious circumstances. But lately, the papers have been saying the incest allegations were all a lie. Something that an incompetent counselor inadvertently stimulated during a hypnosis session . . . False memories?' I questioned.

'My brothers were killed. Not my uncles. But essentially you're correct. And it wasn't an incompetent counselor or false memories. The incest and the child abuse were real. A depravity that went back farther than any public official ever suspected. Generations back.

'Montgomery, one of my brothers, was killed by his wife when she found out he'd molested her daughters. During the trial one of my sisters – Bella Cecile, you met her today – accused all my brothers of molesting their children.'

A breeze sifted through the patio, coming from the open end. The patio was enclosed on three sides, open on one. I wondered how the breeze found the opening and how it would get out. Even the air was trapped. I shivered again. Miles sighed and looked back at his hands.

'I don't know if you noticed, but the Grande Dame is . . . not like the rest of us. She's . . . unbalanced.'

'Either that or very hungry.' It was the kind of dumb statement that often pops out of my mouth when I'm under intense stress. What I wanted to say was that a great percentage of the DeLandes seemed unbalanced. But then, that might have been just as bad. I didn't really want to be rude to Miles. Not with a body lying just a few feet away.

Miles laughed and his eyes met mine again. 'Yeah, well.' He took my hands. Stroked the backs of them with his thumbs slowly, organizing his thoughts.

'My mother molested each of her children as they were growing up. Then gave the girls to their own brothers. In incest. Because of that, we have a very . . . tangled . . . set of bloodlines.'

'My mother . . .' I said. 'She was your . . . sister?' The word tasted strange on my tongue. I had never considered that my mother would have brothers and sisters . . . a family. And then his words penetrated. *Incest*. A soft dread, softer than the breeze, wafted against my skin.

'Yes. She was.' He paused, his thumbs stroking a warm path on my cold hands. He looked at me again. 'My brother Andreu, or maybe it was my brother Montgomery, I never figured out which, was my father. The Grande Dame seduced them and was sleeping with both boys when she became pregnant with me.'

I swallowed. There was a pain across my shoulders from holding still so long. Or maybe the dread had settled there, heavy and suffocating.

'I'm a child of incest.' Miles's hands stopped moving and held mine securely. They were so warm against my frigid skin. 'And so are you.' The silence on the patio grew thick, the air hard to breathe. 'Richard DeLande, my brother, was your father.' Miles pronounced Richard 'Rushar' in the French manner. 'He raped your mother – his sister – repeatedly until she became pregnant. Somehow she got away. And she hid from him all these years.'

My throat worked, dry tissues sticking. Richard DeLande had died in a hunting accident, I remembered from the papers. My real father was dead.

'Why did you want my mother? You've been looking for her.' The words were a whisper, dry and coarse. My throat ached.

Miles nodded. 'I've been looking for all my missing sisters and nephews and nieces.' He squeezed my hands. I took a shuddering breath, surprised my lungs still functioned.

'They're scattered all over the country. Many, like you, are in hiding. Many need counseling or financial help.'

He sounded like a social worker, all caring and concerned. But something didn't fit quite right. Something was wrong with the timber of his voice, the spacing of his words. As if he were lying, or . . . hiding something. I watched his eyes, remembering Dr Tammany Long's lectures on tactics.

Miles lips twisted in a lopsided smile. Charming. Humble. An act? 'Trust me,' he had said. I struggled to remember what Rufus Kirby had taught me about the DeLande Estate and its peculiar inheritance structures.

'I have control of a lot of money and of the DeLande family and estate finances. As the Eldest, it's my responsibility and my right to care for the DeLandes. Bringing them here, gathering them together is a first step.'

It clicked then, the wrongness I felt at his words. We had talked, once, about money and power and control as they related to international finances. Though I hadn't known it at the time, he had been talking about DeLande money, DeLande corporate power, and the Eldest's control of all three. And I knew, suddenly, what it was that Miles DeLande really wanted.

'And with them all gathered together here, you can work on them with all the charm at your disposal, get them to sign over any proxies entitled to them under the original DeLande Estate papers. You can consolidate your control of the DeLande corporate structure and manage to come off like a white knight at the same time.'

His eyes flickered. Something dark moved deep in his thoughts. Something I didn't want to see in the light of day. Something I should have feared. 'Smart girl.' Miles dipped his head in salute. And the dark thing slid silently away. I shuddered, forcing my mind back to practicalities.

Part of my studies with Rufus Kirby had been DeLande papers, those available to the public. I knew at least a bit about the way this family's convoluted finances worked. *My mother's long-term planning?* I tucked that thought away for later study and consideration and returned my attention to Miles. The DeLande Estate was required reading for tax lawyers wishing to practice in the state of Louisiana. Through my studies, I knew that all acknowledged DeLandes were entitled to a share of the DeLande holdings.

'Well, I won't sign over anything. Whatever I'm entitled to as a DeLande is mine,' I said. 'But I won't fight you either.'

His eyes shifted again, as if the light went out behind them. 'You may change your mind.'

'Is that a threat?' I whispered.

He smiled then, that same easy-going smile he had bestowed on me the times we shared breakfast in the Café du Monde. 'Of course not. I'm the good brother, remember?'

I had entered a surreal world, here on the DeLande Estate. A man had just died. I had just learned an awful truth. And I was discussing money with a volatile, eccentric man. A very powerful man, who wanted something from me. Who had an agenda of his own.

He increased the pressure on my fingers, his grip tightening until the bones ground together. Yet his smile never faltered. Moments passed as the pain in my fingers grew to an agony, and though I had no idea why he wanted to hurt me suddenly, or what kind of test I was being subjected to, I didn't resist the pressure of his grip. I didn't try to pull away. Breathing deeply, I simply floated, accepted the strength of his grip, ignoring the bruising, watching his eyes. Slowly they cleared. Sirens sounded in the distance.

Miles stood, nodded and released my hands. The sirens were closer, the sound wavering through the trees at the front of the house. I clenched and spread my fingers to restore the circulation.

'Do me a favor,' he said. 'Don't mention the girl at the top of the stairs to the police.'

'But she pushed Marcus down the stairs. Didn't she?'

Miles studied my face, his dark eyes intent. 'Yes. She did,' he said finally. 'But I think she's a sister. Your half-sister. I've been trying to track her down for weeks. I think she's Richard's little girl.'

Half-sister . . . The words echoed in my mind. *Half-sister?*

'I think Marcus was . . . abusing her. And I don't want her charged with anything.'

I nodded in agreement, looking up at him. *Half-sister* . . .

'We were the only two in a position to see her. Even your bodyguards were too far back to catch sight of her.'

'I won't say anything.' But I knew what I wanted . . . I wanted to find her. And I wanted to be safe from the dangers my mother had run from. I smiled then, even as a new thought occurred to me. Remembering Dr Tammany Long teaching me the art of bluffing with a pack of playing cards and a hand of five-card stud.

'Miles? You might want to think carefully about any . . . coercion . . . regarding my portion of the DeLande Estate.' My smile grew, and I watched his face as I said the next words. 'My mother is still alive. I don't know who is buried in the coffin for Victoria Robicheaux. But it isn't my mother. And I have a feeling she wouldn't take kindly to anyone who might want to hurt me.'

Miles watched me in return, his own eyes hooded as he considered the possibility of my mother's continued survival. He didn't ask how I knew she was alive. He simply never seemed to doubt that I knew. And my mother was a DeLande who had foiled the family for years. She might be a power to reckon with in her own right.

'I have to go inside and confront the police.'

'I'll wait here.'

'When you want to rejoin the family, have a maid show you to the family room.'

Rejoin the family . . .

Miles turned and left, his stride long and smooth. 'Family.' But the word was whispered, and Miles never heard.

CHAPTER 16

Ever since I was fifteen, I had known I wasn't who they said I was. And I had always thought that if I only knew the answer to the great mystery of my life, I would find myself. I would discover who I was and I would *know* . . . so many other things. As if that one bit of information, that one secret explained, would give me myself. Like an epiphany.

And I had always held it against Tee Dom and Tante Ilene because they wouldn't tell me. Hated them perhaps, just a little. Punished them more than just a little. Because they had withheld the truth from me. There had been enigmatic looks between the two, all my life. Secretive, protective and knowing.

Tears threatened, burning against my eyelids. *They had known about my past.* They had known all about me. And they had hidden an awful truth from me. My mother and father had been brother and sister. What did that mean about me? Was I genetically unstable? Abnormal in some way?

I crossed my arms and clasped my upper arms in cold fingers as the night enveloped the world. My mind was moving sluggishly, like it did when I had gone a day without sleep. Was that, in some way, related to my genetic makeup? Did my mind work differently from the rest of the world?

Where were they? These two people who had loved me? My Tee Dom and Tante Ilene.

Out of nowhere, the thought came to me. Miles had missed something. Left it out. Or had never known it. Tante Ilene and I were related. Marie Lisette and Elizabeth Diane Sarvaunt were cousins. Hadn't Miles once said something about his mother's mother being a Sarvaunt? I had brought Beth Sarvaunt's diary with me. I would read until I learned more. Until I learned it all. And the more I learned, the closer I would be to finding my mother. LaVay. The artist. Because she was alive. I knew it.

Shadows, now cast by security lights, slanted across the patio, stripping the paving stones with long dark brush strokes of night-black paint. Mosquitoes buzzed quietly around my head.

The sirens had quieted some time ago. Turning, I looked toward the French doors, tinted pink now with the setting of a late summer's sun. Carefully, I stood and moved across the patio toward the dining room, opened the door and stepped inside.

The room slowly fell silent, yet I heard snatches of conversation.

'. . . crippled since the old girlfriend shot his ass . . .'

'. . . happened in New Orleans, didn't it . . .'

'. . . says he's a *DeLande* and shouldn't be investigated for . . .'

'. . . probable cause of death is a broken neck received from the fall . . .'

Half a dozen men in uniforms and several in street clothes turned as I entered. By the time the door closed behind me, all conversations had ended.

'I'm . . . Bonnie Sarvaunt. I was here when Marcus . . . fell. Would anyone like to take my statement?'

I knew how I must look, the black-tinted windows at my back. My fringed shawl forgotten, hanging off one shoulder. My hair kinked around my face in tendrils, softened by the breeze. My complexion was probably white as a ghost. I'm an artist like my mother. I could picture myself well.

'I'll do it.' Three men spoke at once. I managed a smile. All three pulled clipboards off the Louis XIV table still laden for the main course, clicked open pens, and moved toward me.

'I'll handle Miss Sarvaunt. You gentlemen go start taking statements in the family room.'

'Some fucking family,' someone muttered, not caring if he was heard. The man giving the orders pretended not to notice, and the three uniformed officers moved away.

The order-giver was of average height, average weight, balding, and had clear blue eyes. He smiled as he picked up his own clipboard and crossed the room to me. 'You know cops and a pretty girl,' he said, exposing yellowed teeth in a too-wide smile. 'I'm Captain Murdock.'

'No. I don't.' But I knew to be wary of this one. There was something about him, something in his eyes. He hated the DeLandes. Every last inbred one of us. I laughed then, a shaky slightly hysterical sound. And he laughed with me as if he thought something was actually funny.

I knew without asking that no one would mention my newly revealed ancestry. This was one family which had seen enough of police and heard enough legalese in the past year to last a lifetime. They would willingly volunteer nothing.

I had lowered my eyes at Captain Murdock's first words, and now opened them wide, fighting the tears that suddenly wanted to fall. There was something about the stern-faced policeman that affected me just like Father Alcede. Although there was no similarity between the two men, with Father Alcede being tall and willow-thin and the police captain being average height and balding, the effect of dealing with the two men was the same. I wanted to cry.

And somehow I knew that this man was glad Marcus was dead. Very glad. I had the feeling that when the night was over, Captain Murdock would stop by his favorite bar, order a stiff drink and lift a salute to the demise of one more DeLande. I hadn't seen Marcus mourned by any of his family either, but Captain Murdock went the family one better. He was downright happy.

I took a shuddering breath and wiped my eyes on the back of my hand. There was a smear of mascara on my wrist, and I was certain I already had big black rings under my eyes. I was shaking, and Josh Campos appeared at my side suddenly with a handkerchief and an afghan. His appearance surprised me and I jerked, pulling back as he touched my arm. He grinned that lopsided grin and draped the afghan around my shoulders.

'Shock.' One word, and he was gone. The afghan felt delicious around my body, an insulating layer of warmth I desperately needed. *Shock?* a small part of my brain asked, echoing Josh's comment. *I can use shock. Use it to my advantage with the police.*

'I understand you were the one closest to the deceased when he *fell* down the stairs.' It was obvious from his words and inflection that he didn't believe Marcus had fallen down the stairs at all. My shaking worsened. And that small part of my brain that was still in control, that small part that was still rational, took refuge in the two things Mme Willoby had taught me always worked on men. Tears and stupidity.

'I just got here today, Officer,' I said, blowing my nose on Josh's handkerchief, using my shock. 'I'm an artist, showing with Taber Rhame.' And the tears flowed like a spring in the bayou, a steady cascade of water from my eyes and mucus from my nose. I shook and blubbered and was totally useless. 'I didn't see a thing,' I said, whimpering. 'Except all that blood and the piece of bone sticking through his skin.'

And it worked. All I had to do was give way and let the panic of the evening have free reign. All I had to do was concentrate on the memory of the body, all bloody and bent. Mme Willoby would have been so proud.

I blubbered so much Captain Murdock finally got frustrated, writing up my statement in his own words. Since it basically said that I had seen nothing, I didn't mind signing the document.

When the captain finally released me, I turned away, wiping my eyes, intent on finding the girl who pushed Marcus down the stairs. If she really was my sister, then perhaps she needed me. And I didn't want the police to find her first.

As I rounded the corner by the dining room, I bumped into Miles. An amused Miles, leaning against the door frame, boots crossed, arms crossed, no hat. A quirky twist to his lips and a twinkle in his eyes. He kissed my raw, salty cheek. I wondered how long he'd been there.

'Little lady, are you all right?' he drawled, his voice slightly mocking. 'It just tears my heart out to see a purty little thing like you cry.' He'd been there a while, it seemed. And he knew I had taken refuge in tears to protect myself from too many pointed questions. I blushed and looked away, remembering the crush of his fingers on mine. Tactics . . . Power plays. Establishing dominance like dogs in a pack or hens in a barnyard. My mother had made sure that I would know how . . .

As if he read my mind, Miles's smile widened. He opened his mouth to say something, just as Captain Murdock stuck his head out the door.

'You want to come in here . . . Mr DeLande.' The captain's eyes were hard and his voice sharp on the word 'Mister', as if the word tasted funny as his mouth formed it. Miles nodded and turned his gaze back to me.

'Why don't you go on upstairs and take a long hot bath, Miss Sarvaunt? You can even watch TV in the tub. You know. Upstairs?' He glanced up, over our heads. To the floor where the girl had been. The naked girl only we two had seen.

As I intended to search for her anyway, I nodded in reply. 'Thank you. I will. I think I'll . . . retire early, if you don't mind.' I made the comment to Captain Murdock, meeting his hard blue eyes. He pulled his head back into the dining room, leaving us a moment of privacy.

Miles put his arm around me, his lips at my ear. 'Did you say anything about the girl?'

'No,' I whispered back. 'Nothing. I told him I wasn't in a position to see anything but the body. Did you say anything about me being a DeLande?'

'Absolutely not,' Miles said, chuckling. 'You'd have to be half-crazy to want to join this family.'

He was serious, underneath the laughter. He really believed what he had just said. Shielding the doorway and any probing eyes from the motion of his hand, Miles slipped me a scrap of paper. 'Here's a map to the floor upstairs. Only parts of it have been upgraded and remodeled in this century, so be careful. There should be a flashlight in your room, in the drawer by the bed. You think you can find your way?'

'I'll do all right. Do you intend to come?'

'As soon as I can get away. As soon as the last cop is gone and the Grande Dame is put to bed with a strong sedative.' He squeezed my shoulder, and although the memory of his bruising fingers was still painful in my memory, the gesture was somehow reassuring. 'It'll be late, I'm afraid.'

I hoped that I had found her by then. I wanted to search for her alone, spend time with her, this sister I had never known.

He tilted his head to the side, as if to say, 'Of course,' and stepped into the dining room.

Back in my room, I stared at myself in the mirror over the sink. My eyes were red and swollen, my nose was plumped up like an overcooked boudain. My makeup was ruined. I looked a bit like a sullen twelve-year-old who had been denied an outing.

I'm not sure what I was supposed to be feeling in the aftermath of death and revelation. But I'm certain it wasn't the near-hilarity that possessed me as I stared at my reflection. A giddy elation, half-frivolity, half-panic.

I was devastated. And I wasn't. I was near collapse. And yet I felt a wild exhilaration and a breath-catching thrill. I had found my family. I had finally unraveled all the terrible secrets of my past. And someone had just died. My eyes watered and I laughed at the sight of the tears falling from my hollowed-out eyes. I was the human equivalent of a hard rain from sunny skies. The devil beating his wife, as Tante Ilene might have said. Simply hysterical, as Miss Taussig might have said.

Miss Taussig had long ago replaced my childhood lack of self-control with yoga, proper body mechanics, and breath control. Yet, the longer I lived in the real world rather than the isolated watery world of my youth, the more I realized that she had not been entirely successful. Apparently she had only covered up my unbridled emotions, hiding them beneath a veneer of Oriental influence. Because they were certainly out of control now.

I was shaking and cold all over, visions of Marcus, dead at the bottom of the stairs, competing with the revelation that I had a sister. A sister who had just killed someone. Threaded through all the conflicting thoughts was the new knowledge of my history. My past. My new identity. Myriad new concepts roiling within me.

I changed from my silks into the jeans I had worn driving to the estate, pulled on a long-sleeved T-shirt and tossed a second one over my shoulders. Through the arms of the extra T-shirt, I threaded a pair of underpants, a pair of shorts, and tied on a pair of warm socks. The girl was naked after all.

What would I say to her? How did you converse with a child, a teenager, who had been abused? And what, exactly, did Miles think had been done to her? And how did one talk to a murderer?

It was only after I tied the arms of the extra T-shirt into a knot around my neck that I realized I had been talking to myself. Mumbling. Muttering. Just like Tee Dom had done long ago.

There were two flashlights in the bedside drawer, not just one, and extra batteries that went into my jeans pockets. I looked a bit like a bag lady, one of the strange women who wandered the streets of New Orleans. A lost and slightly off-center woman, mumbling and meandering with no place to go. A vague, forgotten form.

My hair was mussed from pulling clothes off and on. I ran a brush through it, secured it into a ponytail with a padded elastic band, still fighting my tears as I searched for my sneakers. Someone had placed them in the closet. Servants most likely. It bothered me that someone had been in my room, among my things.

I had a mental image of a nosy maid peering into my closet, searching for hidden treasure and fniding m guns. The image was clear and sharp, and the maid in my mind was the same frowzy-haired girl who had called the family to dinner. The one who was so captivated with Josh Campos.

On the heels of that vision was the image of my mother, bruised and bleeding following an attack by her brother. Her face was the face and form I always gave her in my mind, but with her hair tangled, her clothes torn, and her lips swollen.

As an artist, I think and reason in pictures. But I don't know where this thought-picture came from, this vivid impression, this awful fantasy.

I could see the bruises purpling her thighs. The blood at the corner of her mouth. The torn skin of the knuckles of her right hand. In my mind, she lifted the hand and sucked at the knuckles. The sound was like kittens suckling at a mother cat. Hungry. Desperate. Shock. I was still in shock.

It was only then that I smelled the faint scent in my room. Sweet. Vaguely masculine. The same scent I had smelled in my apartment the day Perkins was injured. Who? Who among the DeLandes had my mother run from? And who among them had Miles been trying to protect me from when he hired the bodyguards?

I had smelled that same scent earlier . . . In the dining room. McCallum? *The boy?*

My tears faded, leaving behind a fierce apprehension and distrust. 'Trust me,' Miles had said. But could I trust any of these DeLandes?

I hesitated only a moment before stuffing the .38 into my waistband beneath the T-shirts. If I was lucky, I wouldn't shoot off my ass. Tee Dom's words from my childhood, when he was teaching me to shoot.

'You neva' pu' no gun in you pan's, like dat Magnum PI, no siree, no. You shoot of you ass, gir'. Clean off.' And then he'd laughed. That wonderful, hearty French laugh, with his head thrown back and his mouth stretched wide.

Tears filled my eyes. *Where were they?*

And because there was no answer to my question, I took a calming breath, blew out the tension that had claimed my body, and left the room. But I carried with me the image of my mother, bruised and bleeding. I knew I'd paint that scene one day. Soon. I'd call it *Ugly Truths*.

Halfway down the hallway I realized how cold the air was. Like most Louisianians, the DeLandes kept their house thermostat set at less than seventy degrees in the summer. I went back, stripped the coverlet off the bed, and draped it over my arm. If I found the girl . . . my sister? . . . she'd be cold. Using the map Miles had provided, I set out again.

With little difficulty, I found my way from the East Wing to the wing over the kitchens. I waited in the shadows while a policeman made a circuit of the hallway, checking each room. I knew Miles hadn't told the officers about the girl, so it must have been standard operating procedure. Police trying to figure out why the dead man had been in the hallway in the first place.

I had seen enough TV on the Sarvaunts' old black-and-white set to know that police always assumed foul play. An assumption that would be true enough in this case. When the uniformed officer had disappeared down the stairs to the dining room, I ran through the shadows to the head of the stairs.

The lighting was haphazard on this floor. As was the cleaning. The carpet was a stained old Persian, obviously woven to fit the hall's dimensions. In prime condition it would have been priceless. The state of this one had been ignored for so long that it was beyond repair. The once-rich colors – dark reds and navy and a bright parrot-green – appeared at each irregular light fixture, and faded between them. The dusty Victorian-glass lights cast chaotic shadows, the light dimming to a murky gray before reappearing.

I paused in a shadow and closed my eyes, letting my pupils open to their widest. When I opened my eyes, I saw the pattern of carpet on the shadowed floor, the intricate design, if not the dark-dulled colors.

And the splatter of dampness.

Little droplets, scattered here and there, with a single, larger globule squashed by the smooth bottom of a shiny black shoe. The officer had stepped in the damp spot, smeared it, and moved on, unknowing.

I dropped to one knee and extended a hand. Almost touched the damp place, then stopped, my finger held a scant inch from the floor. Instead, I bent and sniffed. And pulled away, repelled.

I recognized the scent. Acerbic, biting, and sour. Intensely masculine. A scent I recognized from Tee Dom's week-old laundry, and from Elred's unwashed body.

I stood too quickly, the blood rushing from my head. The hallway darkened, my pulse raced, and the blanket felt heavy suddenly. A pressing load. Semen?

I worked at controlling my breathing. Forced it steady. Forced composure in through my lungs.

Had I become the panicky type? *Or was there perhaps something wrong with my lungs? Or my heart? Something inbred?* I pushed the questions away. Miles could live with it. So could I.

On silent feet, I moved to the head of the stairs and turned right. Stopped.

The room was old-fashioned, with an iron bed, a bare mattress, two naked pillows, all hollowed and sunken, stained and frayed. There were two bedside tables, their tops burned with cigar ash, ringed with water stains, the finish long ago eroded to bare wood.

A tattered, braided rug covered the old flooring, the ten-inch-wide boards bearing the wear of generations. The floor was clean. Freshly swept and mopped. More semen, removed by the dependable Jenks?

And wasn't every butler called Jenkins? Was it a rule?

The wall across from the bed was solid shelves, filled with books, games, a twenty-four-inch TV with cable and remote control, puzzles . . . cards . . . A desk top displayed an open coloring-book and scattered crayons, the picture of a Sleeping Beauty neatly filled in with black, dark blue, russet, and deep purple. Angry adult colors. Prince Charming, bending over the princess, was scarlet with devil's horns peeking through his brown hair.

On the far side of the bed was a doorway to the bathroom. Clean. Too clean. As if the old tile and enormous, porcelain fixtures had been steam-cleaned recently. Jenks?

I left the room at a steady trot, looking for my sister. Remembering the body at the bottom of the stairs, bloody, the neck bent back. Vicious. Appropriate. Just.

I searched the entire floor by the light of the Victorian shades and the beam of the flash. Every room had strange locks on the doors. Deadbolts. The double-keyed kind. The kind that could lock someone in as easily as locking someone out.

Every room contained a bare mattress on an iron bed, revealed in harsh detail by the beam of my flash. Many of the bed frames were worn in strange places. As if handcuffs or shackles had scored into the finish. Into the metal itself. Grinding.

How long had these DeLandes practiced . . . whatever they had practiced? How many women had suffered?

The wing was empty. There was no sign of the naked girl. No sign of anyone.

Continuing my search on an adjoining wing, I finally found traces of her. A guest wing, like the east wing, but decades older. The rooms were finished in French country antiques, the décor modern, a forest-green with touches of pale yellow, peach, tangerine and watermelon. Each room was subtly different. Elegant and tasteful.

A decor the Grande Dame might have designed. The thought died aborning.

In the last room, the room before the servants' stairs, I found a bathroom that had been recently used. Someone had showered, dried off on one of the thick, terry towels, used a guest comb, brushed her teeth. And taken off, leaving damp footprints behind to mark her passage. Small, perfectly formed footprints.

I knew it was she. My sister. My *half*-sister. I remembered the halo of hair standing out around her head. Surprised, I realized that my half-sister was half-black, like the Boudreaux boys back home. My childhood friends.

'You were right, you crazy old man,' I whispered out loud to an absent Father Alcede. 'Evil really is out there. But you don't have to leave home to find it. Not if you're a DeLande. If you're one of us, you're born right into it, unless your mother has the good sense to run like hell and hide you from them all.'

The image of *Ugly Truths* returned. A sixteen-year-old pregnant girl had run from them. And been running ever since.

'Yes. She did that. But she paid the price.'

I whirled, my hand moving to the waistband of my jeans, and the dangerous .38 I had hidden there.

The Grande Dame stood, weaving slightly, a half-grin curling at one corner of her lips. Her hair was down, braided and tied with red ribbons at the nape of her neck and the tip of the braid. She was wearing a pearl-colored nightgown with a crocheted lace robe over it. The robe was nubby with a rough, open weave; the pearl shimmered and gleamed through it.

Her feet were encased in high-heeled satin mules the exact shade of the nightgown. Mules like Heddy Lamar or Betty Grable or Dorothy Lamour might once have worn. The sirens, the *femmes fatales*, vamps of a bygone era. The Grande Dame outshone them all.

'Price?' I asked. 'What price?'

Her pupils were open, wider than my own. Abnormally, medically enlarged. A strong sedative had been administered. Miles trying to keep her quiet perhaps? If so, it hadn't been enough.

Perfectly manicured nails gripped the door frame on either side of her head. The grin that crimped one side of her face pulled harder, warping her features.

'I found her three – or was it four? – years after you were born. The little tramp. She was in New Orleans on . . . *business*.' The word was slurred, as if it were dirty. Vulgar. 'She had made a small fortune on the market and hidden it away. But she was still under twenty-one. Still legally mine.'

My mother. She was talking about my mother. My hand

clasped the half-warm, half-cool grip of the .38 at my back. I was trembling.

The emotions I had been numb to all evening flooded me suddenly. A hot surge of fear and anger. Disgust, horror, and outrage thundered through me like a storm on the bayou, roiling in on frothy, muddy waves, destroying everything in its path.

I clenched my hands, feeling the nails of one hand bite into the flesh of my palm. The gun butt was slippery in the other.

I don't think I breathed. I don't think I could have drawn a breath past the surge of tangled emotions.

She was talking about my mother. LaVay.

'I didn' touch her money. All I wanted was you. But she was the best of them all. Stronger. Tougher.' There was grudging admiration in the Grande Dame's voice. A hint of respect. And somehow that frightened me more than anything the Grande Dame had ever said.

I slid the .38 slowly from my jeans. Not thinking. Not planning. I simply pulled the weapon from the restraining cloth.

The Grande Dame's eyes grew dreamy, her voice slurred drunkenly as the drug in her system continued to work. She sounded almost French. Lilting, missing some final consonants. French and familiar. Everything about her was eerily familiar.

'She wi'stood me for weeks. And Andreu, my firs' born. He coul' charm the feathers from a bir', tha' boy.'

My anger began to fade as she spoke. Just a crazy old woman, drugged, faltering in speech. Precariously balanced as her body swayed to the rhythm of her words. Sick. The Grande Dame was sick.

'But she resis'ed him as well. And in the end we ha' no choice bu' to pu' her in a . . . *safe place*.'

The words slithered from the woman's mouth like venom. Poisonous and malign. Her voice cleared a bit then, and grew stronger. Her elegant shoulders again rigid and unyielding.

'Back then we were still a family of power. With a single check I arranged for her to . . . res' . . . for a few month'. Give her time to think. To ponder.' The half-smile that twisted her beautiful features into a rictus smoothed. Softened. 'Bu' she was so strong, tha' one.' There was amazement in the tone. And when she smiled this time, it was a real smile. Touched with tenderness. What looked like pure adoration.

'So strong. One of the doctors – he had been with me for years – agreed to help. But even tha' didn' work. Not with her. Three sessions, and still she was uncooperative. Dr Whitt had assured me that shock therapy would bring all her barriers down. But not her. Not Marie. Not ever, Marie.'

Shock therapy? Like with electricity? But I didn't voice the question. A shadow had appeared behind her, tall and lean. Miles.

Gently, he touched her shoulder. 'Ma'am. It's all right now. Come. Back to bed.'

The Grande Dame tilted her regal head, the silver braid slipping to one side and swinging, the red bow looking perky and youthful.

'Miles?' Her voice was plaintive. Uncertain. Her eyes unfocused.

'Yes, ma'am.'

'You were the other one. So very . . . strong. If I could have had a child from the two of you . . . You and Marie . . . She might have been the one. She might have . . .'

'What?' he asked, his voice curiously flat.

The Grande Dame smiled. It was the beautiful smile, the one that had charmed generations around the world. Serene. Breathtaking. Glorious. 'Taken over for me. And continued the . . . ruin . . . the devastation of the DeLandes. Carried on the curse. It can't die with me, you know. It can't.'

She wavered and would have fallen, but Miles steadied her. 'I had . . . hoped Carin could take her place with you. I had hoped a child from you would . . . do. Tired. I'm tired. I think I'll lie down, Miles. Would you send for my maid?'

Miles took her shoulders and guided her from the doorway, back down the hall into the shadows. Her voice carried back to me, standing in the used bathroom.

'Do you like my Carin, Miles? Would you take her? I think she likes you. I know you could have her if you wanted her. Would you take her, Miles? Please? Just one child. That's all I need. Just one . . .'

My hand had cramped on the butt of the gun, a twisted ache at the juncture of my thumb and index finger. A second cramp tweaked my upper arm. My hand was hot and clammy where the black plastic gun-grip had warmed. I eased the .38 back into my pants and followed my grandmother to the doorway. The hall was empty. Silent. Full of secrets, of tangled lies. Full of ugly truths. False truths.

I knew my sister wasn't far away. The floor had still been damp where she had stepped from the shower. It was only then that I realized I didn't even know her name.

'I'm leaving you some clothes,' I said to the empty hallway. 'And a flashlight with some extra batteries. And a blanket.' My voice reverberated down the silent hall. 'But there's also going to be a map on a little slip of paper. It shows you how to get to my room. I want to help. I think that . . . I think we're sisters, you and I. And I want to help. Okay?'

I walked to the first room on the hallway, the one farthest from the servants' stairs, near the juncture of the wing where my sister had been held captive and abused. Clicking on the light, I went inside. This room looked out over the patio and the French doors leading to the dining room. It was beautiful. Elegant. With a double key deadbolt on the door. Was she still here? Close by? Listening?

'I'm leaving the things here. On the bed. Okay?'

I dumped the blanket, extra clothes, and the flashlight onto the comforter covering the bed. Turned off the light and returned to the hallway.

'I have a house out in the bayou. You'd be safe there. I'd take you there, if you like. Teach you to hunt and fish. And . . . paint and dance and sing. Just the two of us. And maybe my Tante Ilene and Tee Dom, if I can find them. You'd like them. They hid me from her for my whole life. They kept me safe. They'd keep you safe too. Think about it. Okay?'

The words echoed off the bare walls and thinned into silence. I checked the other rooms on the wing, finding them all nearly identical and empty of people.

I wanted this sister, even though she had killed. I wanted her like I suddenly wanted Perkins, who was safely back in New Orleans with Cee Cee Gaudet. I wanted her because she was family and I had been without family for far too long. I wanted her to want me too . . .

Miles reappeared before I reached the end room, the room where my sister had showered, and where the Grande Dame DeLande had found me. His black eyes were dull, like onyx left too long unpolished and dusty, all the glitter and emotion leached away. He looked worn and weary.

His shoulders were slumped, his face haggard, his body clearly fatigued. He looked less like a threat, after his hours dealing with Marcus's death, and more like a little lost boy. The innocent image didn't last.

He smiled, his eyes mocking. The Eldest, the only male DeLande of his generation left alive, leaned against the hall wall. Crossed his boots at the ankle, tucked his fingers into his jeans pockets, and waited. When I didn't speak, and the silence had stretched to uncomfortable limits, Miles shifted.

'So. Now you know all our dirty little secrets.'

'Oh, I doubt that.'

Miles chuckled softly, the sound bouncing along the empty rooms. 'Good point. Among the DeLandes, one nasty secret is always left buried. Hidden. We're a dangerous bunch.' Shifting moods seemed to characterize the man, as the mocking façade faded into something tired and almost approachable. I felt a spurt of sympathy.

'How can you stand it? Living here, I mean.'

Miles shrugged, the action as elegant and fluid as choreography. 'I'm making a difference, finally. As the Eldest, my decisions are final. Unquestioned. I was locating all the lost sisters and their progeny. All the illegitimate offspring of my . . . prolific brothers,' he said wryly, running a slender hand through his hair.

'I had hired counselors, specialists in the field of inter-familial sexual abuse. The Grande Dame . . . my mother,' his lips twisted down in reflex, 'made it a point to molest her children. All of her children.'

I realized then that he meant me to know he had not been excluded from her attentions. I glanced down, away from his face. If it was a tactic, it had worked.

'She thinks it's normal behavior. She thinks that everybody does it, but they just don't talk about it any more than they would talk about their bowel movements in polite company. And she has this . . . bizarre belief that she can breed up some kind of super woman if she just can find the right genetic mix. So she . . . arranges for her children to inbreed with one another when they are too young to know any better. Or when they are old enough to agree to her demands for their own purposes.'

I met his eyes then. Dark eyes with no light in them at all.

'You have no idea of the power she has held over this family. No idea of the damage she has done.' He shifted again, his speech becoming clipped and yet soft. 'She's smart, though. She keeps meticulous records and brings in fresh blood whenever the lines get too tangled.' There was no trace of admiration in his voice. 'And, of course, there's the simple fact that she hates us all, uniformly. And she's crazy as hell.' His mouth curled up on one side in an emotion I couldn't interpret.

'When I became the Eldest, I took away her power. Except for McCallum, and of course Marcus, she has very little say in the running of this house. I had even managed to replace most of her . . . *loyal* servants.' The word was tinged with sarcasm. I didn't ask what he meant by loyal. 'And they were improving, my sisters and all their children. They were talking, sharing it all. Getting it out into the open.'

'So you were doing some good, while you also managed to secure your power base within the family,' I said, leaning on the far wall from him, mimicking his stance. 'Why are you so unhappy now? It would seem to me that you accomplished a great deal tonight. You lost one of your three rivals and found two new DeLandes.' My tone was cool, the single spurt of sympathy somehow destroyed by his monologue. I don't think that had been his intent, but he didn't react to my tone, only to my words.

After a long moment he answered, framing his words slowly, his lips moving as if he had difficulty forming them, or as if they caused him pain to speak them. 'Because there's always *one* more. Always one I've missed. And somehow *she* finds them. And the pain starts over again.'

'So you're going to give up?'

He shrugged again. The elegant, weary monarch. The king who has lost his power to one less capable, but far more cunning. A ruler who sees ominous signs of treachery and deceit all about him. A young Hamlet.

A part of what I was seeing was real, and I accepted that.

But part was fantasy, as if he was trying on different personas to determine which I might respond to. And the strange thing was, some part of me liked Miles DeLande, even now. Responded to him on some deep, intangible level.

This Miles was far different from the Miles I had met in the Café du Monde, the Miles who studied the financial paper with all the diligence of a corporate analyst, who stroked my dog with sensual fingers, who laughed with clear eyes. I didn't like this Miles, this Eldest with his quicksilver personality and lightless soul.

'I guess you could just give up,' I said, my voice hard. 'But then again, you'll outlive her. Winner by default.'

He laughed again and scrubbed his face with a long-fingered hand. His eyes, when he dropped the hand, were clear again. Not lively, exactly, but at least active. 'I suppose I will at that.'

His laughter trailed off, his eyes dark and intense, boring into mine. Eyes a bit more like the Miles I remembered. 'That's the sign of a true DeLande, you know. Finding the monetary benefit in any circumstance. It's why we all stayed here, year after year. Letting them . . . letting *her* . . . carve into our souls. For the profit. A DeLande is always cognizant of the bottom line.'

I nodded back. I had seen the signs in myself since I was a child. The ability to turn any situation to terms of profit and loss. 'So, what about the showing?' It wasn't precisely a question. More in the nature of a challenge. The bottom line after all.

Eyes snapping like coals in a fire, Miles unwound his frame from the wall and crossed to me, taking my arm. He tucked my hand in the crook of his elbow and escorted me toward the light at the end of the stairs. All I needed was a hoop skirt and a fan to make it perfect.

'Well, dear niece,' he drawled, 'while you were skulking about in the historical shadows of the DeLande past, we received the first of the English visitors. Three gallery owners from London. Two from Paris will be arriving around 3 a.m. on the red-eye express, and several dozen more before morning. What's the old saying? The show must go on?'

'Sounds familiar. Has a nice ring to it, actually.'

'We DeLandes *really* know how to give a party.' He grinned at me, standing at the top of the stairs, looking down at the entry gallery. If his eyes had smiled with his face, it would have been a pleasant moment.

'What about Marcus?'

Miles lifted a single shoulder, the motion originating near his shoulder blade in a faint shrug, a gesture I was quickly coming to realize was habitual. It made him look young and harmless. And gave him time to think.

'Funeral on Monday, after the guests have all left.'

'No remorse?'

Miles's eyes hardened, turning to the stone I had compared them to earlier. Onyx. Opaque. Brittle.

'No, little niece. No remorse.'

I shrugged, again copying his gesture, remembering the spots on the rug. Their strong, half-familiar smell. 'Good.'

Miles's brittle laughter floated down the stairs and back the way we had come. Out of the corner of my eye, a shadow separated itself from the others and slid noiselessly forward. Listening. Hovering. But I didn't turn. I pretended not to see. My sister would have to come to me on her own terms. *The DeLande bottom line.*

CHAPTER 17

He slashed, ripping the brocade; fluffy white stuffing tumbled to the floor and foam bulged up from beneath. Again and again he cut at the chair, leaving long gouges and slits. His breathing, usually so controlled, was rough and loud, a dry, angry sob of fury.

'Are you aware that you are hacking into an eighteenth-century wingback once owned by the British royal family?' the Grande Dame asked. Her voice was droll, but slurred, and she laughed, a girlish little titter.

McCallum whirled, the blade held high for a killing strike in the dim light. Candles fluttered, flickering along its length. 'It's just a fucking chair,' he growled.

She reared back, unsteady on her feet. 'Foul language can go outside in the gutter, where it belongs.'

'You said he was in Milan, looking for another one of his long-lost DeLandes,' he said, ignoring her comment.

'And he was.' She shrugged, the nightgown glowing in the uncertain light like a pearl. 'But he's the Eldest. He can do whatever he wants.'

'Including drug you.' It was an accusation, but his voice was less heated and he lowered the blade, dropping the point into the wood floor. It penetrated deeply, though neither noticed.

She smiled then and put her fingers against his cheek. 'I let him give me the drugs, yes. But I have plans for him. For them all. Just leave it to me, Cal. Lovely McCallum DeLande.' She stroked his cheek again and down his sweaty neck to his collar bone, along his shoulder and back again.

'Do you like her, my little Carin?'

Cal shrugged, pulling away, finding the sword sheath and

putting away the weapon. He'd have to return it to the dining room soon, before they noticed he'd taken it again. He tossed the weapon to the computer table where it clattered, knocking over a candle. Wax puddled on the wood surface; smoke spiraled upward.

'She's not Grande Dame material.'

'No, but her child will be. If you're it's father.'

'And the Eldest?'

She smiled again, pouring all the power at her command into the action. 'You are next in line as Eldest, should anything happen to Miles. And I will see to it that nothing . . . no one . . . stands in your way.'

He smiled finally, the angelic smile he knew she loved.

'Come. I'll help you back to bed before he realizes you're gone. You don't want him to know you can still function with that much dope in you.'

I didn't sleep that night. I don't know how I could have slept. My body felt wired, like a watch-spring wound too tight. Like an electrical cord frayed against a sharp corner, smoking and hot.

So, instead, I painted. Rhame had brought along a half-dozen canvases in various sizes, prepared and ready for brush and paint. Unfortunately, we had never off-loaded them from the rented van we drove down in.

MacAloon and Campos, detained by the police even longer than the family, burned off some excess energy by locating the truck parked behind a ten-car garage on the back of the residential property. Grumbling, they brought the truck around and carried three of the canvases and three portable easels up to my room.

Rhame was locked in his suite. Probably not alone. Campos had seen the scarlet-haired Angelique waiting for the artist when he was dismissed by the police. Miles's older sister, sleeping with the same man once seduced by her mother. *Recently* seduced by her mother. But then, Angelique was a DeLande, wasn't she, and Rhame had a reputation as a skirt-chaser. Rhame's passion was his art, his art his passion. Angelique must have stimulated something truly artistic deep in his soul, I thought a bit maliciously. Perhaps they belonged together. I wasn't much surprised by these bizarre people any more.

As usual, when nothing seemed right, and my emotions were charged and yet tattered, I found solace in the scent of paint, the feel of brush against canvas. It was my own most personal and intimate therapy. As relaxing to me as a massage might have been to a harried businessman. And much more productive.

I had never started three new oils at once. Always before, it was a single canvas, a single idea, like the first tightly bound blossom on a spring plant. As the first canvas began to take form, began to bloom open from beneath my brush, others would follow.

But that night painting was inspired. I was impassioned.

I arranged all three canvases facing the windows with a dozen candles scattered around the room. And my face to the door in case she came. My sister. The nameless child.

Most of the time when I paint, I have a certain amount of control over the process. Oh, I know most creative people say, 'It just boiled out of me like steam,' or 'My hand had a life of its own,' or some such thing. And I had felt a bit of that kind of passion when painting *My Hair*. But this . . .

This was an entirely different kind of experience. This was a . . . a magic. A moment when I was not in control at all. When the brush seemed not to lay down color and texture and form, but rather to uncover it. As if the whole scene was there on canvas, hidden from view, and the brush merely exposed it. Stroke by stroke.

The night maid checked in with me near midnight, bearing a tray and talking in whispers. 'The Eldest said you might like a light repast, miss. A bottle of wine, a plate from your . . . er . . . disrupted dinner, and a storm kettle. This candle will keep the water hot for several hours, and here are five tea-bags and a few coffee-bags. The Eldest said you might be up for hours, so if you need anything, just pick up the phone and dial 208. That's my number, ma'am. And I'll bring you anything you might like.'

I glanced away from *Living Sacrifice* to find a view of the night maid's slender rear-end pointed toward me. She was bent over plugging in a phone behind the bed.

Four-star service at the DeLande Estate. All the mysteries, murder, mayhem, and manners you might want all in one place.

I think I grunted and went back to painting. I didn't even hear her leave.

Living Sacrifice was the picture I carried in my mind of my sister at the top of the stairs. Silvered in silhouette, her kinky hair a halo, her body poised like a living crucifix, staring down through the darkness. Deep earth tones tinted the canvas with hints of red, as if the fires of hell were reflected in the shadows.

Ugly Truths was softer, deep, with purples and plums and violets and lavenders, bruises on my mother's thighs and mirrored in her eyes. A haunted scene. Harsh, for all the softness of the satins and velvets on which she was posed. I needed a model to finish *Ugly Truths*, but the rough form and the background were in place by 2 a.m. A form that flaunted sensuality and fear, implied violence and terror and desire and domination.

My Sister's Face was a different matter entirely. A close-up, far bigger than life-size, it was only a smudged shadow peering out of deeper darkness. It was a portrait. One I prayed I'd have a chance to paint.

By 2 a.m. I was deeply involved in the three paintings. So focused I had forgotten the tray of food on the night stand. So centered that I didn't hear the door open. Didn't hear her enter.

Much later, the rhythmic cadence of someone slowly chewing finally penetrated my absorption. I paused, my brush held in the air, a faint smear of violet on the tip, and looked up. She was perfect. An entire series of works all alone, an interplay of possibilities I could almost see. She was utterly beautiful. Her face was rich in emotion, in depths of meaning, in contrast of light and shadow.

Holding myself still, I studied her.

She was swathed in my pale green T-shirt, a size too big, the shorts a muffled shadow covering her legs. One flawless foot was turned so that the high arch was blurred, the toes and heel in harsh relief. Hair mussed. Eyes wary. She watched me. And ate.

The moment our eyes met was . . . what? Like a thunder storm out on the gulf, violent, far-off electric flashes, a sudden tingling in the air. Exhilarating. Magnetic. All that and more. It was provocative and stirring. Filled with deeper meanings than I could have named. And I smiled a tremulous smile with trembling lips, as if I was afraid she would slip away in the night.

She didn't smile back. She just chewed and drank hot tea from my cup, the string dangling down the side, the Lipton Tea tag rotating in the shadows. The beautiful, dusky-skinned girl sprawled on top of my comforter.

The moment stretched. I memorized the shape and texture and hollows of her face. The strange green of her eyes. The fluff of light brown hair, glinting gold in the candlelight. Without speaking, I began the portrait called *My Sister's Face*.

My brush streaking wildly, I sketched her on the canvas, filled in the hollow of eyes, cheeks, and the highlights of cheek bones, brow and forehead, pointy little chin. Wary, frightened look in her eyes. Green, green eyes. *She was exquisite*.

She seemed to know I was painting her. Know and not mind. Holding her pose, her face turned, just so, to the candlelight. She was young. Fourteen? Fifteen? Or perhaps she was older and, like me, looked younger than her years. After all, she was my sister.

For an hour of silence, broken only once when she turned away and filled her cup – my cup – with steaming hot water and a fresh tea-bag, I painted. And she sat. And watched.

A little after three she slipped from the bed and stretched. Sleek and feline, she walked toward me with that smooth DeLande stride. Features coming clear, skin glowing, she reached my side.

With cold fingers, she touched my face. Traced the hollows, the valleys, the fine skin of lips and lid, and smoothed my hair. Her fingers were icy. Nails ragged. Her lips slightly open in wonder.

'Are you sure you're my sister?'

'I think so.'

'You're awfully white to be my sister.'

'Your daddy was my daddy. He was white. So was my mother.'

'My mother was half-black.'

'Oh.' I didn't know what to say to that. My sister was a quarter black. In far-off times she'd have been called a quadroon. 'You're very beautiful.'

'I know.'

I grinned at her. It wasn't vanity that answered. Only certainty.

'I want to be a model when I grow up. My mama says I could be.'

'I think you could be a model now.'

'Yeah?'

'Yeah.' I gestured with the paint-covered brush. '*My Sister's Face*.'

She turned and looked at the portrait. Nowhere near finished, it showed only the promise of the completed work. But it was enough for my sister. She could see beyond the half-formed features to the face beneath. The beauty.

Her face changed as she stared at her likeness. Crumpled and fell, like a small child whose knees are scraped in a fall. 'He's dead, isn't he?'

'Yes,' I said softly, a chill of shock running through me.

'I didn't mean to kill him. I only wanted to push him down the stairs and get away.' She wiped her face with the back of the green T-shirt sleeve. Dark spots appeared on the fabric. 'I thought that if he fell down the stairs it would take a while for him to get back up them. He couldn't walk, you know.'

'I know.' My throat was tight with tears I wanted to shed for her, but she didn't need sympathy, she needed something else right now. And I didn't know what that might be.

'How long before you get done?' She was talking about the portrait and I turned my attention to the canvas.

'By morning if you stay.'

'Okay.' She shrugged. A gesture so like Miles's my heart skipped a beat. 'The old lady won't go out till near morning.'

'What old lady?' I asked, touching the brush to canvas again.

'The beautiful one. The Grande Dame. She goes out every time the moon is full 'round midnight. And when there isn't a moon, at about two hours before dawn. New moon, my mama called it. We used to pick herbs then. During the new moon.'

Her cheek bones took shape under my brush. Her triangular chin. Pointed and adolescent.

'How do you know? No! Don't move. Tilt your head back left.

More. Stop! Don't move. How do you know the Grande Dame goes out at night?'

'My room looked off over the graveyard. I have till about 5 a.m. Then I have to leave.'

'She's drugged. She won't go out tonight.'

'How you know?' Curiosity on the young face.

'Miles told me. And I saw her.'

'Miles. She hates Miles. She can't feel him.'

'What do you mean by feel him?' I could paint a whole series of this girl. More than one series. Dozens. Her face was more fluid and elegant and emotive than any I'd ever seen.

'She can feel most people. Comin' or goin'. She can tell what they're doing. But not Miles. He the guy with you tonight?' Inquisitiveness. Gamin delight laced with pain. Twin emotions pulling at her young spirit. She drank more tea, added hot water to the cup.

'Yes.' I daubed in the eye sockets, drawing their shape. Her eyes were so deep it was like looking into still water at the bottom of a well. 'That was him. He's my uncle. Yours too.'

'Richar' was your daddy too?' She pronounced Rushar the way the Grande Dame had. French. Sophisticated syllables just dripping from her tongue.

'Yes. Or so they tell me. I never met him.'

With a fine brush, I drew on the lips, such perfect lips, the tiny points so balanced, the fine tilt at the corners creating a perpetual smile. Bruised lips. A faint purple spot as if bitten recently. I shivered.

And the door opened. Slowly. A black hole charring the black room. My mouth fell open. My brush paused. A form moved into the light. Miles's pale face a luster of porcelain framed in the center of the black hole. He moved so slowly, even the candles didn't waver in the night. My sister, her head turned toward me, was unaware.

She shrugged. 'He wasn't much. My mama didn't like him. But he was rich so she let him do it to her.' The crudity fell from her perfect lips like dung from fine china.

This was my opportunity to talk about Marcus and what he did to her. The time to bring up a doctor who could . . . do what? Take away the rape? Make it all go away? She needed to see a doctor, but my mouth went dry on the words and I couldn't think. I swallowed against parched membranes, my throat sticky with nervousness. 'She did?'

Miles stayed in the doorway, head cocked. Listening.

'Yeah. But he died and she got lots of insurance money, so it was okay.' The girl was casual. Seemingly at ease. Yet her eyes darted at the flickering shadows, shifting uneasily about the room. Her hands, when she spoke, clenched and relaxed. Clenched and relaxed. As if she had been holding on for dear life to something and had just lost her grip.

'I see.'

'What's your name?'

'I have two. Bonnibelle Sarvaunt and Carin Colleen DeVillier. What's yours?'

'That's weird. I never heard of anyone with two names.' Her eyes flickered, met mine for the first time and danced away. I paused with the brush inches from the canvas. Struggled to remain unaffected by what I had seen in her eyes. Within her was a vast . . . nothingness. Empty and hollowed and dark, exactly like the bottom of a deep, dry well.

I took a breath and placed the brush on the canvas, careful to steady one hand against the other, holding the brush stable. 'I know. But it wasn't my idea. It was my mother's. What's yours.'

'Azalea Demarch.'

'Pretty name.'

She jerked. 'I have to go now.'

'Why?'

'Miles.'

'Oh . . .' I looked up to find the door closed, Miles no longer framed in the dark center. 'What about him?'

'I have to see him.' Her fingers clenched again and this time held on. 'He has to know about the party.'

'What party?' Painting furiously, forgetting even to breathe. Trying to finish her face. Her beautiful seductive face.

'The one for you tomorrow night.' Azalea's face twisted, her beauty contorted with inner pain. She bit her lip, blinking hard. Before I could respond, she continued, 'She's going to poison the food.'

My brush paused. 'She is?'

'Yeah. She wants to get rid of the Eldest and she doesn't care who else gets hurt. She's crazy,' Azalea added, telling me nothing I hadn't determined for myself. 'I have to tell Miles.'

'Miles!' I shouted. 'Miles, come in here.'

The door opened again. Miles stood in the entryway. Face composed, eyes like black holes in a night sky. Dark-on-dark. Instantly, I wanted to paint him too. Would he pose? Would he let me paint him?

'No need to shout, niece.'

I swallowed. Put the brush into a jar of thinner. A cloud of light brown billowed up into the clear liquid.

'Miles, meet Azalea. She also your niece. She'll need to see a doctor soon, but she wants to tell you something.'

Miles bowed easily from the waist. A courtly gesture best suited to the last century, or the ones before that. Yet fitting, flawless, integral to Miles DeLande and the moment. 'At your service, Miss Azalea.'

Azalea looked from me to Miles framed in the doorway and back again.

'He's safe. Besides. If you don't come back, I'll shoot him.'

Azalea smiled. Impish. Charming. Pure DeLande delicious. 'I'll be back before your show. I saw your paintings. You're *so* much better than that Rhame guy.'

My brows went up.

'You got something I can wear?'

'I'll find you something,' I said a bit breathlessly.

'I have to look as good as you.'

'All right.'

And with that, Azalea, my quarter-black, nearly-grown, half-sister, left me, her hand firmly in Miles's. Harmony in their gait, they paced as only DeLandes can, with facile, silky steps. A walk like mine.

And I wondered for a moment how I could have seen Miles walk without knowing, how I could have glimpsed even one DeLande in motion and not known I was one of them.

Only when the door shut, and the candle flames ceased their fluttering, did I realize I hadn't a thing for Azalea to wear. I'd get to take my sister shopping. I would have the opportunity to pamper her and provide for her. Maybe comfort her. The thought made me soften inside, an elastic yielding of the hard knot of emotion I had carried within me since Marcus . . . interrupted dinner.

I smiled at the thought. Interrupted dinner. It was how Mme Willoby might have phrased it, being too proper ever to mention a dead body bouncing down the stairs during a formal meal.

I painted till dawn, stopping only because my hand cramped on the brush just as it had cramped on the butt of the .38. Eating left-handed, I finished off the remains of my meal, picking through the dried-out scraps for anything that didn't have Azalea's teeth-marks on it. And toward 6 a.m., I fell deeply asleep, fully clothed, on top of the comforter, enveloped in the harsh, yet soothing scents of paint thinner.

The average person would have suffered from lack of sleep, but the two-hour nap was more than sufficient for me. By nine, I was showered, dressed, and seated in the dining room, eating from a mountainous plate of food, my back to the door behind which Marcus had died. As I smeared homemade peach preserves onto a buttered bagel, it occurred to me that I should not be so blithe about his death. But I was. And based on the appetites evinced by the rest of the family, Marcus was little mourned.

The kitchen staff had prepared pancakes, pecan waffles, blueberry muffins, bran muffins, a fruit-bowl glistening with honey, eggs, grits, toast, bagels, bacon, hash browns, sausage, tasso spiced ham, cream cheese with onions, brie with herbs, four kinds of fruit juice, an extensive selection of teas, cinnamon coffee, decaf, fresh-ground dark-roast coffee with chicory, real cream, three sweeteners, and a baker's dozen jellies and preserves. I nearly made myself sick trying it all.

Throughout the meal, McCallum followed me with his eyes, watching me, his thoughts hooded. It was a bit like being watched by the Boudreaux boys the summer I began to grow rounded, not just tall. It was those looks that had caused Tee Dom to deny me the joys of playing in the bayou with the Boudreaux boys, leaving me friendless again.

But with McCallum, there was something more. Something penetrating and possessive. Something almost dangerous. I found myself avoiding those eyes altogether, and felt a delicate relief at leaving the table.

When I got back to my room my skirt waistband was a great deal tighter than before my breakfast orgy. I wanted to strip down, shower off the residue of McCallum's gaze, stretch out on the sheets and groan with pleasure. Instead my bed was made, the room neatened, with fresh towels and wash clothes delivered and stacked at the door. And Azalea, curled up on the comforter.

She had turned the portrait, *My Sister's Face*, to the bed, angled so the light hit it squarely. Her face was pensive, yet less vacant than the night before.

Without greeting her, I went directly to the windows, pulled the heavy drapes and lit a candle. Few of my paintings could withstand the light of day, and Azalea's face was no exception.

'Better,' she said, tilting her head to one side. 'I was wondering why it wasn't as good as the ones in the big hallway downstairs.'

'A painting, like a fetus, is seldom improved by displaying it prematurely,' I said massacring someone's famous quote, a quote attributed to the famous personage known as anonymous. The original quote had referred to a manuscript, of course, not a painting, but I didn't think Anonymous would mind. 'I'm not finished.'

'When will you be?'

'Depends on how soon you can pose for me.'

'How about now?' Her eyes met mine once, twice, and settled back on the painting.

'Okay,' I said, a slow grin pulling at my mouth. 'Or, we can go shopping and to the beauty parlor for your society debut tonight. Your choice.'

Azalea's dark green eyes moved from the canvas to me and stayed there. Although her body remained stationary, a sudden energy thrummed beneath the surface of her skin like a soft light glinting from the surface of emerald water. Her eyes swiveled back to her portrait. Her teeth worried her upper lip.

'I want a Cinderella dress.'

'If we can find it.'

'Something silky with skirts out to here.' She held her arms out to her sides showing a full skirt.

A knock sounded at the open door, and we both turned. Miles entered, a maid behind him. 'The nearest town is Vacherie. I don't think you'll find anything like that in your size outside of New Orleans. But perhaps one of these might suffice.'

With his words, the maid entered, opened the drapes, and began laying out size two and size three creations. They hung from the armoire, dangled from the bed frame, and swung from door frame and chair backs. Tiny, delicate creations. I recognized a Versace, an Yves St Laurent and two Givenchy's from my years of studying *Elle*. They were all beautiful. Used, perhaps, but no one would ever know that. Glittering, lovely dresses.

Azalea looked up at me, her mouth tight. 'He has *second sight*, you know. That's how he knew to bring the dresses. But he doesn't like to talk about it.'

Miles lifted a scarlet creation, a skin-tight, latex affair with a full skirt. 'Personally, I've always been partial to red.'

I realized suddenly that Azalea and Miles had talked in the hours we had been apart. Talked, shared secrets and confidences. Private things that Azalea was about to divulge. Things that Miles wanted kept secret. Had he been telling tales to the child? Trying to take something from her, as her Uncle Marcus had done? Who among this family could I really trust? 'Second sight?' I said, my voice carefully neutral. 'Like ESP?'

'Or perhaps this one. It will bring out the emerald in her eyes.' Miles dropped the red dress and held a deep teal up to Azalea.

'Yeah. He sometimes knows things. It's a family trait,' Azalea said, her green eyes like slits. Anger fairly radiated from her. I could feel its heat on my own skin.

'It didn't take psychic powers to know what kind of dress you wanted, young lady. You practically bribed me with the dress last night.' He glanced at me. 'It was the only way I could get her to let a doctor take a look at her.'

'I don't like the red,' Azalea said, her hands on her hips, head tilted to one side. Her eyes were on Miles, a direct and penetrating stare. It was the longest I had ever seen her focus on anything, and I wouldn't have wanted to be the recipient of her gaze, but Miles didn't seem to notice.

'*Second sight?*' I said it a bit forcefully this time.

'I like the teal. It's a maybe. How about the black? No. Too strong.' The swish of silks, satins, and delicate blends whispered behind Miles's words. 'And the silver . . . no. Definitely not. Positively wretched against your skin.'

'Second sight?' I almost shouted.

Miles didn't even glance at me. 'Now, the pink. No. Not *this* one. This one, with the beading. It brings all the warm tones out in your face. And the gold . . . Ah . . . heavenly.'

I rolled up my eyes. Miles wasn't going to answer me. Not right now. 'The teal, the gold, or the pink with the beading. Toss the others out the window,' I said.

The maid's eyes widened, her lips parted. 'But—'

'Take the others away, Anna,' he said to the maid. 'Return them to storage. Now, Azalea. You can't put gorgeous gowns over a filthy body. Shower, wash your hair, shave your legs, all that girl stuff. Here's a bag of toiletries with underthings. Anna picked them out for you, and she has excellent taste.'

There was a silence in the room then, thick and cloying. The silence of two strong wills in voiceless battle. It was a silence I was familiar with. The silence of Tante Ilene and Tee Dom, on the few occasions when they had disagreed. Azalea glanced down, breaking first. Her mouth twisted down in a frown, as if she knew she had lost some important battle but didn't exactly understand why. 'I've never shaved my legs. Mama said I was too young.'

Miles's face twisted suddenly. A terrible expression, half-fury, half-hate, flickered there and vanished so fast I wasn't certain I had seen it. The gaiety he had expressed was back in place, hiding the deeper, darker, clandestine emotions. 'Go draw your bath. Lots of bubbles.'

Azalea shrugged, a gesture pure DeLande, and took the bag, leaving the room. At the door she looked back, a wistful look on her face as she gazed at the beautiful gowns hanging from the armoire. And then her face tightened again, pulling down at the corners of her mouth. She settled a harsh, unforgiving expression on Miles, and she held it a long moment, making certain he understood its meaning. The look said that the dresses were pretty, but they didn't make up for Marcus. Nothing ever would. And there was something else there as well. Something she shared with Miles, something which excluded me. Miles tilted his head in acknowledgment of the secret they shared. The door to the bath closed slowly.

A hoarse breath, more than half-swear, grated from his throat.

'Yes. She was too young to shave her legs, but not too young for her mother to turn her over to the Grande fucking Dame for a sizeable chunk of cash.'

'Is that what happened?'

Miles rubbed his hands through his dark hair, scrubbing his scalp, throwing both light and shadow like sparks into the room. 'My . . . *mother* . . .' The word was so laden with sarcasm and hatred that it was foul, the most sordid and fetid of profanities. '. . . could charm the stars from the sky. The thief from the cross. The Pope to a mad romp in her boudoir beneath the eyes of a camera crew.

'She convinced Azalea's mother that her daughter would be educated and instructed best on the estate, rather than in the public-school system. She hinted that *culture, wisdom,* and *breeding* would be lathered on Azalea like soap on a filly. I don't think Richard's mistress had Marcus in mind when she agreed to let the Grande Dame DeLande take charge of her.'

'You hate her, don't you?'

'Hate is far too *sterile* a term, dear niece.'

When Miles spoke of the Grande Dame his voice changed, became clipped and sharp. An iron-on-iron sound, hot and feverish as a forge.

'We're related in another way, you know.' I don't know where the odd shifts of topic kept coming from, but at least they served as a distraction to Miles. His brows went up.

'Are you familiar with the name Elizabeth Diane Sarvaunt?'

His brows went up higher. 'Your real mother's – my sister's – friend,' he said.

'Well, she was my mother's cousin as well as her friend. Cousin several times removed. And didn't you say your mother's mother was a Sarvaunt?'

Miles's eyes did that shuttered thing again. Took on the lifeless aspect of unpolished onyx. Far-away eyes. 'Ilene. Ilene Sarvaunt,' he said, remembering our conversation from the Café du Monde. 'She married her second cousin, Robert Sarvaunt.'

He looked at me then. Really looked at me with all the power of his gaze. I forgot to breathe. Forgot to blink my eyes. I think my very heart may have stopped while he probed me with his eyes. And I knew somehow that he read more from me than I might really want to give. And then it was gone, that penetrating glare that was like being pierced through with an ice-sickle, and it was just Miles again, and my heart remembered to beat and my breath returned.

'The Grande Dame had siblings. I believe her sister was named Ilene,' he said.

I nodded uncertainly. Wondering what had just happened to me. What he had just done. And then the moment faded. And I couldn't quite remember what had left me so nonplussed.

'And they are missing.'

'Yes,' I said simply.

Miles smiled and stroked my face with a tender hand. I knew then that whatever magic the Grande Dame had in her smile, she had passed down to her son and grandson, Miles Justin DeLande. A double dose of her genes he had. And all the power she possessed as well. He was breathtaking when he smiled. Soul stirring. A very powerful man. The kind of man other men are willing to die for. And women sell their souls for.

'Carin,' he whispered, his breath warm and coffee-scented against my face. 'How did you know that Beth Sarvaunt and Marie were cousins?' Soft voice. Liquid eyes. Sensuous mouth. Hypnotic.

'Her diary. I'm only about half-finished.'

His command was gentle. 'Finish it tonight. Have Azalea read it to you while you paint her. After the party.'

It seemed a strange request, but then everything that had happened to me since I received the fifty-thousand-dollar check from my mother was strange. And he *was* the Eldest, after all.

'Sure,' I said, my voice slightly slurred. 'Tonight. After the party.'

Miles turned to go, his movements poetry, as fluid and smooth as bayou water. Watching him leave, I seemed to wake up, as if a dream had overtaken me for a time. Or a trance. Or a spell of DeLande magic.

'Miles?'

He glanced back, brow raised in question.

'Do you have second sight? Can you see into the future?'

He shrugged, eyes open and honest. Only the barest hint of hesitation to give him away.

'No. Of course not. Just entertaining Azalea.'

The door closed softly behind him.

'Liar,' I said to the empty air. And I could have sworn I heard him laugh, low and throaty, like the Grande Dame, from out in the hallway.

That morning, I taught my sister about shaving her legs, and manicuring her nails, although I seldom bothered with my own. Lali, a black maid, volunteered her services to arrange Azalea's fine, curling hair, and Anna returned with several shades of pantyhose and three pairs of shoes, one to match each dress Azalea had chosen. The shoes didn't quite fit, but the addition of stick-on pads and insoles made them wearable.

The dresses had to be altered, and Anna proved herself invaluable with a portable Singer sewing machine, needle, pins and thread, modifying all three dresses to fit in a matter of hours. Azalea couldn't make up her mind on one single dress, and so the cooperative and willing staff simply refashioned all three for my undecided sister.

Sister. I had a sister.

Miles peeked his head into my room several times during the day. I was certain that pleasing Azalea would cost him dearly. I had a feeling that part of Azalea's revenge against the DeLandes would be developing expensive tastes.

In all of my life, I had never been pampered until I had shopped with Taber Rhame. I knew the sheer joy that could result from that kind of attention, and I enjoyed watching my sister taste and feel that pleasure. The pleasure of being the center of someone's attention.

After all, the DeLandes owed her anything she wanted.

And Azalea bloomed beneath the pampering, the total indulgence, the luxury. Where such opulence of pleasure had stimulated in me a need to paint desire, it had a similar effect on my sister, stimulating her innate talents. And I watched in awe as she used her gifts.

Azalea was indeed gifted. A brilliant girl. A genius with a preference for people.

She could look at a person – a complete stranger – and understand them instantly. *Read* them. Know them – their strengths, their weaknesses, their talents and faults. And then use that knowledge with such dexterity, such delicacy of touch, that they never even noticed they were being manipulated. She was a wizard. A witch. Already a sorceress. And she was only sixteen.

Anna, forfeiting lunch with her waiting family, stayed past 2 p.m. altering dresses just to please Azalea. Lali, who had other duties to complete before tonight's showing, rearranged Azalea's hair twice because some little thing wasn't exactly perfect. And Miles paid for it all gladly, just to see the delight and the rapture on the child's face.

My bedroom in the DeLande Estate became a paradise to Azalea. A place where all her dreams came true. And perhaps, hopefully, all her nightmares began to fade.

For me, the only dark blot on the day was the occasional flash of memory when I would hear her voice floating down the darkened stairs. 'Vengeance is mine, says God.' A child's voice warped by murder. A hollow foreboding would grip me then and I would shudder. Blink away the darkness that threatened me, and look closely at Azalea's joy. Hoping her delight would mute the fury of the remembered words.

Late in the afternoon, when we had chosen the dress that most complemented Azalea's exotic coloring, the dress that contrasted most strongly with my own Versace, Rhame appeared. Knocking at the door, he stepped inside my room before any of us could respond, and stood there, taking in the scenery.

His eyes were haunted, with dark circles beneath, the lids purpled with exhaustion, the skin sagging. The very visage of mortality and ruin. Angelique rested her chin on his left shoulder looking satisfied and sated, peering into the room like a lazy feline predator. The cat who got the cream. I expected at any moment to see her lick her lips and purr.

Without asking permission, Rhame strode across the room and slashed the drapes closed, plunging the room into darkness and silence. He lit a candle. Angled the three unfinished canvases –

my night's work – to the faint light. For long moments he stared at the canvases, his eyes slitted, piercing the darkened room from me to the paintings and back again.

And then, still without speaking, he left. Angelique was close on his heels, laughing softly, her scarlet hair leaving a red glow in the room.

'He's jealous,' Azalea said. 'You can do things with light and shadow he can't, but he didn't know it until *she* told him.' It was the comment an adult might make. Sophisticated, and yet entirely her own.

'Nonsense,' I said, blowing out the useless candle. 'He's Taber Rhame. He's so far beyond me that he could destroy my career with a single snide comment.'

'Not anymore,' a masculine voice said gently from the open doorway. 'Haven't you figured it out yet? You're a DeLande. You don't have to live by the same rules as the rest of society.' Miles stood in the open doorway, leaning negligently against the jamb, booted feet crossed at the ankles, jeans so tight they looked painted on.

I walked slowly from the darkened window to the door, my bare feet sinking into the carpet. As I moved, his brows rose. Suddenly I could picture myself as he saw me. Pacing slowly forward, a yellow-eyed lioness, defending her domain.

Miles and Azalea laughed, a growling, voracious sound, victorious and triumphant, almost feral.

'Maybe what I figured out was that only the rules separate us from barbarism.' I reached Miles and paused, eyes wide, pupils dilated in the darkness. My lips parted.

Placing my hands on either side of his face, braced on the jamb, I leaned in. Closer. 'And that choice is the only thing that draws the line between good and evil.' I lowered my voice, letting the silence in the room work for me. '*Choice and rules* are the only things that humans ever have any control over. Even the powerful, even *DeLandes* have the obligation to follow the rules.'

Suddenly I envisioned Marcus at the bottom of the stairs. Broken and bloody. Above him stood an avenging angel, an unashamed murderer haloed in the light above. My heart sped up, a broken rhythm in my chest.

Here was the inconsistency in my own argument. The rules said

I had to turn Azalea over to the police for murder. Manslaughter at the very least. And I knew I never would.

Miles, his eyes on mine, seemed to recognize the contradiction, the hypocrisy in my words. And it was to that paradox he responded.

'Bravo, little niece. *Bravo*. Perhaps you're a *true* DeLande after all. But you should watch out for Angelique. She likes discord almost as much as she likes power. She'll drive a wedge between you and Rhame just to prove that she can,' Miles said, his voice still amused.

'Why would she?' I demanded. My face close to his, my words a whisper. 'Why go to the trouble of getting me fired? What would that prove?'

'It would prove that she was more DeLande than you, more powerful. Besides, little niece, you're more than employee to Taber Rhame,' he said, his voice mocking. 'Don't forget the hands in *My Hair*. It's his hands you were lusting after. His hands on the woman's body in the painting.' Miles turned, exposing white teeth, his face savage, reckless. 'And Angelique has already taken him away from the Grande Dame. It would prove her conquest if she drove him from you as well.'

I lifted my head and drew back from Miles DeLande, the Eldest. Instantly I was aware of the grain of carpet beneath my feet. The too-warm temperature of my body and the room. The sound of my heartbeat in my ears. The concomitant silence in my bedroom. The pressure of eyes on my back. And the elation wafting from my sister, Azalea.

She was enjoying the confrontation as a hawk enjoys the hunt. The taste of prey. Was it part of her revenge, to watch DeLande war against DeLande? I wondered if she realized that when Miles agreed to keep silent regarding her part in the death of Marcus, he developed some kind of leverage over her. Perhaps for her entire life. Did Azalea realize that Miles had his own agenda?

I took a deep breath. Held it. And reached out to her without turning from Miles. Reached out to the servants, cowering from something they could sense yet never understand. Reached out to calm the room, the air, the three behind me. I straightened my shoulders, dropped my hands and blew out my breath.

Miles cocked his head.

I stared at him, his face framed in the shadows of my darkened room. 'Taber Rhame is my employer. Not my lover. Not now. Not ever.'

Miles's eyes softened. The grimace slipped from his face as if it lost its foothold and fell from a high place. His lips closed, and the dangerous expression was gone.

'But a person of *power*,' I said enunciating the word slightly, 'uses everything in life to learn and grow and expand his horizons. To cultivate himself and his spirit. To foster goodness and promote charity and altruism within himself and the world around him. And that is accomplished by following the rules. Even when we don't have to.'

Miles reached out with his right hand and smoothed my face. 'Well said, little niece. Well said. See that you remember those words. And welcome to the DeLande Estate and your . . . long-lost family.' The Eldest DeLande turned and moved back down the hallway, his steps as fluid and graceful as a dancer's. Or a panther's.

CHAPTER 18

The showing was everything a fairy-tale writer had ever envisioned and more. After it was over, and the guests had departed, I stood in the shadow of *My Hair*, letting the excitement and the near-frenzy drain out of me. Watching the cleanup crews and the remaining family, I tried to focus on the hours of gaiety and exhilaration. Tried to find some moment central to the evening. And couldn't.

It was like a whirlwind that left me with only kaleidoscopic images, disconnected bits and pieces of the evening. Slivers of individual moments and snatches of conversation stood out like bright lights, but the evening as a whole was a blur to me.

The household staff had removed the sheet from the massive chandelier hanging from the ballroom ceiling, polished the brass and crystal, placed a single candle in each of the one hundred candle holders, and lit each one. Tne floor had been waxed and buffed to a high shine. The artificial electric lights for Rhame's canvases had been carefully placed, angled to display the huge art works at their best.

The mansion had been robbed to produce abundant seating, which was scattered about in cozy groupings. An orchestra had been hired for the evening, a twelve-piece group as accomplished in the classics as in classic jazz.

The ballroom had been filled to overflowing with important people. Elegantly dressed gallery owners. Critics in off-the-rack ensembles and low-cost designer knock-offs. Reporters in arty, slightly off-beat attire. Artists wearing the grunge look. The wannabes and the accomplished, the haves and the have nots rubbing shoulders beneath the ballroom's erotic scenes.

And the chef, Delasbour, and his staff had outdone themselves.

There was an ice sculpture on a central table set just below the chandelier. A carving of an artist at his easel, a naked model stretched out just beyond.

In eye-catching groupings on the table surface below the ice sculpture were rabbit pâté, seven varieties of cheese, smoked venison, venison sausage balls, boudin balls, gumbo, rice dishes, cajun meats, apricots, two types of olives, kumquats, asparagus sprinkled with bacon, pickled birds' eggs, fresh cherries, grapes, sliced pears in wine sauce, mangoes, melon balls, and a dozen breads.

Fresh shrimp in crushed ice cascaded from a three-foot-tall crystal conch shell, a spiral-cut, sugar-cured ham rested on a bed of Boston lettuce. A cook in a chef's hat stood ready to carve from a side of roast beef, a rack of ribs, and a side of smoked pork.

There was a vegetable tray so large that a footman stood to one side to turn the tray and serve the requests. And the desserts could not be believed. I had never seen such a selection of sweets. Custards, puddings, pecan pies, chess, cherry, blueberry, and apple pies, bread pudding with rum sauce, whiskey sauce, and what tasted like almond-liqueur sauce. There were ten different cakes, platters of homemade cookies, macadamia nuts, white chocolate mints. Pralines and other candies by the dozen.

Champagne flowed, bubbling, from a stone fountain. White and red wines, decaf and dark-roast coffee, and Evian bottled water was served from a table beside the rotating vegetable tray.

Maids carried food and drinks to small groupings of guests. Footmen brought additional seating. A dance of liveried servants – starched charcoal tuxedos and staid tuxedo dresses with plaid bow ties and cummerbunds – kept the food hot, cold, abundant and the guests content.

Flash bulbs exploded with attention-getting pops. Polaroids snapped. And the rich, the famous, and the nearly-so posed, smiled with false camaraderie or alcohol-induced merriment and then moved on. And, occasionally, someone looked at art.

Rhame's new series was a smashing success – every canvas sold. Ten to private dealers or galleries, two to museums of modern art: one in Paris, one in Washington DC. The announcement of a sculpture series to follow from the artist's studio was greeted with sustained applause.

Angelique, dressed in a flame-bright silk dress hung on Taber Rhame's arm all night. The next morning, her photo would appear beside his in the society columns of ten different countries, resulting in a formal divorce decree from his fourth wife. Or was it his fifth?

As for me, I sold out *Wanton Dreams*, the series inspired by Taber Rhame's hands, and received commissions on three more of a similar nature. *Genesis* sold only two, but of all the sales, I was best pleased with these. A prestigious gallery, well known to be on the leading edge in artistic acquisitions, bought both. Claude Michau, invited to the viewing by me, confirmed that Royal Securities would place a triptych of a bayou scene in the main office. I had won the Royal Securities commission.

The gallery owner who knew LaVay was present, all decked out in school-marm-style finery. Networking. Making contacts with the big boys. She had heard nothing from LaVay, not a word, and that was a disappointment. Yet, all in all, it had been a heady experience for me.

Throughout the evening, Azalea flitted from place to place, eating rich foods, cozening wine from agreeable and accommodating footmen, and learning. Aping the manners of the elite, duplicating the duplicitous, she mimicked the artistic aristocracy, her green eyes alight with an almost frenzied pleasure and laughter.

She could have been having the time of her life, wearing her teal silk gown and grown-up slippers with a malachite barrette in her hair. She had conjured a gold bracelet and two rings from somewhere, and sported the bangles with panache. Her enjoyment could all have been real.

But several times I caught sight of her watching the Grande Dame, her eyes hard and cold. I understood that there was a depth of anger within Azalea. Anger that had not found a release. Perhaps never would.

Yet, except for the rare moment when her gaze focused on the Grande Dame, Azalea seemed like an ordinary sixteen-year-old. Lighthearted and gay, without a trouble in the world.

Miles acted the proud uncle as well as the host. He stood all night in the open ballroom doorway, presiding and overseeing the festivities, his tall form never far from the chaise-lounge upon which sat the legend of Louisiana, the Grande Dame DeLande.

The matriarch of the family was elegant, witty, refined and stylish, wearing an emerald creation with full skirts and a tiny beaded vest, an emerald ring with a rock the size of a pigeon's egg and the pearl and emerald necklace purchased twenty years ago from Cee Cee Gaudet. The Emberville pearls.

She was as perfect and flawless as the stones she wore. And just as cold.

Her eyes were as hard and glacial as black diamonds, glittering like a frozen pond beneath a full moon. Secretive eyes. Darkly amused.

All night, Miles watched the Grande Dame, his own eyes noncommittal, hooded. On the surface he seemed the concerned son, anticipating her every need, her every wish. But beneath the concern lay a watchful adversary, anticipating problems. Evaluating and calculating.

Azalea, all grown-up in her teal dress and jewelry, watched the two DeLandes, the Eldest and the Grande Dame, her young face serious and severe . . . and angry. Only the young can hate with such passion. Such fervor and obsession. I wanted to paint that face, that fury. To capture the intensity that would shape a woman's life through pain.

And so the hours had passed in a whirl of people and success and too much food and wine. A long, courtly evening until at last the guests began to drift away and the exhaustion of the past days began to claim me.

As I stood in the shadow of *My Hair*, my arms clasped around the beaded bodice of the Versace, the weariness seemed to seep into me, rising from the ballroom's rich flooring to climb my limbs in a slow spiral and settle near my heart. A sluggish, somnolent rhythm calling me to slumber. I wandered into the ballroom.

I had played the game with critics and gallery owners, collectors and curators, watching this family into which I had suddenly been born. Protected all my life from the intrigues and power plays, the debauchery and corruption of this bizarre family, I had found I could stand back and watch the maneuverings and diversions, the gambits and ploys, plots and mischief unfold.

And I felt curiously violated by it all. The unwilling outsider sucked inside.

Both Miles and the Grande Dame had wanted me. The Grande Dame wanted to use me in her breeding program. Miles had wanted me . . . for what? '*The bottom line*,' he had said, when we spoke on the patio just after Marcus died. But for Miles Justin DeLande, what, exactly, was the bottom line?

What was the bottom line for me? I had wanted to find my mother and had so far failed. I had wanted to discover why she had hidden me away. I had succeeded, and the truth was ugly. The bottom line was incest. The bottom line was my heritage . . . that my mother and father were siblings caught up in a web designed by the Grande Dame. Obscene. Profane.

As if sensing my thoughts, the Grande Dame looked up, found me in the sparse gathering of servants, and smiled. A vile smile that promised . . . something. Miles, observing that smile, frowned, clearly ill at ease until his duties as the Eldest called his attention away once more.

As he left, McCallum took his place, sliding onto the Grande Dame's chaise, his arm slipping about her shoulders. He spoke to her and they laughed, their heads close together. And then they turned, focusing on me. And laughed again. Unsettled, I went back to *My Hair*, standing in the shadows.

After the last guest departed, the servants slowly cleaned up, nibbling at leftover pâté, drinking flat champagne and warm wine, grumbling about the bad manners and drunken deportment of the rich and famous. All were clearly exhausted. And each one, when he found it necessary to pass close by the Grand Dame, found a reason to be diverted, leaving a space around her. It never failed. It was peculiar, an unconscious reaction that was less noticeable during the crowded evening or at the long formal dining table. But it was very real in the aftermath of the showing.

Miles, aware of the servants' discontent and the late hour, accepted a stack of envelopes from his valet's jacket pocket and made an announcement, his voice ringing from the erotic scenery overhead. 'I thank you all for your efforts tonight. The showing was a fabulous success, in great part because the guests were pampered, well fed, and served with a smile.'

'All that champagne didn't hurt,' a masculine voice called out from the kitchen. Everyone laughed, Miles included.

'Agreed. Nevertheless, I wish to express the estate's pleasure and satisfaction with the extra efforts from all of you. Gather around, people. It's bonus time.'

Formerly lethargic footmen and foot-sore maids were suddenly spry, gathering around the Eldest DeLande as he performed the duties of the master of the estate. The envelopes held green, undeclared income for each of them, from the lowest in-training maid to the head cook himself, who appeared in spotless whites to polite applause.

Standing in the doorway, I saw the Grande Dame watching Miles, her lips curled in disdain. Her fingers twitched, her eyes darted, and a tremor seemed to pass along her frame. McCallum was nowhere to be seen.

Slowly, as Miles played out his role as the Eldest, her left hand lifted to her temple, smoothing the hair back and up toward the sleek French twist at the crown. Again and again. Her eyes never leaving Miles in the crowd of servants.

One elegant finger slipped deeper, through the silver hair near the temple, and scratched. And again. Vicious, unconscious motions, the long, tough nail stabbing, and raking the flesh hidden beneath the hair.

I watched, amazed and repulsed. The Grande Dame's face never changed. I don't think she even knew what she was doing.

As if sensing my eyes, she turned suddenly and stared my way. Found my eyes with hers in the flickering light.

Come here. Her black eyes commanded. Her hands stilled, the nail she had used to savage her own scalp, crooked. *Come. Here.*

There was blood beneath that nail. Blood and tissue and a single, long silver strand.

I smoothed down the skirt of my designer gown, the silk slick beneath my fingers, and walked toward her. The orchestra was long gone, the guests sleeping or cavorting elsewhere as they chose. My slippers clicked steadily, the sound only a bit louder than the beat of my heart.

'So. Do you like all the glitter and power and ceremony of being a DeLande?' she whispered.

I didn't know how to answer, and simply watched her darkling eyes. So dark the pupil was lost in the black sea of iris.

'Did you know that our pretty little colored girl is pregnant?'

The icy shock drenched through me. Hairs raised along the backs of my arms like an animal's fur might bristle in alarm.

She laughed. That low throaty growl, so like a large cat in the wild. 'Oh yes. Marcus was good for something after all. Only minutes before she pushed him down the stairs, he managed to impregnate her.'

It wasn't possible for the Grande Dame to know what she claimed. It was absurd. Yet, *she did know*. The certainty was clear in her eyes. The Grande Dame *knew* that Azalea was pregnant . . .

I remembered what Azalea had said about Miles having second sight. And what Miles had said about the Grande Dame trying to breed up a super woman . . . Were the two connected somehow? I rubbed my palms up and down along the outside of my arms, a steady, reassuring comfort. The Grande Dame watched the motion of my hands, a faint smile on her lips.

Did Miles know? Would he . . . what would he do?

'Miles doesn't know yet,' she said, reading my expression. 'And it will be *such fun* watching him decide what to do.' Her voice was calm now, as if she were talking about the weather or the party or the state of French fashions. 'He doesn't believe in aborting a fetus, you know. Calls it murder.

'So now he'll have to decide. Shall he let his sixteen-year-old niece have her uncle's baby or not? And if he does, what if this one carries the curse of the DeLandes? What if this one is stronger even than he? Oh my. Dilemmas and decisions.' She laughed her throaty laugh. Victorious. Satisfied.

A cold dread, as familiar and close fitting as a coffin closed up around me. It seemed I had been trapped by a sense of dread, a silent, nameless fear, for weeks. Ever since my mother arranged for me to receive the 50,000 dollar check . . .

And suddenly I knew what to do. What to say.

I leaned in slightly, forcing my voice to remain low, forcing myself to smile. Forcing myself to play a game I didn't want to play. The DeLande game, a game of power, of knowledge used or withheld.

A game where people were the pawns, the way they had been pawns in Dr Tammany Long's lectures on politics, revolution, and the power plays of war, those hypothetical questions of so many years ago. 'Did you know,' I said slowly, 'that Marie Lisette is still alive?'

The Grande Dame blinked. The skin at the outer edges of her eyes wrinkled, became textured with age and fatigue.

'She protected me from you for twenty years. And she got away from you twice. Once to hide me, and then again when she got out of the hospital. And she's still out there, beating you at your own game.'

My grandmother rose slowly, her eyes on mine, intense and dark. Reading me. Reading the truth in my words. I stepped back two paces, out of her way.

'Where is she?' Low voiced, a teeth-grinding sound.

'Safe,' I said instantly.

The Grande Dame nodded, lifted her skirts with the bloody fingers and walked sedately out the door and down the hallway, passing through *Genesis* with regal hauteur.

I blinked, wondering what had just happened. Wondering at the power of my mother's name. At her hold over the Grande Dame DeLande.

I looked around for Azalea, so young and gay in a teal dress and grown-up lipstick. But she was nowhere to be seen. She had disappeared several times during the course of the evening. Flitting in and out of the crowd. An almost-woman, introduced to the dark side of adulthood too early, still playing dress-up and model and pretend. But she was gone.

The dread intensified. A sound like nails being driven through wood pounded inside my head. My heartbeat. Too fast. Too irregular.

Oh God. Where was Azalea?

I moved through the servants, stepped on something soft that squished beneath my slipper. A flattened-out glob of something, dropped from a guest's plate. Green. I moved on.

'Miles.'

He looked up, his face changing instantly from benefactor to something else, his features a mirror of my own. 'What.' It was a command, as effective as 'Report, soldier,' barked in a general's stony voice.

'I . . .' I stopped suddenly. I'd feel mighty foolish if my sister had gone to the bathroom or was curled up asleep in my room. 'I just wanted to thank you for a wonderful evening.'

The concern melted from Miles's face to be replaced by something else. Something steely and cold, and a bit mocking. He laughed. I had begun to hate that sound, that disparaging, faintly insulting tone. He had laughed differently at the Café du Monde, and I wondered which Miles was the real one. 'I'm afraid you'll have to thank the Grande Dame. All I did was play host and keep her from poisoning the guests. Little enough.'

It was an indicator of my heritage that I didn't even blink at his comment. Here on the DeLande Estate, one could talk about poison and death and any manner of bizarre behavior with little or no reaction.

I refused to smile. 'Well, thank you anyway.' I had no intention of thanking the Grande Dame. Not for anything. 'If it would be all right with you, I think I'll . . . retire now.'

Miles, distracted by something across the room, patted my upper arm and stepped away as he answered, 'Sleep well, niece. Oh, I had the staff put Azalea across the hall from you.'

A group of servants in regimental gray were waving, demanding his attention from across the room. He waved back, twisted in midstride, and walked backward as he spoke, moving as gracefully as an ice skater across a frozen lake. 'She was asleep on her feet, so they took her up an hour or so ago.' He looked back across the room again, and raised his voice. 'I'm coming. One moment.'

In a softer tone he continued to me, 'I've arranged to have a counselor see her in the morning after Mass. I was told that with the younger ones, it's best to begin counseling right away. Good night, Bonnie Carin.' And he was gone. Miles Justin DeLande. The benefactor and champion of the abused and dispossessed . . . And a man who drank power as most people drink water. A man with two sides to himself, both of them powerful and both desiring control. I wondered if they battled within him, or if they had reached an accommodation, declared a truce.

Still elegant in his double-breasted tux, not a wrinkle anyplace, not a speck of lint to be seen, he paced fluidly across the inlaid floor. Long sinuous strides, patent-leather shoes glimmering.

I watched him a moment, the DeLande, the Eldest, as he handled some small crisis. To one side, a contingent of footmen followed the soft-voiced commands of a maid as she directed in the assembling of a scaffold below the chandelier. I didn't envy the men assigned the job of snuffing out the guttering candles and cleaning out the globs of melted wax overhead.

Nor did I envy Miles Justin DeLande. A young man no more than a year or two my senior, who could speak so casually about 'the young ones needing counseling'.

Had he ever needed counseling? What had the Grande Dame done to him?

Silently, I turned and moved out of the ballroom and down the darkened hallway. The candles in the wall sconce had been removed, the floor swept, the long carpets vacuumed, the stray cups and plates and napkins tossed into a rolling bin.

Except for my canvases lined up along the stretch, there was no indication that an exclusive art showing had just taken place. No evidence that the career of a young artist had just been launched, except the discrete 'sold' tags on the corners of so many of my paintings.

Thank the Grand Dame indeed. I didn't like owing her anything. How does one say thank you to a devil?

The house was silent as I walked through the darkened hallways, my skirts swishing, the occasional tap of the beaded bodice and my breath the only sounds. It would feel like this, sound like this, to walk through a museum after hours, or through a great cathedral. Only here, there was no hushed and peaceful tranquility of a holy place. I paused in the grand entryway and slipped off my shoes. Standing in the stillness, I listened to the hush of the great house. An eerie quiet, almost mystical. I half-expected to see a ghost float down the stairs on soundless feet. But nothing moved.

A muffled crash, like a stack of expensive crystal hitting the floor, echoed from the ballroom, the only distraction. Tired servants growing careless or perhaps drunk on warm, leftover wine. Silently, moving like the ghost I had imagined, I climbed the stairs.

My room had been tidied, Azalea's things removed. I stripped off my Versace after struggling with the zipper, tight against my side, and hung the dress on a padded hanger. The shoes went beneath the dress. Pantyhose and silk underclothes went into the sink with Silk-N-Wash. And I went into the shower, letting the hot water pound against my shoulders and back.

Standing there, wet and steaming as my skin reddened lobster bright, I remembered the voice of the collector who bought the two pieces from *Genesis*. The measured praise. The sober plaudits. And I remembered the guests' response to *My Hair* and her sister canvases. An almost electric reaction, like a sexual reflex. Instantaneous. Startling.

I knew for a fact that one late arrival had tried to buy *My Hair* from the Grande Dame, offering her a substantial profit. She had laughed like a young girl, all gay and lighthearted, touched his arm with trailing fingers and gently turned him down. 'I'm sorry, Emmanuel. *My Hair* is mine. And frankly, in a few years it'll be priceless, so I'd be a fool to let it go now for such a pittance. But I'm certain the artist would paint you something in a similar style. Have Miles here introduce you. She's a charming creature. So young to have such an amazing talent. I swear, she must know magic.'

I smiled as the dense fog from the shower rose around me. I had been standing just behind her, hearing every word, my back turned so Emmanuel never saw my face until later, when Miles introduced us.

Thank the Grande Dame. My smile faded.

I shut off the water, dried off on a thick terry towel and creamed my face. Braided my wet hair. Stared at myself in the mirror for several minutes.

Her face was there, in the bone structure. The shape of brow bone, the high cheek bones. But the fulsome beauty that was the Grande Dame would never be realized in my face. No matter that half of my genes were hers.

Thank the Grande Dame indeed.

The vision of *Ugly Truths* flashed through my mind. My mother's face tear streaked. Her thighs bruised.

Naked, I padded from the bath into the bedroom and stopped. Slowly a tremor ran through my body, prickling on my bare skin into gooseflesh, tightened my nipples. Someone had been in my room.

It's curious how one can always sense an intruder. The air is so still in an empty room, the silence so complete. Both stillness and silence were missing in my guest quarters. The air seemed to move a bit, the silence to ring with echoes of sound.

But my room was empty of uninvited guests. There was no one hiding in the closets or behind the easels.

Quickly I dressed, the warm glow from the hot shower and pleasant memories forgotten. I pulled on an old ragged pair of cotton panties. Jeans, T-shirt, socks and sneakers. Tying the last lace, I reached for the .38 in its hiding place in the dresser beneath my underwear. It was there, a box of ammo beside it. But the shotgun, the .20 gauge I had taken from the shanty so long ago, was gone.

I couldn't remember suddenly what it was loaded with – birdshot or buckshot. Birdshot was useless in self-defense. Buckshot could be deadly. There had been one murder since I came to the estate. Was there about to be another? Who would have taken the gun?

The cold shivers, the fresh sensation of being closed in a coffin resurfaced. *Azalea*.

Throwing open my door, I crossed the hallway at an angle and opened the door to my sister's room. The bed was unmade, pillows placed for sleeping, one beneath her left leg if she slept on her stomach. The way I slept.

The fancy dresses and shoes were arranged so she could see them from the bed, hanging from the rod in an open closet. Shorts, T-shirts, a brand-new pair of Levis, still bearing the tags, were scattered across the floor. Messy, untidy child.

She wasn't here.

Azalea had taken the shotgun. I was certain, although I couldn't have told how I knew.

Running back to my room, I dialed 208. The night maid's number. It rang. And rang. And rang.

I slammed down the phone, hitting the cradle with a solid thump. Too forcefully for the high-impact plastic. I heard it crack as I ran back out my door, tucking the .38 into my jeans waistband.

Why would she want a shotgun? Who would she want to kill? But I knew the answer as surely as I knew she had taken the weapon in the first place. To kill the Grande Dame. To mete out justice. The vengeance of God.

At the front door, I met Jenks, his uniform wrinkled, his ascot askew. The slightly sour stench of wine clung to him, as if he had joined in with the lesser employees to finish off the champagne.

'Ah. The young Miss Sarvaunt-t. Or should I now call you Miss DeLande?'

When most people get drunk, the first thing to go is the diction. With Jenks, alcohol seemed to improve the clarity of his speech rather than distort it. The consonants came out clear and precise. Unfortunately, he still sounded crocked to the gills.

'Either. Have you seen the Grande Dame?'

'Many times, Miss Sarvaunt-t,' he said wiggling the fingers of one hand in the air as if waving at me. 'Many times.'

'I mean in the last hour or so.'

'The Grande Dame went-t up to bed some time ago. I'm not-t privy to her schedule. Did you know she snores?'

I couldn't help it. I laughed. A muffled sound behind my hand. 'No, Jenks. I didn't know that. Which way is her room, please?'

'Second floor, last suite-t of the family wing. Just above the Eldest's suite-t. But no one ever goes there, miss, except-t her maid Rosell.'

'I'll keep that in mind, Jenks. Thanks,' I said as I ran up the stairs for the family wing.

'I live to serve.' At any other time the phrase might have been tendered with withering sarcasm. In the face of Jenks's blood-alcohol level, it was merely bitter.

Rhame had pointed out the family wing to me the day we arrived, during his impromptu tour of the house.

At the top of the stairs, I turned left and ran down the hallway. Every yard or so, a night light came on, the kind that is activated by a motion sensor. No one had been this way recently, or the lights would still be on. The last door of the family wing was on the left, only feet from a narrow set of stairs leading down. The stairwell was lighted.

No body lay sprawled at the bottom. No blood splattered the walls.

Great. I was beginning to think like Alfred Hitchcock, macabre and gruesome. Or perhaps I was just starting to think like a DeLande.

Without knocking, I turned the knob and entered the Grande Dame's softly lit rooms. The dominant phrase in decorator lingo would have been *opulent*. Or perhaps *decadent*.

Pearl tones predominated, from the mother-of-pearl silk bed linens and comforter, to the lace bed drapery at the corners of the massive bed. The carpet was pearl-pink and so plush my sneakers were a flagrant vulgarity each time they touched down. The woodwork moldings were painted white everywhere and polished to a high gloss. The lounge chair was like something out of a Marilyn Monroe film, upholstered in pale pink satin with a down comforter arranged across the footrest. The vanity was antique cherry with adjustable triple mirrors, loaded down with sterling silver brushes, combs, and hand mirrors, crystal perfume atomizers, and an astonishing array of cosmetics.

Clothing was scattered about the room and, except for the glaring disparity in the cost of the garments, the effect was similar to Azalea's untidy room. Maybe it ran in the family.

The tall French windows to the balcony were open, silk drapes crushed to one side, moonlight spilling in. The pale light gleamed from rich cloth and sparkled off sterling. A shimmer of illumination that made the pearly room glow.

Beyond the open windows, an oak tree grew, its ancient branches reaching for the balcony, moss moving vaguely in an almost imperceptible breeze. Drawn by the moonlight, I stepped onto the balcony and looked out over the estate. In the distance was the ten-car garage at the end of a curving drive. A guest house or servants' quarters stood to the side, the windows lightless. And further back, dim in the uncertain light, was the DeLande graveyard.

White marble angels stood guard, wings spread wide at the wrought-iron gates. Moonlight silvered the marble crypts, blazed along milky, raised headstones, traced the hand of death through the generations.

What was it Azalea had said? Something about graveyards.

About the Grande Dame and midnight walks . . . full moons and new.

I couldn't remember.

My hand stroked the railing only inches from the tree's branches. Smooth wood and painted iron, moss and bark and tiny oak leaves. The moon was in front of the house, throwing long tenebrous shadows before me, turning the world into a stark and foreign place.

Moving back through the pearly room I closed the Grande Dame's door and descended the steps to the first level, past blinking lights and a security panel which glowed red on the wall. Without thought, without decision, I moved out of the house into the night.

It occurred to me as I stepped along the dim pathway beneath the overhanging branches of an occasional tree, that for a house so full of guests and family, so crowded with servants, it had been silent and empty wherever I went. And then there were no more rational thoughts. Only the faint breeze ruffling the down along my arms.

My shadow moved before me as I climbed the slight rise to the graveyard. The family plot.

The angels guarding the entry were cold, bathed in the light of the chalky moon. Dead faces. Stone faces. Firmly earthbound, trapped by gravity and service to the DeLandes.

The twisted iron gates hung open like black wings unevenly furled, the fanciful hunting bird of the family plaque worked into the iron design itself. Along the perimeter, black spears pointed skyward as if threatening heaven itself, forming a barrier between dead DeLandes and the rest of the celestial world.

Within, enclosed by cold iron and protected by the unfeeling angels, were the above-ground crypts of the long dead. Manicured lawn and diverging pathways led me deeper, past ancient memorials and weathered markers to the newer region. The fresher dead.

I was related by blood and heritage and a twisted genetic history to every DeLande buried here.

The stone was warm still, where I touched it, holding the heat of a long-vanished sun. Storing the energy and warming the dead, so safely entombed. My footsteps were soft shuffles, as indistinct as the light.

Everywhere there were angels and saints. Pink marble angels flanking the tiny crypt of a DeLande baby. 'Josette Leona DeLande. 1962–1964. Beloved Daughter.' The moonlight behind me carved the words from the naked stone. The pink angels cried dark pink tears. Pebble tears tracing the veins in the natural rock. An Italian masterpiece, so lifelike I expected the mourning beings to lift stone fingers and wipe away the pain etched for eternity.

White saints presided over a larger grave. A Mary Mother in flowing robes. A pale green angel sat, contemplative and serene on the polished top of a twelve-foot crypt. Chin in hand, she looked down over the names of those entombed below her.

A rabid sense of the absurd made me see her as holding these dead in place with her finely carved backside, as though preventing the deceased souls from attempted Ascension. There were twelve DeLandes buried here, one for each foot of height, stacked four deep and three high. And that bored angel holding them all in place with silent finality.

Moving deeper, I skirted an oak. Ancient silvery branches, twisted and sinuous as mating snakes, writhed their serpentine length down, moon-dappled and shadowed. Weighted by time and the sheer breadth of living wood, they curled out and down, resting in some places on the ground itself, letting the earth share the load and weight of the ages. Moss, unmoving in the night, draped in a heavy fringe all around.

It was so still now, my breath was a bellows, my footsteps loud, echoing back from blank stone. Crunching on crushed shell. Bruising the clipped grass in little, crisp whispers of sound.

There were no graves beneath the tree for invading branches and roots to violate. And no grass, as if the massive oak blocked out the sun, claiming this spot as its own from both living things and the dead DeLandes.

I walked among the departed, following the shape of a stone-carved name with curious fingers, reading inscriptions, studying the line and form of statuary nestled among the shadows, working my way to the center of the graveyard. The magnificence of the graves grew as I walked. Bigger angels, larger, grander saints. And once, a single crypt, more elaborate than the others, traced all over with carved stone roses. A climbing rose in rock, blooming forever.

Beside the foot of the crypt lay curled the stone figure of a dog. A Pekingese with wrinkled-up face, little tongue showing slightly, pushed between closed lips. Mourning through the eons for a deceased mistress.

At the center, at the very heart of the graveyard, however, something changed. The marble itself changed. Darkened. Blackened, as if heaven had rained down from a kohl-rimmed cloud, staining the rock, seeping into the stone.

Even the moon seemed not to shine. The light here was dingy. Murky. Like the dull illumination of moon through polluted air and grimy clouds.

In the uncertain light, the crypt didn't rise before me slowly and majestically. It was suddenly just there, dark and cold and bleak. Black stone polished to a gleaming sheen. Monstrous black angels with narrow, tilted eyes, gaunt faces, and sunken cheeks, grim of visage and menacing of posture though they merely stood, unmoving and somber. Guarding the crypt.

Steps carved of black stone climbed the side of the crypt itself as if inviting me to stand atop the deceased. I declined.

Perhaps the strangest thing of all about the crypt, stranger than the darkness that seemed to waft from the stone, stranger than the odd visage of the guardian angels, stranger than the sudden appearance of the grave site like a trick hidden beneath a magician's cape, was the elevation of the tomb. It stood higher than any near it. It stood higher than the house behind me. Higher than the base of the nearby trees. I should have noticed the grave from a great distance. I should have been able to pick it out from the Grand Dame's window. I should have seen it a long way off. And I hadn't.

The southern Louisiana landscape is always perceived as flat, devoid of variations in elevation, featureless and wet. But that perception is an error. It has great highs and lows, dips and rises, but the lows are filled with water, dropping often below sea-level. Below the water table which flows only inches below the surface of the ground.

Low hills would be in evidence, plainly visible if only the pervading water would vanish for a moment and expose the bottom of bayou and swamp to view. And deep crevasses dropping away into underground depressions, small caves in the muck.

True hills are rare, however. Gradual rises of four or five feet above sea-level do occur, but seldom true hills. The black marble crypt, a memorial dedicated to the death of one man, occupied what appeared to be a true hill. Rounded and smooth, the little hillock rose with the perfection of any Indian burial site. And at the top sat the blackness that was Royal DeLande's grave. A grave with steps to the top.

I stared at the message carved into the stone for long minutes before the words divulged their meaning. *Royal DeLande. Father. Husband. Lover. All Three.*

All three? Innocent words anywhere but here, planted in DeLande soil. What was it Miles had said? The depravity went back farther than suspected? Started sooner? Something like that.

A night bird cooed far away. A second one, closer, answered sweetly. I turned, took a breath into lungs that felt leathery and tight. Walked away. I might use this tomb, this dark and oppressive place, in a painting. I would photograph it before I left, in moonlight and darkness.

I moved aimlessly, back along the way I had come, away from the dark heart of DeLande dead. She wasn't here. Neither the Grande Dame nor Azalea. Only the dead, the false truths of my life, and me.

It was only by chance I saw the light. A little flash of brightness to my left. A faint glimmer, then it was gone. Blackness in the trees bordering the graveyard. And then again as I turned and waited. A second flash. Light, hand-held. Low down. Moving through the woods, then gone again.

Fixing the position in my mind, I ran.

CHAPTER 19

With eyes made for darkness I cut through the gravestones, passing older, elegant statues, weathered stone, roses and lilies and irises planted in an old garden. Smelled the sharp green smell of growing things.

The path became narrower, but still smooth, testament to the DeLande gardeners. My shadow, moving with DeLande grace, kept pace beside me, seemingly urging me on. The small light twinkled again just ahead.

The black iron fence stopped me. Blacker than the night, it was suddenly there, given away only by a faint glimmer of moonlight on metal. Grabbing the twisted iron bars, I braked, my body hitting the fence with a low thrum. Black spear-points pressed at my eyes and cheeks and I jerked back, afraid. Of what I wasn't certain.

My heart was pounding, my breath rough. It wasn't a hard run, yet I was winded. Holding the cool metal, resting my forehead against the formed and unsharp spear-points, I breathed, forcing calm into me.

Ahead was a pecan grove, the thin arms of pecan trees fanning open against the stars like the bones of fingers. I pressed my face hard into the iron spears, waiting for the little light. A breeze ruffled through the trees high up, just touching the topmost leaves and they quivered, like the nerves in my body quivered from this nighttime run.

And again the little hand-held light winked. Moving. A flashlight among the trees.

The path bent to the left. My eyes traced the walkway, here little more than stepping stones, and discovered the gate.

Black iron on dry-stone supports. An iron half-circle overhead.

Wisteria, carefully trimmed, grew up on either side, pruned to the bare vine, climbing the rock in a slow, snarled spiral. At the iron, the leaves sprouted, dark and colorless in the moonlight. They grew thick and clinging up the iron gate-supports, met and intertwined at the top. And somehow, the joined vines reminded me of the DeLande curse, though I wasn't certain, exactly, what that was.

Taking a final deep breath I pushed away from my iron support. The wisteria-twined gate was half-open, as if someone had only recently passed through. I slipped through the opening and jogged into the pecan grove, moving at a steady pace among the stately trees.

Pecan trees need lots of sun and plenty of root space to flower and nut, so my passage was wide, smooth and only scantily grassed. The breeze dipped down, cooling my sweaty face. The night bird called. So sweet. A single rich trill, unanswered.

The night, with its heavy shadows and hidden secrets, was no enemy to me. There was no fear in stepping into the unknown. No anxiety. No wariness. Only respect for the unseen and wonder at the shadow-play of silvered light and shades of darkness.

The grove ended suddenly, the perfectly spaced old trees giving way to natural forest. Yet the trail of the light had last flickered deep within the trees.

I closed my eyes, letting my pupils open their widest. Resting my vision.

When I opened them and scanned the edge of woodland, there was the path through the trees. Wide enough to drive a small tractor and bush-hog through. And the tin-roofed shed, nestled in the obscuring darkness.

My breath was steady now, the night birds silent, the breeze stilled.

The shed was dark, only the skeletal frames of equipment, rising like dinosaur bones, proclaiming its purpose. And beyond, a smaller path wound on, narrow and rough, into the forest.

Only yards down the path, the ground dropped. Water, sitting even with the surface, squished. Damp and mud penetrated the canvas of my sneakers, clung to my toes, and compressed along my instep.

The passage of many footprints through the muck had made

the ground uneven, and I slowed. No moonlight penetrated. Only a faint luster before me differentiated the pathway from the darker trees.

The smell of swamp, stagnant, heavy with the scent of rot, filtered in and was gone. A whiff of danger carried on the vanished wind.

I don't know when I stumbled from the path. Only that suddenly I fell, hard, bruising my wrist and turning back my thumb. Wet seeped through my jeans to my skin. I lay there, gasping from the shock of the fall, holding my injured hand. So very glad it was my left.

Down low, the stink of swamp was stronger. And added to the miasma of rotting vegetation was the foulness of an animal, several days dead. Close by. Very close.

Faint moonlight glimmered through the trees, touching the thin layer of wet that coated the ground. And beside my hand, where I pushed myself up, was the glimmer of moonlight on metal. I paused.

A watch. Even in the dark, the watch glowed golden, its luminous dial shining up from the earth. An upside-down 3:45.

The breeze strengthened a moment, bringing the putrid scent close and sharp. I shivered, knowing, and rose to my feet.

Moving cautiously, I found him. A white corpse stretched upon the soil. Bloated, moving with an even greater whiteness. Maggots crawling over the clothing and the great expanse of exposed flesh. Gashes opened across the ruptured belly, spilling out darker organs. Rats had been at work.

I retched. A hard and awful sound. Backed away. Turned and found the sturdy shape of a tree. Wrapping my arms around it, I supported myself. And gagged, fighting to stay calm. To not lose my meal. The astringent smell of moss against my face helped, almost overpowering the smell of the body.

Finally, my stomach quieted. Leaving in its place a vibrating weakness, stretched taut.

And in the distance, the light that was my beacon blinked, blinked and went out. It was as if the person carrying the light had stepped between trees and then stopped, hidden behind the trunk of another.

Pushing away from the rough bark, my left hand twinged

sharply, sending an ache up my arm. I supported the injured limb across my waist as I walked, my right hand out front to protect me from low-hanging limbs I couldn't always see in the black of the shadows.

Carried against the faint and intermittent breeze was a soft humming. The occasional notes of a waltz.

The light appeared again, and moving to my right, I circled around a large copse of young trees rising in a thicket from the roots of an older one, cut away. The older trees were thinner here, as if someone had cut only selected trees, and young ones had quickly sprung up, taking their places.

The light, when it blinked again, was closer now, pointed down. Shielded perhaps from one side by a hand, but still bright from behind and the sides.

The humming, too, was clearer, though the melody was unfamiliar.

Mosquitoes, which had been curiously absent, descended in a cloud, reminding me of the mosquito repellent I hadn't worn. But then, I hadn't exactly been planning a midnight hike when I left my room.

Toads and tree frogs were noisy all around, the heavy concentration of sound indicative of both forest and a body of water. A bat, attracted by the light, dipped and flew on.

Stepping slowly, placing each foot with care, I gained on the moving light.

The trees grew thinner still, and I was again on a path. Whether the same or another I couldn't have told. Without the little light I was most surely lost.

Up ahead glowed a light. A porch light perhaps. Illuminating a small brick house, but turned at an angle from me.

An old sharecropper's cabin, renovated, its trim freshly painted, made its appearance through the trees. The flashlight went out. It had the finality of being shut off.

I took a breath and spat out mosquitoes. A nasty reminder to breathe through my nose. I was stinging all over as the pests bit through the mud, cloth and hair to draw a blood meal.

I fanned the air, batting away at the hundreds, and ran across an ill-kept lawn to the shadow of the cabin.

The humming had stopped. Voices, too soft to identify, took its place. And a soft cry. Like an anguished child.

Rounding the corner of the house into the glare of the bare bulb, I stopped. An almost electric shock shivered up from the earth and whipped through me.

Azalea, her body crouched, arms extended before her, whimpered.

She was on the porch. My shotgun in her hands. Pointing inside. The voice which had hummed that tuneless waltz came clearly from within. In lilting laughter.

'Dear child. Put that ridiculous gun away. You can't kill me, you know.' The Grande Dame, gently amused. Scolding. Her voice coming from within the house. 'I can't die just yet. There's far too much left to do,' she cajoled. Calmly. Sweetly. A tender, nurturing tone.

'Come. Meet these people. They would like you. And they need company. They've been alone so long.'

I stepped forward slowly. Metal bars covered a window close beside me. Spider-webs clogged in the corners. Dirt streaked down the glass, blurring the images within. Dull light filtered out.

Azalea sobbed. A single desperate sound, choked off. Her arms trembled. She took a deep breath, lifted the gun a fraction.

'Move . . . Move away from them.'

'Silly girl. Why would I want to do that? You might really pull the trigger then.' A beguiling voice. Alluring in its rich textures. Its captivating charm. Hypnotic, like the harmonious tones of a snake charmer. 'Now, put it down and come inside. Come.'

'Run, gir'! Ge' away! Run!'

I stopped again, frozen. 'Tee Dom?' Whispered. Tee Dom. Tee Dom's voice. The way he sounded when he had the flu. All weak and quavery. And old. The dread I had worn for so long like funeral wrappings tightened, suffocating, strangling. I put out a hand. Stepped forward, uncertain.

Azalea sobbed again. The Grande Dame laughed, a melodious sound, and over the laughter, the words.

'Run. Go, gir'.'

I pulled the .38 from the waistband of my jeans. There was mud on the grip from my fall. Without looking down,

I wiped it off on my T-shirt, thumbed off the safety and stepped closer.

'Go on, gir'. You ge' away. Go now.'

Azalea fired. The sound ripped the night.

A form launched through the darkness. Caught Azalea. Tumbled her toward me. Into me. And we three fell together.

The gun fired again. Deafening. Close to my face. A blinding flash. A sudden pain, high up on my arm. My shoulder.

I rocked back and rolled. Grabbed my left arm, pulling it close. Elastic pain stretched itself over me, replacing the dread with agony.

Azalea reached out to me, her hands touching mine. Searching. Empty.

Through my damaged ears, I could hear screams. And crying. Miles, rising from the tumbled fall, leapt to the porch. Disappeared inside.

Shoving the hysterical Azalea aside, I found my .38 in the shadows by the porch, and followed, cradling my left arm. Two steps and the darkness that was darker than night swept in from the edges of my vision. Shock and pain squeezed my breath from my lungs. 'Tee Dom . . .' I whispered.

Reaching the porch, I bent over. My head lower than my waist.

More screaming inside. 'Tee Dom . . .' Barely audible.

And Azalea, hugging me, her hands pulling at my clothes. Her words a litany. 'No, no no no no no no no. I didn't mean to. Noooooo . . .' A long drawn-out note of anguish.

The burning in my shoulder spread though my chest. A liquid fire. My arm went numb, a frozen tingling along my fingers. With my good arm I pulled myself into the house and slowly, clumsily, slid to the floor. Azalea crumpled beside me, jarring my injured arm.

The pain was an evolving torture, thrumming now with the uneven beat of my heart. A vicious cadence echoed by the hollow pulse of sound in my ears as I heard again and again the gunshot that wounded me.

And over that awful sound of blood and throbbing torment, the Grande Dame's voice. Screaming, a high-pitched wail of agony, rising and falling and rising again.

I blinked and focused on the scene before me. Miles and Tante Ilene and Tee Dom on one side of the room. The Grande Dame before me. Her face, her beautiful, ageless face, was covered with blood. Blood that ran down her chin and drenched her dress. And where one perfect cheek had been . . . was a hole. The flesh of the cheek was blown away, leaving ragged edges and bright tissue and a glimpse of quick-moving tongue. Blood-stained teeth.

Below the vicious hole was her mouth, opened wide, screaming a high-pitched, soft cry, like a siren, over and over. Her hands were pressing at the wound as if trying to stop the flow of blood. It ran and pulsed thickly between her fingers.

Before her stood McCallum. A sword in his hands. He held it up high, both hands on the hilt. It gleamed in the sharp glare of the overhead bulb.

I lifted the .38. Blinked against the pain. Steadied the gun.

McCallum stepped forward, moving on Miles, who backed away, toward Tante Ilene who sat on a couch against the wall. Stepping quickly, Miles moved around a small table and right, back toward the door, toward me, his eyes on McCallum. They were talking – I could see their mouths move – but the sharp ringing in my ears from the shotgun and from the Grande Dame's screams was overpowering. I couldn't hear what they were saying.

Even if I got a clear shot, who was I supposed to hit? The question was wildly amusing, and I wanted to laugh, but the pain in my shoulder stopped me. The room was getting darker, slowly. I could hear the sound of my breathing, like little puffs of agony.

McCallum passed before Tante Ilene, who cowered down on the couch. Tante Ilene, frightened of Cal? Of a boy not even twenty years old? She looked at me then, her black eyes sharp and alarmed, focusing on the blood that seeped from my shoulder. Tante Ilene was frightened of Cal . . .

I followed Cal with the .38, the weight of the small gun like an anvil in my hand. I was gasping. Azalea, at my side was plucking at my injured shoulder, crying softly. I could hear the sound through the ringing in my ears.

McCallum moved on past Tante Ilene. I steadied the gun.

The sword lifted a fraction. And fell. Toward Miles, who raised his arms to ward off the blow.

I fired, pulling the trigger once in a slow, steady motion, just the way Tee Dom had taught me so long ago. I felt the weapon discharge.

In the room nothing happened. Nothing changed. The sword fell in a menacing silver arc. Miles backpedaled. I pulled back the hammer, my fingers numb. Aimed and fired.

And the sword dropped. Off and away from Miles. Fell and bounced on the floor, throwing reflections.

McCallum stepped back two slow steps, faltered, and sat down, his knees buckling. His body sinking back on the couch, resting beside Tante Ilene. Slowly, his head tilted and rested on the couch back, his eyes staring at the ceiling.

Two little holes appeared in the center of his tux shirt. Blood spreading outward and down.

I blinked. A strange sound filled my head. A roar overlaid with a moan. The sound the wind makes when a hurricane hits the coast. But the roar was from inside my head. The moan from my throat. And we all looked around, watching one another.

The Grande Dame lifted a bloody hand and smoothed back her hair, wiping blood from her face and into her silver chignon. Repeated the process. Again. Hypnotically. Her screams and her hands moved in the same rhythm. Her eyes were on Tante Ilene.

White-haired and shrunken, lost within clothes that once had fitted her so well, was a different Tante Ilene from the one I remembered. Cheeks sunken, skin sallow, she breathed as if the movement pained her. Her eyes were on McCallum, and the dead hand he had dropped into her lap. Slowly, she turned to me.

'Bonnie . . .' Tante Ilene's voice, but changed. Broken. As if she had no strength. No breath.

Miles, his lips parted, watched his mother, mesmerized. His arms dropped slowly and fell to his sides, limply.

Tee Dom, gaunt and haggard, grunted. Shuffled over and took the weapon from my hands. His skin was pale, his eyes weak and watering, rimmed with bright red lids.

Starved. He looked starved.

Slowly I looked around the room. Every window was barred. A heavy double-keyed lock, open now, with the key still inserted to keep them in, secured the door. For furniture, a boneless and sagging couch. Pillows. Beanbag chairs upholstered in black plastic. No lamps. No lights. Only a bare bulb in the overhead fixture casting harsh shadows.

A mattress, lying on the floor, was visible through the doorway in the next room.

Prisoners. Tante Ilene and Tee Dom had been prisoners here. Starved, from the look of them, while I feasted in the main house.

Tee Dom lifted his shirt, a dirty, ragged thing, and wiped off the gun, meticulously removing my fingerprints. And then he fired the gun twice, hitting the wall above McCallum both times. He glared at me, his black eyes sharp, both angry and yet proud of something I didn't understand. 'My job to protect you, gir'. You mama say so. And dis one,' he pointed a thumb at McCallum, 'deserve to die.' Tee Dom's face was horrible, lit from within by an emotion I couldn't interpret.

I groaned. Slid lower to the floor. And let the agony of my shoulder claim me.

The hospital was little more than a twenty-five-bed clinic with two nurses on duty, an antiquated X-ray machine and an even older doctor. Roused from his sleep, Dr Pierron sported a grizzled five o'clock shadow, mussed hair sticking up in limp spikes, a mismatched suit and house shoes. Brown pajama bottoms protruded from beneath the suit pants, dragging on the worn-tile floor. The delicate scent of fine brandy clung to his breath as he probed and cleaned my wound, removing little rounded pieces of metal. They clinked solidly into a stainless-steel emesis basin.

'Not bad for a shotgun wound, young lady. Lucky it was only birdshot or you would have lost your whole shoulder. Lucky placement, too. Missed all the delicate bones in your shoulder joint.'

I grunted as he probed deeply with a pair of long forceps. 'I'll try to remember how lucky I am later. When it doesn't hurt so bad.'

Dr Pierron chuckled. 'That may take a while. But I'll see that you get regular shots of Nubain throughout the morning. That should take the edge off.' He patted my good shoulder in a fatherly manner and turned to the next bed as a nurse began to pack the wound with an antibiotic salve.

The emergency room was one long room. Three stretchers, separated by hanging curtains on chain supports that could be drawn back or opened as privacy needs demanded, took up the floor space. Tee Dom was on the far stretcher, hooked up to an IV which pumped clear liquid into his veins. A silly smile softened his face. He never took his eyes off me.

Tante Ilene, her broken ribs wrapped in a stiff cloth brace, was between us. Broken ribs from a fall in the little prison. Left untreated, jagged edges of bone had rubbed against the lining of her lung until inflammation set in. Pleurisy and a touch of pneumonia. Dehydration.

And her eyes, too, never left mine.

'You come save us,' she whispered, as the doctor bent over her, his stethoscope against her upper chest.

I shook my head, choking. And swallowed down a bitter taste at the back of my mouth. 'I wish I had. But I didn't even know you were there. I was just following Azalea.' If guilt had a taste it would be like this. Sour. Corrosive. But it was surely only medicine coating my throat, acerbic and biting.

Slowly Tante Ilene shook her head. The cords of her neck were sharp and taunt beneath the folds of wrinkled skin. 'You come save us.' When she smiled her black eyes filled with tears.

The sight of her damp eyes reminded me of the dead man in the woods, his body lying on wet, moon-touched ground. Miles was out with the police now, trying to locate it in the early dawn light.

Captain Murdock, his blue eyes furious at the lack of compliant witnesses, had stormed through the emergency room when I first arrived and badgered everyone within hearing until the doctor politely told him to get lost. The captain was not a happy man, even with Tee Dom claiming to have shot McCallum.

And the Grande Dame . . . Miles had taken her away from the little brick house before the ambulance and the police had even arrived on the scene. He said he would fly her in the family helicopter to a private hospital where she could get the medical and psychiatric care she needed. Her name would never be mentioned in connection with the shooting. Nor would Azalea's.

Only the Sarvaunts' condition was the police's affair. Tante

Ilene and Tee Dom had both given statements, claiming that McCallum had held them hostage, and then in a moment of rage, tried to kill Bonnie with the shotgun, and them with a sword. Bizarre story.

But Tee Dom had gunpowder residue all over his hands. And there was the little prison house in all its sordid confirmation, and the body in the woods . . .

Tee Dom wouldn't let me tell the truth. Threatened me when I insisted. 'You go' no reason kill Cal DeLande like you Tante Ilene and me, gir'. No reason. You keep you mouth shut or I beat you within a inch o' you life. You hear? You do as I tell you, keep you mouth shut.'

Miles had agreed, and so I kept my mouth shut at the scene of McCallum's death. Claimed to have been unconscious throughout the event. Shot by McCallum for trying to interfere . . .

Before the police arrived, Miles had loaded the shotgun and fired it again, holding the weapon with Cal's lifeless hands. And then he had washed his own and my hands with warm water to remove the gunpowder residue. When the police tested me with a GSR – a gunshot residue test-kit – they picked up nothing. The little Q-tips coated with nitric acid came away clean.

Bizarre story. Bizarre night. And Captain Murdock wasn't buying it at all. But the story concocted by Miles and Tee Dom covered all the bases.

'How long were you in that house, Tante Ilene?' The shot the nurse had given me was making me sleepy. Tante Ilene seemed to waver in her place on the bed like heat wavering across tarmac beneath an August sun.

'Too long. Tee Dom, he kep' the record of the days. Bu' we run out of food two week ago. Only water lef'. And tea-bags. No coffee.' She made a face as if the lack of coffee had been the greatest hardship of all, and I laughed shakily. For her it probably was. 'So we drank plen'y hot tea and drank plen'y water. And we skinny all over now.'

I laughed outright and scarcely felt the tremor of pain that coursed through my body from the wound. And then, with the Nubain making the lights shimmer and causing Tante Ilene to glow, I said the words I had been thinking for months, knowing it was only the drugs giving me the courage.

'We never talked before, Tante Ilene.' I had no control over the tears that splashed down my cheeks and wet my hospital gown. They ran like a leaky faucet. A steady, irregular drip. Big sparkling tears that caught the light.

'Couldn' answer you questions, gir'. So. We talk all the time now. Okay?'

It took less than twenty-four hours for me to recuperate enough to go back to the DeLande Estate, leaving Tante Ilene and Tee Dom to the tender care of the nurses. I wanted to stay and take care of them myself, to touch their faces, hear their voices, know they were alive and safe and soon to be well.

Dr Pierron had his own ideas. The old doctor sent me home to the estate with Miles, three bottles of pills in a paper bag, and a list of instructions and warnings about signs of infection clutched in my good right fist.

I was well enough to go, and not well enough to assist with the care of my aunt and uncle. I had little recourse.

The reception committee at the estate, however, made me consider a relapse. Miles sat in a rocker on the veranda watching the scene with amusement, one leg draped over the arm of the chair, his booted foot swinging.

MacAloon and Josh Campos were furious at my going off in the middle of the night and getting myself shot. After screaming at me for twenty minutes or so, checking the doctor's handiwork and grudgingly pronouncing it adequate, they packed their bags and took off for New Orleans without me.

One of my cousins went with them, attaching herself to Josh's perfect body and his car like glue. Annabella. Andreu's youngest off of Angelique, the red-haired siren who was keeping Rhame occupied. Another inbred DeLande. Like me. She flashed me a saucy smile as the three drove away, her movements languid, her face sensual and heavy-lidded.

Did I have any of that myself? That sensuality? That luxuriously carnal and provocative passion for life? For men? Or was all my passion swept up in my love of art? My hunger for the canvas. My craving for the oily scent and rich hues of paint.

And if I ever did meet a man who fired my senses like painting did, would I have the courage to go off with him, into the unknown? How much easier to go off alone into the dark of bayou or swamp to photograph and paint. How much less complicated.

Once MacAloon and Josh finished with me, Jenkins lit in. Now that I was unveiled as another of the long-lost DeLandes, it was his apparent privilege to make sure I knew my place in the household. Which was to never, ever, traipse about unattended in the dark. And never to leave the house without deactivating the security panels. I was given a twenty-minute lecture on my responsibilities to the staff and to the estate's complicated security problems.

By the time he finally wound down, my head was swimming and my shoulder had entered a whole new realm of agony. A burning, throbbing, nauseating anguish that pulsed from my shoulder up the back of my neck and into my head and seemed to dead-end in my fingertips in an almost electric vibration.

Just before I thought I would surely collapse from the punishment, Miles unlaced his long fingers, rose from his rocker and swept me up in his arms. There was amazing power in his lean frame, and he carried me past a disapproving Jenks up to my second-floor bedroom, placing his feet carefully, as if he'd carried a wounded child before and knew the agony of a misstep.

'If I vomit on you, will you forgive me?' I asked into his shirt front.

'Certainly. And I'll have Jenks wash the ruined clothing. Personally.' Laughter rumbled deep in his chest, pressed against mine.

I smiled weakly.

'You'll get used to Jenks, Bonnie. He's a persnickety, fastidious mother hen and he'll nurture you to death if you let him.'

'I hope I won't be here that long,' I said dryly.

Miles laughed again. 'You won't. But you'll be back. And you'll bring your mother too. What was her professional name? LaVay? Something like that. Marvelous painter. And you'll find her and bring her home so she can begin healing, like all the others.'

He said it with such certainty. Total conviction. And I shivered in his arms when I realized I hadn't told him about LaVay. I had told no one.

Miles kicked open my door and placed me on the coverlet of my bed. Positioned my pillows behind me. Pulled the extra blanket up over my legs. And caught Azalea in mid-flight when she would have ended her excited dive on my injured side.

'Easy girl. You don't want to make her bleed again.'

'Bonnie. Are you gonna live? Are you gonna be okay? 'Cause I think I'll just die if you don't get better.'

Miles turned her in mid-jump and placed her, kneeling, on the mattress. I'm not sure she even noticed him.

'I'm fine. Or I will be.'

Her small, perfect hands roamed over me, following the outlines of bandages and underlying bones. Her hair was corn-rowed with tiny gold beads all over her head. A golden cap on her light-brown skull. I reached out and touched it. Warm scalp. Cool beads. Soft hair pulled too tight. 'I like your hair. Will you let me paint you with it like this?'

'You got to finish *My Sister's Face* first,' she reminded. And then she placed her open palm on my cheek. Her hand was cool and dry, the bones firm beneath her smooth skin. And tears flooded my eyes for no apparent reason.

'I been feeling like that too,' she said. 'All mushy inside.'

I laughed, and wished I hadn't as pain jolted through me.

'So can I come live with Tee Dom and Tante Ilene and you on the bayou?'

'If Miles says so.'

'She has school.'

'In the summers then,' Azalea quickly bargained, her eyes never leaving mine. A true DeLande. Always aware of the bottom line.

I saw Miles lift a shoulder, that elegant, negligent gesture, out of the corner of my eye. 'I don't see why not. If you learn to swim and handle a gun first, this winter. And if your studies go well.' Miles's tone was strange, as if he was saying more than it seemed.

'I nearly killed Tee Dom,' Azalea confessed, biting her bottom lip. She glanced back at Miles and then to me, tears filling her eyes. 'I didn't mean to. But the Grande Dame told McCallum he could kill them. And then he could . . . have you just like Marcus . . . had me.' Her voice shook, the words thick with tears. 'And then she moved and the pellets only got her cheek. Some hit the wall behind her, close to Tee Dom.'

I closed my eyes as a fresh pain ripped through me, spreading outward from my shoulder. The picture of Tee Dom dodging bullets pasted itself across my eyelids. The memory of Tante Ilene's starved face watched, impassive in my mind.

'*He* said I had to tell you,' she nodded to Miles. 'And you had to forgive me. And then I had to learn all about firearms 'cause I'm such a lousy shot.'

'Oh,' I said. 'Well. I think that's a good idea. And the swimming too.'

And I sounded very grown-up and dignified. One of the adults deciding what's best for the teenagers. Great. Just what I wanted.

'Bonnie.'

I looked away from Azalea to find Taber Rhame standing in the doorway, hands on the door jambs, a serious and reproachful frown on his face.

'Come in. Join the party,' Miles said from the corner, where he'd seated himself.

Taber actually jumped. And the expression he wore went from chiding to guilty all in an instant. He almost turned away, and Miles, as if sensing Rhame's indecision, leapt from his chair, took Rhame's arm and guided him in.

'Come in, Mr Rhame. Bonnie's been through a dreadful ordeal, but she's well enough for company. Here. You take this seat right here next to the bed. I'm sure she wants to visit with her *employer*.'

My brows rose. Miles the solicitous? Not bloody likely. Azalea wiped her face and winked, squatting back on her haunches so she could better see us all. Something was up.

'Rhame,' I said, not knowing what was going on, but feeling sure everyone else did.

'Uh. Bonnie,' he said back in the same tone, and stopped, staring at me. A long moment of silence stretched. And stretched. My brows went up higher.

Azalea sighed in pure frustration, finally breaking the moment. 'Well. Are you gonna tell her or are you just chicken shit?'

'Azalea!'

Miles erupted with laughter.

Rhame flushed an uncomfortable burgundy.

'Well, are you?' When Rhame opened his mouth only to close it again, Azalea turned back to me. 'You're fired. Angelique told everyone at breakfast that she's taken over your job and she's gonna live with Rhame and travel with him and be his assistant and his model and everything. But I really think she's just gonna sleep with him.'

Miles laughed harder, plopping down in his chair again. Rhame blushed deeper, and I shook my head at them all, glad I still had some Nubain in my system. It was difficult being the only sane one in this lot.

'It's not that I don't value your help in the past, Bonnie, and I'll write you a glowing recommendation—'

'She needs nothing from you,' Miles cut in, his laughter gone. In the instant it took to blink he became the Eldest, haughty and arrogant, his eyes like black stone. 'Bonnie – Carin – is a DeLande. If she wants to work it will be as an artist. Not some . . . one's assistant.' The insult was palpable in his tone. Some . . . what had he been about to say? What had he not said? Some . . . fool? Some . . . washed-up artist? Some . . . low-life not worth the dirt I trod on? It was all there in his tone. The insult. His opinion of the man. But unuttered.

'Yes.' Rhame stood, his hands twitching. 'Well. Of course she—'

'And she has enough commissions to keep her busy for the rest of the year,' Miles continued, not letting Rhame talk.

'Yes. Of course,' Rhame said edging to the doorway. 'If there's anything I can—'

'Nothing. There's absolutely nothing you can do.' Imperious Miles DeLande, his voice slicing into a world-famous artist and ripping him to shreds, while his body lounged indolently in an armchair, his feet outstretched, crossed at the ankles, his fingers laced on his stomach.

The DeLande power of the voice. Something else the Grande Dame bestowed on her son. Something else I didn't have. Interesting.

'Yes. Well. Um. Goodbye, Bonnie. Um. Goodbye.' And he scurried from the room.

I remembered the way Rhame had handled Jenks upon our arrival, putting the man in his place. Sending him off chastised, like a kicked puppy. Like a man less than half his years had done just now. Very interesting.

'And thank God he's taking Angelique with him. We'll get a little peace around here for a while. Though I almost feel sorry for the man. Angelique is . . . difficult.'

Azalea laughed and stretched out beside me on the bed, sharing my pillows. 'What he was thinking was, she's a bitch.'

'Mind your manners, girl,' Miles said mildly. And again something was being spoken in the room of which I knew nothing. Something they shared. I wasn't sure I wanted in on it, whatever it was.

'How's your . . . how's the Grande Dame?'

Miles pursed his lips, considering.

'I'll take you to see her. She's . . . Well . . . You'll see for yourself.'

I nodded once. 'And the man in the woods?'

Miles flinched. Literally.

'He was . . . a private detective hired by someone unknown and . . . murdered by McCallum while . . . skulking about on private property.'

I nodded again, watching Miles's face.

'Anthony Aucoin,' I said, naming the detective who drove the brown car, the one that was looking for me in Khoury. The one of whom Elred had snapped a picture or two. The one who supposedly paid a two-bit junky to kidnap me, and then disappeared.

Miles pursed his lips, saying nothing. He didn't have to.

'The Grande Dame paid him to find my aunt and uncle, bring them to the little prison, and lock them in. And then McCallum killed him. Cut him up with the bloody sword in the dining room. The one Jenkins turned white over when Rhame and I told him about it. That sword,' I said, convinced.

Miles finally conceded, tilting his head once to the right. 'Smart girl. Not bad at all.'

'She's pretty good, huh, Miles?' Azalea said proudly. And she patted my thigh with an open palm, her hand hot, now, through my jeans.

How strange, to be touched. How uncommon. And Azalea did it so naturally, as if it meant little or nothing; to me it was a revelation. A rarity and a treasure. I'd have to try it myself. Soon.

'She's very good, actually. Better than I thought,' Miles said. And I struggled to remember what subject had last been discussed. But my mind was Swiss cheese today. Full of holes holding nothing. Then I remembered. The PI, dead in the woods.

'So what do the police think? About the murder. And the fact that he died by a sword.'

Miles shrugged again. Uninterested. And I knew without asking that the Grande Dame would never be mentioned. She was, after all, the Grande Dame DeLande, the legend of Louisiana. She was inviolate. Sacrosanct. A kidnapper and child abuser. I closed my eyes.

'I'm tired. I think I'll sleep a while.'

'Of course.' I heard Miles rise. Heard him walk smoothly to the door, boots on rug, then heavier, hollowly, on the wood floor. 'Once she comes home, she'll never leave this house again, Bonnie. Her doctors are seeing to it that she's involuntarily committed. A full-time . . . nurse . . . will care for her around the clock. She'll be sedated when necessary. And restrained when required. She's . . . no longer herself.' And he left the room.

I understood the meaning behind his words. The Grande Dame would be drugged, watched over by glorified jailers, tied down, and never let loose again.

She was insane. I remembered the hideous wound marring her perfect face and the rise and fall of her screams. And I remembered the sight of McCallum falling. Two neat little holes in the white shirt. I had killed a man . . .

I closed my eyes, remembering the yellow-eyed boy who had kissed the back of my hand when he met me. And I remembered too the elegant, exquisite creature who entered Taber Rhame's door, kicked off her shoes and let down her hair. And smiled so brilliantly and so beautifully it took my breath away.

Azalea laid her head against me and snuggled closer, her body warm. I pulled the blanket up over us both and let sleep take me.

CHAPTER 20

I stared at the Grande Dame one last time.

I was leaving today. Going back to New Orleans to pick up Perkins from Cee Cee, show off my apartment to Tante Ilene and Tee Dom and Azalea. My family.

And I wanted to say good-bye to the Grande Dame. Not that she would remember.

For the last two weeks the Grande Dame had been confined to her room, let out only at night to wander in the graveyard and twice by day to clip roses for her rooms. Followed everywhere by a . . . nurse . . .

Humming her tuneless little waltz, the one I had never been able to identify, she spent the rest of her time in her room. Sitting. And the last two days she hadn't left her suite at all.

Dressed in her pearly silks, her hair neatly braided, her face was perfectly made up around the graft of skin that puckered and pulled over her reconstructed face. Her body was powdered and perfumed and she was sitting on her bed, in the center, surrounded by yards of mattress and silk and lace bedding. Humming as usual.

And carefully, deliberately, pulling out her hair. Strand by strand. Moving as if in slow motion. And each time she removed a strand with a tiny little jerk, she would pause, suck in air and smile. A private, gentle smile. Winsome.

Her skull was visible on the left side of her head from temple to just over her ear. And strands of silver hair were laid out like soldiers across her knee.

When she pulled out a strand, I flinched. Her skull was bloody in the bare spot. Carefully, she tugged on the strand. Easing it from the braid in delicate little tugs. Careful not to break it off part way.

'The doctors agreed it was better to let her pull out her hair,' Miles said softly, his voice at my shoulder. I had known he was there, though he had made no sound, and I had come up alone.

'Better than what?'

'Better than the massive doses of tranquilizers it takes to stop her. Better than the sheer fits she had when we tried to stop her. Or bandage her hands.'

I saw the mitts, padded white cotton with velcro lacings teeth couldn't pull apart, hanging from a chair. 'Have someone cover the mitts with silk to match her nightgown. Sew a few seed pearls and some lace onto them. She'll wear them then.'

Miles looked at me strangely. I could feel it. Though I didn't turn my head to confirm it.

'They aren't pretty enough,' I explained. 'That's why she fights you.'

'I'll . . . try that. Thank you.' I knew he would try it. And I knew it would work.

I crossed the expanse of carpet to the bed, moving up closer, to the head, only feet from her, and waited. The humming slowed. She stopped smoothing the hairs along her leg. After a long, silent moment, she looked up. And smiled. That once-wonderful smile. The smile that captured the hearts of three generations, and now pulled the damaged face in odd ways as the muscles tried to accommodate the damage of a shotgun blast. Her mouth lifted only on one side.

'Marie Lisette. How pretty you look. I always did like you in green. It brings out the green of your eyes.' Such a sweet tone. Rich and savory. The caring, affectionate voice I had never heard as I grew up. Loving and kind. 'And you know, if you want to keep Richard's interest, you have to please him. A woman always has to please a man. No matter what. No matter what. No matter what.' And she laughed as horror twisted through my body. As *Ugly Truths* leapt to my mind.

The picture I had finished and framed and packed in the truck waiting out front. Drawn from a model and from pictures of my mother I had found in the archive room. She did look like me. Amazingly like me. But so sad. And I painted her like that. Sad. Like me but with greener eyes, pupils opened all the way, exposing the blackness painted on her soul.

'I had to please them, you know. Just like you.'

I jerked my attention back to the Grande Dame. She was looking at me now. Her black-on-black eyes, so like Tante Ilene's, boring into mine. *Look at me. Hear me.* I could almost hear her say the words.

'I had to please all three at once. Royal and Nevin and Daniel, all three.' She smiled, as if trying to convince me of some important fact. 'You only have to please one. Richard. Is that so hard? Is it so difficult to just do what he says? I had to.' She leaned forward, grabbing my wrist. Her nails were painted a pale, pale pink. Her pupils were open like mine. Hers drugged. 'I had to. And so do you. Just be glad it's only one.' She shook me gently. 'Just be glad.'

Releasing my wrist, she sat back and ran her fingertips over her bald spot. Satisfied. And started that awful, wordless humming. Demented. Insane.

I backed away from the bed, my body colliding gently with Miles. He caught me by both elbows, holding me, his touch sexless, yet affectionate.

'She intended you for me, you know,' he said, his mouth near my ear. 'When I was growing up, she would say that as soon as she found Marie's child, she'd put us together. Start us out together young. I never understood what she meant until much later. *Much* later. And when I did, I went away.

'I spent a whole summer hiding away in Moisson with my brother's wife, Collie DeLande. She's great. You'll have to meet her one day.' I could feel him smile, moving the hair beside my ear.

'And then I went away to school. The Grande Dame never found you, and she never tried to give me anyone else.'

I shivered, staring at the figure on the bed, and Miles released my arms. Stepped away.

Without looking at him again, I left the house. Drove down the long stately drive between the old oaks. And out into the street. The three in the borrowed classic car with me seemed to sense my disquiet and rode silently for some time, beginning a desultory conversation only miles away, when the fear began to subside. The terror to ebb.

I had to please all three at once.
She intended you for me, you know.

Phrases that intermingled in my mind, beating a dissonant harmony. Off beat. Ugly.

What was I? Is this what it really meant to be a DeLande? Struggling, I tried to put my misgivings aside. And about halfway to New Orleans, I succeeded, joining in the conversation.

Tee Dom and Tante Ilene were telling Azalea all about the cabin on the bayou. And I was telling them about the changes I was planning to make. Electricity. Air-conditioning. At least two rooms added on with a staircase leading to the loft. A good paint job. Steps from below the water line to the dock. A real bathroom with running water and a toilet that flushed. Expensive in an area with such a high water table, but doable.

They all thought it sounded great. Even Tante Ilene.

'I tol' you motha' she shou' bring in 'lectric and air-condition. I tell her. But she say no. She say you do it when you old enough. But I so tire' of the hot. So glad you make it col'.'

And then, as usual, when my mother was mentioned, she started talking about her. How tall she was, like me. How good a painter she was, like me. How she liked being alone on the bayou, like me.

How much she loved me. How much it hurt her to leave me.

And like a sponge out of use too long, I soaked up the stories, the hints, the tidbits of her. And vowed I'd find her. As soon as I got us all settled, I'd start Stocker out on the trail of LaVay. Certain now that the elusive Italian artist was she.

'How's your ribs, Tante Ilene? You look like you're breathing great,' Azalea said, an innocent, open look in her green eyes.

'Eat you breakfas'. You tutor comin' get you in five minute, you lazy bone.'

Azalea grinned. 'I'm not lazy. You are.'

'Not lazy, either. You show proper respec' you Tante Ilene. Mah rib hurt.'

'The doctor said you're fine.'

'Huh. What dat docto' know. His rib neve' broke befor', betcha.'

Azalea laughed, a tinkling little sound, and finished her oatmeal. Oatmeal cooked on the new gas range in the bayou cabin.

The cabin I used to call the Sarvaunt Shanty, enlarged and updated. And really very pretty.

An electric fan purred slowly overhead, distributing the heat from the up-to-the-minute space-heater that kept the former shanty warm, even in winter.

The days of trailer-living were over. We had moved into the cabin – all four humans and Perkins – in December, spending Christmas and New Year's on the water.

Miles had joined us for New Year's, bringing fireworks and so much food that the new refrigerator and chest freezer couldn't hold it all.

Christmas he spent with Collie DeLande, giving her away in marriage to a well-known lawyer in New Orleans. He'd stayed at my apartment for the days of the ceremony and the celebration, leaving a surprise when he left. I was curious what he'd bought me, but not curious enough to go see for myself. Whatever it was, it would be there come spring.

I planned to spend the summer in the city with Azalea, absorbing the culture that was the Crescent City. Seeing the sights. Having fun. Shopping . . .

I had planned many things, however, and the most important one had remained elusive. LaVay. My mother.

She had never returned my calls, the ones put through by the dowdy little gallery owner in New Orleans. And Stocker, armed with only the artist's professional name, had been unable to locate her. LaVay's agent was closed-mouth and uncooperative, although he did agree to forward a letter to LaVay from me.

In desperation, I had even sanctioned an after-hours visit to the agent's office by Stocker. A polite term for a covert breaking and entering. But the man's records were incomplete. I knew how much LaVay made off of her art for the last ten years, what donations to the poor, and what professional courtesies she returned. But not what name she was now using, nor where she lived.

Nor whether or not she was really my mother.

And so Christmas came and went along with the carpenters and painters and electricians and plumbing contractors, earth-moving machines, bilge pumps and a muddy mess out back. And then New Year's with Miles bringing belated gifts for Azalea who was filling out so fast I couldn't keep her clothed, a new boat for Tee Dom, a new sewing machine and Bible for Tante Ilene, and a new commission for me. I was a success, even without resting my laurels on the DeLande name.

Money, the portion of the DeLande wealth that was mine, had made my life so much easier. Michau, who handled my financial affairs in New Orleans, was ecstatic with the portfolio I was building. It seemed his reputation was once again on the upswing, as several DeLande cousins – Azalea included – placed their financial investments in his hands. Where one DeLande ventured, others followed. Wealth, like scandal, was a DeLande genetic predisposition.

But LaVay had not been found.

A boat puttered up to the dock, an ancient johnboat with a tiny two-cycle motor and a top speed of twenty-two miles an hour. At the helm was Temper Darbonne, a red-headed, mild-mannered Frenchman and retired school teacher. He tutored Azalea four days a week, putting up with her tantrums, her grievances, and encouraging her in her studies of French, world history, English and math.

The fifth day of the week she spent in LaRoque at the bank under the tutelage of Rufus Kirby learning stocks, bonds, the ins-and-outs of the financial world, and computers. And she carried a shotgun. Just in case my old tutor hadn't outgrown his groping ways.

'Hello, dat house. De coffee still hot?' Temper wasn't a soft-spoken man, for all his gentle ways.

'Yo' come, Tempe' Darbonne. Si' down. Ilene? Where dis man's coffee? You 'sleep back dere?'

'You wan' hem coffee, you pour hes coffee you'sel',' Tante Ilene shouted back from the bathroom. 'I don' wait on you han' and feet no more! You lazy ol' man!'

From my studio loft, I laughed and called down to Temper. And laughed again when Tee Dom got up to pour the tutor's coffee. It had been this way in the cabin since Azalea moved in. She brought life and fire and joy into the lives of my aunt and uncle. And I didn't look too closely at the impact she'd had on me. Nor at my dependence on her.

Part of the legendary DeLande curse was the ability to be loved.

To make others love. A blessing, some might say. A gift. But for a DeLande, misuse of gifts had brought only misery and torment for nearly a century.

And Azalea knew the full extent of her natural gifts, exercising them, practicing them on me. She had me wound around her little finger.

'Ah know, Rober'. Dose modern women, dey got some stubborn way, yea? Mah Hannah, she de same, only de worse.'

Tee Dom, too smart to comment, just handed him a cup of steaming brew and sat down with a muttered 'oooff'.

Minutes later Azalea called up the stairs. 'I'm outta here, sis. We painting tonight?'

'We painting' meant me with a brush in hand, her on an ottoman posing. And chattering away like a magpie. And, rarely, doing homework. So far I had used Azalea in three of my commissioned works. Her piquant face had captured the heart of more than one admirer. My agent had even received an offer from a New York-based modeling agency. I figured Azalea's head was swelled enough right now just from living with us three doting Sarvaunts.

And then there was the trauma of losing her baby. A baby Azalea had hated upon first confirmation of her pregnancy, and then grown to love. She had planned out a nursery, picked out baby clothes and a name. Several names, all of them for girls.

A scant two months into the first trimester, she lost the child. Her life had taken too many wrong turns and been visited with too much trauma in this last year for me to let her take off for New York and some distant fame and fortune. She needed the stability of a homelife for a while. She needed to be a teenager. She needed me.

And I needed her.

So I wasn't about to let her go. No time soon. I stuck my head out over the balcony.

'Maybe, kid. The weather report's calling for rain, and I need moonlight to paint you by.'

'Yeah. Okay, love you. Bye.' And she slammed out after Temper, banging the door behind her.

'Love you too,' I whispered, so very glad Miles had relented and let her live with me. Content, I went back to the canvases leaning on makeshift easels – a series of two-by-fours hammered onto the roof supports, a quick solution dreamed up by the contractor who renovated my home. Ingenious man.

Half of my paintings these days were actual honest-to-God daylight paintings. And although the moonlit ones still sold best, I was gaining confidence with the brighter ones. Dawn and sunset lent the scenes I painted a certain rosy warmth conducive to the sensual nature of my work.

I was gaining a reputation as an artist with an almost magical control over shadow and light. And passion. One French art magazine referred to me as a wizard, a sorcerer, and my model as an enchantress. So far, my critics had rumbled only softly. I was becoming a Name in the art world.

Bonnibelle Sarvaunt, Cajun artist, talented and young, with close ties to the powerful DeLande family. Ties at least one journalist was trying to unravel. Miles and my agent had decided to eventually reveal to the world that I was a DeLande. They figured it could only help my sales figures, and together they plotted and schemed the how's and when's to the revelation. I let them handle it as they both were more devious by far than I.

All I wanted to do was paint and get to know my family. Spend time becoming acquainted with myself and the two people who had raised me. And my new sister.

Bonnibelle and Carin were no longer two separate identities fighting for living space inside me. They had somehow come to an understanding. Reached an accord, or merged, or at least agreed on harmonious relations. I had come to accept who I was. Who I would always be. Two souls sharing the same body. Bonnibelle Sarvaunt and Carin Colleen DeVillier DeLande.

And my genetic history? I didn't think about it much. But it was always with me. A part of me. A part of the magic I was born with. DeLande magic. And for using magic, there was always a price.

I pulled out my paints, the pinks, both warm and cool tones, the Lamp Black and two shades of white, and checked my brushes. I needed a new fitch, which meant a trip into New Orleans soon. I no longer ordered my brushes hoping for quality, sight unseen. I inspected them personally. And I was picky. After all, the bottom line was my artistic reputation . . .

'Yo' busy now?'

I jerked. A tube of open oil paint vaulted from my hand and skittered across the floor, leaving a smear of Lamp Black on the canvas drop cloth.

'Tante Ilene,' I grabbed my shirt front. 'Why don't you whistle or something coming up the stairs? You nearly scared me to death.'

'I like to see if I catch you doin' somethin' you ough' not to be,' she teased.

'Yeah, well, one day you're going to catch me doing a heart-attack, that's what.'

'I'm a sneaky ol' broad,' she said, agreeing, quoting Azalea.

Great. The kid had the old woman talking like a street person. With my luck they'd join a rap group, have a number one record, tour the country, make a fortune, and leave me here all alone in the bayou. I grunted and picked up the paint, smearing color on my jeans.

'You go' a dress?'

'One or two,' I said absently, returning to my brushes. I needed a fine brush as well. I was getting to the point with the old ones that the tiny lines looked blurred. I ran my thumb across the slightly worn bristles.

'Well, you pu' on a dress and take yo' Tante Ilene to the docta' today.' With those wards she turned and walked back down the stairs.

'Yeah. Okay.' I'd have to take the van to New Orleans this time rather than the car. I had a half-dozen paintings to ship and deliver, and a round dozen new canvases to pick up . . . 'Do what?' I bellowed.

Again the tube hit the floor. At least this time I had managed to cap it.

'Yo' take yo' Tante Ilene to the docta'.'

'What for?' I checked her posture and her coloring with a practiced eye. She had gained back some weight, but not all of the pounds she had lost in the prison on the DeLande Estate. She looked good. Real good.

'Mah reg'lar check-up for the blood press. I go' a new docta' in Grand Isle. A specialis'. 'Poin'men' at two.'

A cold dread descended on me as close and familiar as my own skin. And though I hadn't felt it for months, it was like an intimate enemy, the same dread I had worn like a cloak or a shroud on the DeLande Estate. 'Why do you need a specialist, Tante Ilene?' The words came out steady. Calm.

'You neve' ask why yo' Tante Ilene fall in dat prison house. De docta', dat Pierron man, he say I have small stroke maybe. He make 'poin'men' fo' me.'

'A stroke . . . Why didn't you tell me, Tante Ilene? Why did you wait till the last minute to tell me about all this?'

She shrugged, a very Gallic gesture, rough and rounded. 'Tee Dom take me then, if yo' busy,' and she turned and took the last two steps to the ground level.

'Not on your life. But why do I have to wear a dress?'

'Specialis',' she called back from the kitchen, as if that explained it all. And for her it did.

I changed in record time, trying to avoid stepping on Perkins who thought he was going to go for a ride, which he loved. He danced under my feet, his hard claws tapping on the wood floor. Evading him, I read two parish maps while I brushed my teeth, checking which back roads I'd need to take to avoid going all the way up north to Houma and then east, and back south along Highway 1.

I found I could cut off an hour's travel-time by cutting over to 56, then taking 58 to 55 to 24 to Larose. The rest of the way was easy. Even tourists didn't get lost on Highway 1. Highway 1 was the only way in or out of Grande Isle unless you took a boat and I knew that Tante Ilene would never consider spending several hours in an open boat. Too bad. She didn't know what she was missing.

I wore a gauzy pink print rayon with a beige opaque underslip that I had purchased from a consignment shop on my first week in New Orleans. It looked okay with the silk blend sweater and the overcoat I tossed on top.

January was cold, even in the sub-tropical south. Almost a week ago, a harsh Canadian cold front had howled down from the north, paralleling the Mississippi River Valley. Like most Yankees, it must have decided it liked the south, because it seemed in no hurry to move on. I was sick of clouds and icy rain and slick walks and bad light to paint by. And I was especially sick that Tante Ilene needed a specialist.

Socks and lace-up ankle boots completed my ensemble. When she saw me, Tante Ilene rolled her eyes, but at least she didn't comment. As I helped her into the van, I realized how much between us had changed.

Last year this time she would have said nothing about my dress, and kept her face carefully blank. Of course, last year she would never have asked me to take her to a doctor at all. She would probably have died silently rather than ask me for something.

As we drove away, Perkins came out on the dock that now circled the house – dock in front, deck out back. He barked furiously, angry at being left behind. Yet as we circled around out of sight, down the freshly paved new driveway, he pranced around front and barked at the dark water. Perkins loved watching the fish swim in lazy circles. And loved even more barking at the occasional alligator or goose swimming by. For a city dog, he had adapted quite well to bayou living.

Tante Ilene and I stopped at Golden Meadow for a leisurely early lunch, my shortcuts having shortened the trip considerably. We ate at a seafood place, a little hole-in-the-wall joint that looked dreadful but was packed with cars. It was one long room decorated with plastic checked cloths on picnic tables, with benches instead of chairs. The place was one I could only call trashy (quaint would have been a stretch). But the steamed shellfish and broiled flounder were wonderful.

Tante Ilene wanted her fish fried, but with a stroke in her past, there would be a lot of changes in the future. Starting today.

I was confiscating her new deep-fat fryer when we got back home. Her eyes narrowed even as I had the thought, and I smiled at her sweetly. Her lips pressed together to keep in whatever she was thinking as she finished her catfish.

Comfortably full, we pulled back on Highway 1 and headed south, the radio crooning a soft country tune, covering the silence between us.

'So. How do we find this place in Grand Isle?'

'We stop befo' Grand Isle. We take nex' road afte' 3090. Couple turns later, we there.' She nodded her head as if that was all there was to it, when there was a great deal more.

'That's all you know? A couple turns more! Tante Ilene, let me see the directions.' I held out my hand, waiting.

'Go' no direction'.'

I put my hand back on the wheel. 'Great. Just lovely,' I said under my breath. 'We're gonna get lost and I don't have my gun.' I had left my .38 back at the shanty for use by Azalea, who was being taught the finer points of marksmanship by Tee Dom and one of the Boudreaux boys.

Wiatt Boudreaux had come calling soon after Azalea had moved in, his cowboy hat in hand, his boots polished and his blue jeans pressed to a sharp crease. Older than Azalea by three years, his bright blue eyes and smooth olive skin had charmed me from the start. Tee Dom had tried to chase the young man off with a shotgun, but I had intervened. Azalea needed to meet and get to know men. She needed to discover that they were not all like Marcus. They were not all DeLandes. So she went out to dinner at the Dairy Queen and to the movies in LaRoque with Wiatt. And though she was still shy, she obviously liked him. I thought of it as a step in the right direction.

'Dat gun yo' mama's gun.'

I knew she said it just to get me off the subject of directions. I knew it was a ploy. But any mention of my mother always worked to redirect my attention. And Tante Ilene had been using the ploy shamelessly for months.

I gripped the wheel, determined. 'Tante Ilene, please. Tell me the exact directions. Please.'

She smiled a complacent smile.

I gritted my teeth.

'Tante Ilene—'

'She stole it from the Grande Dame after she run away the secon' time. De police lookin' fo' it still. I don' know why dey not discover dis when McCallum die.'

I ignored the second part of her statement, about McCallum dying. I always ignored the thought of McCallum. 'The police . . .'

'Yes, I 'spec' so. De police she call in afta' yo' motha' lef'.'

'So if I had tried to register the gun as Michau had first suggested—'

'De police call in de Eldest. Yo' fin' yo' family right away.' And she laughed, as if at a sublime joke.

I decided it was time to reevaluate this new family communication we had developed. There was a certain benefit to the old expression 'Silence is golden'.

Two miles or so past the Port Fourchon turn-off on 3090, Tante Ilene directed me to turn right, into the marsh. Still smarting over the gun-registration comment, I did as directed and slowed the van – my nearly new forest-green Chevy van with seating for seven and clip-out bucket seats and a custom-made rack in back for my canvases. The road was a potholed mess.

The house where she directed me was a multiple hurricane survivor. A low-roofed, wood-framed, T-shaped structure on pilings, with floor-to-ceiling windows on three sides and an unpainted façade facing the road. The yard was shell, sand, weeds and marsh grasses. Marsh water licked at the drive itself, ruffled by the icy wind. A pair of egrets huddled together on the bank. The Gulf, only yards from the house at storm tide, lapped the beach, bending tall grasses in rolling waves. A cold salty mist hung in the air.

Before I could question her, Tante Ilene hopped from the van, letting in a blast of frigid wet. She marched purposefully to the house. And around to the side, disappearing from sight.

This was no doctor's house.

I pulled my coat on over my sweater, shut off the van's engine and opened the door. And only then did the possibility occur to me. Only then.

I stopped, my eyes half-focused, one foot on the ground, one in the van. A cold mist touched my face, curled wet fingers through my hair. Could she . . . could Tante Ilene have finally relented? Shaking, I locked the van and closed the door. Followed Tante Ilene's footprints around the side of the house.

I was soaked, not by rain, but by salty mist, by the time I reached the side door. Soaked and cold and scarcely daring to breathe. My fingers were icy and my breath short.

Certain. *Absolutely certain*.

But what if I was wrong . . . ?

Tante Ilene opened the glass door for me, pulled it shut against the wind. Latched the small aluminum catch. Took my coat. Handed me a towel to blot my hair. Not once did she meet my eyes.

'Breathe, gir', or you lose yo' lunch all ove' yo' pretty dress.' A terse command. No pity. But then, pity wasn't what my mother had in mind when she gave me to the Sarvaunts, was it?

And now . . . Was I about to be given back? Was this my mother's house?

I took a deep breath and followed her through the short hallway. My Tante Ilene had been here before. Several times. She knew the layout well.

Her heels tapped with a firm rubber sound on turquoise Mexican tile. Her shadow turned and stopped.

Before me was a studio. Smaller than I would have guessed. Larger than mine at home on the bayou. Mexican tile covered with well-used drop cloths. Canvases stacked along the walls, on easels, on chair seats, on a wheeled drying-rack constructed of padded two-by-twos. My mother – my real mother – had painted. I twined my fingers together. They were so cold that they ached.

At an easel in the center of the room stood a girl. No. Not a girl, a woman, older than she first appeared. Limber, lean, dressed in frayed jeans and an oversized work shirt rolled up at the cuffs. She was barefoot in the cold room, her feet on one small section of floor not covered by oil cloth. A deliberate intention. As if she enjoyed the cold feel of tile on her soles. There was a gun on the paint stand beside her. An automatic, silver and black. A 9mm. My mother painted with a gun beside her . . .

I blinked away tears and tried to focus on her face. She kept wavering wetly. I blinked again and two tears rolled down, clearing my vision.

Her arm was lifted when I entered. Her face intent. Green, green eyes. Green like the sea on a sunny day. Like the foliage of summer. Rich and bright and open.

My heart was pounding, beating out an irregular rhythm. My breath came in a sob, a soft cry echoing through the room. Tears coursed down my face, burning.

Slowly, though she didn't look up, her arm dropped. She replaced the brush in a jar of clear liquid. A green cloud churned up from the bristles. And she simply stood there. Waiting.

The wind howled, roared, and whistled through cracks in the windows. Rain splattered down hard for a moment, stopped. A space-heater somewhere in the room smelled of kerosene. And finally, when my eyes were so hot I thought they would burn in my head, Tante Ilene spoke.

'Yo' say keep her safe. Well, she safe now.'

After a long moment a soft voice asked, 'And the Grande Dame? What of her?'

'She tie' to the bed. Crazy as a loon. Miles, yo' brother, in charge now.'

'I never . . . met Miles.'

'He' okay. For a DeLande.'

The woman smiled. And settled her exquisite eyes on me. The childhood photographs did not do those eyes justice. Open. Exposing her soul to the world. She had pupils even larger than my own, wide and deep, like pools in the bayou.

Everything she thought could be read in her eyes. Everything she felt. Her soul was naked to the world. Stripped. Exposed. Totally vulnerable.

How had she been able to fool the Grande Dame enough to get away twice? How?

'I had to. I had a daughter to protect,' she said softly. Her voice was a spring breeze. Gentle. And she had known what I was thinking. What I was feeling.

She nodded slowly. I knew, somehow, that everything she did, she did slowly. Deliberately. Without fuss or wasted effort.

And then she smiled.

And the effect was blinding.

Marie Lisette, LaVay, had all the beauty of the Grande Dame's smile. All the power and charm and sheer force of the Grande Dame. But this smile was richer, warmer. A flare of loving illumination that lit the room like sunlight.

And with all the grace in her slender frame, she crossed the room to me. A panther dancing the ballet. A dancer prowling jungle deeps. Smooth and fluid as the tides or the slow movement of bayou.

And she put her arms around me. My mother's arms were strong, the bones beneath the skin like steel beneath velvet. I lifted my own arms slowly and touched her on either side, almost afraid she would vanish, only a dream after all.

She pulled me close and her body was warm against mine. I was so very cold that I shook, my breath a constant little sob. She was real. She was really . . . real.

She touched her warm cheek to my wet one and smiled against the side of my face. I could feel the movement of skin and facial muscles. 'The bottom line,' she whispered, 'was your safety.'

I understood instantly that this was apology. This wonderful woman was apologizing to me . . .

I pulled away and focused on her eyes, so green and open. So like my own. My tears had wet her cheek and I touched it, smoothing the fine hairs, blond in the light of a cloudy day.

'I know.' My throat was so tight the words hurt. But I did understand. After all, I had met the DeLandes.

'Well.' She smiled again, that bewilderingly lovely smile, and took my hands in her warm ones. 'Let's go get you warm, then. Tante Ilene, I have coffee made, but I'll pour it out and make fresh.'

Tante Ilene grunted. 'You neve' coul' make a good pot o' coffee. You let Carin make. I teach her up good. An' you turn up de heat in dis place, gir'. It colder than a igloo in here.'

I laughed then. A shaky, tear-rough sound. Girl. My mother was girl to them too. Just like me.

I had found her at last, after all these years. And I was right. Knowing who I was made everything . . . right.

'The DeLande bottom line.' Arms linked, we went into the kitchen and with each step, the joy within me grew.

I had found her at last, after all these years. And I had been correct so long ago. Knowing who I was made everything right. Finding my mother pulled all the disparate pieces of my life together, fitting the jagged ends, mending all the broken and rough places on my soul. Proving to me what I had guessed even as a child – that my mother's abandonment was an act of love, not an act of cruelty. Relentlessly, fiercely, she had protected me, giving me the life of safety and opportunity that she had been denied.

At last I knew all the secrets. At last I knew who I was. Bonnibelle Carin Colleen DeVillier . . . a DeLande.

I had found myself.

STOLEN CHILDREN

GWEN HUNTER

My name is Nicolette Dazincourt Delande, and I have committed murder...

Nicole grows up in the Cajun bayous, fresh and beautiful and as capable with her daddy's shotgun as she is with her mother's sewing machine. Until she meets Montgomery Delande, the son of one of Louisiana's finest and oldest families. He is wealthy. He is charming. And he wants to marry her.

Three children later Nicole is pampered, protected and adored by a husband as graceful and elegant as a panther, a strangely possessive husband who can turn vicious in a soul-freezing second.

But Nicole never dreamed of the evil that lives at the heart of the Delande clan. An evil so foul that not even her babies are safe. And Nicole will stop at nothing to protect her children from a family so monstrous that only an extraordinary woman can escape from it alive...

HODDER AND STOUGHTON PAPERBACKS

THE ITALIAN GARDEN

SUSAN MOODY

Hannah was twenty-two that summer in Italy. Long days of silent, unbreathable heat, violence in the air, nights full of fireflies and explosive prohibited love. It was the summer that she met Lucas and learned the secrets of her own sensuality, discovering herself as he discovered her. And discovering too, that passion can destroy.

Twenty-five years later, Hannah's life is passionless, ordinary, safe. She has been punished for what happened. But others disagree. And when her family is threatened Hannah knows that she must face the truth of that summer in the Italian garden – before it's too late.

HODDER AND STOUGHTON PAPERBACKS

PRAYING FOR SLEEP

JEFFERY DEAVER

Michael Hrubek, a young schizophrenic, has escaped from a hospital for the criminally insane. And he's making his way towards Lis Atcheson, the teacher who testified at his murder trial.

Four people race to intercept him before he reaches her. His psychiatrist; the hospital director; a professional tracker. And Lis's husband, who must get to Hrubek before the madman reaches his wife.

But Michael's mind - with its delusions of murder and betrayal — is crystal clear about one thing. He knows Lis better than she knows herself. And he carries with him a monstrous secret that will tear apart many lives during the course of this single horrifying night.

HODDER AND STOUGHTON PAPERBACKS